Irish author **Abby Green** ended a very glamorous
career in film and TV—which really consisted of
a lot of standing in the rain outside actors' trailers—
to pursue her love of romance. After she'd bombarded
Mills & Boon with manuscripts they kindly accepted
one, and an author was born. She lives in Dublin,
Ireland, and loves any excuse for distraction. Visit
abby-green.com or email abbygreenauthor@gmail.com.

Maisey Yates is a *New York Times* bestselling author
of over seventy-five romance novels. She has a coffee
habit she has no interest in kicking, and a slight Pinterest
addiction. She lives with her husband and children in the
Pacific Northwest. When Maisey isn't writing she can
be found singing in the grocery store, shopping for shoes
online and probably not doing dishes. Check out her
website: maiseyyates.com.

D0656646

REDEEMED BY HIS STOLEN BRIDE

ABBY GREEN

CROWNING HIS CONVENIENT PRINCESS

MAISEY YATES

MILLS & BOON

First Published in Great Britain 2019
by Mills & Boon, an imprint of HarperCollins*Publishers*
1 London Bridge Street, London, SE1 9GF

Redeemed by His Stolen Bride © 2019 by Abby Green

Crowning His Convenient Princess © 2019 by Maisey Yates

ISBN: 978-0-263-27798-2

MIX
Paper from
responsible sources
FSC® C007454

REDEEMED
BY HIS
STOLEN BRIDE

ABBY GREEN

This is for Heidi Rice, who came up with
the idea of giving the jilted fiancée from
Confessions of a Pregnant Cinderella her own story. X

CHAPTER ONE

LEONORA FLORES DE LA VEGA couldn't seem to take her eyes off the man standing at the back of the crowd in the glittering ballroom. He towered over everyone around him, putting him at well over six feet.

He was also scowling, which only made his hawkish good looks even more forbidding and intimidating. And even from here Leonora was aware of his sheer masculine magnetism. As if there was an invisible thread tugging her attention to him whether she liked it or not.

She knew who Gabriel Ortega Cruz y Torres was. Everyone did. He came from one of Spain's most noble and oldest families. They owned huge swathes of the country and generated an income from banking, vineyards and real estate—just to name a few enterprises.

He was an intensely private man, but even so he had a reputation for being as ruthless in the bedroom as he was in business. Single, he was considered one of the most eligible bachelors in Europe, if not the world. But he appeared to be in no hurry to settle down. And when he did it would be with an undeniably well-connected woman who breathed the same rarefied air as he did.

And why should that even concern her? Leonora chastised herself. She might come from a family almost as well-connected as Gabriel's, but there the similarity ended. Her family had lost their fortune, and had been subsisting on scraps and the funds from opening up their *castillo* just outside Madrid. It was an ignominious state of affairs. And one that was becoming increasingly unsustainable.

She had never spoken to Gabriel Torres and was never likely to. A man like him wouldn't lower himself to consort with someone from a family of very faded glory. But she'd always been aware of him. From the moment she'd first laid eyes on him when he'd been about twenty-one and she'd been twelve. She'd watched him play polo—that had been before her family had lost everything due to her father's gambling habit, a long-standing source of shame that had kept her parents from venturing out in public for years.

She hadn't been able to take her eyes off Gabriel that day. He'd been so vital. So alive. He and the horse had moved as one, with awesome athleticism and grace. But it had been the expression on his face that had caught her— so intense and focused.

She'd overheard one of the opposing team say, 'Hey, Torres, lighten up. It's just a friendly game.'

He'd said nothing, just glowered at the man. Leonora could remember feeling an ache near her heart, as if she'd wanted to soothe him somehow…make him smile.

Which was ridiculous.

She became aware of the hubbub in the ballroom. Of the hundreds of eyes looking at her. And suddenly she came out of her reverie and back into the present moment. A moment that was going to change her life for ever.

A spurt of panic clutched at her gut and she breathed through it.

She was doing this for her family. For Matías. She had no choice. She was their only hope of redemption.

A light sweat broke out on her palms as she forced her gaze away from the man at the back of the room and found the man she *should* be looking at. Her fiancé. Lazaro Sanchez. He was devilishly handsome, with overlong dark blond hair and mesmerisingly unusual green eyes. Tall. He was almost as tall as—

She shook her head briefly. *No.* She had to stop thinking about him. She was about to become engaged to *this* man. This man she hardly knew, if she was honest. They'd had some dates. She didn't feel anything when she looked at him. Not like…*him.*

But Lazaro was kind and respectful. And, more importantly, he was prepared to bail her family out of their quagmire of debts and in so doing restore their respectability and secure Matías's future. In return… Well, Leonora was cynical enough to recognise ruthless ambition when she saw it. Lazaro Sanchez wanted to marry her in order to achieve a level of acceptance into the world she inhabited. Her only currency now was as a trophy to someone like him and she had no choice but to accept it.

She noticed then that Lazaro had a glowering expression on his face, not unlike the one on Gabriel Torres's. Something about that caught in Leonora's mind, but before she could unpick what it meant she realised that one of Lazaro's staff was making a motion, as if to say, *It's time.*

She tried to get his attention, 'Lazaro?'

He looked at her. Still glowering.

'Are you all right?' she asked. 'You look very fierce.'

His expression cleared. He held out a hand and she slipped hers into his. *Nothing.* No effect. She berated herself again. People in this world didn't marry for love or chemistry. They married strategically. Exactly as she was doing.

'Yes, fine…just a little preoccupied,' he said.

Unable to help herself, Leonora glanced back across the room, and this time Gabriel Torres's dark, compelling gaze met hers. A flash of heat went straight through her abdomen. Her fingers tightened reflexively around Lazaro's.

'Are *you* okay?' he asked her.

A surge of guilt blasted her. How could she be so compelled by another man when she was about to commit publicly to this one? She looked at Lazaro and forced a smile. 'Yes, I'm fine.'

His hand tightened around hers. 'I'm glad you have agreed to marry me, Leonora. I think we can have a good marriage, I think we can be…happy.'

Did he?

A semi-hysterical bubble rose up inside her. She had a sense of the massive room closing in around her, suffocating her. Lazaro let go of her hand and slipped his arm around her waist. The feeling of claustrophobia got worse.

His hand tightened on her waist, almost painfully, and Leonora hissed at him. *'Lazaro—'*

He looked at her with a strange expression on his face, his eyes burning.

'You're hurting me.'

Immediately he released his grip. 'I'm sorry.'

Leonora forced a smile. The sooner they got this announcement over with, the sooner she could get out of this room and get some air. She resolutely forced herself to keep her eyes averted from where Gabriel Torres stood, towering over everyone else around him. Powerful. Magnetic. Disturbing.

A waiter approached with champagne and she took two glasses, handing one to Lazaro. She saw movement nearby and said, 'Your advisors are making motions that it's time to make the announcement. Ready?'

Lazaro looked at her, and she clung to the resolve she could see in his eyes.

He clinked his glass to hers. 'Yes, let's do it.'

He put his arm around her waist again and Leonora forced a smile through the lingering claustrophobia. He started speaking, but she didn't really take in his words, letting them roll over her.

Against every effort, her eye was drawn back across the crowd to where Gabriel Torres stood. He was still watching her, with a disconcertingly intense gaze. Leonora started to tremble lightly under the force of it.

Suddenly a voice rang out. *'Wait! Stop!'*

It shook Leonora out of her trance. It was a woman, who'd pushed through the crowd near the dais. She was being held back by security guards. She was dressed like the wait staff, in a white shirt and black skirt. Vibrant red hair, up in a bun. She was very pretty. Bright blue eyes.

She was looking at Lazaro, and then she said, 'You need to know something. I'm pregnant. With your child.'

For long seconds time was suspended, and then everything seemed to go into slow motion as Leonora felt Lazaro's arm leave her waist. She watched as the woman said something else, not hearing what it was through the buzzing in her head.

Lazaro stepped down off the dais to talk to the woman, holding her arm. She looked very petite next to him. Vaguely, ridiculously, Leonora appreciated that they looked good together.

She couldn't hear what they were saying, and then the woman was being led away.

Lazaro turned back to look at her, his expression veering between shock, anger and contrition.

He came back up on to the dais and said something to the crowd—she wasn't sure what. Too many feelings were rolling over her—chief of which, she was ashamed to admit, was a sense of relief. But that was quickly eclipsed when she looked around and saw the crowd whispering. Some people were looking at her with pity and others with something far less benign. A malicious glee at the fall of one of their own.

She'd tried to buy her way out of debt and shame and now she felt as exposed as if she were naked. And *he* was still there. At the back. Looking at her with a grim expression.

She turned away and saw Lazaro. She backed away and then she stopped. Maybe this was just some hideous case of mistaken identity.

'Is it true?'

But Lazaro said nothing, and his silence said everything. He looked guilty.

He held out a hand. 'Leonora, please…let me explain.'

It was real.

She became aware of the burn of humiliation. She shook her head. 'I can't agree to marry you. Not now.'

She sent up a silent *thank you* that her parents weren't there to witness this moment. Or Matías. He would see that she was upset and that would upset him.

She cast a look around, instinctively seeking an escape route. All she saw were judgemental eyes. Mocking eyes.

She looked at Lazaro for one last time, dismay and humiliation scoring her insides like a knife. 'How could you do this to me? In front of all these people?'

Without waiting for a response, she put her glass down on the nearest surface and turned and fled, making for the nearest exit with no clue where to go.

The first thing she saw was a Ladies' sign, and she followed it to the bathroom, which was mercifully empty. She locked herself into a stall and sat down on the closed toilet.

She was trembling, her heart pounding. She forced herself to take deep breaths, and just as she was starting to feel marginally calmer the door opened. It sounded as if at least three women were coming in, all chattering. About her and Lazaro.

'Who'd marry her now? She's so desperate she was willing to marry some nouveau riche billionaire...'

'Where did Sanchez even come from?'

'Some say he grew up on the streets.'

'The de la Vegas can't survive this. All they have is her and that brother of hers, who everyone knows is a—'

At the mention of Leonora's beloved brother she opened the door and stepped out of the stall, coming face-to-face with the three gossipers. The chatter stopped instantly.

One blanched, one went red, but the other one was totally unrepentant. Leonora was too upset to speak. She just watched as they collected their things and walked out in silence, taking no sense of satisfaction in having routed them because she knew they'd only start gossiping again as soon as they were out of earshot.

She went over to the sink and put her hands on the counter, looking at herself in the mirror but only vaguely registering that her outward appearance—relatively calm—belied the storm inside. She could only give thanks that the women hadn't witnessed her falling apart.

She took a deep breath and ran some cold water over her hands and wrists. She hoped that by the time she emerged there would be no one else waiting to witness her walk of shame.

At that instant a face popped into her head. *Gabriel Torres.* His hawk-like features were as vivid as if he were standing in front of her. She went hot and then cold at the thought of *him* having witnessed her public humiliation.

But she wouldn't see him again. Because she wouldn't be emerging in public for a long time.

She took a breath and steeled herself before heading back out and into the lobby, hoping for a discreet getaway.

* * *

Where was she?

Gabriel Torres looked left and right outside the function room, but there was no sign of the dark-haired woman in the long strapless red dress. The dress that clung to her elegant curves in a way that had made his blood pound for the first time in a long time. The compulsion to follow her prickled over his skin now; he wasn't someone normally given to such impetuosity.

He had only come here this evening to see for himself what Lazaro Sanchez was up to, because he didn't trust the man as far as he could throw him. Especially when everything he did seemed to be designed personally to get under Gabriel's skin. And because they were both involved in a very competitive and lucrative bid for a public project.

Recently Sanchez had even gone so far as to concoct a story that he and Gabriel were half-brothers. He'd accosted Gabriel at an event they'd both attended and when Gabriel had tried to walk away, disgusted at the insinuation that they could be related, Sanchez had stopped him, telling him of a day, many years before, when he had confronted Gabriel's father, claiming to be his son.

To Gabriel's surprise and shock he'd remembered the incident—and the skinny kid who had been waiting for them outside a restaurant in central Madrid. It had been his birthday—one of the very rare occasions when his dysfunctional family had put on a united front.

Gabriel had never been naïve about either of his parents. It was quite possible that his serially philandering father might have sired a bastard along the way. For a family like the Cruz y Torres, whose vast dynasty stretched back to the Middle Ages, such occurrences by opportunists were frequent and, frankly, to be expected.

So, for all he knew, Sanchez could be his brother but

he suspected it was more likely to be a ruse to get under Gabriel's skin.

Ironically enough, Gabriel's father was at this event too, this evening, but Gabriel had ignored him. They barely tolerated each other at the best of times, and he'd had no doubt that the only reason his father had been there was probably the free-flowing booze or a woman.

Since Sanchez's claim to be related to Gabriel, he'd been kept at a certain distance. But tonight had been one of his most audacious moves yet: announcing his engagement to one of Spain's most well-connected women, whose own family rivalled Gabriel's in lineage and legacy.

Marriage to someone like Leonora Flores de la Vega would elevate Sanchez to a place that would make it that much harder to ignore him. Gabriel had to hand it to him for sheer chutzpah.

Clearly he hadn't been intending on marrying Leonora Flores for her money—her family were famously broke after her father's well-documented gambling problems. Her worth came in her name and lineage.

Gabriel had heard the whispers in the crowd. Whispers that Sanchez had offered her a deal—he'd pay off her family debts and in return buy his way into the world he was so desperate to be a part of that he claimed to be Gabriel's blood relation.

Gabriel didn't know Leonora personally, but he knew *of* her, and their paths had crossed over the years at social events. But coming here this evening, seeing her standing up on that dais beside Sanchez, had reminded him that there was something about her that had always snagged his attention. He'd noticed it again this evening. Enough to distract him from Lazaro Sanchez.

Her beautiful face had been composed. Revealing nothing. Her long dark hair pulled back and sleek, showing off the exquisite bone structure of her face. Wide almond-shaped eyes. Dark lashes. A full mouth that hinted at a level of sensuality Gabriel sensed she wasn't entirely comfortable with.

He'd racked his brains to think of the last time he'd seen her. It hadn't been recent. She'd grown up in the meantime. Now she was a woman—and a stunningly beautiful woman at that.

Gabriel had found himself staring at her, willing her to look at him, *needing* her to look at him. And then she had. He'd felt the impact of that contact from across the room. An instantaneous jolt of sexual awareness surging through his blood.

She'd kept on looking at Gabriel and he'd seen the flicker of panic in her eyes. Along with something else far more potent.

She wanted him.

That awareness, together with seeing Sanchez's arm around her waist, had caught at something unexpected inside Gabriel. Something hot and visceral. A sense of… possessiveness.

When Sanchez had announced their engagement, Gabriel had felt an inexplicable and almost overwhelming urge to disrupt proceedings, but just at that moment another voice had rung out. A voice coming from the petite red-haired woman near the dais, claiming to be pregnant with Sanchez's child.

Leonora had fled, and Gabriel had watched her go, knowing immediately that he would go after her. He'd never felt such a primal pull towards anyone.

He'd looked at Sanchez and the animosity he'd felt towards the man had compelled him to mock him for his abortive attempt to buy respectability and for bringing his domestic dramas into the public domain.

But all thoughts of Sanchez were gone now, as he looked left and right for Leonora Flores.

She was gone.

An alien sensation stopped Gabriel in his tracks and he realised it was the sensation of something having slipped through his fingers.

For a man who generally obtained his every want and desire, it was unwelcome. And an unpleasant reminder that he was acting out of character. Pursuing a woman when he didn't need to. If he wanted a woman that badly he could walk back into the room behind him and take his pick. But a new restlessness prickled under his skin. He didn't want one of *them*. So eager, so desperate. He wanted *her*.

And then, as if answering his silent call, he saw her, standing behind the elaborate foliage screening the lobby and entrance from the rest of the hotel. He saw what she saw: a bank of waiting paparazzi outside the main door of the hotel, and no other means of escape.

There was no way he was going to let her out of his sight again. And if the opportunity presented itself to remind Sanchez of where he belonged, Gabriel would be a fool not to exploit it.

Leonora cursed silently. Between the fronds of the exotic plant she could see where the photographers were lined up, no doubt ready to capture the smiling couple emerging from the hotel. There was no other way out without going through the lobby. One way or another they would see her, either scuttling away as if she was the one in the wrong, or walking out without her new fiancé.

Just as she was steeling herself to run the gauntlet, she felt the back of her neck prickle with awareness and her skin tingled all over.

She turned around and Gabriel Ortega Cruz y Torres was

standing a couple of feet away, looking at her. She gulped. He was even taller up close. Broader. Thick dark hair swept back off his forehead. Deep-set dark eyes. Strong brows. A patrician nose and a firm, unyielding mouth.

His bottom lip was surprisingly lush, though, softening the hard edges of his face and making her wonder what it would feel like to touch…kiss… She could imagine him lounging on jewel-coloured cushions, summoning his minions.

Summoning his lovers.

A wave of heat flashed through her body. She was losing it. She *never* imagined kissing men. She was a twenty-four-year-old virgin, because her life had revolved around her parents, the castle and her disabled brother. She'd been more of a mother than a sister to her brother, since their world had imploded after her father's gambling excesses. She'd literally had no time for anything else. Anything normal. Like relationships.

Before she could even think of something to say Gabriel came forward and his scent reached her nostrils, sharp and infinitely masculine. Exotic.

'Would you like me to get you out of here?'

His voice was deep and compelling.

Leonora's response was swift and instinctive. She nodded.

'We'll go out through the main entrance. Don't look left or right, just let me guide you.'

He plucked something out of his pocket and Leonora saw that it was a phone. He issued a curt instruction and put the phone back, his eyes never leaving hers.

'My car is outside. Let's go.'

Before Leonora knew what was happening Gabriel Torres had taken her elbow in his hand and they were already halfway across the lobby. Flashes erupted from outside, and as soon as they got through the doors there was a barrage of noise and calls.

'Leonora! Where's Lazaro Sanchez?'

Leonora ignored it all and followed Gabriel's instructions, looking straight ahead.

A sleek low-slung silver bullet of a car was parked by the kerb and the doorman sprang aside as Gabriel helped her into the front passenger seat. The door was shut, cocooning her in expensive leather and metal and blissful silence, which was only broken briefly when Gabriel came around to the driver's side and opened the door, settling himself into the car.

Within seconds they were moving through the throng of press, who had to part to let them through. Leonora flinched at the bright flashes from their cameras as the paparazzi pressed cameras up to the window to get their shots.

'I should have tried to leave through a back entrance. I'll be on every front page tomorrow.'

She felt Gabriel glance at her. 'Why should you? You've nothing to be ashamed of.'

Leonora's heart was pounding. She saw Gabriel's hand work the gearstick. Square-shaped long fingers. Short, blunt nails. Masculine.

Her lower body clenched.

'You didn't have to do this,' she said.

Her voice was husky. She looked at Gabriel, whose jaw was tight.

'It's nothing. You shouldn't have been thrown to the wolves like that.'

She got the impression that he was angry. On her behalf. She barely knew him. Her relief at being out of that situation was taking the edges off her own anger at Lazaro.

'Well…thank you.'

She noticed then that they were driving through one of

Madrid's exclusive city enclaves. Leafy streets and chic cosmopolitan bars and restaurants. Expensive antique shops and designer boutiques. Elegant buildings mixed with new architecture.

Feeling embarrassed now, and thinking that Gabriel might be regretting his good deed, Leonora said, 'You really don't have to take me home. I'm the other way, anyway. I can jump out here and get a taxi.'

He shook his head and glanced in the rear-view mirror. 'Not if you don't want them to follow you home, you can't.'

Leonora looked behind them and saw a couple of motorbikes weaving in and out of traffic, following them. Her heart sank at the thought of them outside the family estate. If Matías saw them he'd get confused and upset...

At that moment Gabriel said, 'Hang on,' and then surged ahead as a traffic light turned to red. He negotiated a couple of rapid turns down dark side streets that had Leonora's heart jumping into her throat, but at no point did she feel unsafe. It was exhilarating.

With the next turn into a quiet residential street Leonora sucked in a breath. It looked as if they were going to drive straight into a wall, but it quickly revealed itself to be a door that opened and allowed them entry down into a private garage under the building.

Gabriel pulled to a stop beside a row of equally sleek cars. 'I think we lost them at the last traffic lights.'

Silence descended around them. 'Where are we?' she asked.

'At my city apartment. You can wait here for a bit—let them lose you. I'll organise for you to get home later. If you want.'

If you want.

Leonora looked at Gabriel, still reeling at everything that had happened and at the fact that he was her rescuer.

His eyes were on her, dark and unreadable, and yet she felt as if some silent communication was taking place. Something she didn't understand fully. Or didn't want to investigate fully.

'Okay…if you're sure. I don't want to bother you.'

He shook his head. 'You're not bothering me. Don't worry.'

He undid his seat-belt and uncoiled his tall frame from the car. He came around and opened her door and held out a hand.

Leonora almost didn't want to touch him, afraid of how she'd react. She could still feel the imprint of his hand on her elbow. But she couldn't dither, so she put her hand in his and let him pull her out. And she'd been right to be afraid, because a jolt of electricity ran up her arm and right down into her core.

By the time she straightened up she was breathless. And she was so close to Gabriel that one more step would bring her flush with his body. She could sense the whipcord strength beneath his bespoke suit. Her eye line rested just below his bowtie.

His hand wrapped around hers. 'Okay?'

She looked up and forced a smile, trying not to be intimidated by the sheer masculine beauty of the man. His proximity. 'Fine… Just a bit shaky after the paparazzi. Normally I don't register on their radar.'

Not the way this man did. He was slavishly followed and speculated upon by press eager to get a story on the reclusive billionaire. She thought of the papers tomorrow. Her head hurt at the prospect of her parents' reaction. They were depending on her to redeem the family name and finances, not to embroil them in another scandal.

Gabriel let her hand go and Leonora suddenly realised something with dismay. 'My bag and coat!'

Lazaro had arranged for someone to take them to the cloakroom at the hotel.

Gabriel said, 'Come upstairs and I'll arrange for them to be delivered here.'

He opened a door that led out into a dimly lit foyer. A security guard stepped into the light. 'Good evening, Señor Torres.'

'Good evening, Pancho. One of my team will be delivering something shortly. Let them in and send it up, please.'

'Of course, sir.'

Gabriel put his hand on Leonora's back, guiding her with a barely perceptible touch over to an elevator. Even so, she could feel his hand through her dress, and had the ridiculous urge to sink back against him, let him take her weight.

It unnerved her how much he made her *feel*, so she stood apart from him in the small space as the doors slid shut and he pressed a button. It rose silently and stopped a few seconds later with a small jerking motion.

The doors slid open and Gabriel put out a hand, indicating for Leonora to precede him. She stepped out and into a stunning penthouse apartment. It had all the original features of the building's era—around the nineteenth century, Leonora guessed—but none of the fussiness.

It was a very contemporary apartment in the shell of one of Madrid's classic buildings. Modern art hung on the walls, with spotlights directing the eye to bold slashing strokes and colours. Surprisingly sensual. Something about the design—the lack of clutter, the open spaces—soothed her. The furniture was deceptively plain and unobtrusive, letting the interior speak for itself. She'd never seen anything quite like it.

She watched as Gabriel strode over to French doors, opening them to let some air in. Leonora only realised then how close it was. The late-summer city heat was still oppressive. He took his phone out of his pocket and made a call, speaking in low tones. She assumed he was arranging to have her things collected.

He turned around to face her then, tugging at his bowtie, undoing it. Opening the top button of his shirt. She almost looked away, feeling as if she was intruding on some intimacy.

He gestured with a hand to a couch. 'Please—sit, make yourself comfortable...'

Leonora stepped further into the room, feeling naked without her wrap or bag. 'I'm fine, thank you. You have a beautiful apartment.'

No doubt it was just one of the hundreds of properties owned by him and his family all over Spain and the world.

It was well known that he was seen very much as the patriarch of his family, even though his father was still alive. And Leonora was vaguely aware of a rumour about his younger sister going off the rails and how she'd been sent abroad to clean up her act.

She shivered slightly at the thought of what it must be like to face a disapproving or angry Gabriel Torres. She didn't even know his sister, or if the rumour was true, but she already felt sorry for her.

'Would you like a drink?' He walked over to an elaborate drinks cabinet. 'I have whiskey, brandy, champagne, wine, gin—'

'I'll have a little whiskey please,' she blurted out, needing something to settle her clanging nerves.

He poured dark golden liquid into a small tumbler and brought it over to her. 'It's Irish. I believe it's meant to be very good.'

Leonora took it, distracted by the bowtie dangling at his

neck and the open top button of his shirt. She could see dark bronzed skin. A hint of hair.

'You haven't tasted it?'

He shook his head. 'I don't drink.'

She watched as he moved back, giving her space. It fitted that he didn't drink. He seemed far too controlled. Exacting. Alert. She wondered why he didn't, but wasn't going to ask.

As if he could read her mind, though, he supplied, 'I was put off after watching how alcohol affected people's judgement and their decision-making. Not least my father's. He almost ruined the family business.'

So that was why Gabriel now ran their extensive operation.

'I'm sorry to hear that...' Impulsively she added, 'I have some idea of what you're talking about.'

She wondered why she'd said that, but there was something about being in this space with this man that didn't feel entirely real.

To her relief he didn't say anything, or ask her to elaborate on the fact that her father's vices had driven them to the brink and over. Anyway, he probably knew the sordid details. Most people did. But for the first time she didn't feel that burning rise of shame. Maybe it was his admission that his family wasn't perfect either.

He said, 'I'm sorry for what happened to you this evening. You didn't deserve that. You're too good for a man like Lazaro Sanchez.'

Leonora clutched the tumbler to her chest. She'd yet to take a sip of the drink. 'You don't have to be sorry. It wasn't your fault. And how can you say I'm too good for him? You don't even know me.'

'Don't I?' he asked softly, raising a dark brow. 'We come from the same world, Leonora. We might not have had a conversation before now, but we know more about each other than you realise—and I'm not talking about idle gossip. I'm talking about the lives we've led. The expectations on our shoulders. The life built on legacy and duty. Responsibility.'

CHAPTER TWO

GABRIEL MARVELLED AT how expressive Leonora was. She clearly hadn't expected him to say that. He'd caught her unawares. Her eyes were wide on his, as if he'd shocked her.

He realised now that they weren't dark brown, as he'd assumed. They were grey. Like a stormy ocean. But even as he had that fanciful notion she seemed to come back to herself and her face resumed its serene mask. The same one she'd been wearing earlier, standing beside Lazaro Sanchez. Before all hell had broken loose.

She took a sip of her drink and he noticed her hand wasn't entirely steady. He had to clench his fist to stop from reaching out and taking her hand in his. He saw her throat work as she swallowed and he imagined the burn of the alcohol as it slipped down into her stomach, radiating heat. Mirroring the heat he felt in his blood.

Dios, but she was stunning. Possibly the most beautiful woman he'd ever seen. And she was getting to him in a way that made him distinctly uncomfortable. Usually when he desired a woman it was a manageable thing. Right now it was taking all his restraint not to seduce Leonora to within an inch of her life and demand the satisfaction his body was crying out for. A kind of satisfaction that he knew instinctively would eclipse anything he'd ever experienced before.

He stepped back and gestured to a nearby couch. 'Please, sit down. Your things should be here soon.'

* * *

For a long moment Leonora couldn't move. She was still in shock at how succinctly Gabriel had summed up her existence.

'The lives we've led... The expectations on our shoulders... The life built on legacy and duty. Responsibility.'

She'd never felt that anyone could possibly understand what her life was like. She had very little to complain about and yet sometimes she felt as trapped as if she was in jail.

He was looking at her. He'd just asked if she wanted to sit down.

She shook her head jerkily. 'No, I'm fine. Thank you.'

She felt restless, and she walked over to where floor-to-ceiling windows looked out over a terrace and further, to the skyline of Madrid under a clear starlit sky. She had a very fleeting moment of wondering what Lazaro was doing right now. Dealing with the mother of his child?

A tiny sense of hysteria at what had happened rose up and she took another hasty sip of whiskey to try and force it back down.

Gabriel came to stand near her. She could see him in the reflection of the window. He'd taken off his jacket and his chest and shoulders looked impossibly broad under the snowy shirt.

She saw her own reflection. The strapless red dress. She'd hoped its elegant simplicity would prove to be timeless, because it was many seasons out of date. She saw the glittering drop earrings hanging from her earlobes that looked like diamonds. But they weren't diamonds at all. They were cubic zirconia. It was a long time since she'd worn any real family jewels. They'd all been sold by her father to get money for gambling.

She felt like a fraud, and the humiliation from earlier

rose up again. She quickly downed the last of her drink, guiltily relishing the last dregs of comfort from the alcohol.

She turned to face Gabriel, avoiding his eye. 'I should leave—go home. My mother and father will be worried.'

And Matías.

Just thinking of him made her heart hurt. What would happen to them now? If they lost the castle then that was it. They would have hit rock bottom with no way back. An entire dynasty and legacy wiped out through the actions of her father...

'Don't go yet.'

She looked at Gabriel. Her heart thumped hard. His face was all lean angles and harsh lines. And then softened by that ridiculously sensual mouth.

'We're still waiting for your things.'

Leonora was torn. She wanted to appear totally at ease and sophisticated, draping herself artfully on one of the sofas while wittily regaling Gabriel with inconsequential chatter. But that wasn't her. Had never been her.

'I can get them tomorrow. They're not that important.'

She felt that the longer she stood there the quicker he'd see that he was having an effect on her.

He came closer and moved to take the empty glass from her hand. He put his fingers over hers. A deliberate move? The breath stuck in her throat. He was so...*vital*. Lazaro had never had this effect on her and she'd believed that it would make for a better marriage. No extreme feelings or wants.

Gabriel said, 'The paparazzi will know for sure by now that your engagement wasn't announced. They'll be actively hunting you down. Waiting for you. You should call your parents—warn them to stay inside.'

Leonora swallowed. Gabriel's fingers were still on hers. 'But I can't just...stay here.'

'Of course you can.' He took the glass out of her nerveless fingers and in the same motion, with his other hand, he handed her his phone. 'Use this.'

It seemed to be a foregone conclusion. And she knew he was right. She couldn't go back home now and face a barrage of lights and questions. Out of concern for Matías as much as anything else.

Leonora moved away from Gabriel and dialled her home number. Her mother answered, immediately concerned, and Leonora rushed to assure her that everything was okay. She filled her in on the broad strokes of what had happened and told her not to worry. She told her that she'd spend the night elsewhere, to draw the press away from the de la Vega home. Her mother sounded disappointed—and then just weary. They'd been here before, with the press camped outside.

When she'd ended the conversation, after checking that Matías was okay, Leonora handed the phone back.

Gabriel said, 'Your brother is not well?'

Leonora gave a small tight smile. 'He has…learning difficulties. Since birth. He's home at the moment—from the school he attends just outside Madrid.'

The school that was paid for out of the receipts from tours around the Flores de la Vega castle. And with the money from the designer clothes and jewellery Leonora sold over the years online. The school that he loved and thrived in. The school that was offering him a real chance at a life in the outside world as he moved into adulthood.

The school that they would no longer be able to afford if they had to sell the castle—the only thing keeping them afloat in a sea of debts.

'He picks up on moods and tension very acutely, so he'd be upset if he knew the press were outside, or if there was anything wrong with me.'

'You're close?'

Leonora looked at Gabriel, expecting to see the same look most people had when they heard about Matías, varying between mild disdain and salacious curiosity. Or pity. But Gabriel's face and eyes held none of those things. Just a genuine question.

She nodded, feeling emotional. 'The closest. He's eighteen now, and when he was born I was six. He was like my baby more than my little brother.'

'That would have been before your fortunes…changed.'

Leonora appreciated his attempt at tact. He was obviously referring to the fact that her parents had once been such fixtures on the Spanish social scene that they probably hadn't been around much to parent. Making their fall from grace even more explosive. They'd gone down in a ball of flames and infamy when her father had been thrown out of the casino in Monte Carlo with his wife clinging to his coat, weeping uncontrollably.

That was one of the reasons for their reclusiveness these days. Her parents' shame. Hence their desire and need for redemption. Through Leonora.

She diverted her mind from that and said, 'Something like that. Yes.' She looked away, embarrassed.

'That was them—not you. You're not like them.'

Leonora looked at him. Had he moved closer? The way he made her feel—the way he seemed to be looking deeper into her than anyone else ever had—made her prickly.

'You don't know that I don't have a gambling habit.'

He seemed to consider this for a moment, and then he said, 'True, I don't. But I don't believe you do.'

He was definitely closer now. Close enough for Leonora to see the stubble lining his jaw. And that his eyes had golden flecks—they weren't just brown.

She shook her head. 'Why are you doing this? Why do

you care what happens to me? We've never met before this evening. I mean…not properly.'

Even with Leonora's family connections they'd moved in a lesser sphere than the Torres family.

'No. But our paths have crossed—even if just peripherally. I realised something this evening—I have always noticed you…on the edges. As if you'd prefer to disappear.'

Leonora blushed to think she'd been so transparent.

'And I realised something else.'

She looked at him.

'You have become a very beautiful woman.'

A tingling rush of heat coursed through her blood. The way he was looking at her was so…*intense*. She could almost feel it…as if he was touching her.

He took another step closer. Almost close enough now that she could imagine him bending down and pressing his mouth to hers.

Leonora was barely breathing. She was hot—so hot. All over. Deep down where no man had ever had any effect on her before.

'I want you, Leonora.'

For a long, suspended moment neither one of them moved. Gabriel was watching her as she struggled to absorb this information. So, all these sensations making her melt from the inside out…it wasn't just her.

For a second it was too heady to consider. The fact that he thought she was beautiful. And that he wanted her. *Her.* A woman who lived a more sheltered existence than most nuns.

At that moment there was a chiming sound. Gabriel emitted a curse under his breath and said, 'Don't move. That's the concierge with your things.'

He turned and she watched him walk across the vast room with athletic grace. He disappeared and she heard a door open, low voices. She saw the French doors and suddenly needed—craved—oxygen. She walked outside, drawing in deep lungsful of the night air. The sounds of traffic floating up from nearby streets helped to ground her in reality a little.

What was she doing? Practically falling into Gabriel Torres's arms after mere words? He was probably just being polite, helping to soothe what he assumed was her damaged ego. But in all honesty relief was her overriding feeling when she thought about Lazaro and the wreckage of their engagement.

It had been an audacious plan in any case—agreeing to marry a man purely for strategic reasons. Because it would benefit them both. It shamed her now. Yet she knew it was silly to feel shame, because her parents' marriage had been a strategic one. In their world *every* marriage was a strategic one. Too much was at stake when legacies and dynasties had to be passed down to the next generation for emotion to be involved in making a marriage.

The fact that her parents got on and had some affection for each other was just a bonus. It had helped them weather the storm of infamy and their son's vulnerabilities.

But Leonora—much to her eternal embarrassment—had always secretly harboured a desire for more. For a *real* relationship. For love. Happiness. She saw visiting tourist couples walking through the castle and its grounds, sharing kisses, holding hands. Whispering things to each other.

She'd met an old English couple, married for fifty years. They'd exuded such an aura of contentment and happiness. She knew what they had was rare, but not unobtainable. For normal people. Not for her.

When Lazaro Sanchez had shown an interest and taken her on a few dates, and when he'd put forward his proposal and the fact that he was offering to pull them out of their quagmire of debts, Leonora had known that she had no choice. She had responsibilities, just as Gabriel had said. The Flores de la Vega legacy was bigger than her secret hopes and dreams for a different life. A more fulfilled life.

'I want you, Leonora.'

She shivered, even though it wasn't cold. She shivered with awareness. With desire.

'I have always noticed you...on the edges. As if you'd prefer to disappear.'

How could a man who was little more than a stranger— no matter how much their worlds might have collided over the years—*get* her? More than anyone had ever got her before?

She'd never felt seen in her life. She'd hovered on the edges, exactly as he'd described. Out of the innate shyness that she had to work hard to overcome. Out of her concern for Matías, who found social situations very challenging.

And also because she'd never really enjoyed the social scene of their world. It had always reminded her of a medieval royal court, with its intrigue and politics. Petty cruelties. The way so-called friends had treated her and her parents and her brother like pariahs ever since they'd become *persona non grata* had been a formative lesson in human nature.

Had Gabriel Torres really told her that he wanted her? So bold? So direct?

Yes. He was that kind of man. He would just say what he wanted and expect results.

Leonora looked out over the city stretching before her. Millions of people living their lives. Millions of possibilities.

It was as if she'd stepped out of her life and into an alternative realm. Where anything could happen. She was in a moment out of time. In a place she'd never expected to be. With a man she would never in a million years have expected to know her name. Let alone...*desire* her.

Unless it wasn't desire.

It must be pity.

A wave of humiliation rose up through her. Oh, God, was she so desperate that she really believed—?

She heard a noise and tensed to face Gabriel again. She needed to leave. *Now.*

Gabriel saw the moment Leonora heard him return. Her slim shoulders were suddenly a tense line. He stood behind her, drinking in her graceful figure. The smooth pale olive skin of her back. The sleek dark ponytail that he wanted to wrap around his fist so he could tilt her head back, giving him access to her lush mouth.

He might have started this evening fixated on Lazaro Sanchez, and wondering what the man was up to, but now all he could see was this woman.

'I have your things.'

She turned around but he noticed that she avoided his eye.

She held out a hand. 'Thank you. I really should go now. There's a back entrance into the estate. I can use that. I'm sure they won't see me.'

Gabriel handed her the wrap and bag, noting how she avoided touching his hand. A novelty when he was used to women throwing themselves at him. Especially if he told them that he wanted them.

'Are you really willing to take that risk?'

She put her wrap around her shoulders, covering up her skin, crossing it over her chest like a shawl.

Eventually she looked at him. 'Look, thank you for helping me, but you really don't need to go out of your way to do any more.'

Gabriel moved closer to her, watching how her eyes

flared and colour tinged her cheeks. She wanted him. He knew it.

'Did you not hear what I said?'

She swallowed. Her fingers clutched her wrap.

For a second the possibility trickled into Gabriel's mind that she was different from other women he knew in terms of experience, but he batted it away. She was twenty-four. To be inexperienced at her age, with her stunning beauty, in this modern cynical world, was practically an impossibility. Far more likely she was playing him. She knew he wanted her and she was getting off on watching him work to seduce her.

There was little novelty in Gabriel's world and he suspected it was the same for her. She was hardly a wide-eyed innocent when she'd been about to announce a business arrangement masquerading as a marriage.

'I want you, Leonora. You felt it too this evening. I saw it.'

She flushed and her eyes were huge. 'But…we don't even know each other. How can—?'

'How can it be possible?' Gabriel decided he'd indulge her faux innocence. 'Because chemistry transcends such mundanities.'

Every line in her body was tense.

'You don't have to do this, you know.'

There was a fierce pride in the aristocratic lines of her beautiful face. Her eyes had turned stormy.

'I don't need your pity, Gabriel.'

Leonora was resisting the pull she felt to this man with every atom of her being. He was toying with her. He had no clue how inexperienced she was and she wasn't about to let him expose her any more than she'd already been exposed tonight.

She went to move past him, intent on getting out of there

before she could unravel completely, but he caught her hand, stopping her. Heat travelled up her arm. She clenched her jaw.

'You seriously think I *pity* you?'

The incredulity in his tone compelled her to face him, her hand still in his. He was frowning. Suddenly she was very aware of their proximity, and of the darkness of his chest under the white shirt.

She swallowed. 'Maybe you just feel sorry for me…for what happened. You feel some kind of responsibility to make me feel…better.'

Even as she said this out loud she wanted to cringe. It sounded ridiculous.

He shook his head. 'You give me far too much credit. I'm not that nice. I told you I want you because I meant it. And I believe you want me too. You wanted me even as you stood beside your fiancé.'

Leonora flushed with guilty heat. She tried to pull her hand back but Gabriel didn't let go. He tugged her closer. She couldn't breathe.

'You don't believe I want you? I can prove to you that I do. And that you want me.'

Leonora knew that if she tugged hard she'd be free. She knew that if she did that, and if she turned and walked away, he wouldn't stop her. He was too proud for that. Too sophisticated to chase a woman or force her. And yet…she couldn't move. *Didn't want to.* That sense of being in a moment outside time, outside of her life, was acute.

As if sensing her vacillation, Gabriel said, 'Here you are beholden to no one. There's no duty or responsibility. We're just two people. A man and a woman who want each other. Who are free to indulge our mutual desire.'

Leonora searched the hard planes of his face, those dark eyes. Was it really that simple? Could it be that simple? *Was* she free?

She thought of where she would be now if that woman hadn't interrupted the announcement of her engagement.

She would be in a very similar situation with a man she'd liked, but hadn't wanted. Maybe he would be kissing her now and she would be feeling nothing, resigning herself to the fact that this was as good as it would get. Because so much more was at stake. The future of her family. Her brother's security.

She considered the vagaries of fate and timing and how she might not be here at all, how she wouldn't be feeling this terrifying but exhilarating wildness coursing through her blood right now.

But she was. And it sank in that Gabriel Torres was deadly serious. He wasn't being nice. Or pitying her. He wanted her. And she wanted him. For one night. One night out of time.

The wildness rushing through her body turned into something far more reckless. Tonight she really was free. Tomorrow she would return to reality and pick up the pieces of her life.

She wanted to seize this moment that fate had handed her. A chance to experience true desire with a man who wanted her for *her*. Not because of who she was or what her name represented.

Gabriel was watching her. Reading her.

Without saying a word, letting his actions speak for him, he let her hand go and reached for her wrap, tugging it out of her hands, pulling it off her shoulders slowly. The silk trailed across her skin and she shivered minutely at the sensation. She'd never thought of herself as sensual before, but she felt sensual now. Under his gaze.

His eyes not leaving hers, he draped the wrap over the back of a nearby chair and Leonora could see it out of the corner of her eyes, a vivid red splash of colour.

Danger. *Passion.*

He took her bag out of her hand and put it down. Anticipation built inside her, deep down. Coiling tight. She couldn't take her eyes off his face.

He said, 'I've told you I want you and I mean it. I haven't wanted a woman like this in a long time. But you owe me nothing. I brought you here to give you refuge, and my guest suite is at your disposal for as long as you need it. It's your choice what happens next.'

She let out the breath she'd been holding unconsciously. She hadn't expected that kind of consideration. And at that moment Leonora almost resented him for not just kissing her and taking the decision out of her hands.

She knew it would be so easy to gather up her wrap and bag and say, *No, sorry...not now.* But something inside her had bloomed into life and she suspected he knew that very well. Better than she did.

She felt totally out of her depth. Another woman, more experienced, would no doubt be sliding her arms around his neck, pressing herself against every hard muscle of his body. But she felt paralysed with sudden shyness.

Gabriel's gaze narrowed on her face. He frowned slightly. 'Leonora, if you don't want to—'

'I do,' she blurted out before she could lose her nerve. 'I do...want you.'

She stepped closer. They were almost touching. His sheer physicality was overwhelming but it didn't intimidate her. It excited her.

He put his hands on her arms and tugged her closer. She rested her palms on his chest. It was like steel. A spasm of sheer lust gripped her insides in a vice of tension. She pressed her thighs together to stem the heat flooding her core. But it was impossible. Every nerve quivered with anticipation and her heart was thumping so loudly she was sure it had to be audible.

Slowly, Gabriel took his hand off one of her arms and brought it up behind her head. She felt him undo her hair, so that it was loosened out of the ponytail. He massaged her scalp, his long fingers strong but surprisingly gentle. It made something else quiver inside her. Not just desire. *Emotion*.

But before that could really register he was lowering his head to hers, and as if in some desperate bid to cling on to a semblance of reality she kept her eyes on his, on those gold-flecked pools of brown. Intense and direct. Anchoring her to the moment.

But any hope of clinging to reality dissolved in a flash flood of heat when his mouth touched hers. Firm and un-yielding. Soft but hard. Masterful. She was helpless against the giddy rush of desire that ripped through her body as his mouth moved over hers, enticing her to further intimacy, coaxing her to open up to him, pressing her closer so she could feel every inch of his long, lean body.

She opened her mouth, and even though she wasn't a total novice—she had kissed boys a long time ago before her life had been reduced to staying in the shadows—she wasn't prepared for Gabriel's expertise.

His mouth and tongue demanded a response she wasn't sure how to give. She could only react instinctively. Tasting, exploring. Mimicking his movements. She felt rather than heard a growl deep in his throat as he pulled her even closer, delved deeper.

She couldn't breathe, couldn't think, but she knew she never wanted this moment to end. She'd never experienced anything so thrilling. Transporting.

When Gabriel took his mouth off hers she moved with him, loath to let the contact end. Her heart was pounding.

It was a struggle to open her eyes. When she did, it took her a second to focus. Both her hands were clinging to his shirt. She was pressed so close against him that she could feel his desire, long and thick, against her belly.

It should have shocked her. But she pressed closer in an instinctive move, emboldened by a feminine rush of confidence she'd never known before. By the evidence of this man wanting her.

He smiled, but it wasn't a gentle smile. It was hard. Knowing.

Not even that could dent Leonora's desire. She wanted this man to be her first lover, so that whatever happened next she'd always have this experience locked inside her. That was why she'd said *yes*. Because she'd realised how close she'd come to never experiencing this.

'Make love to me, Gabriel.'

He picked up one of her hands and interlocked his fingers with hers. A pulse throbbed between her legs.

His mouth quirked on one side. 'Your wish is my command.'

Even through the haze of arousal and desire making her feel drunk, Leonora doubted that this man was anyone's to command.

He kept their hands linked and led her from the living area, down a hall and to a door. He opened it and Leonora took in a vast bedroom. In contrast to what she'd seen of the apartment so far, this room was almost ascetic. Nothing but bare white walls and a few pieces of modern furniture.

Gabriel let her hand go to switch on a light. It sent out a warm golden glow, softening the hard edges in the room. She wondered about that. About its starkness. And yet it soothed her, coming from a castle stuffed to the gills with oversized furniture and dark décor more suited to the Middle Ages.

Her eyes fell on the bed—the most decadent thing in the room. Massive, and luxuriously dressed with sumptuous dark grey sheets and pillows. Unashamedly masculine. And modern.

'Come here, Leonora.'

She took her gaze off the bed and looked at Gabriel. She sucked in a breath. He filled the space. She pushed down her trepidation and walked the couple of feet over to where he stood. He was taking his cufflinks out of his shirt and placing them on top of a chest of drawers. She stood before him.

'Take off your jewellery.'

She didn't think. She obeyed. Giving herself up to this night and this man with total commitment. She took out her earrings and placed them down next to his cufflinks. Then she removed the matching bracelet. He'd probably already guessed they weren't real, but she didn't care any more.

'Take off my shirt.'

Leonora stepped closer, some of her bravado faltering as she reached for his buttons and started undoing them, revealing his impressive chest. She hoped he wouldn't notice the faint tremor in her hands. When it was open, she pushed it back and looked. Her mouth went dry. He was more like a warrior than a civilised businessman. Hard muscles. Hair curling over his pectorals and descending in a dark line at the centre of a six-pack to disappear under the waistband of his trousers.

He tugged his shirt off completely, letting it drop to the floor. 'Now you. I want to see you.'

No one had ever seen Leonora naked. Not since she was a child. When she was a teenager, fooling around with boys at after-school parties, it had always been an awkward fumbling in the dark, under clothes. Not this stark *'I want to see you'* while standing in the golden glow of a lamp in front of the most intimidating man in the world. A connoisseur of women, by all accounts.

Before Leonora could overthink it she turned around, presenting Gabriel with her back and the zip to her dress. She pulled her hair over one shoulder and steeled herself for the moment she would feel his hands at her zip. But instead of going there first, his hands landed on her shoulders, and then she felt his breath at the back of her neck, before he pressed his mouth there, the moist tip of his tongue flicking out to taste her skin.

Her legs nearly gave way completely.

She was dealing with a consummate seducer—not an over-eager boy.

His hands trailed over her skin as if he had all the time in the world to learn her shape. Goosebumps popped up even though she was warm. *Hot*. Melting…

Then his hands moved to the top of her dress and he started to pull her zip down, all the way, until it stopped just above the curve of her buttocks. His knuckles brushed her skin there and it felt as intimate as if he'd kissed her.

The dress was loosened around her chest but she brought her arms up, stopping it from falling down.

'Turn around.'

Her heart pounding, Leonora turned. After a moment she looked up and saw Gabriel's face. It was…stark. Hungry. She shivered.

He put his hands on her arms and slowly pulled them apart. The dress stayed up for a moment and then, under its own weight, fell down to her waist. She wore a matching strapless bra. Red lace.

Gabriel let her arms go and reached behind her to undo her bra. It fell away to the floor before she could worry about him noticing how frayed and worn it was.

He looked at her for a long moment. Saying nothing.

And then, 'You are more beautiful than anything I've ever imagined.'

Gabriel reached out and reverently cupped her breasts. Leonora had always felt self-conscious about their size, but they fitted Gabriel's palms perfectly. He rubbed his thumbs across her nipples and she had to bite her lip to stop herself from moaning out loud as they stiffened under his touch, almost to the point of pain.

He stopped for a moment, bringing his hands up to cup her face before seeking her mouth again and drawing her deep into a drugging kiss. Her hand clasped his wrist, needing something, anything, to root herself in this dream.

The friction of her bare breasts against his chest was sensory overload. But that was nothing… He stopped kissing her and trailed his mouth across her jaw and down the side of her neck to her shoulder, and then down to her breast. He cupped the plump flesh again and lifted it to his mouth, teasing her stiffened flesh with his tongue and teeth.

She couldn't stop the moan this time. It came out like a guttural plea to stop…never to stop…to keep going. Her hands were on his head, her fingers in his thick hair as he lavished the same torture on her other breast until they were both tingling and wet from his mouth.

When he stopped and lifted his head Leonora could barely keep standing. Gabriel pushed her dress down the rest of the way, over her hips. It fell to the floor with a barely audible swish of silk.

Now she wore only panties and stockings. Her shoes. She kicked them off, dropping a few inches in height. It made Gabriel seem even taller, more impressive.

Then, before she could worry about how to stay standing on her wobbly legs, she was lifted into the air against his chest and carried over to the bed, where he lay her down as reverently as if she was made of spun glass…

CHAPTER THREE

GABRIEL WASN'T SURE how he'd managed not to ravish Leonora before now, but he knew something was holding him back. Her reticence—which he felt sure had to be an act—was having an effect on him.

For a man who had slept with some of the world's most beautiful women, and who'd been sexually active since he was a teenager, he was finding lately that sexual liaisons had become merely satisfactory. More often than not disappointing. But here, now, he hadn't done much more than kiss Leonora and already he was having the most erotic experience he'd had in a long time. If ever.

His instincts about her had been right. She was exquisite. Every line of her body sleek and perfect. Her skin was like silk. Her breasts were perfectly shaped. And her nipples—His mouth watered again, just at the thought of how they'd tasted and stiffened against his tongue.

She was looking at him with huge eyes. As if she'd never seen a man before. Part of him was irritated that she could get to him with such a rudimentary act—was he so jaded that faux innocence turned him on?

Enough playacting.

Gabriel divested himself of the rest of his clothes.

Leonora watched as Gabriel efficiently undressed, revealing a body honed and densely muscled. And hard.

She couldn't stop her eyes widening on his arousal, thick and long.

He came down on the bed, resting over her on both hands. She suddenly felt trepidatious. What if he noticed straight away how inexperienced she was? What if it hurt? What if he was too—?

'You don't have to do this, you know...'

He bent down and surrounded one still sensitised nipple in the hot wet heat of his mouth. Leonora's back arched.

She panted, 'What...? Do what...?'

He lifted his head, a sexy smile playing around his wicked mouth. 'Put on the innocent act. You don't have to play games to entice me, Leonora. I'm enticed.'

Before she could respond to that he was ministering the same exquisite torture to her other breast. *Act? What act?* She couldn't think straight. Not when he was massaging one breast with his fingers and nipping at the other with his teeth before soothing it with his tongue.

His tongue trailed down under her breasts to her belly, dipping into her navel before moving further. Leonora tensed as he came close to the juncture of her legs. He tucked his fingers under her panties and tugged. She lifted her bottom off the bed in silent acquiescence. He pulled them down her legs and off completely. Then one stocking and the other followed them to the floor.

Now she was totally naked—like him. And yet she didn't feel self-conscious. Just...hungry. Aching. Empty inside. As if something was missing.

He was looking at her, his eyes roving over her body, and her self-consciousness returned. She was suddenly acutely aware that she didn't conform to current beauty trends by waxing every inch of her body. But Gabriel wasn't looking remotely repulsed.

He came down beside her, his hand resting on the cluster of dark curls between her legs. 'I like a woman to look like a woman.'

He kissed her then, stopping any words or more coherent thoughts. The feeling of pleasure that he liked her as she was quickly became something far more urgent as he pushed her legs apart and his hand explored further, through those tight curls to the secret place where she ached for his touch.

She gasped into his mouth when his seeking fingers found her, wet and ready. He massaged her, stroking her with expert fingers into a level of excitement that had her arching off the bed, pleading incoherently for something just out of reach, a shimmering promise of ecstasy she could almost taste.

He was relentless, teasing her to the point where she thought she would die if he didn't just—

But then, with one deep thrust and a twist of his fingers, Leonora was finally released from the tension, and she soared high on a wave of pleasure so exquisite she cried out, her hands instinctively reaching for Gabriel's wrist to stop his movements, her throbbing flesh over-sensitised.

Gabriel looked down at Leonora, transfixed by the pleasure suffusing her face. Her skin was dewed with perspiration, her cheeks pink. When she looked at him her eyes were unfocused.

'That was… That was…'

He shook his head, trying to fathom how she could manufacture a response so…earthy. Responsive.

He answered for her. 'That was amazing.'

It had been. And he was literally hanging on to the last shred of his control. Seeing her like this, her breasts moving up and down jerkily with her breaths, long dark hair tumbled across the pillow, it was all he could do to find and roll on protection.

He settled between her legs, where the core of her body was still hot and damp. She looked at him, her mouth swollen from his kisses. He'd never seen a more erotic sight, had never felt such a visceral need to join with a woman.

He couldn't wait any longer.

He put his hands on her hips, positioned himself where she was so wet and ready, and plunged deep into the hottest, tightest embrace he'd ever known.

The sensation was so exquisite that he almost climaxed in that moment.

It was also unexpected.

She was innocent.

Unbelievably.

Her eyes were wide and shocked. He saw her silent entreaty to move…to do something to alleviate this alien sensation. And Gabriel could no more deny her that silent plea than he could force his mind back to some rational place and absorb this revelation fully.

It took supreme skill and control to claw himself back from the brink and move slowly in and out…

Leonora's brain was white-hot with the sudden pain of Gabriel's body thrusting into hers and now, as the pain ebbed, with the building of a whole new level of tension. He'd looked at her just now as if he'd realised she was a virgin, but to her profound relief he hadn't said anything…

She didn't want him to say a word to take them out of this moment. She was joined with this man who had taken her over, body and soul. He lifted her buttocks up, so he could deepen his thrusts, and every single part of her body spasmed with a wave of pleasure, cancelling out any last vestige of pain.

He caught her hands, both of them, and twined his fingers with hers. He brought them over her head and held them there as he moved in and out in a relentless rhythm that made her writhe against him, seeking release from the growing tension.

She could do nothing but hold on as he wound her so high she thought she would break into a million pieces—and then, with no warning, she did break apart, on a thrust so deep that she gasped at the majesty of his body pulsing deep inside hers. She saw an expression of almost pain on his face as he stared down at her, as if he'd never seen a woman before.

Wave upon wave of ecstasy racked her body. She could feel her inner muscles clamping around Gabriel's hard length. She was his captive of pleasure and yet she'd never felt more free as she soared on a high that was breathtaking.

He jerked against her and she bit her lip to stop crying out as yet another mini-orgasm wrenched her apart all over again.

She had been so totally unprepared for this overload of sensation that she didn't even notice when Gabriel extricated himself from her embrace, slipping into the deep oblivion of deep and total satisfaction…

When Leonora woke the faint light of dawn was painting its pink trails across the sky. It took her a second to absorb the fact that she wasn't in her own bed and that she felt different.

Because she was different.

She was no longer a virgin. She had been thoroughly initiated into the art of lovemaking by a master.

She turned her head and saw Gabriel's dark one beside her. Even in sleep he looked powerful. Her gaze moved down his naked body hungrily, lingering over the densely packed muscles of his abdomen and lower, to where his masculinity looked no less impressive at rest.

Her lower body clenched. After they'd made love that first time she'd fallen into a pleasure coma. And then she'd woken a couple of hours later with her bottom tucked into Gabriel's body, his growing erection stirring against her. He'd demonstrated that that wasn't the only way to bring about intense pleasure and had brought her slowly and inexorably back to life with his hands and his mouth, showing her that what had happened hadn't been a dream.

No. It hadn't been a dream.

It had been very much an explosive and transformative reality. She held the sheet to her body, going cold inside as the full significance of the night sank in. Just hours ago she'd been about to be publicly betrothed to Lazaro Sanchez. And yet here she was, having been thoroughly bedded by a totally different man.

This behaviour was so out of character for her. She hadn't even kissed Lazaro beyond one chaste kiss on the lips. And yet she'd spent mere hours in Gabriel's company and tumbled into bed with him with barely a moment's hesitation.

She'd felt responsible for so long—since her parents had lost everything when she was a teenager—that she'd almost forgotten what it was like to want something just for herself. And now she felt supremely selfish. The paparazzi had probably been camped outside the *castillo* all night, while she'd been here indulging in sheer sensual decadence.

She felt as if millennia had passed since the previous day, when she'd set out from her home ready to commit to Lazaro Sanchez. And here she was in another man's bed.

She put a hand to her burning face.

She thought of how Gabriel had looked at her with that single-minded intensity. No one had ever looked at her like that before. As if they truly *saw* her. As a woman. Independent of her name and the scandal that had rocked her family.

And then she cursed herself.

Gabriel Torres was an experienced man of the world. A consummate lover. He probably looked at all his lovers like that. She was just one in a long line. She'd intrigued him last night, but even if he hadn't figured out she'd been a virgin she doubted very much he'd be expecting to see her again.

Terrified that he would wake and look at her, and see how profoundly he'd affected her, she stole out of the bed as quietly as she could. She held her breath when he moved, saying something incomprehensible in his sleep. When he didn't wake Leonora gathered up her things and tiptoed out of the bedroom, finding a guest suite down the hall where she dressed and repaired herself as best she could.

She avoided looking at herself in the mirror. She tried to ignore the tenderness between her legs. But then she caught a glimpse of the redness around her jaw and neck. The burn from Gabriel's stubble. The burn of shame.

She quickly pulled her hair back and tied it into a rough bun. She put her wrap around herself, hiding as much of the evidence of the passion of the night as possible. Then she crept out of the apartment and down to the lobby, where she got the concierge to call her a taxi.

Thankfully she didn't have to wait long. As it drove through the quiet early-morning streets she took a deep, shuddering breath, hating the awful bereft feeling stealing over her.

She thought of the man sprawled sexily in bed in his stunning apartment. He would wake up and get on with his life and not think about her again. Of that she was sure. Last night would barely register on his radar. How could it when she'd been such a novice?

She'd made a pact with the devil, agreeing to sleep with

Gabriel Torres, telling herself that one night would be enough. Because now the empty feeling inside her mocked her. One night with Gabriel Torres had ruined her for ever.

Gabriel woke slowly, through layers of a deep sense of satisfaction. Not just any satisfaction. Sexual satisfaction. It was a long time since he'd felt like this.

His mouth curved into a smile as images came tumbling back into his head. Long dark hair, elegant curves, high, firm breasts with deliciously hard nipples... Brown curls covering the apex between her legs—the place where he'd lost himself and found ecstasy. The best sex he'd ever had.

With a virgin.

His eyes snapped open on that thought and he jack-knifed up in the bed, instantly awake.

She'd been a virgin.

He hadn't been able to process that information fully in the midst of the hottest experience of his life. She hadn't asked him to stop. She'd entreated him to go on with those huge grey eyes. And he'd tipped over the edge of his legendary control.

Uncomfortably, he had to concede now that he didn't think it had been her innocence that had elevated the experience beyond the realms of normality. It had been *her*. And their unique chemistry. He'd had no idea it would be so explosive.

Where was she?

There was a stillness in the bedroom that extended out into the apartment. He stood up from the bed and pulled on a pair of jeans, and only then noticed that it was bright outside. Already morning. He could hear the faint hum of city traffic.

He felt discombobulated. He always woke at dawn, if not before. He never slept in.

He padded through the apartment, an uneasy and unfamiliar feeling of exposure sliding into his gut.

There was no sign of her. Literally no sign. Had he dreamt it all? Then he saw the small tumbler that still held some alcohol. He didn't like the sense of relief.

He went back into his bedroom and something glinted in the morning light on his cabinet. Her jewellery. She'd left it behind. He went over and picked it up and recognised instantly that it wasn't real. Costume jewellery. To create a façade.

Leonora Flores de la Vega. The heiress with nothing to her name except her name. And her astonishing beauty. A virgin who'd left him behind in his bed.

No woman ever left him. *He* left women. And no woman left him with this hungry, clawing ache of need.

Even after only one night he could sense that the more he had of her, the more he would want. Unprecedented. One night with her was not enough. Not nearly enough.

As he stood under the powerful spray of his shower a few minutes later Gabriel knew that Leonora Flores was not like his usual women. There was a wildness under her serene exterior and it resonated with something inside him—a wild streak he never allowed to surface in his day-to-day life, when he had to be supremely controlled and on guard at all times. Too many people depended on him.

He'd been her first lover. And he couldn't deny that, along with the erotic charge he felt thinking of that, he also felt something else totally uncharacteristic. *Possessive.* It had been there the previous evening too, when he'd felt the electric current between them as she'd stood beside Sanchez with his arm around her waist.

Gabriel emerged from the shower and slung a towel around his waist. He caught a glimpse of himself in the mirror over the sink and stopped, looking long and hard at his reflection. He was thirty-three years old. He'd been ignoring his advisors' not so subtle whispers for some time now. Whispers that had been getting more insistent. Whispers about settling down. Putting forward a more respectable image. Being a family man.

Something lodged in Gabriel's gut at that thought. *Family man.* He'd always known that he would have to have a family some day. After all, he was the last in his line. But after his emotionally sterile upbringing, with two parents who had despised each other, he'd never relished the prospect.

And he'd never fully admitted to himself that while the thought of a family terrified him on one level, on another he'd always wondered if he could do it any differently? He'd grown up with one assertion—never to bring children into this world and leave them to their fate as his own parents had.

His younger sister had suffered more than he had, and he still felt guilty that he hadn't noticed her descent into chaos. But by then he'd been the only thing holding the Cruz y Torres empire together...

Both his parents had conducted extramarital affairs for as long as he could remember, and he'd routinely witnessed them lying to each other about their activities to the point when it had become farcical.

Gabriel was ashamed to recall that when he had been much younger, he'd had a fantasy of a relationship far removed from what he'd seen with his parents. Uncynical. Respectful. Kind. But life had shown him that he was a fool to have such dreams when he'd found his first lover in bed with his so-called best friend.

She'd told Gabriel she'd seduced his friend to make Gabriel jealous. He'd thrown his lover and his best friend out, and from that day forward had ruthlessly quashed his silly teenage fantasies.

But perhaps he had finally met someone with whom he could envisage embarking on the next phase of his life. He wasn't such a fool as to equate physical innocence with honesty, but there was something special and unique about Leonora Flores de la Vega.

She was stunningly beautiful, and she oozed elegance and class in spite of the fact that she was all but penniless. They had the most insane chemistry Gabriel had ever experienced with a woman.

And clearly, if she'd been prepared to marry Lazaro Sanchez, she was in the market for marriage.

The thought of her with that man made Gabriel's hands clench into fists. His expression in the mirror turned hard.

Sanchez had obviously been ready to make a lifelong commitment in a bid to garner respect. Perhaps it was a sign that Gabriel finally needed to deal with something he'd been pushing away for a long time. Saying a curt *Not yet* whenever another advisor tentatively mentioned the notion of settling down.

But maybe 'not yet' had become now.

Leonora Flores de la Vega was perfect on every level for what he envisaged in a marriage. He had never been so old-fashioned as to have expected a virginal wife, but he couldn't deny that her innocence appealed to a deeply masculine part of him. As did the knowledge that she hadn't slept with Sanchez.

She was from *their* world. She knew how these marriages worked. And after last night he didn't have to worry about compatibility.

Last night he hadn't seduced Leonora for any other reason than because he wanted her. Sanchez had been the last person on his mind. But now...

He relished the perfection of timing and serendipity. And the opportunity to show Lazaro Sanchez in a very comprehensive way that a woman like Leonora Flores de la Vega was out of his league.

For ever.

When Leonora arrived back at the *castillo* after driving Matías back to his school, she found her mother waiting for her, looking pale and agitated.

'What is it? Is it Papá?'

Leonora always had the fear that something would set her father off again. Something like this—his daughter getting jilted in public by her fiancé.

Her mother shook her head. 'No, nothing like that. Papá is having a nap. You got a phone call...from Gabriel Torres. He wants you to call him back.'

Her mother was handing her a note with a number on it before Leonora could fully register it. It had been two days since that cataclysmic night. Two days of feeling alternately shocked and shamed and giddy at what had happened. And two days of the knowledge sinking in that of *course* Gabriel wasn't going to be chasing her down.

Except now butterflies exploded in her belly. Along with a far more carnal tug of awareness. And the man wasn't even here.

She looked at the number. A cell phone number.

Her mother gripped her arm. 'Oh, Leo—*Gabriel Torres*. You must have made an impression.'

Leonora's face burned and she avoided her mother's eye. She'd been vague about Gabriel's involvement the other night, making it sound as if he'd just offered her a place to hide out. But she knew he'd offered her so much more. And delivered.

She scrabbled for something to say. 'Mamá, I'm sure

he's getting in touch for something quite boring. Let me go and call him back.'

Her mother shooed her off, two bright pink spots in her cheeks, making her look girlish for her fifty-four years.

Leonora's insides cramped as she went into the castle's office, the administrative centre where they took bookings for tours. Tours that were falling increasingly in numbers because people inevitably wanted to experience something more exciting than just walking around a dusty medieval castle full of antiques and scary-looking portraits of long-dead ancestors and a tired and wilted walled garden.

Her family's dependence on her sat heavily on her shoulders today. She'd just had a painful conversation at Matías's school about overdue fees.

She sat down at the desk and put the piece of paper in front of her. She pulled her cell phone out of her pocket and keyed in his number. For an age she sat there, a little paralysed at the thought of hearing that deep rumble of a voice again.

Then, before she could lose her nerve, she pressed the key and after a second heard the long ring tone.

The call was picked up almost immediately with an impatient, brusque tone. *'Si?'*

She almost cut off the connection, he sounded so forbidding, and then his tone changed and he said sharply, 'Leonora, is that you?'

She gulped. 'Yes, it's me.'

'Thank you for calling me back.'

She thought she detected a dry tone in his voice. She didn't imagine he had many women doing a disappearing act on him.

'I'm sorry for...for leaving the way I did the other morning...but I felt it was for the best.'

'For who? You? Or me...?'

Leonora squirmed in the chair. 'Both of us… It was—'

She stopped. She'd been about to say *just a moment out of time,* but that sounded far too whimsical.

'It was just one night.'

'An incredible night.'

His voice was low and it seemed to rumble down the phone and across Leonora's skin. Her mouth went dry and her palms got clammy just thinking about it.

Then he said, 'I'd like to take you out for dinner.'

Leonora pushed aside the X-rated memories. 'Dinner?'

'Yes…' He sounded amused.

'When?'

'Tonight. I'll pick you up at seven.'

'I…'

'Do you have plans, Leonora?'

Was it her imagination or was there a mocking tone in his voice now? Of course she didn't have plans—other than the endless worrying about what was to become of them.

She tried to sound as nonchalant as possible. 'No, I don't have plans this evening.'

He became brisk again. 'Good. I'll see you at seven.'

CHAPTER FOUR

BY ALMOST SEVEN that evening Leonora was a bag of nerves at the thought of seeing Gabriel again after sharing such intimacies, and also wondering what he wanted. A repeat of that night? Or was he just intrigued because she wasn't like his usual lovers?

The thought had slid into her mind over the past couple of days...wondering if he'd noticed her innocence. But he hadn't said anything. And certainly any pain had been fleeting.

She tensed when she heard the low purr of a powerful engine and crunching gravel, not remotely ready to see the man again.

Liar.

She went to the window and peeked out, feeling like a coward. She watched him step out of a low-slung sports car—a different one from the other night. This was black.

He was dressed semi-casually, in dark trousers and a lighter toned long-sleeved top. She could imagine the material was expensive, the way it moulded to the muscles of his chest as he came around the car.

He looked stern. Austere. But then she remembered how he'd smiled wickedly. Sexily. Her insides spasmed.

She was about to go into the hall to answer the door when he rang the bell, but just then she heard quick footsteps cross the marbled hall and cursed silently. Her mother.

Seizing on the opportunity to meet the man who had been Leonora's knight in shining armour the other night.

Her mother's disapproval of Lazaro Sanchez's behaviour, as compared to the gallant actions of one of their own, had spoken volumes about what she'd really thought of Leonora's first fiancé. And yet, Leonora thought cynically, her mother would have been only too happy to have Lazaro's money paying off their debts and restoring their reputation.

The front door opened and Leonora heard voices—her mother's too high and girlish, and Gabriel's much lower. A light sweat broke out on her brow. She wished there was a mirror to check her reflection again.

Her black silk shirt dress with its wide belt had at one time been fashionable, with its thigh-high slit, but now she was afraid it was far too provocative and out of date. She touched the buttons again, to make sure they were done up as far as they could go—which didn't feel high enough. And should she have put her hair up?

Footsteps approached and she realised she was clasping her hands like a schoolteacher. She unclasped them just before the door opened.

Leonora only saw Gabriel, filling the doorway as if this massive house had been built around him.

Her mother said redundantly, 'Leo, Mr Torres is here.'

Leonora moved forward, shaky in high heels. For a ridiculous moment she wasn't sure if she should put out her hand to shake his, but then he reached for her, taking her shoulders in his hands and bending down to kiss her on each cheek.

His scent caught her unawares, hurtling her back in time to the other evening. She put her hands up to his arms—in a bid to stay standing as much as anything else.

'Señorita de la Vega. Thank you for agreeing to come and have dinner with me.'

There was a tone in his voice that made her look at him. Intimate. Complicit. It sent a flash of heat between her legs.

He straightened up and let her go. 'Shall we?'

Leonora gave her mother a quick kiss and walked out ahead of Gabriel while he exchanged a few parting words with her mother. He came out and opened the passenger door of the car, waiting until she got in. She tried to gather herself as he came around the car and got in.

He sat behind the wheel. But instead of starting the car he looked at her and said, *'Leo?'*

It took her a second to understand his meaning. 'Matías called me Leo when he was small. It kind of stuck…in spite of my father's distaste for shortening names.'

Leonora couldn't look away from those mesmerising gold-flecked eyes. His jaw was clean-shaven, but she could still remember the way her skin had felt so tender after kissing him. It had burned. Like she burned now…deep inside.

'Leo…' he said. Slowly. Testing it out. And then, 'I like it. It suits you. Makes me think of a lioness.'

His mouth curved into a small smile and then he turned the ignition on and drove down the drive and out of the property.

Leonora was breathless. So much for trying to regain her composure. She'd never thought driving a car could be considered sexy, but watching the way Gabriel drove, with nonchalant confidence, was undeniably compelling.

She was able to study him as he drove, taking in the thick hair swept back off his forehead. The long aquiline nose, more than hinting at his exclusive lineage. The hard jaw and that sensual mouth, made for sin. And that powerful body. Hard and honed. Not an ounce of spare muscle.

A warrior's body in the guise of a very modern man. All in all, an intoxicating package.

He glanced at her and she looked away, face burning.

She realised her thigh was bared in the slit of the dress and hurriedly pulled it together, holding it with her hand.

'I've seen your thigh, Leonora.'

Her face burned hotter. She didn't know how to handle this…this flirting.

She blurted out, 'The other night… It wasn't… I don't usually behave like that.'

Something shifted in the atmosphere as Gabriel pulled up smoothly to a red traffic light. She risked a look at him and saw he was staring straight ahead, hands on the wheel.

'I thought as much,' he said after a moment, the car moving forward again.

Now she felt even more exposed. Clearly her inexperience had been woefully obvious. But hopefully not the full extent of it.

'Why didn't you tell me you were a virgin?'

Leonora felt the blood drain from her face. From hot to cold in seconds. 'How did you know?' she asked through bloodless lips.

Thankfully Gabriel needed to focus on the traffic, so he was looking ahead and not at her.

'Because I've never slept with a virgin before.'

Leonora wanted to slip down in the seat and disappear altogether, drowning in a pool of humiliation. But she forced herself to sit straight.

'Why did you ask me out this evening if you know I'm such a novice? I'm sure there are many women who can provide more experienced entertainment.'

She felt him glance at her but she stared straight ahead.

'You misunderstand me, Leonora. I did not say this was a negative thing.' He waited a moment and then he said, in a low voice that rubbed along every nerve-ending, 'In fact it was the most erotic experience of my life.'

That made Leonora even more rigid. 'If you've asked

me out because I'm some kind of novelty to you—' Her flow of words halted when Gabriel swung abruptly into a layby and he came to a stop.

She looked at him and he turned to face her, the car idling. He looked stern and she swallowed.

'I did not ask you out because you're a novelty. I asked you out because I desire you very much.'

His gaze dropped to her mouth and he muttered something unintelligible to himself. Then, before she knew what was happening, he closed the distance between them, snaked a hand under her hair to the back of her neck and his mouth was on hers, possessing her so thoroughly that by the time he broke the kiss she was pressed against him, hands clutching at his jacket.

She was gasping, dizzy. After mere seconds. Her mouth throbbed. His kiss had been swift and explicitly sexual.

He raised a brow. 'That is no novelty. That is the kind of chemistry and desire that comes along very rarely. Trust me. And I want much more than one night with you, Leonora—much more.'

Leonora couldn't speak as Gabriel pulled back out into the traffic as if nothing had happened, his enigmatic comment reverberating in her head.

I want much more than one night...

What was he proposing? An affair? For her to become his mistress?

Everything in her balked at that because she knew she was not mistress material. She was a world away from the sophisticated women of the world he would know, in spite of her privileged upbringing. Until they'd lost all that privilege.

But then maybe he was only talking in terms of days... weeks. Gabriel Torres didn't flaunt his affairs. He was discretion personified—which was largely how he'd built up such a mythical reputation. And a man like him wouldn't be satisfied with one woman for long.

It was only when she saw that they were veering away from the city centre that she asked, 'Where are we going?'

He glanced at her and she felt it like a searing brand. *Dios.*

'We're going to my home. My family home.'

'Castillo Torres?'

Leonora was immediately intimidated. She'd visited the estate a few times in her lifetime, for social events with her parents. That long-ago polo match. Fundraisers. Galas. She hadn't been in a long time, but she remembered it as being a huge and intimidatingly grand place.

In comparison, it made her own family *castillo* look like a cosy country cottage.

'Yes. I trust that is okay?'

Leonora nodded. 'Of course.'

The truth was that even if he'd taken her to a busy restaurant full of people it wouldn't have lessened his intensity, or his power to intimidate. Maybe this was how he flew under the radar? He kept his liaisons confined to his elegant apartment or the *castillo*. Well out of the public eye.

Leonora didn't like to think that she was the latest in a long line of women who had been invited back to the *castillo*, but she told herself she was being ridiculous. There was a long line of women before her and there would undoubtedly be a long line after her. She didn't see a man like Gabriel Torres settling down to a life of domesticity any time soon.

She couldn't even imagine him in such a milieu.

He was turning off the main road now, onto a smaller road which led to a huge set of iron gates that opened automatically as soon as they drove up to them. Gabriel low-

ered his window and saluted the security guard in the box
on the other side of the gate.

Leonora's family used to have security at their *castillo*—
not any more. There was nothing of value left.

They drove in and Leonora tried not to let her jaw drop
at the verdant splendour of the grounds. Tall trees lined the
drive and beyond she could see lush landscaped lawns and
blooming bougainvillea.

The winding drive opened into a massive courtyard with
a fountain in the middle, behind which the *castillo* rose ma-
jestically. Not unlike Leonora's home, but on a far grander
scale, it had a distinctly Moorish shape. And she noticed
immediately that it was in pristine condition, which made
her heart ache as she acknowledged how far her family
had fallen.

Gabriel stopped the car at the bottom of the steps leading up to the main door. He got out and came around the
bonnet, opening Leonora's door and helping her out.

A young man materialised seemingly out of nowhere
and Gabriel tossed him the keys, asking him at the same
time how his exams had gone.

The young man grinned and said, 'Passed them all,
boss!'

Gabriel responded, 'Good for you,' and the young man
jumped into the car and drove it around to the back of the
castillo—presumably to a garage similar to the one under
Gabriel's apartment, filled with expensive sports cars.

Keeping her hand in his, Gabriel led her up the steps.
The door opened as they approached, as if by magic, and
a uniformed butler bowed to them as she stepped over the
threshold.

Gabriel said, 'Ernesto I'd like you to meet Leonora
Flores de la Vega. Leonora, this is Ernesto, the only person holding this whole place together.'

'Not true, sir, but thank you. Señorita de la Vega, pleased to meet you.'

He bowed again and Leonora was charmed. She smiled shyly, 'Lovely to meet you too.'

She liked the way Gabriel acknowledged his staff. She was ashamed to remember how her parents had treated their own as very much beneath them. And now they had none. Karma?

Her hand was still in Gabriel's as he led her through a vast stone hall and out to an inner courtyard with a pool filled with colourful fish and lotus flowers. Stone pillars around the edges led up to a balcony running around the space.

Then they walked through to the other side and back into the main building, where another reception area led off to more rooms and a grand staircase up to the first level.

'This is…beautiful. I was here before, but only in the grounds.'

Gabriel stopped walking and grimaced as he looked around them. 'I've been working on bringing it into the modern era. For years it was dark and dank, full of useless antiques and mouldering paintings of long-dead relatives.'

Leonora couldn't help a small wry smile. 'That sounds like *my* family home.'

She caught Gabriel's eye and his gaze dropped to her mouth. Suddenly he looked…*hungry.* Leonora's heart thumped. Was he going to kiss her right here? Now? She wasn't ready—

But then the look on his face passed and he kept walking, saying, 'It's a painstaking and expensive process. I've been working on this for the last decade and we're not nearly finished.'

Leonora stayed silent, following where he led her, through a confusing labyrinth of corridors. She could see now why he might like his very sparse and elegant city apartment. It was a direct contrast to what he'd grown up with. That was why *she'd* liked it.

A sense of affinity struck her again...disconcerting.

They were approaching the end of the corridor now, and Gabriel pushed open a door which led into a massive drawing room, full of light and huge windows that looked out over the back of the *castillo*. All she could see was acres of lush green, trees, and what looked like an orchard in the distance.

'We grow lemons and olives here. Sell them to an organic company. Part of my restoration is an attempt to make the *castillo* and its grounds as self-sufficient and environmentally friendly as possible.'

He let her hand go and went over to a drinks cabinet.

Leonora said wistfully, 'That's what I'd love to do too. The day when these kinds of buildings can justify themselves by merely existing has surely ended.'

He cast her a look over his shoulder. 'Exactly.'

He came back then, with a glass of what looked like champagne in one hand and water in the other.

He handed her the tall elegant flute and said, 'Dinner will be ready in a short while, but first I have a proposal to put to you.'

Leonora took a sip of champagne and it fizzed down her throat. She swallowed, genuinely intrigued. 'A proposal?'

He looked at her carefully. 'Yes, Leonora. A proposal. Of marriage.'

CHAPTER FIVE

A PROPOSAL OF MARRIAGE. If Leonora had still had some of the champagne in her mouth or her throat she would have choked or spat it out. The shock of his words thumped her in the gut. She felt winded.

He was just looking at her. Assessing. As if he *hadn't* just said the most audacious thing she'd ever heard. A sliver of ice went down her back when she thought of the possibility that she might have hallucinated briefly.

'Did you just say—?'

He cut in smoothly. 'That I'm proposing marriage? Yes, I did.'

Leonora clutched the glass as if it was a lifeline. Her brain wouldn't seem to work. It felt sluggish.

'Do you…? *Why?*'

'For many reasons—chief of which is because I think we'd be a good match. I've known for some time now that I need to settle down, but it's always been an unpalatable prospect…until we met and connected.'

Connected.

Leonora's head was suddenly filled with X-rated images of them in bed, limbs entangled, his powerful body thrusting in and out of hers, transporting her to heights of ecstasy she'd dreamed about every night since.

Something else struck her and she felt slightly sick. 'Is

this just because I was a…a virgin? Maybe you're old-fashioned and that kind of thing—'

He held a hand up, eyes sparking. 'Stop right there. This has nothing to do with your sexual innocence.' He lowered his hand. 'Although I have to admit that knowing I was your first lover is incredibly satisfying in a way that I never would have thought possible.'

Leonora's insides clenched. She had to admit that losing her innocence under the expert tutelage of Gabriel hadn't exactly been *un*satisfying. Far from it. But…*marriage*? And yet why should it be such an alien concept when she'd agreed to marry someone else only recently?

She struggled to understand Gabriel's motivation. 'But I'm not remotely suitable.'

He frowned. 'You couldn't be *more* suitable for my requirements.'

Requirements.

A cold weight lodged in her chest. And it mocked her. Because she realised that for a moment she'd fantasised that this might be a proposal stemming from emotion. Feelings. When she'd never even considered that with Lazaro Sanchez.

But you didn't sleep with him, reminded a small voice.

Leonora lifted her chin. 'Do I need to remind you that my family are considered pariahs in society? We haven't been invited to an event in years. I don't see you sullying the Cruz y Torres name by association with us.'

In answer he pulled out his phone from his trouser pocket and after a few seconds handed it to her, 'Have you seen this?'

'This' was a grainy paparazzi picture of her getting into his car that night outside the hotel. She looked like a rabbit caught in the headlights and he was staring directly down the lens of the camera, defiantly.

She handed it back, feeling sick. 'I tend to avoid looking at those websites or their headlines, considering my family were their sole fodder at one time.'

'I'm showing it to you to illustrate my point that I really don't care what anyone thinks of us getting together.'

Leonora looked at him. 'What would your parents think?'

Gabriel's expression hardened. 'My parents are not remotely involved in the running of my life and haven't been since before I came of age. If anything, I run *their* lives. My father spends most of his time in his city townhouse and at this point in time I'm not even sure where my mother is— she usually has the decency to conduct her illicit liaisons in discreet locations. They have no jurisdiction over me.'

Leonora shivered slightly, recalling how serious he'd been at twenty-one. No wonder, if he'd been running a massive business on his own.

'Don't you have a sister? Younger than you?'

His expression immediately softened. The cold weight in Leonora's chest warmed slightly.

'Yes. Estella. The bane of my existence.'

And yet clearly she wasn't, if that softened look was anything to go by.

Intrigued, Leonora asked, 'Where is she?'

'She's in New York, working as a model. She went through a rough patch a few years ago. Fell in with the wrong people. But she's doing really well now.'

The pride in his voice was evident. Then his focus came back to Leonora.

He said, 'Your family might have fallen from grace due to your father's actions, but whose grace? And who else hasn't? I despise that hypocrisy.'

At that moment there was a discreet knock on the door

and Leonora looked around to see Ernesto enter. 'Dinner is ready, Señor Torres.'

'Thank you, we'll be right there.'

Leonora turned back to Gabriel, still feeling slightly winded, absorbing his words. She would never have expected him not to care about his family's reputation, but conceded cynically that he had that luxury because they were so powerful.

He said, 'I know you weren't expecting this when I brought you here, but I don't believe in playing games, Leonora. Life is too short. You're the first woman I've ever brought to the *castillo*. And you're the first woman I've ever proposed to.'

Gabriel was not used to being unable to read a woman easily. Usually they were so *unsubtle*. But Leonora was like the Sphinx. All cool and serene. He'd put a marriage proposal to her and she'd recovered quickly after her initial shock.

Their dinner plates had just been cleared away by his housekeeper and he asked, 'Did you go to university?'

A faint wash of colour came into her cheeks. She avoided looking at him and he had to curb the urge to tip her chin up so she had no choice. Once again, not usually an issue for him with women.

She shook her head. 'No. I wanted to do a business degree, but by the time I left school…things had changed. Matías was in school, but he came home every weekend and he needed me. And I had to work at the *castillo*—try to get it to make us some money.'

'I can imagine that experience probably taught you as much as a business degree.'

Leonora smiled ruefully. 'Perhaps, although it hasn't exactly been a resounding success. The *castillo* needs serious investment—like what you're doing here.'

Gabriel seized the opportunity she'd presented him with. 'I can help you with that kind of investment, Leonora.'

Now she looked at him, eyes wide, the flush in her face deepening. She stuttered, 'That isn't... I didn't mean to make it sound like—'

'I know you didn't. I'm merely stating a fact. If you become my wife, naturally your security and your family's, and the restoration of your *castillo*, become my responsibility.'

His cool, emotionless logic and the word *responsibility* made something snap inside Leonora. She blurted out, 'Why do you want to marry now?'

He sat back and looked at her. 'To be perfectly honest, because you're the first woman I've met who has inspired me to consider it.'

Leonora felt light-headed. 'Me? I inspired you?'

She really wasn't that special.

'I always knew I'd have to marry. I'm the last in my line. Not marrying and not having a family isn't an option for me. But it's something I've preferred not to think about. Until now.'

'But if it was an option you'd prefer not to?'

'I don't deal in *what ifs* or unknowns. I deal with reality, and this is my reality. And yours too, Leonora. Or are you going to tell me your engagement to Sanchez was born out of emotion or desire?'

Leonora flushed. 'No, of course not.'

She felt exposed, and tense. He knew full well she hadn't slept with Lazaro.

A sense of something that felt like hurt compelled her to push back. 'What makes you think I'm available? Just because I agreed to marry Lazaro? The other night you were reminding me that we're bound by duty and responsibility, but maybe I want more than that. Maybe I don't want to just become someone's *responsibility*.'

Or, maybe, she realised in the same split second, she didn't want to become Gabriel Torres's responsibility, because already she was feeling things for him that were dangerous and disturbing.

Gabriel sat forward. 'Are you telling me that you hadn't agreed to let Lazaro Sanchez take responsibility for your family's debts?'

At that moment the housekeeper came back into the room with a tray that held coffee for Gabriel and tea for Leonora.

Without taking his gaze from Leonora's, Gabriel said, 'We'll take it in the lounge, thank you, Tulia.'

He stood up and Leonora followed his lead from the dining room, glad of a momentary reprieve from the growing tension.

They followed the housekeeper into another surprisingly airy room, adjacent to the dining room. Sunset was bathing everything in a pink and golden hue. The furniture was classic, elegant. Timeless.

The woman set the tray down on a coffee table between two couches.

Gabriel said, 'Thank you, Tulia. That will be all.'

The woman left the room.

Gabriel said, 'Please, sit down.'

Leonora hesitated for a moment, torn between telling Gabriel that she wanted to leave, so she could get out of his disturbing orbit, and the stronger pull to stay. Hear him out.

Let him seduce you again?

Leonora sat down quickly before he might see the turmoil he'd unleashed inside her. Before he could see the want. Even now, despite his disturbing proposition. *Proposal.*

Thankfully he sat down on the opposite couch. She felt as if she could get her breath back and gather her wits as long as he kept his distance. She picked up her cup of tea and took a sip, hoping it would ground her.

He seemed to be waiting for her to speak. It unnerved her. She hadn't had so much focused attention on her from anyone, ever. And from a man like Gabriel Torres it was more than a little overwhelming.

She looked at him. He was sitting back, holding his tiny espresso cup in one big hand but looking no less masculine. One arm was stretched out along the couch, pulling his top tight across his tautly muscled chest.

She swallowed. *Focus.*

'Why do you want to marry me when you could marry any number of far more suitable women?'

He took his arm down and sat forward. A muscle ticked in his jaw. 'Why are you resisting my proposal when you agreed to marry a man you hadn't even slept with?'

Leonora tensed even more—so much that she felt as if she might splinter into a million tiny pieces. It was precisely because she'd slept with Gabriel that she was resisting this proposal. Because she was still reeling after what had happened and how explosive it had been.

She put her cup down and stood up, pride stiffening her spine. 'Maybe I should go. Just because I agreed to marry one man, it does not mean that I'm automatically going to agree to marry the next man who asks me.'

She turned, but stopped when she felt Gabriel's hand on her arm. Gentle, but with enough force to stop her. Reluctantly she faced him, and he let her arm go. She was surprised to see an expression of humility on his face.

'Wait—please.'

He ran a hand through his hair, mussing it up. It gave

him a more approachable air. Less stern. Despite herself, Leonora felt something inside her weaken.

He said, 'I haven't articulated myself very well. Just hear me out...please?'

Leonora had the sense that this didn't happen very often with a man like Gabriel. She nodded her head slightly and sat down.

He sat down again too, but sat forward, with his hands clasped between his legs. He looked at her.

'It was not my intention to make you feel as though I thought of you as a wife for hire, based on your recent history. As I told you, there's been pressure on me for some time to marry and start a family, but no woman has ever made me feel remotely inclined to do so—until the other night and *you*. Every moment in your company only makes me feel more sure that this is the right decision for both of us.'

Leonora cursed him silently. His deep mesmeric voice was drawing her in, making it all sound so reasonable. Logical.

'You know this world, Leo, and you know how to navigate it. I think you share my disdain for it, and yet understand that we need it too. We are bound to it whether we like it or not.'

Leo. She should feel irritated by the way he'd shortened her name—only ever done by her family—but, dammit, she *liked* it. It felt intimate in a way that it didn't feel with her family. Private.

'You and your family need urgent financial help. Matías can't afford to stay at that school for ever. And what will you do if the bank takes your *castillo* as payment for the debts still outstanding?'

Leonora went cold inside. 'How do you know about Matías's school?'

'I know someone with a child in that school, so I know how expensive it is.'

Leonora refused to let herself feel vulnerable. 'I'm sure if we lost everything and Matías had to come out of the school we'd manage.'

'I don't doubt *you* would. But would they? Your parents? Who have only known a life of privilege and luxury, even in spite of what's happened? And would Matías survive without the care of special teachers and assistants? You'd have to work—you wouldn't be there all the time.'

Leonora knew he was right. Her parents would never survive in the real world, in a small apartment—if they were lucky enough even to get one. Neither would Matías. She had less sympathy for her parents, but Matías... She'd do anything for him. To keep him safe and secure.

Gabriel said, 'And there's something else you're not acknowledging.'

His voice was lower. Seductive. Leonora really wanted to avoid his dark, knowing gaze, but she couldn't.

She feigned nonchalance even as her skin tingled with anticipation. 'What's that?'

She knew, though.

She knew with every gathering rush of heat that pulsed through her body.

'We want each other.'

Just that. Stark. To the point.

'I don't like to play games, Leonora, life is too short.'

'And believe me,' he said, 'that's as solid a reason as any to embark on marriage. We have social compatibility and mutual chemistry. A powerful combination.'

Not really understanding why she felt such a need to resist his pull, Leonora said, 'But it won't last—it never does, does it? And what then?'

Gabriel raised a brow. 'This wasn't a concern of yours

when you agreed to marry Sanchez? A man you hadn't even slept with?'

Leonora stood up abruptly, feeling cornered. She paced away to a window that took in the expanse of the *castillo*'s impressive back lawn. She was being a total hypocrite— she knew she was. And she was deluding herself. She *did* know why she was resisting his pull. But how could she explain that she had found it easier to agree to marry a man she hadn't been intimate with, who she hadn't even wanted, than *this* man, with whom she had been intimate and who she did want, with a hunger that made her feel so many things it was overwhelming?

She realised that Gabriel was infinitely more disturbing to her on so many levels because he affected not only her equilibrium, physically, but also her emotions. She'd grown up in a world where you kept your emotions hidden behind a polite front.

Her parents had never really approved of Leonora and Matías's affectionate relationship. But Matías didn't understand about keeping his emotions hidden and Leonora loved him for that. When her parents had sent Matías to the special school they'd told her that it was because he was becoming too attached to her. Too dependent. She'd always felt guilty that her need for his uncomplicated love and affection was the reason he'd been sent away, and while she knew now that he'd been sent away for lots of other reasons, to do with his own self-development in the right environment, she still felt guilty about that need in her for emotional sustenance. As if it was a weakness.

And that was why Gabriel scared her. Because he touched on those needs and wants inside her. That was why it had been easy to say yes to Lazaro. Because he hadn't disturbed her emotions on any level...

* * *

Gabriel looked at Leonora's graceful, willowy form. She oozed elegance in spite of the tense lines of her body. She was perfect. For him. For his life. And yet she resisted.

Irritation spiked in his gut when he thought of how she'd been willing to marry Sanchez with far less to go on.

He stood up and walked over to stand beside her. Her arms were crossed tightly over her chest. The irritation got stronger.

Before he could stop himself he said, 'Were you in love with Sanchez? Is that what this is about?'

She turned to look at him and he saw shock on her face. 'No! How can you even ask that? You really think I would have slept with you if I'd loved him?'

Gabriel didn't like the way her words soothed something jagged inside him. *Jealousy.*

She bit her lip. 'I just… I'm ashamed to admit it now, but I think I found it easier to make a commitment to him because it felt like a sterile business agreement. It's not as if I'm under any illusions. I know that people like us have to marry for reasons that are far removed from love…but I hadn't expected that I would…*want* my husband.'

Gabriel clenched his hand into a fist by his side to avoid reaching out to touch her. She reminded him of a nervy foal. Ready to bolt at the slightest sound.

'Is that such a bad thing?'

She looked at him and her eyes were dark pools of grey, searching his as if for answers. 'Maybe not…'

Gabriel took a step closer. 'Let me show you how it can be, Leo…'

Despite the turmoil in her head and her gut Leonora didn't move when Gabriel took a step closer. Close enough to touch. Her traitorous body craved his. Part of her wanted him to convince her, show her again how he could transport her. Transform her.

He was going to convince her to acquiesce—and, heaven help her, she was going to let him.

Desperately, at the last moment, she tried to assure herself that she wasn't saying *yes* yet. She was just allowing him to…to persuade her. But as his hands cupped her face and his mouth landed on hers she knew she was lying to herself.

She'd already made her decision and it was based on many logical reasons—everything he'd outlined. But it was also based on *illogical* reasons—reasons that had to do with motivations that came from a far more secret place. A place where she harboured dreams that she'd be a fool to believe a man like Gabriel would be able to fulfil.

Dreams of a happy marriage—of an old couple walking hand in hand together after a long life lived in love…

But he was kissing her now, and all those dreams dissolved under his hot touch.

When her legs no longer felt capable of holding her up Gabriel lifted her against his chest and carried her through the vast and echoing *castillo*, with the weight of history all around them, into his bedroom.

He undressed her. Undid her belt and pulled it off. Opened the buttons of her dress and pushed it apart, baring her to his gaze before tugging it over her shoulders and down her arms. Then undid her bra, releasing her breasts to his hands and mouth.

He laid her on his bed and pulled down her panties, pushed apart her legs and tortured her with his mouth until she was gripping the sheets and trembling with the effort it took not to shatter. But of course he wouldn't allow her that mercy, and he pushed her until she came in great shuddering waves, against his mouth.

And then, when she was still pulsating and dizzy from

that shattering peak, he wound her up again, demonstrating the ease with which he could manipulate her. He thrust into her, stealing her breath and robbing her rational mind of any last coherent thought. He wound her higher and higher, until she was thrashing under him, begging, pleading for mercy.

And that was the moment when he stopped and said, 'Look at me, Leo...look at me.'

She forced her blurry vision to take him in, and it was a majestic sight as he reared over her, his body embedded in hers, every muscle straining with the effort it took not to let go. His face was flushed. Eyes burning.

Her whole body was poised on the precipice—one more thrust and she'd be set free. But he wasn't moving. She raised her hips but he pulled back. She scowled at him and he smiled wickedly. She was laid bare. Exposed. Nowhere to hide. And yet she felt a measure of power, the same power she'd experienced the first night they were together. A very feminine power.

Gabriel's body trembled against hers with the effort it was taking him to stop moving, over her, in her, and that gave her some solace.

And then he said, 'What do you want?'

His question got to her, breaking some last vestige of resistance. She suspected he was asking something deeper than just if she wanted release, but her brain was too melted to study it.

'You...' she said brokenly. 'I want you, Gabriel.'

For a moment he still didn't move. And then, just when she was about to beg him to release her from the tension, and from his too intense gaze, he finally moved, and with a broken cry she soared into bliss.

It was raw and visceral and she suspected that she'd just acquiesced to everything he'd asked of her without even saying *yes*.

* * *

The next morning when Leonora woke she felt deeply sated and at peace. It took a long moment for her to figure out where she was and why she was feeling like this. Then it all rushed back.

The proposal.

Making love.

She shivered under the thin sheet. 'Making love' sounded so…so benign, when it had felt more like breaking her apart and putting her back together in a new configuration.

She was alone in the room. She looked around it in the early morning light. It was surprisingly bare—not unlike the bedroom in Gabriel's apartment in the city. Like the man—no frills or flounces or flowery words. Just direct words like *I want you,* or *A proposal of marriage.*

Leonora got out of bed, afraid that Gabriel might appear at any moment and find her feeling so raw. She pulled on a robe that had been laid at the end of the bed—*considerate*—and went into the bathroom.

She looked at herself in the mirror, expecting to see a bedraggled mess. But her eyes were shining and her cheeks still had vestiges of pink in them. She cursed herself. Betrayed by her own body. She paced back and forth, knowing that Gabriel would be expecting an answer when she saw him again.

She sent up silent thanks that he hadn't extracted an answer from her in the throes of passion last night. She would have said anything not to have him stop his particular brand of passionate sorcery.

He made her feel as alive as she'd ever felt and he also made her feel scared. Scared for herself. For her heart. The heart she'd hidden for so long and the heart that longed for more than she'd witnessed growing up.

A little voice popped into her head: *Maybe a family can give you that if Gabriel can't?*

Before she could stop her wayward imagination she saw Gabriel in her mind's eye, returning home from work and scooping a dark-haired child up into his arms, before tugging Leonora close so that he could kiss her.

Leonora caught a glimpse of her reflection again and this time she looked slightly wild-eyed. This was precisely why she should say no to Gabriel. He stirred up too many illicit dreams and fantasies. Fantasies that could never materialise. No matter what she felt when they made love-like the only woman in the world.

And yet…did she have a choice? She had to marry. That was her duty and her responsibility. If it wasn't to Gabriel then it would have to be someone else. Because, no matter what she'd said to him the previous evening, the truth was that she *was* a bride for hire—whether she liked to admit it or not.

Was it so bad that she and Gabriel had this insane chemistry? Wouldn't it help a marriage? At the start at least… It couldn't last. He wouldn't want her like this for ever. But maybe by then they'd have children…

There was a knock on the door and Leonora jumped like a scalded cat. 'Yes?'

A woman's voice. 'Señorita de la Vega? Breakfast is being served downstairs in the dining room.'

Leonora's heart was thumping.

Not Gabriel.

'Thank you. I'll be right down.'

Footsteps went away.

Leonora got herself together and washed, and then went back and dressed in her clothes from yesterday, feeling the sting of shame that everyone would know.

But no one looked at her strangely when she went downstairs. If she passed anyone they just smiled politely, clearly busy with the upkeep of the *castillo*. That reminded her of what Gabriel had said about helping with their *castillo*'s renovations. How could she deny her family that?

She entered the hall and Ernesto appeared.

'Please, Señorita de la Vega, this way.'

Leonora forced a smile, even though inside she was cringing at what Ernesto must think of her. 'Please, call me Leonora.'

He smiled benignly at her as he opened the door into the dining room. She walked in and Gabriel stood up from where he was sitting at the head of the table, dressed in a pristine white shirt, tie and waistcoat, which only empha- sised his lean body.

'Good morning.'

She avoided his eye, coming into the room, and wished she'd had more make-up to put on, or tied her hair back. She felt dishevelled. Undone.

'Good morning.'

She sat down and the housekeeper appeared with an array of food.

Leonora smiled at her. 'This looks delicious.'

The woman was pleased. 'Let me know if you want anything else.'

When she was gone Leonora still avoided looking di- rectly at Gabriel.

Until he said, 'Look at me, Leo.'

See? Direct.

She put down the coffee pot and looked at him. All strong lines and that sensual mouth. Those mesmerising eyes. Her lower body spasmed reflexively with the memory of what it had felt like to have his powerful body thrusting in and out of hers.

Dios.

'You're a nice person, Leo.'

She blinked. That wasn't what she'd expected to hear. 'Well, I…thank you.'

'You notice people, acknowledge them.'

Now she was embarrassed. 'So do you,' she said, thinking of his interaction with the boy who had parked his car last night.

'See?' he said as he lowered his coffee cup. 'We're well matched.'

Leonora wanted to look away again, but she couldn't. She felt a sense of fatality wash over her. In all honesty, even though the thought of marrying Gabriel scared her to death, because he made her long for so many things, the thought of walking out of his *castillo* this morning and never seeing him again was nearly more terrifying. Never touching him again? *No.*

Before she could really think it through she blurted out, 'Yes.'

'Yes…to what?'

He arched a brow even as his eyes darkened with something that looked like desire but which she suspected was satisfaction. A part of her wished she could say no, just not give him that satisfaction. Did *anyone* say no to this man? She couldn't blame them.

She took a breath. 'You know what. Yes, I'll marry you.'

Gabriel was surprised at the level of tension he'd been feeling, which suddenly dissipated. He hadn't been sure what Leo would say even after last night.

He reached for her hand and lifted it, leaning forward to press a kiss into her palm. He saw how her eyes flared and an answering rush of desire made his blood hot. He wanted to tug her over onto his lap and crush that soft mouth under his, but he forced the desire down. They would have a lifetime for that. Right at that moment he couldn't imagine a day when he wouldn't want her with this fierce hunger, and surely that had to be a good indication that this union would and could work?

It was time to progress—with this woman by his side.

Not wanting to waste another moment of time, he said, 'Would you object to a private wedding service here in the *castillo*'s chapel at the end of the week?'

CHAPTER SIX

LEONORA'S HEAD WAS still reeling a couple of days after she'd agreed to a private wedding which would take place that very week. She'd protested, of course, but with his particular brand of cool logic Gabriel had asked her what advantage there could possibly be in prolonging the wait.

Gabriel had worn her down all too easily, and in the end she'd agreed—it had been the prospect of securing Matías's future sooner rather than later.

She'd come to Gabriel's office in Madrid this morning, to look over a prenuptial agreement. Cruz y Torres Enterprises was housed in a sleek and modern building made of glass and steel. Everyone looked very serious and efficient. She'd been whisked up with a private escort straight to his massive corner office that had a terrace overlooking the city.

'This is impressive,' she said, walking over to a window.

She could feel Gabriel looking at her and her skin prickled with awareness. They hadn't slept together since the other night.

'It's not bad.'

He came to stand beside her and she glanced at him. 'Not bad…? A slight understatement.'

He turned to face her. 'This will be your world too when we're married.'

Leonora balked a bit at that. Somehow she hadn't fully absorbed that aspect. She would be Señora Cruz y Torres.

Suddenly she felt conscious of her very worn suit. It was designer, but practically vintage at this stage, one she wheeled out when she had to look smart. And she'd wanted to look smart today. Professional. Because essentially this was just a business agreement, right?

It might be for Gabriel, but her thumping heart said something else.

A moment of panic made her turn to him. 'Gabriel, I know you think I'm suitable, but really—'

He put a finger to her mouth, stopping her words. He said, 'You're going to be absolutely fine. Trust me.'

He took his hand away.

Leonora swallowed. 'I just don't want to let you down.'

He shook his head. 'You won't.'

There was a taut moment when she thought he was going to pull her close and kiss her, but then there was a knock on the door and she looked around to see a series of officious-looking men and women enter. She was glad of the inter-ruption. She didn't want Gabriel to see how needy she'd felt just then, for reassurance.

The prenup.

She calmed herself and took a seat at Gabriel's desk, where he'd pulled out a chair. She'd looked over the agree-ment herself at home, when Gabriel had emailed it to her, and she had no issues with it. It was exceedingly generous, actually, with provisions set out for her family and Matías in the event of their divorce. Essentially, he was promising to look after them for their lifetimes.

After she'd signed the agreement, and the legal staff had left, Leonora put down her pen and looked at Gabriel. She felt ridiculously emotional to think that this man, who really barely knew her, was making such a commitment to her family.

'Thank you—you've been very generous.'

He shrugged. 'Your family will become my family, Leo.'

She shook her head, 'But you haven't even met Matías.'

He paused for a beat and then said, 'So take me to meet him.'

Leonora's heart tripped. 'Now?'

'Why not?' He glanced at his watch. 'I can cancel my afternoon meetings—they're not a priority.'

Leonora put in a call to Matías's school. They had no problem with visitors that afternoon, so after some lunch in Gabriel's office they left the city in one of his sleek cars.

They were walking down the corridor, about to meet Matías in the common room area of his school, when suddenly Leonora stopped and said, 'Wait.'

Gabriel looked at her. 'What is it?'

Leonora was suddenly aware of the magnitude of introducing this man to Matías. 'You need to be gentle with him. He can be nervous with strangers and especially protective of me.'

Something crossed Gabriel's face. 'I have a younger sister. I know that's very different, and Estella doesn't have a learning difficulty, but I do know what it's like to worry...'

Leonora couldn't quite compute that Gabriel Torres was here, reassuring her about her own brother. 'Okay.'

She needn't have worried. Within mere minutes Matías was in thrall to Gabriel in a way she could only sympathise with. Staring at him as if he was a god.

It made Leonora's heart twist, because she'd witnessed so many people over the years shunning her brother because he was different. Gabriel seemed to have no such issue, and was talking to Matías as if he was any other young man of eighteen.

They were having an in-depth conversation about football and it turned out they both supported the same team—much to Matías's ecstatic excitement. When Gabriel offered to take Matías to a match some time, the young man—almost equalling Gabriel in height—launched himself at Gabriel, hugging him tightly.

Leonora immediately tensed, waiting for Gabriel to pull back at this display of affection from a stranger, to extricate himself, look awkward, but he didn't. He just hugged Matías back.

To her shock, instead of feeling reassured, she found that watching Gabriel so at ease with her brother was setting her on edge and bringing up emotions she wasn't sure she wanted to identify.

When they finally left, Leonora sat tensely beside Gabriel in his car.

'What is it?' he asked. 'I would have thought you'd be happy to see that Matías and I get along.'

'He really likes you,' she had to admit.

Gabriel shrugged nonchalantly. 'You say that like it's a bad thing.'

Suddenly she realised what was at the root of her unease. Gabriel was too used to getting his own way, having people fall in slavish devotion at his feet. He'd taken Matías's reaction for granted. She was aware that she was irrationally angry with him about that. But it was as if introducing him to Matías had brought home just how quickly and easily she'd let him upend her life. How quickly she'd let herself fall in with his plans.

She looked at him. 'Matías is vulnerable. If you say you'll take him to a football match he expects that to happen. If he likes you he trusts you implicitly, which makes him even more vulnerable. Once we marry, my responsibility to him doesn't disappear. He's only ever known me as his main carer outside of the school.'

Gabriel shot her a glance. 'Are you sure we're just talking about Matías, here?'

Leonora flushed.

'I have no intention of sidelining anyone once we're married, but the fact is that you will have other responsibilities. You'll be my wife, and I have a hectic schedule at the best of times. And once we have children, they'll obviously take precedence. We'll have as much support as we need, but I don't want to entrust my children entirely to the care of staff, as I and my sister were. And as I suspect you and your brother were, until there were no staff.'

That stunned Leonora slightly. 'You want to be involved in your children's lives?'

For a moment he said nothing. She saw his jaw clench, and then he said, 'My parents all but abandoned me and my sister. Left us to our own devices, sent us to schools as far away from them as possible. I was able to handle it. But Estella…she was more vulnerable. I had no idea how badly she was affected. Because of our age gap, when she was a teenager and home for the holidays I was already working in the business. I missed the signs…'

'The signs of what?'

'Signs that she was falling in with a wrong crowd. People happy to take advantage of her limitless wealth, her name and vulnerability.'

Leonora's chest tightened. 'What happened?'

Gabriel was grim, hands tightly on the wheel. 'I found her passed out at home a few years ago. She was unconscious. Nearly dead. I got her to hospital and into rehab and since then she's been doing really well. But the neglect of our parents was a direct cause of her pain and I'll never forgive myself for not seeing it.'

'You weren't her parent. It wasn't your job.'

He glanced at her, and the look on his face made her shiver. 'No. But I knew she wasn't like me. I won't lie—I don't know the first thing about relating to children—but I know that ours will not be neglected and left to fend for themselves.'

Ours. Their children.

They stopped at traffic lights and he looked at her. 'Unless you have other ideas?'

Leonora was still reeling from what he'd just said. She realised he was waiting for an answer. 'No. I want to be involved. Our upbringing wasn't so dissimilar. Until my father lost everything my parents were absent a lot. It was just me and Matías until he went away to school. I can't imagine having children and letting someone else raise them.'

Some of the harshness in Gabriel's expression softened. 'I know Matías is vulnerable and that he takes everything literally. I've made a commitment to you and he's part of that. All your family are.'

Emotion rose inside Leonora. For the first time in years she felt a weight being lifted off her shoulders. She looked away in case he saw it.

The lights turned green.

A car beeped behind them and Gabriel said, 'Leo, we're not moving till you look at me.'

She swallowed her emotion and turned her head. The car beeped again.

Gabriel was unfazed. 'Do you trust me?'

More cars beeped. But the awful thing was that Leonora didn't need the pressure of the traffic building behind them to tell her that *yes*, she did trust him.

She felt as if she was falling off a cliff edge, with nothing to hold on to. When had she allowed herself to trust him so implicitly? How had that even happened? Had it been just now, when he'd spoken of his sister? Or the moment she'd decided to sleep with him? Or the moment she'd seen him being so kind with Matías?

She nodded.

He said warningly, 'Leo... I need to hear it.'

More cars beeped.

A bubble of euphoria was pushing its way up from her chest and she blurted out, 'Yes! Yes, I do... Now drive! Please!'

They moved off smoothly back into the traffic. Cars were overtaking them, beeping their horns, but Gabriel showed no sign of being bothered. A small wicked smile played around his mouth and Leonora felt a lightness she'd never felt before, with anyone.

'You like causing havoc, don't you?'

He glanced at her and his smile grew more wicked. 'Always.'

Instead of being taken home, though, Leonora found herself being driven into the city centre—specifically to an exclusive shopping street in Salamanca. A place she'd avoided for some time, without the funds to purchase designer clothes.

'Why are we here?' she asked as Gabriel navigated expertly into a small parking space right outside one of the world's most expensive designer shops.

He turned off the engine and faced her. 'I've taken the liberty of organising for you to meet with a stylist. Unless you've already sourced a wedding dress and trousseau?'

Leonora flushed. Of course she hadn't. She'd been in denial, wondering how far her dressmaking skills would get her, cobbling together things from her wardrobe and her mother's.

'You'll be back on the social scene as my wife, and you'll need to maintain a certain...standard.'

Leonora swallowed. Again, that was something that had only hit home in that moment of panic at his offices earlier. Uncomfortably, she said, 'I don't like the idea of you buying me clothes.'

A slightly exasperated look came over Gabriel's face. 'You *would* say that, wouldn't you?'

'What's that supposed to mean? I'm sorry if I'm not making this easy for you by merely acquiescing to your every demand.'

Gabriel snaked out a hand and caught her behind the neck. He tugged her forward gently, so gently that she could easily have resisted, and yet treacherously she didn't want to. She *knew* this was part and parcel of marrying a man like Gabriel—so why was she winding him up? Because she wanted to provoke him?

'As long as you acquiesce to *this* demand we'll have no problems.'

His mouth landed on hers like a hot brand, immediately cauterising her thinking process.

'And Señor Torres said that we need to fit you for a wedding dress, yes?'

Leonora's attention came back to the efficient stylist, who had spent the last two to three hours helping her select more clothes than she thought she'd ever know what to do with. Or wear.

'Yes. I'm getting married this weekend.'

Leonora ignored the way the stylist paled slightly. She recovered herself and said, 'Very good. Please, come with me across the road to our bridal selection and we'll see what we have there. Luckily you'll fit most sample sizes.'

Leonora smiled weakly, following the woman across the road to another exclusive boutique. The stylist looked her up and down critically and Leonora said quickly, 'I don't want anything fussy. It's not that kind of wedding.'

What kind of wedding is it, then? a snarky inner voice prompted.

She ignored it.

The stylist disappeared behind a rack of voluminous dresses and Leonora called out, 'Honestly, the more simple the better. In fact maybe it could just be…'

The words died on her lips when the woman reappeared, holding a long dress under protective covering. 'Let's try this, shall we? And go from there.'

Afterwards, when Leonora was changing back into her clothes, she had to admire the skill of the stylist. They hadn't had to go anywhere after that first, perfect dress. Leonora scowled at that. She didn't want a perfect dress. She wasn't like other wide-eyed brides, believing in love and happy-ever-after. Her marriage was a business transaction, pure and simple. Gabriel was going to provide a dowry to save her family and she would bear him heirs to continue his line.

So why, when she had stood on the raised dais in the shop and looked in the mirror, had she felt ridiculously emotional?

Was it because she knew it was the perfect dress for a *real* wedding? Because in spite of everything she wished this was a real wedding?

Just because she trusted Gabriel Torres, she'd be a monumental fool to hope that trust would become something more substantial. If anything, what he'd told her about his parents only gave her more insight into why he was so self-contained. He'd had to learn from a young age to depend on himself. At no point had he mentioned love, wanting it or needing it.

She was still feeling a little raw when she walked back

into the main area of the wedding boutique, and she wasn't at all prepared to see Gabriel sitting on one of the dusky pink chairs, reading a newspaper. He should have looked ridiculously out of place, but of course he didn't.

He looked up when she emerged, and immediately he frowned, standing up. 'What is it? Did something happen?'

She realised she must be still scowling and she forced a smile. 'Nothing is wrong. Everything is…fine.'

The stylist came out behind her, immediately fawning. 'Señor Torres, what an honour. Is there anything we can get for you?'

He glanced at the stylist, and then back at Leonora, a small smile playing around his mouth, as if he knew exactly the turmoil he caused in her heart and her gut and it amused him. She fought not to scowl again.

The stylist was saying, 'Purchases can be delivered to wherever you like.'

He said, 'Have everything but the wedding dress delivered to my *castillo*. After all, that's where you'll be living from next week—isn't that right, *querida?*'

Leonora felt dizzy at that reminder. But she refused to show it.

She went over and slipped her arm through his. 'Yes, of course it is, *mi amor*.' She wanted to see him as off-balance as she felt.

His jaw clenched, but instead of feeling a sense of satisfaction that she'd got to him, all she felt was an ache near her heart.

He thanked the stylist and then took Leonora's hand in his, entwining his fingers with hers, and led her out of the boutique to the street. She slipped on her sunglasses, wanting some kind of armour against Gabriel.

He stopped outside the shop and looked at her. 'You

weren't lying when you said you didn't like the idea of me buying you clothes.'

Leonora's heart thumped. 'It's not that. I'm very grateful—and I know I have to maintain a certain standard. I've just got used to doing without all the fuss and anxiety about what's fashionable and what's not…'

He made a non-committal sound and then he said, 'There's one more place I need to take you.'

He was walking down the street at a brisk pace before she could ask him where they were going. She saw women doing double-takes—men too, for that matter—as they cut through the shoppers. Leonora felt dowdy in her jeans and plain shirt and suddenly lamented that fact, in spite of her words to Gabriel. Right now she wished she was wearing something more flattering. And her hair was still in a rough bun, after the stylist had asked her to put it up to see how the veil would look.

'Where are we going?' She hoped it wasn't somewhere too public.

'My bank.'

Leonora rolled her eyes behind her glasses. Only someone like Gabriel could actually say *my bank* and literally mean *his* bank. The bank that he owned.

The ornate façade of Banco Torres, one of Spain's oldest financial institutions, used mainly now as an investment bank, rose up before them at the end of the street. And Leonora couldn't help but be intimidated as they went through the revolving door into the hushed exclusivity of the marble foyer. Classical statues were dotted around the space. Huge paintings hung on the walls. Presumably Gabriel's ancestors.

A woman approached them, beautiful and sleek in a dark suit. 'Señor Torres, the item you requested is ready in the vault.'

'Thank you.'

Still holding Leonora's hand, Gabriel led her over to where a uniformed security guard was holding an elevator for them. They got in and it went down to the basement level. They were met there by another sleek employee, male this time. He led them through open steel doors and into a long room filled with security boxes. There was a box on the table, and after unlocking it he left them alone.

Gabriel said, 'This is the family vault.'

Leonora looked around. 'Oh...' *Their* family vault had been cleaned out by her father.

Gabriel let her hand go and went over to the box, opening it up. He lifted out a tray and laid it down in front of Leonora. She sucked in a breath. It was a tray full of sparkling rings. Antique rings. Sapphires, rubies, diamonds.

'These rings have belonged to Cruz y Torres brides down through the generations. But if you don't like any of these we can buy a new one.'

Leonora shook her head faintly. As much at the thought of the unnecessary expense as because one ring in particular had immediately caught her eye. It wasn't as ornate as the others. It was much plainer. And yet it stood out.

It was an emerald cut diamond in a gold setting, with a detail of three smaller diamonds either side of the main stone. Classic and elegant.

Gabriel must have seen where her gaze was resting and he picked it out, holding it up. 'This one?'

She looked at him and nodded reluctantly, feeling like a fraud.

He took her hand and said, 'Let's see if it fits.'

Leonora held her breath as he slid the ring onto her finger. It fitted perfectly. She felt a shiver go down her spine as it sparkled up at her benignly.

'This ring belonged to my great-grandmother, actually.

My father's grandmother. Apparently her marriage to my great-grandfather was a rare love-match. She died at the age of eighty, and he died less than a week later of a broken heart. Or so they say.'

Leonora looked at Gabriel suspiciously but he didn't look mischievous. He looked serious.

He said, 'This isn't a love-match, Leo—you do know that, don't you? We have insane chemistry...but that's just desire. I'm not denying that it's a boon for our marriage, but that's all it is. A boon. The important things are our compatibility and the fact that we come from the same world. We both want a different life for our children. But as for love... It's not something I've ever really hoped for or believed in. Sweet stories about my great-grandparents are just...fairy-tales.'

She pulled her hand back, the ring feeling heavy on her finger now. 'Why did you tell me about them?'

He looked at her far too assessingly. 'Because I think you want more from this marriage. More than I'll ever be prepared to give. And you need to know that now.'

Leonora's insides clenched tight. Was she so transparent? She felt the weight of the ring, the cold of the precious metal against her skin. He wasn't telling her anything she didn't already know, but her treacherous heart was shrinking in her chest at his words. In spite of everything, she had hoped for more.

She forced all emotion out of her voice. 'I know what's expected just as much as you do. I've never been under any illusions about what marriage means for me. Do I need to remind you that if the announcement of my engagement hadn't been so rudely interrupted I would be engaged to Lazaro Sanchez right now?'

His expression darkened. He moved closer. 'Do not mention that man's name again.'

Leonora tipped up her chin. 'I've known you intimately for less than a week—do you really think mere sex would turn my head so much that I'd forget a lifetime's lessons and start believing in fairy-tales?'

Gabriel looked at the woman in front of him. She was wearing a plain button-down shirt. He could see a hint of the lace of her bra. She wore faded jeans. Not a scrap of make-up. Her hair was up in a messy knot. She could pass for a student, and yet she had the innately regal grace that belied her lineage.

She was also the most exquisitely beautiful woman he'd ever seen. And every moment he thought he could read her, or figure her out, she slipped through his fingers like quicksilver.

The ring sparkled on her finger in his peripheral vision and something about that was immensely satisfying. Even though he still felt the spike of irritation at hearing her mention Lazaro Sanchez's name. Just the thought that she might possibly be with that man was enough to make Gabriel reach for her, tugging her into him so their bodies were flush.

'It's not *mere* sex—it happens to be amazing sex,' he said in a low, rough voice, already feeling the inevitable rush of blood to his groin.

Colour tinged her cheeks. 'We can't—not here.' She put her hands on his chest.

Gabriel clenched his jaw. She was right. As much as he'd love to turn her around, pull those provocative jeans down and bury himself inside her, he wasn't about to be the first of his line to desecrate the family vault in such a carnal manner. The fact that this behaviour was also totally out of character was something he didn't want to investigate.

'My apartment is less than five minutes from here.'

Leonora desperately wanted to pull back and say something cool, nonchalant. She still stung inside from his warning not to fall for him. But the sting was melting under the rush of blood to every nerve-ending. And she realised that she'd never felt so alive. Fizzing.

She was not a spontaneous person, and she wouldn't have figured Gabriel to be one either. But she was suddenly filled with an urge to unsettle him as he did her every time he looked at her. So she moved her hands down his chest to his waist and then cupped the growing bulge under his trousers.

Instantly his eyes flared with surprise and he sucked in a breath. 'Witch...you'll pay for this.'

Leonora smiled, even though she knew that every time she savoured a small victory like this she was fooling herself if she thought Gabriel's warning would serve as a deterrent. Nothing could save her from herself.

The thing that struck Gabriel most on the morning of his wedding was the equanimity he felt. He'd always imagined that on his wedding day he'd be suffocating with claustrophobia and chafing at the demise of his freedom.

But he wasn't feeling any of those things. He was feeling impatient.

Leonora was ten minutes late. And, while he knew that was traditional, this was hardly a traditional wedding, with only a handful of guests in the Cruz y Torres family church in the grounds of the *castillo*.

He'd managed to drag his mother back from the tropical luxury outpost where she was conducting her latest affair. His father was beside her, glowering. A parody of a united front.

All the more reason why Gabriel felt sure that Leonora was right for him. They wanted the same things for their children. A more holistic upbringing. They had respect and compatibility and that insane chemistry.

He shifted uncomfortably in his morning suit, recalling his totally out-of-character behaviour the other day—taking her back to his apartment mid-afternoon, where they'd lost themselves in a mutual frenzy of need. He couldn't remember feeling that desperate even when he'd been a hormone-fuelled teenager with his first lover.

Leonora's parents were here too. He'd talked to them the night before, when he'd hosted a dinner here at the *castillo* in order to meet them. He liked them. They'd been humbled by their experience and had paid a price that was disproportionate to what they'd done.

There was movement just beyond the church door and Gabriel tensed, surprised to find himself actually experiencing something that felt like…anxiety. A very unfamiliar sensation.

And then she appeared in the doorway. A graceful silhouette. Long white dress, veil obscuring her face. She was on the arm of Matías, whom she'd nominated to be her attendant. Gabriel's sister had desperately wanted to be here, but she was on a fashion shoot in South America and logistically wouldn't have made it in time.

Music began and they started walking down the aisle. Gabriel's breath stopped when Leonora was revealed more fully. The dress was a plain white column—no frills or flounces or ruffles. Just straight, elegant lines, skimming her perfect figure. Long sleeves and a round neck. And yet even from here he could see how the material clung to every dip and curve.

He forced his eyes off Leonora and acknowledged Matías as they arrived at the front of the church. He shook the young man's hand and then Matías went and stood beside his parents.

Leonora stood before Gabriel, face downbent. He willed her to look up at him. She finally did and he saw the shape of her face, the cheekbones, firm jaw. Lush mouth. Huge eyes.

'You look…stunning.'

The priest coughed and Gabriel turned to face him—but not before he found Leonora's hand and wrapped it in his, as if needing to touch her to make sure she was real.

Most of the wedding ceremony was a blur to Leonora. Gabriel taking her hand had been the only thing keeping her anchored to the spot as the enormity of what she was doing had sunk in when she'd reached the altar. She was committing herself to a man who would never love her. She was setting fire to all those secret hopes and dreams she'd nurtured deep inside her for years.

Somehow all this hadn't occurred to her with Lazaro Sanchez. Because she hadn't cared for him as she cared for Gabriel. That unwelcome realisation had made panic flutter in her chest. But then Gabriel had pulled up the veil obscuring her vision and she'd looked at him. And all she'd been able to see were those dark, fathomless eyes, and her panic had dissipated…

'You may now kiss your bride, Señor Torres.'

It was over.

But it was only beginning.

Gabriel cupped her face and lowered his mouth to hers, so slowly and deliberately that she was quivering all over by the time he made contact. Damn him. He knew exactly how to play her.

The kiss was short, but just as devastating as if he'd pulled her close and taken it all the way to deep and explicit. When she pulled back his eyes were glittering. Until now she'd barely even taken in his steel-grey morning suit or the white cravat. It made his skin look very dark.

He took her hand again and led her back down the aisle. Leonora smiled tremulously at her parents and Matías. He was the reason she'd been late. He'd been confused by all the activity and wondering why Leonora was dressed so strangely, and he'd wanted to know what it meant that she would now be living in this new place and not at home.

Very considerately, Gabriel had arranged for one of Matías's favourite teachers from his school to come to the wedding so she could keep an eye on him.

Leonora sucked in big breaths of fresh air once they were outside. A professional photographer took some pictures and then they were ushered into one of the *castillo*'s dining rooms for the wedding breakfast.

Leonora saw her parents awkwardly conversing with Gabriel's parents, who were looking unbearably aristocratic. As if all this was beneath them.

She had caught Gabriel's mother looking expressly at her midsection at one point, and had realised that she must suspect that Leonora was pregnant. Well, she wasn't. Not when she had the all too familiar cramps to prove it.

Leonora had always suffered from particularly painful periods, but it had never been diagnosed as anything but mild endometriosis. She hadn't even considered that she might be pregnant—Gabriel had used protection every time—but she'd been surprised at the tiny dart of disappointment when her period had arrived as usual just the other day.

Was she really ready for babies? Children? The thought was alternately terrifying and awe-inspiring.

She put a hand to her belly now, as she took a sip of champagne, unconsciously easing the lingering ache of the end of her period.

The wedding breakfast was nearly over, so she was surprised when Gabriel tapped his glass and stood up. He looked down at her and then he said, 'I would like to take this opportunity to welcome Leonora into the family, and also to welcome her parents and her brother Matías.' He looked at her and raised his glass. 'You're the future of this family, Leonora—you and our children.'

He took her hand and kissed it and the dull ache inside her was forgotten. She was curiously touched by his public endorsement of her, and the welcome he'd offered to her family. But she could see that his parents didn't totally approve, and they wasted little time in leaving once the party started to break up.

Gabriel had told Leonora that they would be leaving after the wedding for a short honeymoon—again, not something she would have expected of him, having assumed he'd waste no time in getting back to work.

She knew she should be grateful for this time to get to know him better, but as they set off for the airport later that day she couldn't control the butterflies in her belly at the thought of time alone with her new husband.

CHAPTER SEVEN

PARADISE. THAT WAS the only word Leonora could think of as she took in the sight before her. Gabriel had brought her to a paradise that had only ever existed in her imagination. It had a name of course. Costa Rica. They'd flown into the lush tropical country, bordered on two sides by sparkling oceans, late last night, and had then taken a smaller plane to the west coast, where Gabriel owned a villa.

They'd arrived so late and Leonora had been so exhausted that she'd barely noticed Gabriel taking off her outer clothes and laying her down on the softest surface imaginable. But now she was awake. Or was she still dreaming? She wasn't sure.

She'd woken in a massive four-poster bed, with muslin drapes gently moving in the warm breeze. When she'd pushed them back she'd seen the bedroom—wooden floors, rustic furniture. Then wide open doors leading out to a terrace and a glimpse of what could only be described as heaven.

A robe had been laid across the end of the bed, and Leonora had realised she was in her underwear. The strapless white bra she'd worn under her wedding dress and matching lace panties. Refusing to linger on thinking about Gabriel undressing her, she'd pulled the short robe on, and now she stood on a wooden deck, with an infinity pool in

front of her, overlooking a forest and beyond that the sparkling Pacific Ocean.

'Not a bad view to wake up to, hmm?'

Leonora started and turned around with a hand to her
chest. Gabriel was standing a few feet away, holding a cup
in his hand. His hair was damp and he wore casual board
shorts and nothing else. All she could see was that impressive expanse of hard-muscled chest.

She fought for composure. She was still disconcertingly
in that space between waking and sleeping, and the view
in general was not helping to bring her back to reality. *Either* view.

'It's absolutely stunning.' She turned back to the other
view.

He came and stood beside her. 'Did you sleep well?'

Leonora smiled a little sheepishly. 'Like a baby.'

'Good. You deserve a break…'

Leonora didn't like the little warm glow near her heart
when Gabriel said things like that. It was too…seductive.

She forced a breezy smile. 'I'm fine—why would I need
a break?'

'Because you've been carrying the weight of your family's responsibilities for years.'

She rushed to defend them, but Gabriel put a finger to
her mouth before she could.

'I'm your husband now, Leo. You're not on your own
any more. It's not down to you. It's down to *us*.'

Leonora looked up at him. It would be so easy to lean
on this man. So easy to let him just take her burdens and
anxieties. And it was already happening. Her parents had
told her that he'd already set up a meeting for them to talk
with his assistant with regard to carrying out renovation
work on the *castillo* and hiring staff again. And she knew

their association with the Cruz y Torres family would soon have them accepted back into Spanish society.

Familiar anxiety knotted her belly, though. 'What if my father—?'

Gabriel shook his head. 'He won't. I spoke to him and he's agreed to get counselling to try and figure out why he became addicted to gambling. He's learnt a harsh lesson. I'm sure he won't go down that route again.'

Leonora was shocked that he'd discussed it with her father, who had always turned to obdurate stone when she'd tried to broach the subject of counselling or therapy. Perversely, she felt slightly jealous that he'd made more headway than she or her mother ever had.

As if reading her mind, he said, 'Sometimes it takes a person on the outside to communicate a little more effectively. Your father is ashamed of what he's done.'

Leonora swallowed her defensiveness. She realised that after living her life solely in service to her parents and her brother and their huge unwieldy home it would be a challenge to let someone else into that space.

'Thank you for talking to him. I think he does want to get better.'

'They're all thousands of miles away and being perfectly well looked-after. Forget about them now. Breakfast? Or would you like to work up an appetite first?'

Leonora's heart sped up. 'An appetite?'

He nodded. 'You owe me something.'

'I do?'

He nodded as he put down the cup and reached for the tie on her robe and undid it. 'You owe me a wedding night. But first…let's take a little dip.'

He pushed back the robe and it fell off her shoulders and down to the ground. Leonora blamed her semi-awake state for the fact that she felt so languorous as Gabriel looked her up and down while she stood there in nothing but two flimsy scraps of lace.

As she watched he opened the top button and his shorts dropped to the ground. He was naked, and she took in the magnificence of his naked form as if she'd never seen it before. *Now* she was wide awake. Her body humming with electricity.

'Turn around,' he instructed.

She did, revelling in the warmth of the morning sun and the humid air. He undid the clasp of her bra and it fell away, floating gently on the breeze. He came up behind her and wrapped his arms around her, his mouth searching for and finding the sensitive spot between her neck and shoulder. She shivered in reaction. All that was separating them was that flimsy scrap of lace, and Gabriel's hands were there now, pulling it down over her hips.

Her panties fell to the ground at her feet and she turned around, heart beating so fast she felt light-headed. He stood back and held out a hand. She took it and followed where he led her to the pool.

As they descended the stone steps leading down into the clear cool water, with the backdrop of nothing but lush nature around them, she felt as if they were embarking on something very elemental.

The fact that this was so far removed from what Leonora might have imagined of a marriage was too huge to absorb at that moment. So when Gabriel reached for her she went willingly, wrapping her legs around his narrow waist, her arms around his neck, mouths fusing and passion drowning out all and any disjointed thoughts except for *this* bliss.

Breakfast turned into a very late lunch that day…

A few days later Leonora was dozing on a lounger under an umbrella by the pool. Since that first cataclysmic morning she'd discovered that Gabriel had a discreet, friendly staff, who melted in and out of the villa every day, leaving food and tidying away the evidence of the previous night's passion.

At first she'd been mortified, but now she was ashamed to say she was already used to the sensation of invisible hands keeping her world pristine. It was a novelty after years of hiring only the most minimal help at the *castillo*, because she literally had not been able to do all the work alone.

Their days had fallen into a lazy, sensual pattern. Leonora would wake late, as she was generally only falling into an exhausted sated slumber as dawn was lightening the morning sky, and Gabriel would already be up, taking calls or doing some work in his airy study on the other side of the villa. He would join her for a late lunch, which would invariably end up with them back in bed.

Leonora blushed now under the umbrella. They were insatiable. She'd never known sex could be like this—so all-encompassing.

The previous night he'd been about to automatically don protection when she'd acted on impulse and put a hand on his, stopping him.

He'd looked at her for a long moment and then he'd put the protection aside and lain down beside her. 'Are you sure about this? Are you ready?'

Leonora had looked back at him, and even through the haze of desire she'd known they were crossing a line. She'd nodded and said, 'Yes. I want children with you. I know it's hard work, because I looked after Matías when he was younger, but these are different circumstances.'

Gabriel had put a hand on her belly. 'These are very different circumstances, *querida*. You're not alone any more. Our children will have two parents who want the best for them, who will support them no matter what. You'll be a great mother. You're amazing with your brother and you love your parents…'

Leonora's heart had felt suspiciously full. She'd reached for Gabriel, pulling him over her, opening her legs around him, guiding him into her body. Skin on skin. No barriers. Telling him without words that she wanted all those things too. *And more.*

That was why she'd stayed silent—for fear of what she might say.

She hated to admit it now, and she told herself it had only been because of the unique sensation of not using protection, but making love to him last night had felt almost…spiritual.

She put a hand on her flat belly, imagining a baby already taking root inside her. And then she told herself she was being ridiculous. It wasn't the right time. But it could happen within the next cycle. Soon.

She realised how badly she wanted it now. She wanted to show Gabriel that their family could be different. That there could be love. Her heart clenched. Her fantasy of a fuller, richer life wasn't just a fantasy any more. No matter what he'd said or how much he'd warned her not to build castles in the air. If Gabriel wanted a different life for his children then who was to say he couldn't fall in—?

'Afternoon, sleepyhead.'

Leonora's eyes snapped open behind her shades. Gabriel was standing beside her sun bed, tall and broad. Barechested. She was glad that the oversized glasses hid what had to be the soppy expression on her face.

She snatched her hand off her belly and sat up. 'Afternoon. Did you have much work to catch up on?'

Gabriel sat down on the lounger next to hers and reached for some of the fruit that his housekeeper had left out for

Leonora in a bowl. He shook his head and his mouth tightened almost imperceptibly. 'A phone call about a project with someone from the other side. Intensely irritating but unavoidable.'

'That sounds...unpleasant.'

He dismissed it with a hand. 'It's not important.' He stood up, holding out that same hand. 'Come on, I want to take you somewhere.'

Leonora stood up, conscious of his eyes running down her body in the cutaway swimsuit. She let him take her hand, hating the way her treacherous heart tripped. He instructed her to put on a caftan and shoes, and then he took her around to the front of the villa, where there was a sturdy open-top four-wheel drive with a wicker basket in the back. She threw a sunhat in the back with the basket.

'Come on—jump in.'

Gabriel swung into the driver's seat, his naked torso gleaming. He looked like a buccaneer.

Leonora got in and Gabriel took off down the winding path. She put her head back and looked at the canopy rushing overhead, the sun breaking through every now and then in a bright flash. She felt...free. Unencumbered.

She didn't want to ruin the moment by saying anything so she let Gabriel drive, noticing his powerful hands on the wheel, the way he drove with speed, yet precision. There was a shadow of stubble on his jaw. His hair was messy in the breeze. He looked younger. Less...stern. When she'd seen him across that ballroom on that fateful first night she never would have imagined him in this kind of environment...carefree.

She had a sudden thought and hated herself for it. But she couldn't help asking, as massive trees rushed past the Jeep on either side, 'Have you ever brought anyone else here?'

She almost hoped he hadn't heard, that the breeze whipping past their faces might have snatched her words away, but she saw his hands clench on the wheel, momentarily.

'Have you ever brought anyone else here?'

The words landed straight in Gabriel's gut. No. He hadn't ever brought anyone else here. Because this was his secret private sanctuary, where he could get away from everything and everyone. And yet he hadn't hesitated at the thought of bringing Leo here.

That question from any other woman would have made him feel as if there was a hand around his neck, squeezing slowly. But this was different. *She* was different. Which was why he'd married her, he told himself now. Because she didn't induce that feeling of claustrophobia. The opposite, in fact.

Seeing the shock and awe on her face that first morning had been worth it alone. He was jaded, and the people around him were jaded. Yet Leo, even coming from the same world, was remarkably *un*-jaded.

He took her hand in his, slowing the vehicle as they veered off the road and onto a dirt track that ran deeper into the jungle. He looked at her. 'No, I've never brought anyone else here.'

She couldn't hide the relief on her face, even though she quickly masked it. And then she surprised him.

'Good,' she said. 'Because if I thought this was just some routine you've done a thousand times I think I'd have to kill you. And those other women.'

Gabriel threw his head back and laughed. Leo was grinning and his chest tightened. She was so beautiful. The sun had added a golden glow to her skin. Her hair tumbled over her shoulders, its normally sleek glossiness untamed in loose waves. And he wanted her with a hunger that only seemed to grow the more he had of her.

On that unsettling thought he let her hand go, ostensibly to put both his hands on the wheel in order to control the car on the rougher terrain. But it was also because he'd just realised how far under his skin she'd reached. All the way so that for the first time in his life work wasn't the first thought of his day. Or his last. It was *her*. And then, when he was sated, he thought about work again. As if he needed to take that edge off before he could think clearly.

He'd had to take a phone call with Lazaro Sanchez just now, and Sanchez had goaded him about using Leonora to score points in their rivalry. Just hearing her name on that man's lips had made Gabriel see red, even as his conscience had pricked when he'd recalled being very aware of how it would look to be photographed with her leaving the hotel the night of the failed engagement.

That felt like a long time ago now. He'd never envisaged then, that Leonora would become his wife.

He'd told Sanchez that Leonora was *where she belonged*. And he'd really meant it. He felt a possessiveness that he'd never felt before—for a woman or anything.

Gabriel shoved aside the niggling prickling sensation that felt like exposure. He was on his honeymoon. It was natural and expected to be captivated by one's wife. Possessive.

Leonora gasped out loud as they burst through the thick trees and onto the edge of the most pristine beach she'd ever seen in her life. Gabriel stopped driving and she stood up in the vehicle, scanning left and right. She could see nothing but sea, white sand and the line of trees bordering the beach. It was completely empty. The waves rolled in with a rhythmic *whoosh*.

Gabriel got out, picking up the wicker basket. Leonora

got out too and stuck her sunhat on her head as she walked to the start of the beach. She slipped off her shoes and dug her toes into the soft warm sand.

It was beyond idyllic and there wasn't another human in sight. Just her and this charismatic man who had come into her life only a couple of short weeks ago and comprehensively turned it upside down and transformed her, inside and out.

Impulsively, she pulled off her caftan and threw her hat down on the sand. She started running backwards towards the sea. 'Last one in is a loser!'

Gabriel stood stock-still for a moment and then he put down the basket, kicked off his own shoes and started running after Leonora. She squealed and turned around, but it was no use. Gabriel caught her all too easily and lifted her up, over his shoulder, and carried her into the crashing surf of the glittering Pacific Ocean, dunking her mercilessly under the foaming waves until she begged for mercy.

He pulled her out, laughing and spluttering, and then she saw the intensity on his face, the way his eyes burned. She reached for him, seeking and finding his hot mouth, revelling in his whipcord body as he lifted her against him, wrapping her legs around him.

The waves crashed around them unnoticed as Gabriel pulled her swimsuit below her breasts, feasting on her wet flesh. The stark contrast of his hot mouth against her sea-cold skin made her head fall back…she was in paradise with the most exciting man she'd ever met and she never wanted it to end…

The knowledge that she'd never felt happier than in that moment was bittersweet. Because she knew it wasn't the same for Gabriel. What he was feeling was purely physical, evidenced by the way he couldn't take his hands off her, or she off him. But, weakly, she avoided thinking about that and gave herself up to the moment, like a miser with her gold.

A couple of hours later, after they'd made love under the shade of the trees on the edge of the beach, Leonora sat with her knees tucked up under her chin, her arms around them. She wore her caftan over her naked body while her swimsuit dried on a nearby rock, with Gabriel's shorts beside it. He wore a towel, tied precariously around his narrow waist.

The detritus of a delicious picnic lay around them. Fruit, bread, cheese, cold meats. Ice-cold water and sparkling wine. Of which Leonora had had a little.

The feeling of happiness lingered in her chest. It was unsettling, because she realised now how little she'd ever felt truly happy in her life. She'd always been so worried about her parents and Matías. And before they'd lost everything she'd always been far too reticent to let her emotions free rein.

'What are you thinking about?'

She glanced at Gabriel, who was sitting back, leaning on one elbow, watching her. He popped a piece of pineapple into his mouth. The thought of blurting out exactly what was on her mind made her break out in a sweat.

She shrugged lightly. 'Just about life…'

'Oh, just about *life*? Nothing much, then?' Gabriel mocked her easily.

Leonora smiled. 'I was thinking about how I used the *castillo* to hide away for a long time. I was so shy… I never felt as if I truly belonged in our world. Everyone else seemed so much more confident than I felt.' She looked at him almost accusingly. 'You even noticed it.'

He sat up too. 'Our perception of other people is usually wrong, you know. Some people just manage to put on a more convincing act. I don't think you're that shy, really. You didn't like being the centre of attention that evening in the hotel, but you did it because you felt you had to. For your family.'

Leonora absorbed that. She hadn't thought about it like that before. He was right—she hadn't liked it, but she hadn't been crippled by it. Maybe her shyness had dissipated over the years and she hadn't even noticed. And he was also right that when it came to doing something for her family she didn't hesitate.

Maybe it would be different if she felt she had a role. A reason to get up in front of people.

She looked at Gabriel and said grudgingly, 'You're very observant.'

He arched a brow. 'I'm observant because I have to be. If I can't read people and I don't see what's going on around me I lose my edge. And if I lose my edge I risk losing everything. My father lost his edge and I had to take over. Too many people depend on me. My family legacy depends on me.'

Leonora touched her belly under the caftan. 'And me too.'

He turned to her and she saw the seriousness of his expression. It cleared, and he smiled, but it was wicked.

'Yes. And you too, Señora Torres.'

He lay down again and pulled her with him, so she was sprawled across his chest. Her breasts were flattened against him and he funnelled his hands through her hair, pulling her head down to his.

'About that legacy... I think it still needs work...'

When his hands reached for her caftan, pulling it up and off her body, she helped, throwing it aside. He removed the barrier of the towel between them and she sat astride him and took him deep inside her on a gasp.

Afterwards, when the sun was setting and it was warm on her naked back, where she lay sprawled across Gabriel's bare chest, she knew she was in deep trouble. All the warnings in the world couldn't stop her falling for this man, because she was already deeply and irrevocably in love with him.

A couple of far too short days later they took off from San José airport. Leonora felt nervous at the thought of leaving behind the idyllic bubble they'd inhabited these past few days. Nervous at the thought of going back into the real world with a man who was still an enigma to her in so many ways—in spite of their physical intimacy, and in spite of her getting to know him in a little better.

They'd discovered similar interests in everything from art to books, movies and politics. But she couldn't afford to forget that the very urbane and seductive man she'd come to know hid a ruthless streak. How could he not be ruthless when he'd shouldered such responsibility for so long and when he was so successful? When he had a legacy to continue?

Physically, their obsession with each other didn't seem to be waning. Far from it. They'd been ready to leave for the airport, dressed and packed, and all it had taken was one burning look from Gabriel and they'd been back in the bedroom, on the bed, clothes ripped off in minutes.

Maybe Gabriel was right, Leonora told herself now. Maybe all they needed was this insane chemistry and mutual respect. And a willingness to commit to bringing up their children differently than they had been brought up in order to have a happy life?

But she couldn't shake the hollow feeling inside her that it wouldn't be enough.

In a bid to try and distract herself, she reached for

the pile of newspapers and magazines left out by the plane's staff.

Almost immediately she noticed a picture on the front page of a tabloid magazine. It was Lazaro Sanchez and the red-haired woman who had crashed their engagement party. They were emerging from what looked like a town hall. She was wearing a cream dress and matching jacket, her bright red hair pulled back into a low ponytail, clutching a posy of flowers. He was in a suit and putting out a hand as if to ward off the paparazzi from getting too close. They'd just been married, clearly.

Leonora couldn't remember him ever looking as intense with her as he did in the photo. She could see the faintest outline of the woman's pregnancy bump. So he *was* the father. No wonder he'd married her so quickly. Her name was Skye O'Hara.

Leonora knew she should be feeling *something* at the sight of her recent almost-fiancé marrying another woman, but all she felt was relief. And a kind of terror to think that she might very well have not had that night with Gabriel which had led to their marriage.

'What's that?'

Leonora looked at Gabriel. She handed the magazine across and he took it, taking in the front cover.

He looked back at her, spearing her with those dark eyes. 'Does this bother you?'

She shook her head. 'No…actually, not at all.'

Gabriel crumpled up the magazine and tossed it in a nearby bin. Then he reached for Leonora, undoing her seat belt and tugging her all too easily out of her seat and into his lap. She blushed and looked around, but there were no staff.

'Sanchez's loss is my gain. He's a fool.'

Leonora looked down at Gabriel. There was a tone in his voice that made her want to ask if he knew Lazaro Sanchez personally, but before she could he was pulling her head down and pressing hot kisses along her jaw and neck. Her head fell back and every coherent thought was wiped out as the last, lingering effects of their magical honeymoon were continued in the luxurious bedroom of the private plane.

Almost a week after they'd returned from honeymoon they were having dinner in one of the *castillo*'s less formal dining rooms.

'How are you settling in?' Gabriel asked.

Leonora thought of the way he'd woken her this morning—the way he woke nearly every morning, actually—in a very sensual way that inevitably put her back into a satisfaction-induced coma for a couple of hours while he got up and went to work. She'd never behaved so decadently in her life.

He was watching her closely and she suspected he was even smirking slightly, which helped her not to blush.

Airily, she pretended not to be thinking about sex. 'Fine, thank you. Ernesto has been very kind. He's shown me every part of the *castillo*. Including the vaults where you store the wine that you don't drink and your family portraits.'

Gabriel took a sip of his sparkling water. 'The portraits are scary, aren't they?'

They were. And they were a sober reminder of the sheer weight and extent of Gabriel's family's legacy.

Unconsciously she put a hand to her belly, thinking that it would have to be miracle if she hadn't fallen pregnant on their honeymoon, given that they'd made love every night and every morning. She'd know in about ten days, anyway.

Now she did blush, which she deflected from by asking hurriedly, 'Why don't you drink—is it just because of your father?'

Gabriel put his glass down. 'That, and I don't like the sensation of not having my wits about me. I once got very drunk when I was a teenager and I never wanted to feel like that again.'

She could understand that. Even though she'd never really been drunk herself, she felt as if she lost her wits every time Gabriel looked at her.

Curious, she asked, 'Why did you get drunk?'

He looked as if he didn't want to say anything, but then reluctantly he said, 'My first lover. She was a bit older than me. I was besotted with her. Until I found her in bed with my best friend.'

Leonora felt her insides plummet. 'You were in love... once?'

He made a face. 'Was it love? It was more like an obsession. And even if it was love she merely confirmed for me that it doesn't exist.'

It was a sign, as if she'd needed one, not to look beyond the physical intimacy of their honeymoon.

She changed the subject and forced a neutral tone into her voice. 'I saw Matías today. He's so excited about the football match in a few weeks. Thank you for getting the tickets.'

Gabriel shrugged nonchalantly. 'I have a box at the stadium. He'll be treated like a king.'

Emotion caught in Leonora's chest. Gabriel really had no idea how a casual gesture could mean so much. 'He'll love it.'

Gabriel asked, 'How are renovations coming along at the Flores *castillo*?'

'Really well. They've done so much already. I think my parents have decided to keep doing the tours. They have plans to make them more dynamic—add in wine tastings, overnight stays, that kind of thing. The fact that they'll be able to hire staff makes all the difference. It's given them a new lease of life. Thank you.'

Gabriel inclined his head. 'It's all part of the agreement.'

That dented a little more of the hazy glow surrounding Leonora. Gabriel wasn't doing this out of the goodness of his heart. He was doing it because it was part of their pre-nuptial agreement. Laid out in black and white. Okay, so his relationship with Matías was something he *was* doing out of the goodness of his heart…but she needed to remember that this marriage was very much a transaction for him. Much as it would have been for Lazaro Sanchez.

She was a commodity who had value in her background, her name, and in how she looked and could conduct herself. And she was lucky that Gabriel found her attractive or she wouldn't be here.

His hand came over hers and she felt that all too familiar tingle of electricity. She almost resented it for a second.

'Where did you go just then?' he asked.

She cursed the fact that she couldn't seem to hide her expressions around Gabriel, when for years she'd perfected the art of not showing anyone what was going on inside her.

She forced a smile. 'Nowhere.'

Gabriel lifted his hand off Leonora's. It was disconcerting to feel so attuned to another person. She'd retreated just then, closing herself off right in front of him. He'd immediately wanted to know why. Even though he was more used to people trying to read *him* for his reactions.

It was also disconcerting how quickly he'd adjusted to having Leonora here at the *castillo*. He almost couldn't remember a time when she hadn't been there. When he arrived home in the evening the first thing he noticed was her light scent. Floral, with musky undertones. Like her—

serene on the surface but full of complexity and fire underneath.

The captivation he'd felt in Costa Rica didn't appear to be diminishing. During a board meeting earlier his mind had wandered all too easily to remembering how he'd woken her that morning. It had started slow and sensuous but had quickly become urgent and explosive.

She was addictive.

He assured himself that this was normal. He just hadn't expected that he would *want* his wife this much. He'd imagined a far more sedate arrangement, if and when he married, with sex turning into a function more than an indulgence. But this was a *good* thing, he assured himself now. He and Leonora had something to build on. A connection that went beyond what most couples in their world had.

Leonora said, 'Your assistant called me today—about a function in Paris at the weekend?'

'Yes. It's a gala in aid of a charity. It's on at the same time as Fashion Week, so it'll be pretty high-profile.'

Leonora immediately felt intimidated. Which was ridiculous. She'd been bred for this sort of thing.

'When do we leave?'

'We'll fly out Saturday afternoon, and come back on Monday. I have some meetings there on Monday morning.' He put his hand over hers again. 'You'll be fine.'

She looked at him. 'I don't want to let you down. I've never been the most gregarious person in a group.'

He shook his head. 'I don't want gregarious. I want you.'

The hazy glow was back. He interlinked their fingers and Leonora felt a pulse throb between her legs. It was as if her body had been made uniquely to respond to his. It was maddening—and utterly thrilling.

He stood up and held out a hand, the look in his eye very explicit. Unmistakable.

Her body reacted predictably, her blood growing hot, moving faster through her veins.

They'd just finished dinner. Leonora usually liked to relax, watching a boxset or reading a book before bed. But that had been before Gabriel had awoken this needy and insatiable side of her. And right then the thought of losing herself to his expert touch was a very enticing prospect. She really didn't want to think about their first official public outing together as a couple.

So she stood up and let him lead her up the stairs and into their bedroom. She tried to feel cynical about it and remind herself that this attention from Gabriel was in part to ensure a quick result for an heir, but when he touched her, or looked at her like he was doing now—as if, like her, he couldn't quite understand this *thing* between them—it was very hard to be cynical. It felt so pure. And raw. And necessary.

CHAPTER EIGHT

'YOU LOOK BEAUTIFUL, LEO.'

She tried to feel confident under Gabriel's approving gaze but a million butterflies were fluttering around her belly. No, buzzing. Fluttering was too gentle. She felt as nervous as she had the night of her engagement announcement.

She checked her reflection again. A styling team had come to get her ready and her hair was in a simple chignon. Her dress was a dark royal blue. Floor-length and fitted, it had three-quarter-length sleeves. It was modest at the front, with a high neckline, but it was backless at the back. A more risqué design than she would usually wear but the stylist had insisted.

Gabriel had surprised her with sapphire drop earrings and a matching bracelet and necklace. The jewels glittered against her skin. She knew she looked the part—she just didn't feel it.

She forced her gaze back to her husband's. 'Thank you. So you do.'

And he did. She'd seen him in a tuxedo before, but he still took her breath away. He wore a white bowtie this evening, and the white of the shirt and the tie made him look very dark.

'Shall we? My driver is ready downstairs.'

Leonora took a breath and slipped her arm through his,

hating how much she liked it that he reached for her hand and held it in the lift on the way down. A little extra touch.

They were staying in a hotel not far from where the function was taking place. An exclusive hotel overlooking the Arc de Triomphe. Gabriel had an apartment in Paris, of course, but it was undergoing refurbishment. He'd taken Leonora there earlier to meet with the designer and get her input on the design. Another unexpectedly thoughtful gesture.

They were in the back of his sleek chauffeur-driven luxury car now, her hand still in his. She wanted to be able to pull away, tell him she was fine, but she wasn't. She saw the flashing of the paparazzi cameras in the distance. The sleek line of cars. The beautiful people getting out.

Bizarrely, at that moment she thought of the picture she'd seen on the magazine cover, of Lazaro Sanchez's new wife… Skye?…and of how terrified she'd looked. Leonora felt a spike of empathy for her.

It was time to get out.

Someone had obviously caught a glimpse of Gabriel inside the car and the camera flashes went crazy.

He looked at her. 'Ready?'

She nodded.

'Wait here. I'll get out first and come around and get you.'

He got out and the shouts were deafening.

'Gabriel! Over here!'

'Where's Leonora?'

'We want to see your wife!'

He came to her door and she sucked in a big breath and stuck on a smile—just as he opened the door and the world became one huge bright flash of light.

After about an hour of milling around the thronged ballroom, after the charity auction had taken place, Leonora's smile felt like a rictus grin on her face. Gabriel was deep in conversation with some very serious-looking individuals, and she'd spied some open doors leading out to a terrace that looked blessedly airy and empty.

She caught his attention and motioned that she was taking a little break, and then made her way through the crowd of well-known faces from film and politics. When she reached the doors she stepped outside, relief flooding her to find the space was indeed empty. Nothing but fresh air and the lights of Paris glittering as far as the eye could see.

She ventured further and then stopped suddenly—because there *was* someone else out here. A woman in a strapless black dress. Petite. Very pretty. With bright red hair. Looking at her with big blue eyes. Shocked eyes.

The woman said, *'You.'*

Recognition was swift. It was Skye O'Hara. Lazaro's pregnant wife.

Leonora looked down and saw the small bump. Inexplicably, she felt a spurt of something that felt like jealousy.

She spoke in English. 'Sorry, I didn't realise there was anyone here.'

She turned to leave, but she heard from behind her, *'No. Please, don't go.'*

Leonora stopped. Tension thrummed through her. She turned around again, schooling her expression to be as noncommittal as possible.

Skye said, 'I just want to say how sorry I am... I never intended to ruin your engagement like that. I just... I'd tried to get in touch with Lazaro but it was impossible. I sneaked into that room and saw him... I had to let him know.'

The tortured look on her face and the sincerity of her words made Leonora do a double-take. She was used to a different breed of female. Like the ones who had been gossiping in the bathroom the night she'd met Gabriel. Clearly

Skye was not in their league, and something in Leonora relaxed.

'I know. I get that now. You met before he proposed to me.'

'Yes!' The relief was evident on her face and she smiled ruefully. 'I would have hated it if you'd been with him then.'

Leonora moved closer to Skye. 'No, that would not have been nice. But he would not have done that. These men... they have integrity, at least.'

'You mean Lazaro and...?'

'Gabriel—my husband.' Leonora couldn't stop her gaze from dropping again to Skye's pregnant belly. She looked up. 'Congratulations. I wish you all the best in your future with Lazaro.'

Skye put a small pale hand on her belly. She smiled shyly. 'Thank you...' Then she blurted out, 'I felt it move just now...a proper movement.'

The evidence of Skye's pregnancy only drove home the fact that no matter how in tune Leonora might feel with Gabriel, she really only had one function to fulfil as his wife. Bear him an heir. And she was in danger of forgetting it.

Skye must have seen something on her face. She looked anxious. 'I'm sorry—did I say something...?'

Leonora forced a smile. 'No, not at all. I really do wish you all the best in your future with Lazaro and the baby.'

She turned away to leave but Skye reached out and took her hand. 'I'm sorry again...and I wish you all the best too.'

Leonora was surprised at the surge of emotion she felt at the other woman's touch and sincerity. She squeezed Skye's hand and said, 'Thank you,' and turned away before she could notice the moisture springing into her eyes. Crazy. What was wrong with her? She'd never really had a close female friend, but she realised now that if she had, she would have wanted her to be someone like Skye.

She walked back into the room, her eyes searching out her husband. She didn't have to search for long because he was the tallest man in the room. Well, him and the man he was talking to. Lazaro Sanchez. What on earth would he be talking to *him* for?

Suddenly concerned, Leonora made her way over, seeing the tension in Gabriel's body. And in Lazaro's. The grim looks on their faces. This was not a friendly chat. Far from it. They seemed to be locked in some private battle of wills.

She drew closer and they were still oblivious to her. She picked up their conversation.

Lazaro Sanchez was saying, 'Maybe this time you'll be surprised, Gabriel, and maybe the best bid will win—the one that has the good of the city at its heart, not just the insatiable Torres need for domination in all things.'

Gabriel took a step closer to Lazaro, his face etched in stark lines. 'I do remember you, you know. I remember that day when you confronted my father in the street and claimed to be his son. You have a chip on your shoulder, Sanchez, and it's time to get over it and stop telling yourself you've been hard done by.'

Leonora couldn't believe what she'd just heard. The two men obviously knew each other. Had history. The tension between them was palpable.

She took a step into their space, but even then they didn't notice her. She said, 'Hello, Lazaro, it's nice to see you.'

Lazaro Sanchez blinked and seemed to come out of his angry trance. So did Gabriel, and he immediately reached for Leonora, pulling her close with an arm around her waist.

Lazaro echoed what Skye had said. 'Leonora. I'm sorry for what happened. It was never my intention to do anything to hurt or embarrass you.'

She smiled tightly. 'I know. I just met your wife. Congratulations on the baby.'

'Thank you.'

Lazaro looked at Gabriel and Leonora could feel the tension in her husband's body. He was rigid with it. She'd never seen him react like this to anyone else.

'Till next time, Torres.'

Lazaro walked away.

Leonora looked up at Gabriel, who was staring after Lazaro with a hard expression. Almost bitter. She said, 'I didn't realise you knew each other.'

He looked at her, jaw tight. 'I'd prefer it if we didn't but, yes, we do.'

'You've known him since before the night of the engagement party?'

'Yes, for a few years now.'

Leonora felt sick as things slid into place in her mind. 'A few *years*?'

Instinctively she moved out of his embrace and stood apart. 'You know him and you didn't think it worth mentioning?'

'I didn't think it was relevant.'

Confusion and hurt and other emotions were swirling in Leonora's gut now. 'Not *relevant*? I slept with you on the night I was due to announce my engagement to him—the night you seduced me—and you didn't think it was relevant?'

Gabriel looked around and took Leonora's elbow, guiding her over to a corner of the room where a large plant shielded them a little. That only made her feel more incensed.

She pulled away again. 'Why didn't you tell me you knew him?'

'Because he's not someone I think about unless I have to.'

'You don't like him—that much is obvious.'

'No, I don't.'

The implications of this were huge. 'Why were you even at the engagement announcement if you don't like him?'

Gabriel's jaw clenched. 'Because I needed to know what he was up to.'

Leonora shook her head to try and understand. 'You came after me…after the interruption. I thought it was co-incidental…but it wasn't, was it?'

'I came after you because I wanted you. You felt it too that night. And, I was concerned about you.'

But Leonora wasn't hearing him. She was reliving what had happened in slow motion. She looked at him, feeling the blood drain south through her body, leaving her cold all over. 'You seduced me just to get back at him. You seized an opportunity.'

Gabriel shook his head. 'No, I seduced you because I wanted you—for no other reason.'

Leonora was aware of a sharp pain near her heart. 'Are you telling me you weren't in any way aware of the fact that it might get to Lazaro if you were seen with me?'

Gabriel flushed. 'I admit I wasn't *un*aware that it might irritate him if he saw pictures of us together, leaving the hotel. But once we got back to my apartment Lazaro San-chez was the last person on my mind.'

Leonora shook her head. 'You've used me from the very start—like a pawn. Is that why you proposed? Because it was another way to strike at your adversary?'

Leonora backed away from Gabriel. She had to leave before he saw how devastating this knowledge was to her. She turned and fled, apologising as she bumped into peo-ple in her bid to get out of the function room.

She emerged into a corridor and saw an elevator. The doors were closing and she ran, catching it just before they closed all the way. She stepped in, aware of people looking at her. Her heart was pounding. She felt wild. Undone.

She'd just been a pawn all along.

She saw Gabriel emerge from the room just as the doors closed. In that moment, when their eyes met for a split second, she hated him.

She didn't think when she got out on the ground floor. She went straight to the entrance and jumped into the first taxi she saw...

Gabriel cursed loudly and colourfully enough to make people stop and look at him at the entrance of the grand hotel. He'd just seen a flash of blue dress and bare back disappear into a taxi and the car was already merging into the heavy Paris traffic.

He tried calling Leo's phone but it went straight to voicemail. Gabriel was not unaware of the irony of his wife being pretty much the only woman who had ever consistently demonstrated that he wasn't as irresistible as people liked to make out.

He summoned his own car and got into the back, instructing the driver to go to his hotel. All he could do was hope that she had returned there.

But she hadn't.

He paced up and down, trying her phone again and again. Eventually he gave up. She'd run because she needed space. He couldn't blame her. His conscience stung hard. He *had* gone after her that first night because he'd wanted her, but he'd also seen an opportunity to stick the knife into Sanchez by letting them be photographed leaving the hotel together.

He just hadn't realised how much he would want her. Sanchez had become very much peripheral to everything once he'd slept with Leo and decided to ask her to marry him.

But could he convince her of that?

'Où allez-vous, madame?'

Leonora looked at the driver and blinked. Where *was* she going? Her instinct had been to get as far away as possible from Gabriel. But she had a limited amount of cash in her clutch bag and she was dressed in an evening gown. Hardly appropriate to roam the streets, even though she felt it would take miles to work off the anger she felt towards Gabriel.

Anger. *And hurt.*

She knew she had no choice but to go back to their hotel, so she gave the address reluctantly. The taxi did a U-turn in the road and went back the way it had come.

She felt sick. Bruised. And, worse, like a monumental fool. From the moment Gabriel had spoken to her he'd relished her strategic importance in scoring points against a rival.

Would he really be so petty?

Leonora ignored the question. Her anger was too fiery for her to try and be rational, to think this through. Lazaro had seen her as a pawn to use to get him accepted in a world closed to him. And Gabriel had seen her as a pawn to use to get back at Lazaro.

She knew she wasn't a helpless victim in all of this, but the revelation tainted every single interaction she'd had with Gabriel since they'd met. How he must have laughed at her the morning after that first night together when he'd realised that she hadn't even given her virginity to Lazaro. Another point scored.

For a moment she thought she might actually be sick, but she managed to control it. The hotel came into view, glittering in the distance. The taxi pulled up outside and Leonora paid the driver and got out.

As she ascended to their room in the elevator she nurtured her anger, feeling as if she needed some kind of armour against Gabriel's inevitable effect on her. When she reached the door she realised she didn't have a key, so she knocked on the heavy wood.

It opened almost immediately. Gabriel filled the doorway, jacket off, tie loose, top button undone. His hair was messy, as if he'd been running a hand through it. He held his mobile phone to his ear and he had the grimmest expression she'd ever seen on his face.

He said curtly, 'She's here. It's fine. Thank you, Marc.'

He stood aside and took his phone down from his ear. Ridiculously, Leonora felt like a rebellious teenager who'd been caught sneaking home from an illicit party. She refused to let Gabriel make her feel as if she was in the wrong, so she tipped her chin up and stalked past him into the suite.

She turned around to face him. He'd followed her and she could see the anger on his face.

'Don't *ever* do that again.'

Leonora was genuinely confused. 'What?'

'Run away and turn your phone off. We had no way of tracking you or following you.'

'*We?*'

'My security team. The same security team that protects you without you even knowing it. You're a target, Leo, because *I'm* a target.'

To her surprise, although she could still see the anger, she could also see something else. Fear? And Gabriel looked slightly pale. Or was it just a trick of the light?

But his revelation just stoked her anger. She welcomed it. 'Well, if I had *known* that you had a security team I would have been more considerate. And I didn't turn off my phone when I left. It's been off since we arrived at the event.'

Gabriel ran a hand through his hair, mussing it up more. Leonora hated how fascinated she was by this far less urbane incarnation of Gabriel Torres.

Had he really been concerned?

She pushed that notion down, remembering seeing him go toe to toe with Lazaro Sanchez. The bristling tension between the men.

'Look,' he said, before she could say a word, throwing his phone down on a nearby chair, 'I'm sorry I didn't tell you that I knew Sanchez. I didn't realise how it would look. Or how it would make you feel when you discovered we did know each other.'

She asked tautly, 'What is it between you?'

Gabriel stuck his hands in his pockets. 'Ever since he arrived on the scene a few years ago he's made a beeline for me. Shadowing my every move, trying to disrupt deals I'm involved in. We're both currently involved in a bid to redevelop the old Madrid marketplace.'

Leonora had heard about that bid. It was huge. 'I had no idea you were involved in that.'

The hurt she was feeling intensified. While she'd been thinking that she was growing closer to Gabriel, developing an intimacy that might one day extend beyond the bedroom, he had basically told her nothing about his day-to-day life. It was like a slap in the face.

He looked at her. 'I didn't think you'd be interested.'

'I'm your wife. I think I should know what you're involved in.'

Gabriel walked over to the window. He said, 'I've never had to answer to anyone. I've never had to explain myself.' He turned to face her. 'It didn't occur to me to let you know about these things.'

The anger in Leonora diminished slightly. She could appreciate how a lone wolf like Gabriel might find it hard to adjust to being in a relationship.

Still... 'That doesn't excuse you not telling me about Lazaro. It's too much of a coincidence that we ended up in bed together the same night my engagement was meant to be announced.'

Gabriel shook his head. He came closer, but Leonora backed away. He stopped.

'I went there that night because of Sanchez, yes. But as soon as I saw you I got distracted. It became about you, not him.'

Leonora cursed the fluttering in her belly. 'It was about him when you walked me out through the front door of the hotel.'

His mouth tightened. 'I was aware of how it would look, yes. But I was also conscious of wanting to get you out of there, and getting to know you.'

His straightforward honesty deflated her a little. Her heart beat fast as she recalled how she'd felt the pull between them that night. She'd felt guilty, standing next to her fiancé and being mesmerised by another man. And as soon as he'd asked if she wanted his help in leaving she hadn't hesitated.

As if sensing her weakening, Gabriel said, 'I swear to you, from the moment we got to my apartment Sanchez was not in my head or my thoughts or my motivations. I wanted *you*. Do you really think I would have seduced you into my bed just to get back at him?'

Pride oozed from every inch of the man in front of her. But she resisted the urge to let herself weaken too much.

She remembered something. 'You were saying something to Lazaro earlier...about meeting him in a street with your father. What was that?'

Gabriel's jaw clenched. 'He claims to be my half-brother on my father's side.'

Leonora sat down on the seat behind her. 'What?'

'He confronted us in the street years ago. It was my birthday. He accused my father of being *his* father...but then two of my father's men took him away and I never saw him again until a few years ago.'

'So...he *could* be your half-brother?'

'It's quite possible. My father could have sired any number of illegitimate children.' The bitterness was in Gabriel's voice was palpable.

'Who is his mother?'

Gabriel shook his head. 'I don't know...and I don't care.'

But Leonora saw something. A flicker of emotion. And the fact that Lazaro Sanchez could inspire emotion in Gabriel made her feel almost...jealous. Which was crazy. Jealous of a business rival!

'Did you marry me to get back at Lazaro?'

He took a step forward, a fierce look on his face. 'No. I married you because you were the first woman who made me even want to think about it.'

Suddenly she felt weary. She stood up abruptly. 'I'm quite tired now. I think I'll go to bed.'

She turned before he could see the emotion she was feeling. She suspected deep down that Gabriel wouldn't really have gone so far as to seduce her and marry her just to score points, but it still stung.

He called her name just as she reached the door. She stopped reluctantly but didn't turn around.

He said from behind her, 'You were never a pawn. I went to the engagement announcement that night because of Sanchez, yes. But then I saw you, and I wanted you from that moment. I went after you because I wanted you. I seduced you because I wanted you. And I married you because I knew we'd be good together. Because I want you more than I've ever wanted another woman.'

Leonora's heart beat a little faster. Her hand tightened on the door handle. Gabriel had really hurt her this evening. And his power to hurt her only reminded her of how far she'd fallen. She had to protect herself.

She said, 'I'll take the spare room tonight.'

She walked out with her head held high and didn't look back. But it felt like a pyrrhic victory, because every instinct was urging her to go back and seek solace and oblivion in the arms of the man who had hurt her. Ironically, he was the only one who could help her to forget.

Leonora lay awake in the spare bed for a long time. It was the first night since she'd married Gabriel that she'd spent alone. And her body ached for him.

Dammit.

The hurt she'd been feeling had dissipated. She believed Gabriel. And she knew in her heart of hearts that if she was offered the choice of a sterile, emotionless marriage with Lazaro Sanchez over this...this sea of emotions with Gabriel, she would choose Gabriel again.

Something she'd been clinging to—a sense of injury— dissolved. She realised that her reaction would only reveal to Gabriel that she had feelings for him. Why else would she have been so affected? She thought of his anger because she'd disappeared. The expression of what had looked like fear on his face.

Impulsively, she got up from the bed and went outside the bedroom. The suite was dark. Quiet. She hovered uncertainly outside Gabriel's bedroom door, not even sure what she was going to do, but then she heard a sound coming from the living room so she went in that direction.

She found him sitting on the couch, watching a black

and white movie on TV. One of her favourites. A classic. Her heart clenched. He was still wearing his tuxedo trousers and his white shirt was open at the neck by a couple of buttons, revealing the strong column of his throat. Stubble lined his jaw and her skin tingled with awareness.

Then he looked up and saw her. He stared at her for a long moment, almost as if he wasn't sure she was real. She was very aware of her flimsy silk negligée. Then he slowly sat forward and muted the movie.

He put out a hand and Leonora took a breath and moved towards him. He caught her hand and tugged her down onto the couch beside him. Electric heat flooded her body. Instantaneous. Addictive.

She opened her mouth but he put a finger to it, stopping her. He shook his head. And then he said, 'Let me show you how much I want you. *You*, Leo, no one else.'

Weakly she gave herself up to the temptation she'd denied herself earlier, and with every touch and kiss she blocked out the hurt and the fact that she would undoubtedly face more hurt in the future.

When Leonora woke the next morning the sun was up. She was disorientated, and then she realised where she was and remembered the previous evening. She looked around but the room was empty. She was naked and her body ached all over. They'd made love on the couch, like teenagers, and then Gabriel had taken her into the bedroom and they'd made love again. And then again, as dawn had been breaking. Each as insatiable as the other.

Leonora groaned and rolled over, burying her face in the pillow. She didn't recognise this wanton side of herself. In fact she barely recognised herself at all. Her emotions were so raw and all over the place.

The revelation that Gabriel had known Lazaro all along

still had the power to hurt, in spite of his assurances. He wouldn't be human if he hadn't been aware that seducing Leonora might affect Lazaro's pride. But, having met Lazaro's pregnant wife, Leonora figured Lazaro had more important things to consider than hurt pride.

She put a hand on her flat belly. Could she and Gabriel have conceived a child? Last night? She had to be ovulating around now... Her pulse quickened. Even though everything logical told her that they weren't yet ready for the seismic reality of a baby—they were still getting to know one another!—nevertheless she had to admit that she'd felt a pang of jealousy when she'd seen evidence of Skye's pregnancy.

Leonora suddenly imagined Gabriel appearing and finding her dreaming of becoming pregnant with his baby. She scrambled out of the bed and grabbed a robe. She went into the opulent bathroom and took a shower, standing under the hot spray for a long time, relishing the jets of water on her pleasantly aching muscles.

When she soaped herself she saw the signs of Gabriel's lovemaking: stubble rash on the inside of her thighs. She blushed and quickly rinsed off and got out. She roughly dried her hair and pulled on the robe again.

She steeled herself before she left the bedroom, wishing she could feel blasé and nonchalant after a night like the one they'd shared. They were married, hardly illicit lovers, and yet she felt like a jittery teenager.

When she emerged into the living area she saw the dining table was set up for breakfast. A hotel staff member was there, pouring coffee for Gabriel, who stood up when he saw her.

'Good morning. I ordered a selection of everything. I wasn't sure what you'd prefer.'

Leonora smiled at the staff member as she poured her

coffee and then melted discreetly away. She took in the array of food laid out—fresh fruit, yoghurt, pastries, pancakes, bacon, eggs, toast—and to her mortification her stomach rumbled.

She sat down quickly, avoiding Gabriel's eye, putting some fruit pieces in a bowl and helping herself to some yoghurt.

'How are you feeling?'

Gabriel's question seemed innocuous enough and Leonora risked a glance at him, relieved to see him buttering some toast and not looking at her.

'Fine, thank you.'

Tired. She fought not to let the blush inside her rise to the surface when she thought of why she was so tired.

After a moment Gabriel said, 'I thought we'd spend a lazy day just wandering around the city. If you like?'

Leonora's heart thumped. She swallowed her food. 'You don't have to work?'

He shook his head. 'My meetings are tomorrow and everything is set up for them. It's Sunday—who works on Sundays?'

She'd used to. It had usually been quite a busy day for tourists visiting the *castillo*.

Gabriel said, 'You look surprised?'

Leonora felt self-conscious. 'I think I'd just assumed you'd be more of a workaholic.'

Something fleeting crossed his face, but it was gone before she could decipher what it was.

He said, 'I probably would have found an excuse to work today, but now I have a reason not to.'

It was ridiculous that she felt so excited and yet so trepidatious at the prospect of a day in Gabriel's company. Hadn't she spent a honeymoon alone with him for the best part of a week? But that had felt different—out of reality.

It had all been so new. All-consuming. She hadn't been in love with him then.

She hid her trepidation and said lightly, 'Then I'd like that.' She thought of something, 'What if the paparazzi spot us?'

Gabriel was one of their favourite subjects to follow as he was usually so elusive. But there had been plenty of paparazzi outside the hotel yesterday evening so they knew they were there.

Gabriel wiped his mouth with a napkin and stood up. He said with a wicked smile, 'I thought of that and I have a plan...'

CHAPTER NINE

GABRIEL'S PLAN HAD been to order up some casual clothes from the hotel's boutique, and now he and Leonora, dressed in jeans, shirts, light jackets and baseball hats, were ducking out of the hotel via a back entrance.

Leonora's hand was in Gabriel's as he led her around the side of the hotel. She could see the paparazzi waiting at the front, looking bored, checking their watches, and she couldn't help the small giggle rising as they made their escape. She felt as if she was playing truant from school. Giddy. And even giddier at this unexpected side of Gabriel.

To her surprise, he took her to the nearest Métro station saying, 'It's quicker than a taxi—do you mind?'

Leonora grinned up at him. 'Not at all.'

And that was the start of a magical and totally spontaneous day. They travelled around the city totally unnoticed, blending in with the crowds. Well, as discreetly as a six-foot-plus man *could* blend in with the crowds. Gabriel drew plenty of looks, but not necessarily looks of recognition. And if someone did do a double-take Gabriel and Leonora were usually gone before they realised who it was, having slipped down a side street.

Gabriel had left it to her to decide where to go, so they'd started at the Eiffel Tower and then wandered to the museums, going into the Rodin Museum, where his famous sculpture *The Kiss* had suddenly taken on a whole new significance for Leonora.

They'd stopped for delicious coffee and pastries on the Île de la Cité, near Notre-Dame, and now they were wandering through the leafy Jardin du Luxembourg, chatting easily about inconsequential things.

For the first time Leonora was acutely aware of families. Men carrying toddlers on their shoulders. Babies in prams. Her insides clenched. This could be them some day. And she appreciated more than ever Gabriel's desire for their children to have a different kind of upbringing.

On impulse, when they were standing by the lake in the park, Leonora turned to Gabriel and blurted out, 'I want to have a baby with you.'

He looked at her, a slightly nonplussed expression on his face, his firm mouth twitching. 'Well…that's…*good*…'

Leonora cursed her impetuosity. 'I mean, I know we have to have children, for so many reasons, but I actually… *want* to have a child with you.'

Her heart was pounding so fast. She tried to blame it on the coffee they'd just had. But she knew it wasn't the coffee.

Gabriel suddenly looked more serious. He twined his fingers with hers. 'I know,' he said. 'Me too.'

Leonora felt as if something intensely precious and delicate had been strung between them. And then she saw it: the heat in his eyes. The intent. It sparked the fire inside her and within seconds Gabriel was striding out of the park and flagging down a taxi.

He bundled Leonora in and she looked at him, taking the baseball cap off her head, half terrified and half exhilarated at the urgency suddenly beating between them.

'Where are we going?'

But she knew.

He gave directions to the driver to go back to the hotel, which wasn't far. They were there within minutes.

As they got out Leonora said, 'What about the paparazzi?'

But Gabriel just growled as he tugged her out. 'They don't matter.'

Within a short minute they were back in the hotel suite and Leonora's back was against the door, her mouth under Gabriel's and his hands roving over her body, removing her clothes with ruthless efficiency.

By the time they reached the bedroom, with a line of clothes strewn between the bed and the main door, they were naked.

They fell on the bed, limbs entwined. Leonora didn't know where she began and Gabriel ended. She'd never felt so primal in her life. When Gabriel joined their bodies in one cataclysmic thrust Leonora gasped. It was swallowed by Gabriel's mouth as he started to move in and out, taking them higher and higher, until they could go no further. After a taut moment, every muscle straining against the oncoming rush of pleasure, they fell into it, down and down... and Leonora wasn't even aware that she was crying as her emotions overflowed onto her cheeks.

It was early evening when Leonora woke in the bed alone. She realised her face and eyes were a little sticky and touched her cheeks, horror dawning on her as she realised she'd cried tears of pure emotion while making love to Gabriel.

She got up and dived under a steaming shower, as if that might wash away the signs of her weakness. She prayed that he hadn't seen her emotion. The thought of him realising he'd moved her to tears made her scrub herself even harder.

Eventually she got out, and only emerged into the living area once she'd put on some make-up and pulled back her damp hair. She dressed in casual dark trousers and a thin grey long-sleeved top. Clothes not remotely designed to entice.

Gabriel was standing looking out of the window, and for a moment before he heard her she drank in the tall, broad-shouldered magnificence of him. She wanted him. Again. Already. *Always.*

A sense of desperation mixed with panic gripped her and she felt like fleeing, as if she could escape the way he made her feel, but then he turned around and saw her.

She couldn't help the heat rising into her cheeks and was glad of the dusk outside and the low lighting hiding her reaction.

'I didn't want to disturb you,' Gabriel said.

Leonora's self-consciousness was acute. He hadn't wanted to disturb her—in case she started crying again?

She forced a bright smile. 'I'm awake now.'

He looked at his watch. 'I don't know about you, but I'm famished. We can eat here or go out. It's up to you.'

Leonora's relief that he wasn't making any reference to her tears was short-lived when she imagined sharing an intimate meal in this suite while she still felt so raw. And with the bedroom so near.

She said quickly, 'Let's go out.'

In the back of the chauffeur-driven car on the way to the restaurant, Gabriel found that he was ever so slightly piqued that Leonora seemed so eager to venture out to less inti-mate surroundings. Previous lovers would have been only too happy to capitalise on his undivided attention. But then, Leonora wasn't just a lover. She was his wife. And even as a lover…the lovemaking they shared was nothing like any kind he'd experienced before.

When he thought of this afternoon, and how desperate he'd been, his only consolation was that she'd been as hungry as him. He could still feel her nails digging into his buttocks and hear her rough entreaties. *'Please...don't stop...'*

Gabriel shifted in the seat, irritated. He was regressing. He was no more in control of his body now than he had been when he was a lusty teenager. *Por Dios.*

The car pulled to a stop and now Gabriel was the one who relished getting out of the intimate space. He went around and helped Leonora out.

She looked around her. 'Where are we?'

'Montmartre. There's a good place I know up here.'

He took her hand in his—a gesture that came to him as naturally as breathing air. A gesture he would never have allowed with previous lovers. Somehow it felt ridiculously intimate. But they were married, so that changed everything...didn't it?

They turned a corner and a beautiful square opened out before them, lined with trees and restaurants and bars, music drifting out into the warm evening air.

'Oh, this is lovely!'

Gabriel watched Leonora's face as she looked around, a rare kind of pleasure flowing through him at her reaction.

She caught him looking at her and she blushed.

He said, 'You're unbelievable—do you know that, Leo?'

She looked genuinely confused. 'Why?'

'You were born into one of Spain's oldest dynasties and yet you're not a snob, or spoilt—which, notwithstanding your father's fall from grace, you could very well be.'

Leonora wasn't sure how to respond to that, but she took it as a compliment.

Gabriel led her to a restaurant on the other side of the

square. It looked discreetly expensive. The maître d'
greeted them effusively and showed them to a table that
was artfully screened off from the other diners, while giving them a view of the charming square.

They were seated and had been handed menus when Gabriel said, 'You could very well have sought out a suitable
husband at a much younger age. Why didn't you?'

Leonora hadn't been expecting such a direct question.
No one had ever asked her that before. But she'd certainly
always been aware of people's looks and speculation whenever she'd appeared in public.

She took a breath. 'I think for a long time I was angry
with my father for failing us like that. For being...fallible.'

A cynical expression flashed across Gabriel's face. 'I
can attest to just how fallible fathers can be.'

'Once it became apparent that I was the only potential saviour of my family I resented it for a long time. I
resented the structures that haven't changed much since
medieval times. This notion of having to be married off
for the good of the family name. I was made very aware of
the fact that our—*my*—only real currency was our name
and our lineage.'

'If it's any consolation, things weren't much different for
me. I alone am responsible for carrying on the illustrious
Cruz y Torres name. My sister doesn't bear that responsibility and I wouldn't put it on her.'

Leonora shook her head. 'And you never minded?'

Gabriel picked up an olive and put it in his mouth, chewing for a moment. 'I never said I didn't mind. When I was
younger I contemplated running away many times. That
day when Lazaro Sanchez confronted my father in the street
and said he was his son... I actually felt slightly envious of
him—that he wasn't burdened by the family name.'

Leonora looked at Gabriel. 'Maybe that's what's at the

root of your issues with him. The fact that you're a little jealous of him.'

Gabriel leaned forward and took Leonora's hand. He brought it to his mouth and pressed a kiss to the back of it. He said, 'I was jealous of him that night when he announced your engagement.'

Leonora's heartrate picked up. All she could see were Gabriel's intense eyes, the gold flecks giving them a leonine quality.

There was a discreet cough and with a struggle she looked up at the waiter, for a moment feeling dizzy. Forgetting they were in public. Had they even ordered? She couldn't remember...

Gabriel let her hand go. Starters were placed down in front of them. They ate in silence, and Leonora was glad of a moment to absorb what Gabriel had said, and to tell herself that his admission of jealousy didn't mean anything. He had decided he wanted her that night. That was all. He had an ongoing rivalry with Lazaro. That was all.

As if to reinforce that assertion in her head, their conversation didn't stray into personal territory again. But after the main course had been eaten and taken away Gabriel's gaze narrowed on Leonora.

'Did you enjoy today?'

Leonora was immediately rewarded with a flashback to when they'd arrived back at the suite earlier, ravenous for each other. She took a quick sip of wine—anything to cool her insides.

'It was lovely, thank you.'

He leaned forward. 'I want you to feel valued, Leo. You're not just a pawn. We both grew up knowing we bore a responsibility that most people don't. Our privilege isn't something we got to choose. But I'm glad that I bear this responsibility with you. I think we can be happy together.'

A chill breeze skated across Leonora's skin and she shivered slightly. Gabriel's words circled in her head sickeningly. *'I think we can be happy together'.* Lazaro had said almost exactly the same words just before the engagement announcement.

The truth was no matter what Gabriel said, or how many assurances he provided, she *was* just a pawn. But then, as he pointed out, so was he in many ways. They were both pawns. Somehow that didn't give her much comfort.

It was clear now that today hadn't really been born of a spontaneous desire to spend time with her. It had been a calculated move to make her feel valued. Wanted. Desired. Maybe he hadn't planned that explosive interlude back at the hotel, but all that confirmed was that they wanted each other.

Leonora cursed herself for being so sensitive. She had to develop a thicker skin if she was going to survive in Gabriel's world. The fact that she felt a growing intimacy with him beyond the bedroom—worse, a growing friendship—was all just an illusion. Gabriel was looking on her as an investment to nurture.

Leonora pasted on the brightest smile she could. 'I think we can be happy too.'

Gabriel smiled approvingly.

This was her life now and she had to come to terms with it. To want more... Well, that was just foolish.

In a bid to deflect Gabriel's attention, because he saw too much, Leonora said, 'So, tell me about this bid you're involved in...'

Ten days after they'd returned from Paris, Gabriel was at the public bid for the market space. A project he'd been working on for over a year.

For a man who wasn't used to being unsure of outcomes,

he didn't like to admit that the bid might very well go Lazaro Sanchez's way. The man had come up with a decent plan. A plan that Gabriel could grudgingly respect even if he didn't agree with all of it.

But for the first time in his life the prospect of losing to someone else wasn't his main concern. Something else was distracting him and taking precedence over the bid. *Leonora*.

Things had been slightly *off* ever since Paris, and Gabriel couldn't figure it out.

That Sunday they'd spent together had been one of the most enjoyable days Gabriel could remember in a long time. He didn't have close confidantes. He'd always trodden his own path and had learnt very early on not to trust people. Women or business peers. Everyone wanted a piece of him or to best him.

But he trusted Leonora. Enjoyed spending time with her. *Wanted* to spend time with her. He never would have taken a day off like that before. It had been years since he'd taken the Métro or just wandered around a museum.

But when they'd returned to their suite after dinner on the Sunday night she'd been slightly withdrawn. He'd taken a call, and by the time he'd gone to bed she was asleep. The first night they hadn't made love since they were married.

And then, this week, he'd been busy preparing for the bid, and each night when he'd come back to the *castillo* she'd been in bed, asleep. So he'd hardly seen her. Or touched her. He could feel his hunger for her gnawing away inside him and she should be here by his side today, but she wasn't.

She'd been pale this morning—out of sorts. She'd said something about period pains and had assured him she just needed to rest. So he'd left her behind.

He'd found to his surprise that the evidence that she wasn't pregnant had made him feel conflicting things. Because, as much as he knew he had to have children, he was aware that it was too soon. He wanted more time with Leonora. Alone.

And yet they weren't using protection, so if she wasn't pregnant this month the likelihood was that it would happen very soon. Unless they made a decision to wait for a while, which would go against one of the reasons for this marriage: to have heirs. To continue the family legacy.

This revelation was disconcerting and it made him feel off-centre.

There was a movement in his peripheral vision and he saw Lazaro Sanchez walk over to where his wife had just arrived. Her bright red hair was distinctive. And the small bump of her pregnant belly.

He had to concede that she was not the kind of woman he would have expected Sanchez to go for. She looked... *nice*. Kind. She was smiling, and he could see from here that it was genuine. Warm. Leonora had a similar quality but she was more reserved.

Leonora.

He took out his phone and sent her a quick text, asking how she was.

She replied almost instantly.

Feeling okay, thanks. Good luck with the bid. Sorry I'm not there with you. x

To his surprise, that small 'x' impacted him in his gut, taking his breath for a moment.

Someone approached him. 'Señor Torres? It's time.'

Gabriel saw Sanchez moving towards the stage and

knew he couldn't afford to lose focus now. Sanchez was married, having a baby. Gabriel was also married, and even if Leonora wasn't pregnant now, she would be soon.

There was a lot riding on every decision Gabriel made now. His responsibilities and his legacy were growing exponentially and he wasn't going to let anything distract from that. Not now, not ever.

When Gabriel returned home from the public bid he was met by Ernesto, who looked anxious. 'It's Leonora, sir, she hasn't left the bedroom. She tells me she's all right, but I'm concerned.'

Immediately all thoughts of the bid and the brief altercation he'd had with Lazaro Sanchez afterwards left Gabriel's mind. He looked at his watch. It was early evening. That meant she'd been in bed all day with these pains. Surely this was not a usual menstrual problem?

He took the stairs two at a time to their bedroom and opened the door. Leonora was just a shape under the covers and he went over, his gut clenching with concern. She turned over and he could see even before he reached her that she was pale.

He sat down and automatically put a hand to her brow. It was clammy. 'What is it? Is this a regular occurrence?'

She shook her head, dark hair slipping over one shoulder. Her cheekbones stood out starkly. She was clearly in pain.

'Not every month. Some are worse than others. I have a history of bad cramps. They usually pass within a couple of days. How did the bid go?'

He waved a hand, dismissing that and asked, 'Have you ever seen a doctor about this?'

She nodded. 'When I was younger. He told me it was mild endometriosis.'

She tried to sit up and winced, sucking in a breath.

Gabriel made a split-second decision, pulling out his phone.

Leonora heard him, and went even more ashen. When he'd terminated the call she said, 'Hospital really isn't necessary, Gabriel. I just need to take some more painkillers and I'll be feeling much better by morning.'

Gabriel stood up and said tautly, 'We're not debating this, Leo. You need to get checked.'

Leonora was in too much pain to argue with Gabriel, much as she'd have liked to. She couldn't deny that she was a little freaked out herself, because this month her cramps seemed even more acute than normal.

She got out of bed slowly, trying not to show how much of an effort it took. Gabriel found some shoes and laid them by the bed. As she stood up a wave of dizziness hit her.

Immediately Gabriel was scooping her up into his arms and Leonora realised she was too weak to argue. Most likely from not having eaten all day.

She tried to protest, but he was already out of the room and down the stairs, walking into the main hall, saying something to Ernesto, who leapt to attention, opening the passenger door of Gabriel's car.

Gabriel put her in as carefully as if she was made of fine bone china.

She said, 'Really, there's no need for this…' But he didn't listen to her, strapping her in and closing the door.

Leonora kept her mouth shut as Gabriel drove into the city and stopped on the forecourt of a hospital. People were there to greet them and Leonora was embarrassed—until a wave of pain from her abdomen made her grit her teeth.

An orderly appeared at her door with a wheelchair for

her to sit in, and suddenly she was glad that they were there. Because this was definitely not normal any more.

The following few hours became a blur as she underwent a series of tests. There was a lull while they waited for the doctor to return with some results. Wanting to divert her mind from all sorts of scary possibilities, she asked Gabriel about the bid again.

He turned around from where he was standing at the window, hands in his pockets. His tie was pulled loose, the top button of his shirt open, jacket off and thrown on a chair. His hair was mussed because he'd been running a hand through it.

He said, 'We won't know for at least another month. The two bids have gone on public display at City Hall and the public now has a chance to see both sets of plans and to vote for their favourite. Their vote, together with the city councillors, will decide who gets the commission.'

'Was Lazaro there?'

Gabriel's expression darkened. He nodded. 'Yes—and his wife.'

Leonora plucked at the sheet, feeling guilty. 'I'm sorry again that I wasn't there.'

After all, wasn't that her role now? To be by her husband's side to show support? Lazaro's wife might not have the right name or lineage, but she appeared to be fulfilling her brief far better than Leonora was—on every level.

Gabriel shook his head and came and sat on the end of the bed. 'Don't be silly. It really wasn't that important.'

'But you've been working on it for a year and you hate Lazaro.'

Gabriel stood up, hands dug deep in his pockets again. His jaw was tense. 'I don't *hate* Sanchez...but he winds me up like no one else.'

Leonora squinted at him. 'Are you *sure* you're not related?'

Gabriel made a face, but before he could respond the doctor arrived in the room.

He looked at Gabriel. 'You should go home for the night, Señor Torres. I'm afraid we'll have to do more tests in the morning before we'll be able to give you any conclusive results.'

A sense of dread filled Leonora and she forced herself to ask, 'What do you think it is?'

The doctor looked at her, and she could see the gravity of his expression. 'I'm sorry to say, my dear, that your endometriosis is no longer mild, and probably hasn't been for some time. It appears to be extensive and acute. The fact that your symptoms haven't necessarily been severe up until now is atypical. But every woman with this condition is different. We'll know more tomorrow, when we conclude the tests. I'm sorry I can't tell you more right now.'

A week later

A kindly voice came from a great distance. 'How are you feeling, Leonora?'

She knew it wasn't Gabriel. It was too kindly and he called her Leo.

She struggled to open her eyes, feeling the huge effort it took. When she opened them she shut them again quickly. It was too bright. She was aware of pain...dull, down low... in her abdomen.

There was something pressing on her mind—something urgent—but she knew she didn't want to think about it.

She managed to croak out, 'Thirsty...'

Whoever was there held her head up and pressed something to her lips. A straw.

The kind voice said, 'Drink, Leonora, you'll be feeling better soon.'

But she knew she wouldn't be.

Before she could figure out why, she slipped back down into the dark, comforting place.

'How are you feeling, Leo?'

Gabriel. She knew it was him because she'd been feigning sleep since he'd come into the room, like a coward. But she couldn't keep hiding.

She opened her eyes and blinked in the light.

He looked huge, standing at the end of the bed. Worried. There was stubble on his jaw. For a moment emotion threatened to overwhelm her but she pushed it down. She remembered everything now. She had done as soon as she'd woken properly from the anaesthetic, two days ago.

He said, 'The doctor said you can come home today. But there's no rush. As soon as you're feeling up to dressing.'

She opened her mouth. 'We should...we need to talk about—'

Gabriel shook his head. 'Not now, Leo. We can talk about it when you're feeling better.'

Leonora might have laughed if she'd been able to. Right at that moment she couldn't imagine ever feeling better. But she forced herself to push back the covers and swing her legs over the side of the bed.

Immediately Gabriel was there, but she put up a hand, terrified of what his touch would do to her in her emotionally brittle state. 'I'm fine. I'll have a shower and pack. You should go...have a coffee... I'll be ready when you come back.'

He left the room and she let out a shuddering breath. She felt hollow. Aching. A kaleidoscope of images and memories from the past few days came back into her head before she could stop them.

A doctor standing by the bed, saying, *'I'm so sorry, Se-*

ñora Torres, but tests have confirmed that your fallopian tubes are beyond saving. The endometriosis has caused too much damage...surgical removal of the fallopian tubes... you'll still have your uterus and ovaries...'

She was infertile. At the age of twenty-four.

Unbeknownst to her, because her symptoms hadn't been severe, the endometriosis had been quietly and devastatingly wreaking havoc on her insides, cruelly targeting her fallopian tubes, rendering them useless. Beyond saving.

She knew she was still in shock. It hadn't sunk in fully. Nor had the ramifications. She hadn't been able to deal with seeing her parents, though she knew they were worried. Too afraid of what she'd see on their faces. Their terror that this might change everything.

Leonora pushed herself up from the bed and walked over to the private bathroom, locking herself inside. Physically, the doctor had said she should be fully recovered within a couple of weeks. Emotionally, however...

She turned on the spray of the shower and stripped off, stepping into the small cubicle. She used the shower head to clean herself, careful to keep the wound dressing dry.

When she was finished she wrapped herself in a towel and washed her face, brushed her teeth, avoiding looking at her face in the mirror. But then she caught her reflection and stopped. Her eyes looked like two huge pools of pain. Her skin was white, stretched taut, her cheekbones standing out starkly.

All of a sudden she couldn't contain it any more. The emotion rose up and came out of her in great, shuddering sobs.

Gabriel came back into the hospital room carrying coffee for Leonora. He stopped when he heard the sobs coming from the bathroom. His blood ran cold. He'd never heard such a raw outpouring of emotion before, and every instinct in him told him to go to her…but he knew she wouldn't welcome it. This was a very private pain, and for the first time in his life he knew what it was to be helpless.

A week later

Leonora was sitting on a chair on the back terrace of the *castillo*. The late-summer early evening still held lots of warmth, but nevertheless Ernesto had insisted on putting a rug over Leonora's legs.

The spectacular grounds of the *castillo* soothed Leonora's ragged emotions, so she'd taken to sitting here every day, while her body healed on the outside. She was still numb on the inside, though. Still trying to compute the catastrophic loss of her fertility. Every time she tried to dwell on it her mind skittered away.

Her parents had come to visit and her mother had been pale. She'd said, '*Por Dios,* Leo…he'll have to divorce you if you can't give him an heir. What will happen to us?'

Leonora's father had taken her mother away after that, telling Leonora not to listen to her. But her mother was right. And it was something Leonora knew she'd have to discuss with Gabriel sooner or later. The fact that she was no longer capable of providing her husband with an heir.

At that moment she heard footsteps and her skin prickled with awareness. Still. Even after what had happened.

Gabriel came into her field of vision, tall and broad. Dressed in a three-piece suit. His long fingers were tugging at his tie, opening it and the top button of his shirt.

'How are you today?'

Leonora nodded. 'Feeling much better, thank you.'

Gabriel sat down on the lounger beside her, his dark

gaze roving over her face. Leonora knew she must look pale and wan.

'The doctor came to see you today?'

She nodded. 'He was here earlier. I'm healing well.'

Physically.

Gabriel nodded. 'That's good.'

Leonora forced herself to look at him. 'We should talk about—'

He held up a hand. 'We're not talking about anything until you're back on your feet. All you need to think about now is recuperating.'

Leonora swallowed her words.

Gabriel stood up. 'Dinner will be ready shortly. I'm just going to take a shower and change and then I'll come back down.'

Leonora watched him walk away, athletic grace in every move he made. She turned her head, eyes stinging suddenly. She pulled her glasses down over her eyes in case anyone saw her emotion.

Dealing with this diagnosis would be massively disrupting to the best of relationships, founded on love, so what hope could they possibly have? Gabriel could delay the conversation for as long as he wanted, but ultimately Leonora knew this spelled the end of their marriage.

CHAPTER TEN

GABRIEL WAS IN his office, staring out of the window, which took in a spectacular view of Madrid. Sunlight bathed the city in a golden glow. But he didn't see any of that. His thoughts were inward.

It had been two weeks now since Leonora's operation, and physically she seemed to be fine. But emotionally…

Gabriel couldn't begin to fathom what she was going through, and the feeling of helplessness he'd felt that day in the hospital when he'd heard her crying was still there.

Helplessness was totally alien to Gabriel. He was used to being able to influence things, events. And yet even he had to concede that this was entirely out of his control.

There was no amount of money he could throw at the situation to make it better. To restore Leonora to full health.

Unsurprisingly, she'd been withdrawn for the past two weeks. She'd been sleeping in one of the guest suites, in spite of Gabriel's insistence that he would move rooms.

He hadn't liked not having her in his bed. Not at all. It made him feel even more helpless as he watched her retreat further and further to some place he couldn't reach.

There was a knock on his door and he turned around, irritated at the interruption. It was his secretary.

'Sorry, I know you don't want to be disturbed…but it's Lazaro Sanchez.'

Literally the last person Gabriel wanted to see right now.

But to his surprise, instead of issuing an immediate rejection, he heard himself say, 'Send him in.'

Sanchez walked in. Familiar tension and something much more ambiguous mixed in Gabriel's gut.

Leonora's words came into his head. *'Are you sure you're not related?'*

He said, 'To what do I owe this pleasure?'

Lazaro walked over to the desk, and as he did so Gabriel noticed that he looked a little less cocky than normal. As if some of the stuffing had been knocked out of him. He almost felt compelled to say something, but then he noticed a padded envelope in Lazaro's hand.

Lazaro put it down on the desk and tapped it lightly. He looked at Gabriel. 'There is all you need in there to prove that we are related. Which we are. Again, I don't want anything from you or your family—simply an acknowledgement that I am of your blood. It's the least I'm due, I think. Also, I've decided to pull out of the bid for the market. I still think my bid was the better one, but it's not my priority any more. And, yes, you're right. A big part of my motivation *was* in going up against you. You're a worthy adversary, Gabriel, but I've lost the appetite for battling with you.'

Lazaro was almost at the door before Gabriel had recovered enough to say, 'What's changed?'

Lazaro turned around and smiled. 'I've just realised what's truly important in life...that's all.'

He walked out before Gabriel could get his wits back together. Very few people surprised him. But Lazaro Sanchez had just blindsided him. Rapidly, Gabriel tried to assess what Lazaro's agenda might be...but he couldn't come up with anything.

He walked over and picked up the padded envelope. Inside was a piece of paper with the information for a doctor who had a sample of Lazaro's DNA in storage. All Gabriel had to do was provide his own sample of DNA for comparison and they would know if they were related.

But Gabriel didn't need to do the test. He knew in his gut what the result would be. He'd known that day in the street, when he'd first seen Lazaro, that the possibility that he was his kin was very real. In fact, on the other side of the animosity that had played out between the two men, there had been a sense of affinity that he'd never wanted to acknowledge.

It was an unsettling revelation.

Gabriel put down the piece of paper and walked back over to the window. He should be feeling triumphant because he was going to be awarded the bid for the market. But he wasn't feeling triumphant. He was feeling deflated. As if something had been taken out of his grasp.

He realised that he'd relished the fight with Lazaro. The chance to prove himself. Because it happened so rarely.

And then an insidious suspicion came into his mind. Had Lazaro found out about Leo's diagnosis, somehow? Was this why he'd gone a step further in his claim to be of Cruz y Torres blood? Because he knew that if Gabriel didn't have an heir, then any child of Lazaro's would therefore have a claim on the Torres inheritance?

Gabriel shook his head. He was being paranoid. There was no way Lazaro could have found out. It was just coincidence…

But, the fact remained that without an heir, the family name would die out. Even if Lazaro *was* his half-brother, he might not want anything to do with the Cruz y Torres name. Especially after the way he'd been treated…

Gabriel thought of how only a couple of weeks ago he'd been almost hoping that Leo wouldn't be pregnant, so they could have more time alone together. Fate was laughing in his face. Because now they had all the time in the world.

* * *

Leonora sensed Gabriel before she saw him, but she kept on reading aloud to Matías, who had come to the *castillo* to visit her. He'd always loved being read to, and she still did it on occasion. It was like a security blanket, and he'd obviously sensed that something wasn't quite right with his big sister. She hadn't told him about her operation, he'd be too upset.

But Matías had spotted Gabriel and he jumped up from the seat they were sharing and went over, throwing his arms around Gabriel's neck. Gabriel looked at her over Matías's shoulder and she could see it in his eyes.

Now he was ready to discuss things with her.

She'd been feeling perfectly well again for a few days now. Apart from the small scar on her abdomen it would be hard to know that anything had happened. But it had. And it had had catastrophic repercussions.

They both had dinner with Matías, and then he was taken back to his school by one of Gabriel's staff.

Gabriel turned to her at the door, from where they'd waved him off. 'Come and have a nightcap on the terrace?'

Leonora's hand gripped the door for a moment, and then she let go and nodded. 'Sure.'

She followed him out to the terrace, peaceful and fragrant with blooming flowers and plants. Candles flickered gently in the light breeze. Leonora sat down in a chair and tucked her legs underneath her. She watched Gabriel pour himself a coffee and then he looked around.

'What would you like?'

'A little port, please.'

He poured some into a delicate glass and brought it over. Amazingly, considering how battered and bruised her insides were, Leonora felt a flicker of response. She took a sip of the sweet alcohol.

Gabriel came over and sat down on a chair at right angles to hers. His shirt was unbuttoned at the top, revealing the strong bronzed column of his throat and a glimpse of curling chest hair. His sleeves were rolled up and the muscles of his arms were a distraction that sent further tendrils of awareness to Leonora's core.

To her surprise he said, 'I had a visit from Lazaro Sanchez today.'

'Oh?'

'He told me he was pulling out of the bid…that he no longer cares about it.'

'That's…strange.'

From what Leonora had learnt about Lazaro during their short and very chaste relationship, he was ruthlessly ambitious. He'd been willing to marry a woman he hardly knew, after all.

As had Gabriel, pointed out a small voice.

'Yes…it is,' Gabriel said, and took a sip of coffee.

They sat in silence for a while, and then Gabriel put his cup down and sat forward.

Leonora tensed. He looked at her and she saw compassion in his eyes.

He said, 'I'm so sorry, Leo, for what's happened to you. If there was some way I could reverse the diagnosis or offer you a solution then I would.'

He stood up and she realised how agitated he was when he ran a hand through his hair. He cursed and walked over to the wall, placing his hands down on it.

Leonora untucked her legs and sat up, putting down the glass. She wasn't sure what to say.

He turned around and there was a bleak expression on his face. 'I've never felt so helpless in my life. And it's not a nice feeling. To know that there was literally nothing I could do. You were at the mercy of the doctors.'

A little of the ice that had been like a block in her chest for two weeks started melting slightly. She hadn't really thought of this impacting on Gabriel, but of course it must have.

'I know…and thank you for wanting to do something. But nothing could have been done.'

He came back over and sat down. 'It's not fair, Leo… I see you with Matías and know that you'd be a wonderful mother. Loving, caring, compassionate…'

Leonora had been trying not to give in to anger after her diagnosis, so hearing Gabriel articulate it for her was like a balm to her jagged edges.

'Thank you.'

But suddenly he was too close. Emotions were threatening to crack her open from the inside out—emotions she'd been clamping down on for fear of what would be unleashed. Like that day in the hospital, when the storm of grief had left her weak and spent.

She stood up and went to take his place at the terrace wall. She looked out at the view for a long moment, as if hoping it might give her strength, and then she turned, wrapping her arms around her midriff.

'This changes everything, Gabriel. I'm not the woman you married. I can't give you what you need. The sooner we file for divorce, the sooner you'll be free to move on.'

Gabriel stood up. 'Divorce?'

Leonora's arms tightened around herself, as if that might help her contain the rising emotion. 'Yes. Of course.'

He shook his head and came over to where she was standing. 'We don't need to divorce.'

'I can't give you what you need. An heir. Heirs. You're the last in your line and I'm infertile.'

He looked at her for a long moment as the word *infer-*

tile hung starkly in the air between them. Then abruptly he turned away to look out over the gardens.

Eventually he said, 'The doctor assured us that all was not lost. We have options—IVF, adoption...'

'An adopted child wouldn't be of your blood. And IVF is a long and arduous process that may never work. I worked with an IVF charity for a while and I saw the devastation it can wreak on couples, families. Even when it works it takes a toll on the strongest of relationships.'

Gabriel's jaw clenched. 'You don't think *we* have a strong relationship?'

Leonora swallowed, thinking of how rocked she'd been by the revelation that Gabriel knew Lazaro. How hurt.

'I think, like you said, we have a lot going for us... But this was one of the fundamental requirements, and I can't deliver.'

He looked at her. 'Do you want to divorce?'

Leonora couldn't escape that dark gaze. *No.* The word beat through her blood. She'd imagined a life with this man; a life beyond anything she had believed she could have with someone like him. But those fragile dreams had died two weeks ago.

'I think it's the only option.' They'd been married for almost three months, the legal requirement for granting divorce.

Gabriel looked away. His jaw was tight. Leonora knew that for a man like him it was difficult to admit defeat. As he'd said himself, he hadn't liked feeling helpless. But they were both helpless here.

He said, 'I have a full social schedule coming up. Now would not be a good time to draw adverse press attention. We will discuss this again when you are feeling stronger. A lot has happened in the past two weeks.'

Leonora desperately wanted to say, *What is there to dis-*

cuss? But she knew she didn't have the energy to deal with that conversation. So maybe he was right.

'Of course. Goodnight, Gabriel.'

Gabriel watched as Leonora walked back into the *castillo*, effortlessly graceful in a long flowing maxi-dress, her hair loose and slightly more unruly than its usual sleek perfection. Her face was bare of make-up but no less hauntingly beautiful.

'Do you want to divorce?'

'I think it's the only option.'

He still felt slightly winded by the punch to his gut at her suggestion of divorce. Not once since her diagnosis had that possibility even entered his head. But evidently it was the first thing she'd thought of.

He had thought they were building a solid basis for a long and enduring marriage. Solid enough to weather this storm.

Gabriel felt disorientated as he took in the full meaning of the fact that Leonora's diagnosis of infertility hadn't impinged upon him in the same way it had her. She'd been looking for the first opportunity to leave this marriage. And he hadn't.

Fool.

All sorts of insidious suspicions came into his mind. Maybe she'd played him from the start? Just looking for a way to save her family and ensure their security before seeking her freedom via divorce? Even if they'd had children? Maybe she'd just told him what he wanted to hear?

He cursed himself. He more than anyone knew they hadn't married for love. They'd married for myriad reasons—one of which, as she'd pointed out, was to procreate. Have heirs. Continue the line. The legacy.

Now that had been ripped away from them. Leaving... what? The reality that chemistry and mutual respect and friendship weren't enough? He'd mentioned the options that the doctor had given them—IVF, adoption... Gabriel didn't know much about IVF, but he knew enough to agree with Leonora. It was a hugely invasive and precarious method of having children, and she would be the one to bear the brunt of the pain and the procedures.

If she wanted out of the marriage she was hardly going to put herself through those procedures.

An emotion Gabriel had never felt before burned down low in his gut. It felt a lot like hurt.

He slammed his hand down on the terrace wall. No woman had the power to hurt Gabriel. She had made a commitment to him and she would honour it.

He wouldn't accept anything less.

It took hours for Leonora to fall asleep that night. The pain in her heart was almost physical. She couldn't believe how far she'd let herself fall for Gabriel. How far she'd let herself dream that even without his love they could have a good life together. She'd imagined that when the desire burned out they'd have a family to care for, to unite them.

She considered the fact that he'd mentioned IVF. Adoption. Maybe she owed it to him to give it a shot? But then maybe he'd only mentioned it because he felt duty-bound?

She thought of the families she'd met through that charity. She knew what a toll it took, and how it caused huge fissures in relationships and families.

Of course it could be successful, and many people went on to have children, but people who underwent IVF ached to have children and had exhausted every other possibility. They did it for love. And that was not what this relationship was about.

Even if she did agree to undergo IVF and they had children, she realised now that it wouldn't be enough for her to have children without Gabriel's love. It would kill her. She wanted the dream.

Gabriel would move on. He would find another suitable wife and have children. Of that she was sure. He deserved that.

He'd never made her any promises. She would do her duty as his wife for the next few weeks and then they would file for divorce. There was no other discussion to be had. Her infertility wouldn't have magically healed itself in a few weeks.

'You must be very proud, Torres, your wife is stunning.'

Gabriel looked at where Leonora was standing a few feet away. She was a vision in a long ballgown with a fitted sleeveless bodice and chiffon skirts falling to the floor. The gown was ice-blue. Her hair was pulled back and long diamond earrings glittered when she moved her head.

She was indeed stunning. Without a doubt the most beautiful woman in the room. She had an effortless kind of beauty that he could see people noticing and envying. What they didn't know was that her beauty wasn't just skin-deep. Or that she hid a very painful and devastating secret.

He glanced at the man beside him. A business acquaintance who was looking at Leonora far too covetously for Gabriel's liking.

He made his excuses and walked over to her, slipping an arm around her waist.

He felt the tension come into her body at his touch and everything inside him rejected it. It was a over a month now since they'd had that conversation about divorce. They'd been existing since then in a kind of sterile civil environment that was driving Gabriel slowly around the bend.

They were still in separate bedrooms—and Gabriel fully respected the space that Leonora had needed since the operation. But sexual frustration was a constant gnawing ache, exacerbated by the fact that she had retreated to some icy, closed-off place that he couldn't seem to reach.

She was always in bed when he came home from work. She busied herself at weekends at her parents *castillo*, helping with renovations and plans for the business. Or she spent time with Matías.

For someone like Gabriel, who had never envisaged marriage being anything but a means to an end, to find himself *missing* his wife was not a welcome revelation.

The closest they got to any kind of intimacy was at moments like this, when they were amongst hundreds of people. And everything in Gabriel rejected it. Rejected her closing herself off and retreating to a place he couldn't reach. Rejected the notion of divorce.

Leonora was holding herself so stiffly she could hardly breathe. Gabriel's arm was around her waist, and the urge to melt into his side, let him take her weight, was almost overwhelming.

The urge to touch him, kiss him…make love to him was even more overwhelming.

But she couldn't.

The only thing keeping her upright and able to function for the past few weeks was the block of ice in her chest. Keeping her emotions in a kind of deep freeze.

Gabriel represented heat and pain. She couldn't go there. Not when the time was approaching when they would file for divorce. Surely in a matter of days. Once that had happened, and she could maintain her distance from him, she would allow herself to breathe again. To feel the pain she knew she was avoiding.

But it was getting harder and harder. And tonight was worse than any other night.

It was as if he knew how tenuous her self-control was. At every opportunity he was touching her—her back, her arm—taking her hand, massaging her neck.

His touch was like a hot brand through her clothes. As if her body was conspiring with him to just melt and give in.

It would be so easy, whispered a little voice.

But she couldn't. She knew Gabriel wanted her. It was in his eyes every time he looked at her. Or maybe that was just her desire projected onto him?

She was going crazy.

After the operation she'd thought she'd never *feel* again. Feel desire. Hope. Sensation. But the human body was a fickle traitor. Her body seemed disinclined to remember those painful days. It was as if normal operations had resumed in spite of Leonora's emotional trauma.

'Are you ready to go?'

Leonora blinked. As much as she dreaded Gabriel's touch, because of what it did to her, she realised now that on some level she craved these fleeting moments for a few hours every week.

She moved out of his embrace and saw how his jaw tightened. 'Yes, I'm ready to go.'

He put a hand on her elbow and led her out through the crowd. She could feel the tension in his body, reminding her of that night when she'd seen him and Lazaro together.

The function this evening had taken place in the same hotel where her engagement to Lazaro had almost been announced. She'd been so distracted that she only really noticed when they walked outside and there was a barrage of flashes and questions from the paparazzi.

'Leonora! Gabriel! Over here!'

And then there was one voice which seemed to be elevated over all the rest.

'Are you pregnant yet, Señora Torres?'

Gabriel bundled her into the car and Leonora was tight-lipped as he sat into the driver's seat beside her. She was desperately trying to stem the hurt blooming inside her.

He was looking at her. She could feel his gaze on her. Concerned.

'Are you okay? I'm sorry about that—they're idiots.'

Leonora looked straight ahead. 'Just drive. Please.'

Her tenuous hold on her emotions was breaking. Like taut wires finally snapping under the pressure.

Leonora wasn't even aware of where they were going until Gabriel pulled into the underground car park of his city centre apartment. A sense of *déjà vu* slammed into her, further diminishing her sense of control. The memories here—

'Why have we come here?' she asked Gabriel.

He turned off the car engine and looked at her. 'I have an early meeting in town in the morning. There's a fully stocked closet here—it's not a problem, is it?'

Leonora shook her head quickly, in case he might see something. 'No, not at all.'

There was a touch of weariness in his tone, 'There's a spare bedroom here too, Leo. Don't worry, I'm not trying to seduce you again.'

He got out.

For some reason his words felt like a slap in the face. Even though she'd been the one putting distance between them.

He opened her door and put out a hand. Leonora recalled that first night, when she'd been afraid to touch him. She'd been right to be afraid. And she was afraid again now. But she couldn't avoid it.

She put her hand into his and let him help her out.

He let her go again almost immediately, and Leonora

curled her fingers over her palm as if to keep the sensation of his skin on hers a little longer. But it wasn't enough.

In the elevator on the way up she could feel the tension pulsing between them. Like a heart. Beating. A live thing. She studiously avoided looking at Gabriel but she could smell him. Sense him. *Imagine him.* Touching her, removing her clothes, devouring her...transporting her to a place where the pain didn't exist.

The bell chimed, signalling the elevator's arrival at the apartment, and Leonora flushed at her wayward mind.

She stepped out and was acutely conscious of Gabriel behind her. His sheer size and bulk.

This was her first time back in the apartment since that night. She stopped at the entrance to the living area, almost as if she could see in her mind's eye how events that night had unfolded, like a movie. He'd seduced her from the moment their eyes had locked that night at the hotel. Even though she had been about to be betrothed to another.

She turned around and saw him yanking at his bowtie, opening the top button of his shirt. Their eyes met and his movements slowed to a stop.

The words *Goodnight, Gabriel* were stuck in Leonora's throat. She'd said them after every other event. Every night. As she'd made her escape. But tonight...she couldn't say them.

Gabriel frowned. 'Leo...?'

She was breaking apart inside. All the ice was melting and flowing into the whirlpool of emotion she'd been holding back.

She struggled to say something. Anything. 'I can't... I don't know...'

He moved towards her, taking her arms in his hands. His touch burned.

'Leo...what is it? What do you want?'

She couldn't speak.

He came closer. 'Shall I tell you what *I* want?'

Weakly, she nodded, needing him to articulate the turmoil inside her.

He said roughly, 'I want *you*, Leo. I want you so much it hurts.'

He lifted a hand and cupped her jaw. It took every ounce of strength she possessed to try and hold firm. Resist. Not to turn her face into his palm and taste his skin.

'But what's the point?' she asked.

He took his hand away from her face. Something flickered in his expression. Hurt?

'Does there need to be a point? I want you and you want me. That hasn't changed.'

After a long moment of silence he stepped back, and immediately she felt bereft.

He said, 'Go to bed, Leo. It's late.'

He was walking around her and into the apartment and suddenly everything in her rejected him moving away from her. Even though she knew she was the one who had caused him to do it.

She turned around. 'Wait…stop.'

He had taken off his jacket and thrown it aside. She could see the powerful muscles of his back through his shirt.

He turned around.

'You're right,' Leonora said. 'There doesn't need to be a point… I want you, Gabriel.'

For a long moment Gabriel said nothing. It looked as if he was wrestling with something. But then he said, 'Are you sure?'

No.

Yes. She wanted him too much and the floodgates had opened. She needed him to set fire to the emotional turmoil inside her so it would be transformed into something other than this…pain.

She nodded.

He held out a hand. 'Come here.'

She walked forward, her eyes never leaving his face, as if he was a port in the storm. He drew her close and after a torturous moment lowered his head and settled his mouth over hers.

She'd expected instant conflagration. But it was far more subtle than that. His kiss was like a benediction. And it soothed her as much as it frustrated her.

She pressed closer, hands finding his shirt, gripping it tightly. Her tongue sought his, and that first contact was like a match being thrown onto dry tinder. The kiss went from gentle to carnal in seconds and Leonora relished it, seized it.

Gabriel pulled back his head, breathing fast. 'You… Is this what you want?'

Leonora nodded jerkily. 'Please don't be gentle with me. Not now.'

He looked at her as if trying to figure her out, but then he took her hand and led her into the bedroom. He undid her hair, letting it fall loose around her shoulders. Then he pulled down the zip at the back of her dress. It fell to the floor in a swathe of silk and chiffon. She kicked off her shoes and stepped out of it and turned around to face Gabriel, lifting her hands to his shirt.

She tried not to think of that first night when he'd brought her to life. It was too cruel when they couldn't create life.

She almost faltered at that point, but Gabriel took her ineffectual hands from his shirt and undid his buttons, opening the shirt and pulling it off. Then his trousers. Everything until he was naked. And her mind was wiped clean of anything but *this*. Perfection.

Her inner muscles clenched with anticipation. It had only been a few weeks but it felt like a lifetime. Suddenly she was the one who wanted to go slow. She reached out and touched him reverently. Trailing her fingertips over his chest, tracing his muscles.

Then he caught her hand and lifted it to his mouth, pressing a kiss to her palm. Her heart ached. She pulled away and lay down on the bed, slipping off her panties. She hadn't been wearing a bra.

He looked at her for such a long moment that she almost begged him to stop. But then he moved towards her, kneeling on the bed between her legs, pushing them apart so he could come down between them, pressing kisses to her inner thighs.

Leonora caught his hair in her hand, lifting his head. He looked at her, sultry and sexy. Her heart broke.

She said, 'No. I want you…now. Please, Gabriel…'

Because in that moment she knew this was it.

The last time.

He moved up between her legs, taking himself in his hand to guide himself into her.

At the last moment she said, 'Wait, let me…'

He took his hand away and she put her hand on him, around his length, savouring the sheer majesty of his body.

She stroked him until he said, 'Leo…'

And then she took him and guided him home. He seated himself inside her, as deep as he could go. And then, with slow and remorseless precision, he moved in and out.

Leonora could feel the storm building, gathering pace inside her. She desperately clung on, wanting to record every tiny second onto her brain so she could take it out and remember what it felt like. But she knew her memory would be cold comfort…

The point came when she couldn't hold back any longer.

With a sob, she let the energy rush through her, incinerating everything in its wake, and waves of pulsing pleasure made a lie of the pain in her heart…

When Gabriel woke at dawn he knew immediately that he was alone in the apartment. A sense of *déjà vu* mocked him. He opened his eyes. He could still smell Leo's scent. He could still feel her nails scoring his back as her body clamped down on his, so tightly that he'd not been able to hold on, falling over the edge and down into an abyss of pleasure so intense he was still wrung out.

He got up and pulled on jeans. As he'd intuited, the apartment was empty. Like last time, he almost had a moment of wondering if he'd imagined it—but, no. There was a note on the table in an envelope.

Gabriel.

He went over and opened it. There was a card inside. A short note.

Dear Gabriel,
I'm so sorry. I can't do this.
Leonora

His first instinct was to leave immediately and find Leo, track her down and make her say that to his face while that sensual satisfaction still lingered in her blood.

He walked over to the window and looked out at the view. A view he'd always taken for granted until Leo had come into his life and made him see things with new eyes. Unjaded eyes.

That unwelcome sense of helplessness was back. He'd broken through the ice last night but now he was being punished for it. He'd known Leo had been fighting some internal battle when they'd arrived back at the apartment. She'd wanted him but hadn't wanted to articulate it. So he'd walked away. And then she'd said, *'I want you.'*

And he'd wanted to resist. Not to give in. To demand if she was just making the most of the arrangement she wanted to be set free from. But there had been something so raw on her face, in her eyes. And his need for her had been too great.

So he hadn't resisted, even though he'd suspected that he would pay the price. And the price was this.

He looked at the note in his hand again and then crumpled it up.

She just needed space. She'd been through a lot. He would give her a few days and then he would go to her and tell her— *Tell her what?* interjected an inner voice.

Gabriel knew what he had to tell her. He'd known for some time now. But he wasn't sure if she wanted to hear it.

A few days later, after no contact with Leonora, who had gone back to her family *castillo*, Gabriel's assistant came in with a package from a courier. Gabriel opened it and took out a sheaf of papers.

Divorce papers from Leonora.

Something snapped inside Gabriel.

Enough.

He pulled out his cell phone and made a call, standing up and walking over to the window as he waited for the person at the other end to pick up.

If he didn't answer—

But he did.

He heard Lazaro Sanchez drawl, 'Gabriel Torres, to what do I owe the pleasure?'

Gabriel took a deep breath. 'Can we meet, please?'

CHAPTER ELEVEN

'AND THIS PART of the *castillo* was built in the twelfth century—'

Leonora was used to gasps of awe at this point, but not gasps that loud, followed by excited whispers.

She turned around to see that a new visitor had joined the group. *Gabriel.* She put a hand on the wall beside her to steady herself. Maybe it was a hallucination.

But then he spoke. 'Sorry I'm late. Please carry on.'

How on earth did he expect her to just 'carry on'? But then she saw the far too innocent look on his face and a far steelier look in his eyes.

The divorce.

Leonora turned around again quickly, struggling to find her way back into the spiel which she could narrate in her sleep in three different languages.

Somehow she managed to conduct the rest of the tour without making eye contact with Gabriel or tripping over her words.

After the small group of visitors had dispersed and left, she faced him reluctantly. 'Did you get the papers?'

'Yes. Can we talk somewhere private?'

No.

She could see he was angry. Leonora led him into one of the reception rooms and he closed the door behind them.

She moved away from him and folded her arms. 'I don't know why you're here. We've discussed divorcing.'

He came into the room, pacing fast. 'No,' he said, 'Actually we didn't discuss it. You brought it up, I asked if you wanted a divorce, and you said you thought it was the best option. I then said we'd discuss it at a later date. Sending me papers is not a discussion, Leo.'

'I left you a note. I thought that made it pretty clear where I stood. I didn't hear from you.'

He arched a brow. 'Oh, so you're taking that as a signal of my acquiescence? I was giving you space, Leo. Space to think things over. Clearly that was a mistake.'

Leonora's heart thumped. It was heaven and hell to see him again. 'Okay, well here's the discussion—I want a divorce.'

'I don't.'

Leonora looked at him. 'That's crazy. We both know that I can't have children and you need heirs.'

'There are options. IVF. Adoption.'

Leonora turned around to face the window, afraid of her emotions. Damn him. Ever since she'd slept with him they'd been impossible to close off.

'I already told you—they're not viable options.'

'I thought you were better than this, Leo.'

She whirled around, hurt. 'I'm just not—'

He cut in. 'Willing to give us a chance?'

'It's not that.'

'What is it, then? I know IVF is a hard process, Leo, but I know you're strong. And I'd be with you every step of the way.' He continued. 'Did our vows mean nothing to you? For better or worse? In sickness and in health?'

Leonora could feel her blood draining south. 'That's not fair.'

'Isn't it?' He moved closer. 'Why don't you want to try, Leo?'

'It's not that I don't want to...'

'Then *why?* Are you just looking for an excuse to get out? Now that your family are provided for?'

She was horrified. *'No.'*

He was a lot closer than she'd realised. His scent wound around her and she fought against his pull. She stepped back. She had to be strong. Gabriel was just doing what he always did—not taking no for answer. Refusing to see Leonora's infertility as something that couldn't be surmounted.

'No, Gabriel—just *no.* Can't you understand that one little word?'

He was grim. 'I can understand it. What I can't understand is why my wife doesn't think our marriage is worth fighting for.'

He turned away as if to leave and his expression was so stony that Leonora couldn't bear it.

She said brokenly, to his departing back, 'I *would* fight for it. I would do everything in my power to give us a family if I thought for one second that you loved me. But I won't put us through a process that might never work for anything less than love. You deserve a family, Gabriel, and you can have that with another wife. Just not with me. I wouldn't survive it. If it worked we'd have a family, yes, but I don't want to bring a child into the world just to act as the glue in our marriage. And if it didn't work you'd resent me—' She broke off and turned away, trying to stem the sobs working their way up her chest and into her throat.

She expected to hear the door closing behind Gabriel as he made his hasty escape now she'd uttered the word *love*, so she wasn't prepared when she felt his hands on her and he swung her around to face him, his eyes more intense that she'd ever seen them.

'What did you just say?'

She hiccupped.

Gabriel took her over to a couch and sat down, pulling her with him. He took her hands in his. 'What did you say, Leo?'

Her vision was blurry. 'I said, I won't do it for anything less than love.'

He gripped her hands tight. 'Are you saying that you love me?'

She debated denying it for a second. But how could she? She'd just exposed herself spectacularly. She nodded.

Gabriel let her hands go and rubbed the tears she'd shed from her cheeks with his thumbs. She couldn't read his expression. It was something she'd never seen before. A kind of emotional nakedness.

He looked at her. 'I love you, Leo.'

At first his words didn't impact, and then they did. She pulled back instinctively, disbelieving. 'You don't. You're just saying that.'

He shook his head. 'I'm not lying. I would never lie to you.'

'But you don't believe in love. You never wanted it.'

'I didn't. Until a dark-haired temptress captivated me and ruined me for any other woman. I think I fell in love with you the moment I saw you that night in the hotel. I've never had such a visceral reaction to anyone. I had to know you, follow you. *Have you*. And the next morning I knew that this was different. I wanted more.'

Leonora looked at him, searching his eyes, his face. Searching out insincerity. But she couldn't see it. She could only see *him*.

'Why didn't you say something?'

'Why didn't you?' he countered.

She flushed. 'I was scared.'

He said, 'I was in denial. I kept thinking my feelings for you were strong just because you were my wife. It was natural. Expected. I only realised what they truly were when you suggested a divorce... I was so angry. I suspected you of marrying me solely to secure your family's fortune. But mostly I was hurt, and I had to acknowledge that you only had the power to hurt me because I'd fallen for you. And then afterwards...when you closed yourself off...'

'I'm sorry... It was too hard. I was afraid of what would spill out if you touched me. I was barely holding it together. But that night... I couldn't not touch you.'

'And then you left.'

She took his hand. 'Because I knew that I wouldn't survive a loveless marriage. That's my weakness.'

He shook his head. 'It's not weak. It was self-preservation. I was the one who was weak. I was prepared to bully you into staying married to me in the hope that if you agreed to try for a family you'd learn to love me.'

Leonora took her hand from his. 'There's a very strong possibility that we won't ever have children, Gabriel, no matter what we try. If that happens...how do you know I'll be enough for you? What will you do about having no heirs?'

Gabriel took her hand back, lacing his fingers with hers. 'You *are* enough for me. If we never have a family but I have you that's all I need. I've met with my board and we've drawn up a document that details what will happen in the event of my having no heirs. The Cruz y Torres name won't die out. It's a brand now, and brands last far longer and far more effectively than mere humans. And I've also been in touch with Lazaro Sanchez.'

Leonora instinctively held tighter to Gabriel's hand. 'And?'

He smiled a rueful smile. 'He *is* my half-brother. I did the DNA test. He wants nothing to do with the family name or any inheritance. It's a point of pride with him. Even when I told him our situation, and that any children he has might be the only heirs to the Cruz y Torres name. We've also teamed up for a bid on the marketplace. We're going to work *together*.'

Leonora shook her head, as if that might help her to understand everything Gabriel had just told her. 'You did all of that...before you knew...?'

'That you loved me? Yes, I did. I'm not as selfless as you. I wasn't prepared to let you walk away. Ever. You're mine.'

Leonora's vision was blurring again.

Gabriel said, 'You haven't actually said it yet.'

'What?' Leonora could hardly speak over the way her heart was expanding in her chest.

'That you love me.'

Leonora moved so that she was straddling Gabriel's lap. She cupped his face with both hands and pressed a kiss to his mouth. The she pulled back. 'I love you, Gabriel Ortega Cruz y Torres. With all my heart. Is that good enough?'

His hands cupped her buttocks and he expertly manoeuvred her so that she was under him on the couch. He smiled down at her and she could see the sheer love and joy in his eyes, on his face.

He said, 'I want for ever, Leo, is that good enough?'

Leonora looked up at him and saw the intensity blazing from his face and in his eyes. But a tendril of doubt and fear made her say, 'What if we don't—?'

But Gabriel cut her off with his mouth. With a kiss. He pulled back. 'For ever, Leo. No matter what. You are all I need. Anything else will be a bonus.'

She looked up at Gabriel. She saw love and commitment in his gaze. It had been there for weeks, but she hadn't wanted to believe in it. She'd shut it out.

She smiled up at him and wound her arms around his neck as tears pricked her eyes. 'For ever it is, then.'

EPILOGUE

Three years later
Lazaro Sanchez Torres's hacienda in Andalusia

'GETTING YOU TO agree to take on the Torres name was the most difficult negotiation I've ever conducted.'

Lazaro grinned at his half-brother and clinked his beer bottle against Gabriel's glass of water. 'You didn't think I was going to make it easy, did you?'

Gabriel smiled back. 'God, no. That would have been far too predictable. All I can say is that I'm glad we're on the same side now. It makes life so much easier.'

A moment passed between them. Deeply felt emotion. And then a baby's gurgle made them both turn back to the tableau in front of them.

Dragged out onto the back lawn of Lazaro's *hacienda* was a couch, overlaid with colourful throws. On the couch sat Lazaro and Skye's almost three-year-old son Max. He was looking very serious, because lying in each of his arms, propped up by cushions either side, was a baby, the two of them blinking contentedly and kicking their arms and legs in the shade under a huge tree. They were three months old.

'Okay, Max, you're doing so well—just another few seconds.'

Leonora chuckled beside Skye, who had become a good

friend. Her sister-in-law was moving around, getting lots of pictures from different angles with her camera.

Leonora said, 'Poor Max looks terrified.'

Skye groaned and stood up. 'He does, doesn't he?'

She was wearing faded loose dungarees and a bright yellow T-shirt that should have clashed with her red hair but didn't. The swell of her second baby was evident under her clothes, at nearly eight months along.

'Max, smile, sweetie! It's okay—you won't drop them. Honestly.'

Tentatively Max smiled, his blond, slightly reddish hair blowing in the breeze. His blue-green eyes were full of pride at his responsibility as the older cousin.

After another few shots Skye straightened up. 'Okay, that should be loads to work with.'

Skye, who had built up a name for herself as a talented portrait artist, was going to do a painting of Max and his baby cousins, Sofia and Pablo.

After Leonora and Gabriel had made the decision to try IVF, it had taken two years and three painful miscarriages before it had worked, on their last attempt. Gabriel hadn't wanted to put Leonora through even another attempt but she'd insisted. And, happily, that last round had brought them a successful pregnancy and the twins, and every time Leonora looked at them her heart was so full of awe and love that she almost couldn't breathe.

An arm snaked around her waist now and she turned to look up at her husband. Her life.

'Okay?' he asked.

She nodded, feeling emotional. She had a family now, and more fulfilment than anything she'd ever imagined or fantasised about. And a love that she knew would last for ever.

'I'm fine. You?'

Gabriel looked at her and she saw all her thoughts and feelings reflected in his eyes.

'I'm fine too. More than fine. I love you, Leo.'

'I love you too.'

She reached up and pressed a kiss to Gabriel's mouth, and he caught the back of her head, not letting her pull away, deepening the kiss.

'Ugh, kissy-kissy.'

They broke apart, laughing at Max's disgusted pronouncement, and went to rescue their babies, taking one each.

Lazaro said, all too innocently, as he scooped up his own son, 'Honestly, I don't know where he gets that from.'

Skye rolled her eyes and came over to her husband putting her arms around his waist. 'He gets it from seeing his mother being kissed by his father on a regular basis.'

'Oh, and you're a passive partner in that, are you? As I recall, this morning...'

Gabriel and Leonora watched as Lazaro and Skye walked back into the *hacienda*, with Max perched on Lazaro's shoulders. Their voices faded and Gabriel tugged Leonora over to the couch. The sun was setting, bathing everything in a golden and red glow.

Leonora's breasts were heavy with milk. Just as she became aware of that Sofia made a mewling sound. She deftly undid her sundress and placed Sofia on her breast. The small baby suckled hungrily, dark eyes gazing up at her mother.

Pablo snuggled against his father's chest, eyes closed. Leonora and Gabriel shared a look and smiled, not needing words to articulate the love flowing through them and their babies...

* * * * *

CROWNING HIS
CONVENIENT
PRINCESS

MAISEY YATES

For Mr. H, my 4th and 5th Grade teacher. I remember you teaching us about pseudonyms, and you said if we didn't use one you might be able to find us and read our books someday if we ever became authors. Unless we wrote romance, which you didn't read. Now you're mentioned in a romance—bet you didn't see that coming.

CHAPTER ONE

LATIKA BAKSHMI TOOK a deep breath before steeling herself to open the door. She knew exactly what she would find behind it.

Or rather, *who*.

Prince Gunnar von Bjornland, her boss's brother, dissolute rake, and general disgrace to his country. A man she despised with every fiber of her being. And, a man who was her current project.

Queen Astrid, who was not just her boss, but also her friend and confidant, had asked her to take on the task of reforming Gunnar, and she was going to do it.

In a minute.

"Stop lurking outside my door."

She jolted. "How did you know I was outside the door?"

The door swung open, revealing a man who was more Viking God than mere mortal. His blond hair was pushed back from his face, a slightly darker beard covering his jaw. His light blue eyes were the color of ice, but somehow contained heat nonetheless.

And his *body*.

It was an assault to all her good sense and she hated and loved it in equal measure. She both prayed he would find some sense of decorum in himself and learn to put on a shirt whenever they might encounter one another.

And prayed he would not.

Ever.

His chest was broad, and currently bare, a light dusting of hair over the toned, taut skin there. He took a breath, his well-defined abs shifting as he stepped to the side, as if allowing her entry into his bedchamber.

"How did you know I was out here?" She asked again, not making the move toward entering.

"I could feel the tension radiating through the door. And only you give off tension quite like that, Latika."

"Ah, yes," she said, giving a slight nod of her head. "You're very funny."

"I can *hear* you. You do not wear sensible shoes, like my sister. You wear those hard, spiky heels, and they make a very particular sound on the marble. I suppose, were I given to any great sense of shame, I would be concerned that sound can travel so freely through my bedroom door. One assumes then the sound can travel out just as well."

"A *grave* concern for you," she said, clipped. "I can only imagine."

He shrugged a broad shoulder, making all the muscles in his body shift and bunch. "It isn't really."

"It should be." She looked around the room. There were no signs of recent debauchery, at least. By that she meant, there wasn't a redhead or a blonde lying sprawled out in his bed, or anything quite like that.

However, the bed was unmade, and he had clearly just arisen from it, and likely just pulled the jeans he was wearing on.

It made her wonder if there was anything underneath.

She gritted her teeth, angry with herself without thought. "Astrid has asked me…"

"I would like you to find me a wife," he said, cutting her off and silencing her effectively.

"You… What?"

"I would like you to find me a wife. I understand that my reputation has become of some concern to Astrid. She's married, had a child, and our nation is on the brink of a great and modern future the likes of which would probably make my father rotate in his grave were he not so busy burning in hell."

"Astrid has asked me to help you reform," she finished.

"I know," he said. "And I think there's only one way to do that."

She had expected resistance. She had expected him to balk. To banter. To use excessive double entendre. She had not expected him to see her coming, to anticipate her words, and raise her.

"Why? Why are you suddenly interested in marriage?"

"I didn't say I was suddenly interested in marriage. But I do know that a fairytale is the quickest way to capture the hearts of the people. Is it not?"

"Well, judging by your sister's experience, I would say you are correct enough."

"I am not the heir. That is something that has always sat comfortably with me, but the burden that Astrid carries does not. And for my part, if I can alleviate some of what she carries, then I will do it. I can see that the simplest way will be for me to find a wife."

"A bizarre leap in logic."

"I know you don't respect me, Latika, and I have

never asked you to. Moreover, I've never behaved in a way that might invite you to. Oddly, though it may seem to you, I'm not overly concerned with your approval. But, I do wish to make Astrid happy, and I do wish to bolster the standing of my country in the world. So, you must help me find a wife."

"Is there a particular brand name you are drawn to?" she asked, her tone caustic.

"Yes," he said, not missing a beat. "I would prefer a philanthropist. I do not require that she be in mint condition, so to speak."

It took her a moment to catch his meaning. "You do not expect a virgin? How progressive of you."

"Well," he said. "As I myself am not a virgin, it seems a bit of a double standard to demand my wife come to me untouched."

She tried to keep the flush out of her face, and tried to keep her tone sharp. "You are not untouched?"

The corner of his wicked mouth turned up. "I've been touched one or two times."

"Shocking," she returned.

"I expect that you possess ample channels through which you might find a woman interested in marrying me."

The very idea of arranging marriages didn't sit very well with Latika. Not given her experience surrounding such things. Of course, Gunnar didn't know anything about her real life. Or her real identity. Fishing around in the sorts of circles that might require him to find a wife in might present a problem for her as well.

Considering she was technically in hiding.

But then, she could find ways to be discreet. Find

ways to make sure that she avoided any places that might be problematic.

Just one grim corner of Europe, and the East Coast of the United States. She imagined that Gunnar wouldn't mind her fishing around for an English debutante, rather than looking on the Upper Eastside of New York City.

"Blonde? Redheaded? Brunette? Do you have a preference?"

"None," he said.

"You don't have a type?" she pressed.

"*Female* covers it."

She fought against rolling her eyes. Instead, she made a very officious note on her clipboard. Then treated him to a smile. "A female philanthropist. Hymen not required."

"In fact, I would prefer that there were no hymen present at all," he said. "I'm not a patient man. I'd rather not have to instruct a woman on how to please me."

"Indeed," she said flatly. And she managed to hold back: *that rules me out handily then.*

As if she would ever, in a million years, with flying pigs in the sky, consider being Gunnar's bride.

He turned away from her, his broad back filling her vision. His muscles moved in very interesting ways and she attempted to study the ceiling, rather than his skin.

But it was hard, because his skin was so much more compelling.

And he began to move around the room. He opened up a dresser, pulled out a T-shirt, and shrugged it over his body.

Something about the flex of those muscles caused an answering flex between her thighs, and she did her best to ignore it.

Her emotions were so very charged in his presence, always. And it was her preference to play off the heat as anger. And to pretend that there was no other layer to it.

That there was no part of her—not even a tiny part— that wished to bite down on that insolent mouth of his.

And then bite his chest.

And then lick it.

No. No part of her at all.

She forced a smile. "Anything else?"

"No. I believe that covers it."

"Then I shall begin putting out inquiries, Your Highness. And very soon, I will have found a wife for you."

"It may also bear mentioning," he said, "That I am the owner of my own multibillion-dollar company."

Latika froze. "You... You're what?"

"Yes. I suppose it's about time that came out."

"How... How did you keep that a secret?"

"No one is looking for that bit of dirt. Honestly, it isn't dirt. Why would anyone care? My company has a name, obviously, and *my* name is buried beneath it. But the only thing anyone is ever interested in is who I'm sleeping with. Not the fact that I am the CEO of a multibillion-dollar corporation that deals in green building."

"I..."

"It's part of revamping my reputation, Latika. These things must be made public. I assume you're the person to speak to about the press release regarding that as well."

"I will take care of it," she said, blinking.

"See that you do."

Those blue eyes caught hers and held for a moment, and Latika did her best not to pay attention to the slight shift she felt in her stomach. Did her best to ignore the fact that suddenly the air felt a little bit thicker.

And she really tried not to examine what any of this new information—that he was not going into any of this kicking and screaming, that he had an endeavor that went somewhere beyond gambling and whoring—made her feel.

She was much more comfortable when she disdained Gunnar.

Anything else was unacceptable.

Prince Gunnar von Bjornland had settled into debauchery for far too long. He was at an end with it.

It had been one thing to engage in it when his father was living, and indeed it was something that he had enjoyed.

To throw in the face of his father, even as the old man attempted to sabotage Astrid. Their father was a relic of the highest order. A man who had not been able to fathom that a woman could possibly do a good job of running the country, regardless of the fact that there were many examples that proved they could, and just fine thank you.

No, his father had never gotten over the fact that his heir was a woman. And the fact that his only son had refused to take his side and engage in a coup, overthrowing his twin had been something that the old man could not accept even in the end.

Gunnar had never risen to his father's bait, and to the contrary, had taken a perverse kind of delight in behaving in every way that Astrid did not.

As his sister had lived a serious and contemplative life, dedicating herself to service, Gunnar had waged an all-out war against propriety.

He had taken every sacred tradition and broken it at least once, had taken delight in running roughshod over deeply revered customs, and in general putting Bjornland on the world stage in the context of his behavior.

He had imagined that if nothing else he would be a rather colorful footnote in history.

But of course, it had never been enough for his mind. Hence the secret business endeavor.

But now that Astrid was Queen, and now that various and sundry accusations were being thrown at him as the narrative around his country shifted, he could see that it was time for a change.

This latest debacle had only served to highlight it.

A woman had come forward alleging that he was the father of her child. And no matter that Gunnar had never seen the woman before, there had also been a seed of doubt in him. He always used protection. But condoms weren't entirely reliable, and he'd had to concede that there was a possibility the child could be his, no matter that he was always as responsible as a man could be while being indiscriminate.

The headlines had been scathing, the very fact that a paternity test had been conducted had been cause for scorn among the people.

And now the conversation had become that Astrid could not control her wayward brother. That her own brother despised every value held dear by the country. And when that had been aimed at his father, Gunnar had been happy enough.

But his entire reason for his behavior, his entire reason for being, had been to protect Astrid. Astrid was a strong woman, and always had been, but there had been a war waging beneath the surface of the polished exterior of the palace that she'd had no idea existed.

A war that Gunnar had been on the frontlines of.

He had always protected her. And if protecting his sister now demanded he behave differently, so he would.

And if it meant employing the use of his sister's delectable, and irritating, assistant, then he would do so.

Latika might be delectable, but she was also as stiff as a plank of wood and no less bland.

She was beautiful. There was no argument to be had about that.

In fact, she was uncommonly lovely, and he had always found it a strange thing that a woman of such brilliant beauty be relegated to such a *beige* sort of job.

Though, he imagined a great many people would not find being personal assistant to a queen a *beige sort of job.* But in his world it certainly was.

A woman like her should be wrapped in silk, should be in jewels.

She should spend hours soaking in perfumed baths, readying herself for a lover.

She should *not* spend hours contemplating the merit of clipboards. Though, he had a feeling that was how she spent much of her time.

Her beauty was, in the end, a terrible farce anyway. She looked like a woman built for such things, with her generous mouth and beautiful curves, but she was through and through a woman of practicality and severity.

And he did his very best not to think about how much he would like to test that severity.

He did his very best not to think about just how satisfying it would be to tease that mouth out of that firm unnatural line she kept it in, and torment her until it became a soft "O" of pleasure.

Yes, he did his best not to ponder that.

His world was changing. He would need to find a wife, and he would need to be faithful to that wife.

The very idea of such a chore set his teeth on edge. He could think of no woman at all that would amuse him for the rest of his life, and if he quit engaging in risky behaviors such as racing cars around the autobahn and jumping out of helicopters, his life would likely have a longer expectancy.

Really, this was a terrible plan, but it was the only way he could see to help Astrid.

Though she did not know it, his life had been devoted to that protection.

He would not falter now.

Marriage was, in the grand scheme of things a small price to pay. And for her he would do it. Perhaps not happily, but it would be done.

Because Gunnar von Bjornland might never be King, but he was the master of his own life. And once he set his mind to something, he would damn well see it done.

This was no exception.

CHAPTER TWO

"HERE YOU HAVE IT," Latika said, setting a stack of folders onto Gunnar's desk. "Veritable binders of women."

He looked at the stack, then back up at Latika, one elbow resting on the desk, one brow raised in an impudent manner. "I'm rather insulted you have brought me so much choice," he said.

Latika blinked. "How is that insulting?"

"I should think that the criteria for becoming my bride would be so exacting that you would have little more than a slim volume to present me with."

"I should have thought you would want choice," she said, bristling against his rather pronounced lack of gratitude.

She had gone to a lot of trouble to dig up so many eligible women, lacking in scandal and in possession of beauty.

"I haven't time to do so much reading," he said.

"Do you find it so laborious? To read profiles on women you might marry."

"I find it *boring.*"

"I have here in these folders options, for a woman that you might be tasked with sleeping with for the rest of your life. How is it you find that dull?" she pressed.

"When one turns sex into homework even that can be boring."

He was *impossible*. He was impossible, and he was ridiculous, and she had half a mind to kill him where he sat. She could do it with a letter opener, a paperweight or half a dozen other items on his desk.

As solid as her friendship with Astrid was, she had a feeling that Astrid would take a dim view to Latika assassinating her brother. Just maybe. If Astrid only knew the surrounding story she might forgive her.

"Who do you think the top five are?" he asked. "Use your knowledge of me to guess who I might find the most likely five."

"Gunnar," she said, keeping her tone frosty. "If I had that kind of insight into who you are as a person… Well, I would probably throw myself off the nearest cliff."

"A test then." He folded his large hands in front of him and it didn't escape her notice they were scarred. Odd for a man of his position, she would think. "Who do *you* think my top five would be?"

Latika gritted her teeth. She would lie back and think of Bjornland. She would do her very best to remind herself she worked for the palace.

And this was service to Astrid.

And for Astrid, she could do anything. The other woman had essentially saved Latika's life. And it was something that she was not going to forget anytime soon. Or ever. She was eternally grateful for all that Astrid had done. Working with Gunnar on this marriage project was a small thing to ask.

"All right," she said, doing her best to cover up just how aggrieved she felt. "If I had to choose, I would choose not so much to please *you*, but to give maximum improvement to your reputation, and to the reputation of the country. Therefore, we can set aside your personal preferences as secondary."

He rubbed his chin, the light in his blue eyes wicked. "*Can* we?"

"Yes," she said decisively. "This marriage is for the country, after all."

"And yet, I feel that if I am to be shackled to one woman for the rest of my life, it will have to be a marriage bed that I enjoy the idea of being shackled to." His lips curved upward. "Rather, a woman not averse to being shackled to the marriage bed for my pleasure. I've never been one who enjoyed being shackled. But I have nothing against doing a bit of shackling."

Yet again, she ignored the searing heat in her body, and affected an incredibly bored expression. "Yes, yes. I and the rest of the world are aware of the fact that you are shocking, and love to engage in *edgy* sexual activity. I promise you that if a double entendre presents itself you do not have to be so obvious as to speak it."

"Oh, but I enjoy being obvious."

"Do you?" she asked. "Because I would say that the fact you own your own company was not obvious at all."

She hadn't intended to bring that up.

In fact, she had every intention of ignoring it completely in the conversation today, if only to spite him slightly. And herself. Because the fact that he was a secret mogul fascinated her. And the one thing she was eternally trying to ignore when it came to Gunnar was her fascination with him. And anything that seemed to foster further fascination she resented.

There was something about him that enticed her to act in ways she knew she should not. She didn't like it.

It made her feel like she was not above the rest of the female population of the world in any way at all. And she liked to think that she wasn't that basic.

"That's the trick," he said. "Be obvious enough over here that you can have your secrets where you choose."

"I see." She took a breath. "Well. That aside." She shuffled through the folder and plucked out one. "I would choose…these."

"Explanations," he demanded, taking the stack of folders in his hand. "Or do I have to do everything myself."

"You have done absolutely nothing for yourself since I walked in," she said.

"That isn't true. I've been breathing the entire time. I'm keeping myself alive. For which you and the rest of the world should be supremely grateful."

"I'm about to expire from gratitude," she said. "The first candidate is Hannah Whitman, an English rose. She will compliment you well. Though, your progeny will likely burst into flames in the sun."

He laughed, explosive and deep, hitting her in unexpected places.

"Well," he said. "Melanin deficit aside, she is pretty. And what attributes do you suppose she would bring to our alliance?"

"She's extremely wealthy in her own right, her family is very successful in manufacturing. She has started several charities, with a focus on educating children with special needs. She is more than willing to do the work, not simply write a check."

"I imagine that means there are many photographs of her with grateful children."

"You are correct. She is a light to all the world."

"Well, I have always thought that one's wife should be able to double as a flashlight."

"Best of all," Latika continued, "she's scandal free."

"Excellent. Because I have enough scandals for ten people. It's one thing I do not need a wife to bring to our marriage."

"Next is Lily Addington."

"Another Brit?"

"Yes. Her family owns horses."

He frowned. "That sounds like an awful lot of time spent at racetracks."

"Would you not find that enjoyable?"

"No. I prefer my gambling to take place in a casino. It's much more civilized."

"All right. Bim Attah. She is a Nigerian heiress and UN ambassador for women's rights. She has a PhD from Oxford, and has been instrumental in supplying feminine hygiene products to impoverished girls throughout the world."

He leaned back in his chair, placing his hands behind his head. "She sounds a bit overqualified, don't you think? PhD. I'm not sure I'm equal to that task."

"You have a title. I suspect that in many ways that outstrips a PhD."

"One you are born with," he pointed out. "One you must work for."

She arched a brow. "Shall I take her off the list?"

"Oh, no," he said. "I feel nothing if not entitled to things that might be too good for me. Leave her on the list."

She cycled through the rest of them quickly with Gunnar vetoing all but numbers one and three.

"Okay," she said, sighing heavily. "I will attempt to

arrange a meeting for you. Whatever you do, try not to be yourself when you meet them."

"I never am," Gunnar said. "Why, when there are so many other interesting people to choose to be?"

Latika gritted her teeth. "Why indeed."

She turned away from him, and her phone buzzed in her hand. She looked down and saw that it was an unknown number.

"Oh, don't decline the call on account of me," Gunter said. "There's no need to worry about manners in my presence."

"I wouldn't," she said, answering the phone decisively. It had nothing to do with her anyway. She worked for Astrid, and she couldn't afford to miss any kind of communication just in case.

"Hello?"

"Latika Bakshmi."

The voice was strange, low and husky, and something about the accent sent a familiar sliver of dread beneath Latika's skin.

"Yes?"

"Check your email."

The line went dead. Latika lowered the phone and stared at it, feeling like she lost herself for a full thirty seconds. She had no sense of where she was, or what she was doing.

Until she felt the intensity of Gunnar's gaze on the side of her face. She looked toward him. "What?"

"Are you all right?"

"I'm fine."

"You've gone very pale."

"No. A strange phone call. Likely a prank of some kind." She tried to force a smile. In spite of herself, she swallowed hard and guided her thumb over the email icon on her phone.

She prayed that Gunnar didn't notice the slight tremble in her hands.

She did indeed have a new email.

From an address she didn't recognize. She opened the email, it had one line of text. And a photograph.

So there you are.

And beneath those words was a picture. Zoomed in tightly and cropped close. Latika could just see the edge of Astrid's dress, and that gave her an indication of the event.

The wedding.

Astrid and Mauro's wedding. Latika had been standing just behind the Queen, and she had been sure that she was not in any sort of limelight position. She had been with Astrid for nearly four years and never had been.

But they had found her. Finally.

She swallowed hard, fear like lead in her stomach.

The worst part was, it hadn't been her parents who had found her. She was sure of that. Because while her parents would have happily hauled her away from her newfound life, they wouldn't engage in this level of theatrics. That she knew.

They would still cling to the idea that this was all for her own good, for their own good as well, but also for hers. They would lie to her, lie to themselves, all the while using soft, soothing voices and telling her to think of the future.

No, this kind of threatening language was definitely

the work of the man who was supposed to be her husband by now.

The man she had run away from.

The man she would rather die than find herself joined to.

Latika took a breath and put her hands down, holding her phone closely to her thigh.

"What is it?" Gunnar asked.

"Nothing," she said. "I will make the necessary inquiries, and make arrangements for you to meet these women. In fact, I think we will organize a ball."

"A ball?"

"Yes. For all the eligible ladies in the file."

"I said that I'm only interested in these two."

"But why limit your options, Your Highness. You're correct. The chemistry that you may feel with one of them is important to explore. Allow me to take care of it. I will handle everything."

Her mind was spinning as she walked out of Gunnar's office. On the one hand, creating such a spectacle around the country at this time was possibly unwise. But on the other hand... Well, on the other hand an event like this would necessitate an increase in security. And with so many eyes on the country, she imagined that Ragnar would be loath to attempt to take her now.

No, he preferred to do things secretly. In the dark of night, essentially.

His position as Norwegian nobility mattered far too much for him to go and create bad blood between himself and the Royals in Bjornland.

And in truth, Latika had counted on that. Always. When she had first come to Astrid for the job, it had been on her mind. The fact that Bjornland was politically involved with Norway, and that it would put Ragnar in a bad position should he cross the Queen, had mattered to her.

Because she needed protection.

The palace guards would provide it. The increased attention would provide it. She had to believe that.

The alternative was far too awful to consider.

CHAPTER THREE

THE ENSUING WEEK was a whirlwind. At least, it looked as though it were one for Latika.

Gunnar did nothing but sit back and enjoy the show.

Over breakfast one morning, Astrid commented on it. "I don't think I've ever seen her work so hard at anything. And that's saying quite a bit."

"Yes, she has taken control of the task admirably," he said, not rising to his sister's bait. Because he knew there was bait. Even if he wasn't sure what the hook buried in said bait was meant to drag him toward.

"Are you assisting her at all?" Astrid asked.

"Do *you* assist her in the planning of parties?"

Astrid gave him an icy look. "She is *my* assistant."

At that moment, Astrid's husband came into the room holding Gunnar's nephew. It had taken Gunnar a time to accept his brother-in-law. He had not trusted the man at first, but then, given the way that his sister had met him, Gunnar felt he could hardly be blamed.

Astrid had engaged in subterfuge, essentially tricking Mauro into getting her pregnant. And when he had discovered the ruse, Mauro had been decisive in his action. He had demanded that Astrid marry him, and that, was what Gunnar had taken exception to.

The man was common born, and it wasn't as if Gunnar was any sort of snob, but he had grave concerns about anyone seeking to use his sister. As it had turned out, his feelings for Astrid had been genuine and their marriage had become a very happy one.

But, Gunnar was still getting used to the situation.

"That's different," Astrid said, rising from her seat and crossing the room, giving Mauro a kiss on the cheek before taking her son into her arms. "You should be helping her. Since she is helping you clean up your mess."

For Astrid.

He wasn't going to say that. He didn't care what anyone thought of him. And were it not for his sister, he would happily go on not caring.

"I'm sorry, what exactly did you want me to do?" he asked. "Ensure that the punch is spiked?"

"I don't know, something that wouldn't send my assistant to an early grave. Since I am quite attached to her."

"Yes," he said. "Something that I'm not sure I understand. You seem more fond of her than you are of me at times. And yet, for all I can tell, Latika seems to lack a sense of fun, or humor."

"That's a phenomenon that only presents itself in your presence, Gunnar. I find her amusing and delightful." His sister's gaze was glued to him. "Perhaps it's just you."

"Everybody likes me."

"Everyone thinks you can do something for them. That's different. I don't think Latika cares one way or the other whether or not you can do something for her."

That wasn't true. Everyone was an opportunist. And

everyone would use a person if the need was great enough. He'd learned that early, and he'd learned it well.

Nothing could insulate you when someone decided to use you as a tool. Not even family. Not even blood.

"She works for you. If she needs a favor… You're the one she'll go to," he pointed out.

"Are you implying she doesn't actually *like* me?"

"Did you not just imply that none of my friends actually like me?"

"Are either of you going to threaten to have the guards shoot the other this time?" Mauro asked, his brother-in-law's expression one of amusement.

"Probably not," Astrid said.

"The two of you make me so sad that I was an only child," Mauro said.

"I can see where you would be jealous," Astrid responded serenely.

They settled in to eat breakfast then, and Gunnar was bemused by the domesticity before him. It was difficult to imagine himself settling into such a life.

And yet, he didn't think it would make him entirely miserable. Of course, he would never feel for his wife the way that Mauro and Astrid seemed to feel for each other.

And there would be no children in his marriage.

The line was guaranteed to continue without his help, and he was not the heir. Therefore the task wasn't his.

After the childhood he'd endured, he had no interest in exploring the relationship between a parent and child again. Even from the opposite side.

The door opened, and Latika entered, her black hair swept back into a twist, her makeup sedate. And yet, she glowed. He ignored the tightness that he felt in his stomach. In his groin.

"I do hope I'm not interrupting," she said. "Queen Astrid, we have an appointment with your stylist. We must ensure that you are appropriately outfitted for the ball."

"What about me?" Gunnar asked.

"You will wear a black suit," Latika said, each word crisp.

She was like a tart apple. Then he desperately wanted to take a bite of her.

It was a shame. For with this new endeavor now before him, he never would.

For years now, his dearest fantasy had been getting down on his knees before his sister's prim assistant, pushing one of her tight pencil skirts up around her hips and draping her legs over his shoulder, her back against the wall, as he licked his way into her center.

As if she sensed his thoughts, her gaze landed on his, locked there. She looked startled, like a deer caught in the headlights.

"It seems to me that you are avoiding having to dress me," he said.

"I'm not avoiding anything," she said. "Believe me, Gunnar, if you required dressing, I would accommodate. I'm sorry if that wounds your fragile masculinity in any way."

"Good to know," he said.

On a tightlipped smile, Latika turned and walked out of the room.

Astrid fixed her cold gaze on him. "Can you not deliberately poke at her with a stick?"

"I'm not poking her."

"You're a pain in the ass. She's been through enough without you harping on her constantly. Be a decent human being."

"That is, dear sister, the point of all of this."

If he could not fashion himself into a decent human in the realest sense, he would make himself look like one.

In his world, facade was better than reality anyway.

Two hours after the encounter with Gunnar in the dining room had left Latika trembling and feeling hollowed out, she found herself standing in Astrid's chamber while her friend tried on a myriad of dresses.

"It seems strange," Astrid said, currently admiring a white gown with delicate silver beading that clung to her curves. "To draw attention to myself on what should be a ball in my brother's honor."

"Yes," Latika said. "I can see that. But you know, it is about improving the way people look at all of Bjornland. We have essentially put out a call to all the eligible ladies of the world that Prince Gunnar is looking to settle down. The media attention alone demands that you shine above all else. Especially all those eligible ladies. It won't do to have anyone in attendance be more beautiful than the Queen."

Astrid laughed. "I imagine there will be a great many women there who are more beautiful. My brother attracts rare beauties like honey attracts bees."

"Yes," Latika said. "Pity he is not actually sweet."

"I don't think anyone would find him half so compelling if he were."

Compelling.

That was an appropriate word for the man.

Of course, there were other words too. None of them fit for polite company.

"I think this color washes me out," Astrid said. She looked over at the rack that was entirely filled with gowns. "And that orange would be hideous on me. It would look lovely on you."

She gestured to a gown with a long bodice and a full, sheer skirt that gathered at the side, with a close fitted lining beneath. It was orange, with shimmering gold geometric detail over the top of it.

And, Latika *knew* she would look good in it.

But, she needed stay in the background. Desperately.

"I think I will opt for something black," she said decisively.

"Well," Astrid said. "I will not. I would look like a ghost."

Astrid sighed and then looked over at Latika thoughtfully. "Are you all right?"

"I'm fine," Latika said.

"You don't look fine. In fact, you seem very tense. And not simply because you're planning a party. Usually, you enjoy that."

"Well, it's just Gunnar. You know he and I don't exactly see eye to eye. But it's normal. Nothing out of the ordinary." Except the threats to her safety. But she was choosing to handle that herself.

Astrid blinked. "Yes. I do know that the two of you get on like angry ants trapped in a jar. I also don't think that's the real problem."

"Why?" Latika asked.

"Because I know you. Because we're friends. Latika, don't you trust me?"

Latika shifted uncomfortably. "Of course I do."

"Are you upset about Gunnar getting married?"

Latika sputtered. "What?"

"I'm not a fool," Astrid said. "I know that he irritates you, but I also know that there is something underneath that. I can never tell if the two of you are going to start yelling at each other, or start tearing each other's clothes off."

Latika stiffened, her face getting hot. The fact that Astrid had noticed that she carried some sort of shameful…fascination with Gunnar was truly alarming. It was somewhat refreshing to be able to be alarmed about something other than the email she'd received a few days ago, though, she would not have chosen this. "I can honestly say that I am not upset about Gunnar choosing to get married."

"Then what is it? Please don't tell me it's to do with your parents."

Latika sighed. "Not as such."

"It's related to that, though."

"I… I have reason to believe that my former fiancé knows where I am."

"Latika, that's terrible. You should have told me immediately. I will do whatever I have to, to protect you."

"And I will do whatever I need to, to protect *you*. You don't need to worry about me, or the issues that I'm having. The scandals in my life were never meant to touch you."

"That's not how friendship works," Astrid said. "Yes, you have been an employee, but more than that. And you know it. You are the single best friend I've ever had. It's because of you that I found my husband."

"In fairness," Latika said, "it was highly unlikely any of that would work, and I feel it was only a stroke of incredible luck that saw it all come together. Or fate, perhaps. But either way, I cannot take credit. And had everything gone awry, I would have been responsible for your most disastrous decision ever. We could have damaged the whole of the country over a one-night stand."

"But it was meant to be," Astrid said. "And you trusted me. You trusted me when I said I needed your help, and believe me, the people in my life who have trusted me, who have taken me at my word, have been in short supply. For the most part, people have doubted I know my own mind because I am a woman. Really, only you and Gunnar, and my mother, ever treated me as though I had the head on my shoulders required to run a country. Or, to make any decisions on my own."

"Yes," Latika said. "Well."

It was one of the difficult things about Gunnar. He had always been incredibly supportive of his sister. And though he had been angry over the incident with Mauro, and Latika colluding with Astrid to sneak her into his club so that she might engage his services in the making of an heir, in many ways, Latika couldn't blame him. And indeed, would possibly respect him less if he'd had no issue with it whatsoever.

Latika had helped Astrid accomplish that for her own reasons, but it certainly wasn't in the interest of her finding love with Mauro. No. It was only that she understood what it was like to feel that you had no power in your own life.

An ancient law written into the code of the land of Bjornland had stated that the Queen could declare herself the sole parent of her issue. With that goal in mind, Astrid had set out to get pregnant by the most disreputable man on the planet, thinking he would want nothing to do with the child. Of course, he had. And Astrid had not ended up with a child, and no man, but with a husband. One that she loved very dearly. Nothing had gone quite as they planned, but in many ways, it had gone better.

Latika had never seen Astrid so happy.

And that—she had concluded—was what happened when people were allowed to live. To make their own choices.

To make their own *mistakes*.

Sometimes even a mistake—in the end—was perfectly all right because it led you to where you had always been meant to be.

But choice, that was what Latika wanted. Eventually. A life of her choosing, with a man of her choosing.

She wanted children.

Watching Astrid with Mauro all those desires had only become more pronounced.

She was tired of surviving.

And with Ragnar coming after her those dreams seemed farther away than ever. Dreams other people took for granted.

"What can I do to protect you?" Astrid said. "Your problems are mine. Because we are friends."

"Honestly, this ball is going to offer me a modicum of protection I would not have access to if it weren't for my position here. We will, of course have to increase security. Seeing as we are inviting every eligible woman in the world to come and have a chance with Gunnar. And those who haven't met him will surely jump at the opportunity."

Astrid erupted into a peal of laughter. "You do protest too much, Latika."

"Perhaps my protestations are honest," she said.

"You find my brother attractive. Whether you want to admit it or not."

"A spider can be beautiful in its web," Latika said. "But that doesn't mean I want it on my skin."

Astrid shook her head. "But see, that's where you have him wrong. He's not a spider. Any more than you're a fly. A predator, possibly. But maybe more like the wolves we have here in the mountains. Deadly if necessary, surely. But more than willing to put everything on the line to protect his pack. Gunnar is a true alpha. Leader and protector."

"Perhaps that's the problem," Latika said. "It is difficult for two alphas to get involved."

"That would be the story of my marriage," Astrid said. "But what Mauro and I have learned is that sometimes it can be quite pleasurable to let the other take the lead."

"Yes, well." Latika firmed her lips into a straight line. "I will take the lead by finding some other woman for Gunnar to harass."

"Are you sure you don't want to wear this?" Astrid asked, gesturing to the orange gown again.

"No," Latika returned. "I am not one of the women vying for your brother's attention, and I will not dress like one. It would have to be a moment of true crisis in order for me to turn to him."

"Well, let us hope we had don't have any crises ahead of us."

CHAPTER FOUR

THE EVENING OF the ball, everything was going according to plan. Latika could find no fault with anything.

And she ignored the orange and gold gown that Astrid had sent up for her, in favor of a long, formfitting black dress and simple gold accessories. She would look appropriate, and she would *blend*.

And that was the idea.

She bustled around, making sure that everything was in place, pacing the length of the ornate ballroom, examining it from the gilt-edged ceilings, all the way down to the marble floors.

The massive, golden chandelier was lit, and it was like a sun burning brightly at the center of the room. Perfect. Gleaming and lovely. And in the next twenty minutes the ball would be full of fluttering flowers, all vying for Gunnar's attention.

She heard footsteps on the marble floor, and turned.

And there he was.

He was devastating in that custom cut black suit, the one she had dismissed with a wave of her hand, saying that men needn't be so concerned with such things.

There was nothing *plain* about Gunnar in a black

suit. He was a weapon against all good sense, his broad
shoulders waging war on every prudent thought.

His hair was still overlong, brushed away from his
face, his beard just a bit unkempt.

And it put her in the mind of a Norse marauder, and
she found that however she tried, she could not dislike
the image.

And for the first time, a strange pain hollowed out
her stomach.

Another woman would dance in his arms tonight.
Another woman would dance with him from tonight,
possibly into forever.

And she would never know what it was like to be
held by those strong arms.

She clenched her teeth. That was an empty fantasy,
driven by hormones. And she was not a slave to her
hormones. She was a woman who never had such a luxury. She had been driven by the need to survive. By the
need to press forward, always, and make for herself a
life that she could not only stand, but that she enjoyed.

She had found a way to live.

It might not be her ideal life, yet. But it was wonderful.

And she was only ever proud of herself for that fact.

Gunnar served no purpose. Attraction to Gunnar
served no purpose.

She did not even like the man.

"You have done a spectacular job," he said, and she
ignored the slight thrill of pleasure that went through
her midsection.

"Thank you," she said.

"Soon, I will be like a steak put out before the dogs."

The wicked glint in his eye bade her stomach turn over. She ignored the sensation.

"You will find there are no dogs here. Only a wolf," she said, harking back to Astrid's earlier words.

He grinned, and Latika thought it was decidedly wolfish. "Perhaps."

"Sheep," Latika said. "Sheep going before a wolf."

"Very evocative. Does that make you Little Red Riding Hood in this fairytale of a metaphor? Because I must tell you, I feel my mouth is all the better to eat you with."

And that was when she realized, he was not simply engaging in empty banter. No, there was a gleam in his blue eyes that spoke of intent. But there was no point to him making sexual promises toward her. Not when tonight, of all nights, moved any possibility of something happening between them out of reach.

She ignored the jolt of irritation that she felt over that. The intense regret.

Every time he had ever traded barbs with her she had assumed it was simply who he was, what he did.

She had never once thought that he might… That he might actually want her.

"I am not anyone's version of a fairytale. And you would find, that I bite back."

He moved closer to her, and a thrill shot down her spine. "Pity for you, that what you intended as a threat only sounds like a promise to me. I like a woman who gives as good as she gets."

"Then I suggest you find one here in the room full of them."

"I doubt there will be one sharp as you."

"The trade-offs you make for respectability," she said.

She turned away from him and began to busy herself with details that did not need her attention.

"Are you not respectable?"

"That depends, I suppose," she said, "on your definition of respectability."

Those blue eyes regarded her with open interest. "Someday, I should like to find out."

She locked her teeth together. So tight her jaw ached. "Oh, but there is no someday. For you are getting married. And we all know your life will end as we know it."

"A tragedy," he said.

"Well," she said, brushing her hands down the front of her dress. "It's time to bring in the staff. And then it will be time to open up the doors. I suggest you get in position."

He arched a brow, a wicked smile curving his lips. "Missionary? Did you have something else in mind," he said.

Latika ignored the sharp shock of pleasure that shot straight down through her core. It was wrong for them to talk like this worse to be talking like this tonight. Though in some ways, it pushed it further out of the realm of possibility than ever. Which made it…almost less wrong maybe? Or less dangerous.

"You will look a bit silly in missionary position on your own," she shot back, unwilling to let him see that he had affected her.

"I suppose that depends on who you ask."

The doors opened then, and the staff began to filter inside. Latika managed to busy herself and soon her interaction with Gunnar was forgotten. She had work to do. It distracted her, both from the strange sensation she felt whenever she was around the man, and from the underlying sense of fear she'd been feeling ever since she received that email.

The many, many palace guards in attendance made her feel safe.

No one would do anything to her while she was here.

She repeated all those things to herself as she made sure the food was in place, as she made sure all was well. And then, went back to the antechamber to ensure that everything was ready for Astrid to make her appearance.

Several guests arrived before the Queen was to be seated. And Latika had the task of making sure that Astrid's entrance went smoothly, and according to plan.

Astrid and Mauro looked beautiful, the pair of them absolute perfection. Astrid had ended up choosing a deep emerald gown, and her husband was in a black suit. Mauro was a handsome man. There was no denying it. Tall, dark and Mediterranean, with wicked eyes and a mouth that looked like it was made for sin.

And yet, it was no particular sin that called to Latika. No, there was something about the cold, wild beauty that Gunnar possessed that seemed to ignite thoughts of sin.

Sin that sorely tempted her.

She put her head down, resolutely making her way through the ballroom, now filled with women that were bedecked as tropical birds, fluttering about in bright colors.

She knew that Gunnar had expressed a preference for two women in particular, but the guests did not. And every one woman—single or not—had dressed to impress him.

Latika cued everyone to Astrid and Mauro's entrance, and the royal couple alit, walking through the crowd and taking their positions in their honored seats.

It was all going so smoothly Latika wanted to celebrate. That was the thing. She might not have a husband or children yet. She might not be fully living the life of her choice, but she was living well.

She'd been seen by her parents as a bargaining chip. Her only value had been how she could marry. And here she was, operating in a very stressful and important career.

And she did it well.

She allowed that to buoy her mood. To take away the sour feelings that had begun to roil in her stomach earlier.

With them settled, Latika felt the need to check on the kitchen. She turned and slipped out a side entrance, heading down the hall. And what she saw there made her stomach twist. It was him.

Ragnar.

He didn't have the decency to be hideous. No, instead he was a severe looking older man with salt-and-pepper hair and a neat beard. He was handsome. And a great many women—regardless of their age—would have been thrilled with his attentions. But Latika knew how cruel he could be. And she knew that a life with him would be equal to misery.

The fact that he had come after her after all this time, likely less out of an attraction for her specifically, and more because he wished her harm, sent fear rattling through her.

"My dear, Latika," he said. "It has been quite some time."

"Not accidentally," she said, stopping in her tracks

and beginning to edge back toward the ballroom. There was security there. And she would be able to call for help.

"Do not think I'm so foolish as to try and take you from the palace. I simply wanted you to know how close I am. If you try to leave the country, my agents will intercept you. And I know you are here. Ultimately, as long as I can reach you, you are not safe. I will have you brought back to Norway, and married to me before you could ever protest."

"And why would I marry you?" She asked, fighting to keep her composure.

He liked fear. He liked to cause pain.

She would allow him to see neither in her.

"Because you will find the alternatives so unpleasant. You have made for yourself a little problem here. You thought that by making yourself invisible you would become invisible to me, but you are not just invisible to me, but the whole world. And that is where you have failed yourself, my darling girl. Because when I take you, I will be able to hide you. Your Queen may miss you, but how will she mobilize forces beyond the borders of her country? The public outcry will never be sufficient enough."

The words settled down to her bones, the truth of them making her feel fear. Real and heavy.

He continued. "I have you between a rock wall and me. And you know that it is true. For now... I will be here all night."

"I can have you removed," she said, craning her neck.

"I have done nothing," he said. "And my removal would create an international incident. As you well know. I know you do not wish for an incident. You are too smart of a girl for something like that." She swallowed hard, and turned and fled, running back into the ballroom, shutting the door behind her, pressing her hand to her chest.

And she saw Gunnar. At the center of the room dancing with a woman. The brilliant Nigerian activist.

And suddenly, she had an idea.

Times were desperate. And so was she.

She made her way across the ballroom, heading toward the opposite door she had just come in. A door that would take her away from Ragnar.

With purpose, Latika left the ballroom, and headed toward her room.

Though she didn't know it at the time, Astrid had given her an escape. And Latika knew well enough to take it.

Gunnar was dancing with his third potential bride of the night when a hush fell over the ballroom. He turned, following the gazes of everyone in the room. And there he saw her. Standing at the entrance to the ballroom, dressed in orange and gold, her black hair a glossy wave over one side of her shoulder.

Latika.

She did not look like an assistant. She looked like a princess.

And when she began to descend the stairs, the crowd parted for her as if she was. And then she looked at him. Deliberately. Intentionally.

And a fire ignited in his gut.

He had no idea what game she was playing. He had made it plain earlier that he was attracted to her, because he had never been the sort of man to be coy about such things.

She looked completely different than she had earlier. Though, she had still been delectable in the slinky black dress she'd been wearing, it was the sort of dress designed to make her blend in. And had she been a different woman, it might have been successful. For him, Latika would never blend in.

His greatest concern in life at this moment was that she would go on always as an unanswered need.

And he was not a man who understood denial. Not in his adult life. When he'd escaped his father's power, when it had become clear to the man that Gunnar could not be manipulated, and when it would have taken the involvement of palace guards to continue his grand experiments on Gunnar, Gunnar had taken the chance to escape into a world of sensual pleasures.

Food. Drink. Women.

Luxurious surroundings.

Most of his time spent in warm climates rather than the harsh chill of Bjornland.

He had forgotten denial. He had forgotten need.

Until her.

And while he had no moral qualms about taking Latika to his bed between now and his wedding, he did feel that perhaps the ball where he was supposed to meet his future wife was perhaps not the ideal venue for such an encounter to begin. But Latika didn't seem to agree.

She crossed the room, heading straight toward him, the expression on her face one of seductive intensity.

He wanted her. And he had, ever since she had come into his sister's employ. Every time they had sparred, it had only increased his desire for her.

And now, she paraded herself before him. As if she thought he would not be able to take action here. As if she thought he would be leashed.

"If you would excuse me," he said to his partner, a woman whose name he could no longer recall.

He stepped away from her, making his way toward Latika. And much to his shock, she increased her pace and nearly flung herself into his arms. "I would be delighted to dance with you," she said.

"What are you doing?" he murmured.

"I am sorry," she said. "You have no idea how much. But I need you. Desperately. And I think that I will not harm your objective. I think that I will further your cause."

"Do you?" he asked, keeping his voice low.

"I need you to marry me," she said. "And I need you to announce it now."

"Latika…"

And then, she did something truly shocking. She launched herself forward, and captured his mouth with her own.

Gunnar was a difficult man to surprise, indeed, until this moment he would have said it was impossible.

People were boring in their predictability.

And up until this point, Latika had been scarcely different.

She had bantered with him. She had brought their exchanges of wit to the edge of propriety, but she had never crossed it. And while he found her enjoyable, she had never truly shocked him.

But in this moment, she turned the whole ballroom— maybe the world—on its head.

There was something desperate in her kiss, and he

responded to it. He wrapped his arm around her waist, pressing her tightly against his body, forgetting they had an audience. Because what else mattered when he was finally tasting this woman that had vexed him for years.

He took control of the kiss, tightening his hold on her and angling his head, taking advantage of her surprise, of her slightly parted lips, and slipping his tongue between them.

She gasped, and he took it deeper.

And only then did he fully realize that while he might have ensnared her at this very moment, she had caught him in her trap.

"Everyone has seen," she said. "If you were to reverse course now, no one would believe you. You have clearly staked your claim on me."

"Minx," he said. "Was this your game all along?"

"I promise you it was not."

"Does my sister know that you are little more than a fortune hunter?"

"Your sister knows the truth."

He looked over at Astrid, who was seated in her throne still, watching what was taking place before her with a surprising amount of equanimity. If Astrid suspected that Latika was trying to snare him as a fortune hunter in some way, he knew that she would be on her feet.

That she would have crossed the room, making her way to him, and to Latika, demanding that the farce be ended.

But she was not. Instead, she was sitting and watching. Waiting. Clearly.

"You must say that you'll marry me," she said. "Because if you do not, there is another man here. And he is going to take me away. Not from here, but if I ever set foot outside the palace, he has promised that he will take me. If I ever leave the safety of your land. And he said... He said that my anonymity is what has cursed me, and he is not wrong. If I were to go missing, no one would know. No one would care. But if I was your wife... Gunnar, if I was your wife not only would I improve your standing in the world, but you would save me from this man. If I was your wife, I could hardly go missing without notice. Then he could not force me to marry him. I need you to protect me."

On this, Gunnar did not need a moment to think. They could work out the details later, and they would, but if what Latika said was true, she needed protection. And it was no matter to him which woman in this room he married. It might as well be the one who needed help. It might as well be the one who lit his body on fire.

"Very well," he said. "You have yourself a fiancé." He took her hand and led her over to where Astrid sat. Latika, for her part, was ashen at his side, and did not look the part of blushing bride at all. She was going to have to work on that.

"I have an announcement for you to make," he said to his sister. "It seems that I did not have to look far and wide to find my bride, as she was here the entire time."

Astrid's gaze shot to Latika. "Are you in danger?"

"I will be. If measures are not taken."

"Hello," Gunnar said. "I am the measures being taken. I assume you know about this?"

"Yes," Astrid said.

"We will speak later," he said to his sister. "For now, just make the announcement."

"I think, it's time for you to make your own."

Gunnar turned toward the crowd of people. He was not a stranger to being the center of attention, and in fact, in many venues had courted it. But never here in Astrid's domain. He had been very careful about that fact. That he never assume too much authority in his sister's presence.

Mostly, because it had angered their father.

But he was certain. Certain in this decision, whatever the eventual outcome would be.

There was no other logical choice.

"Thank you all for coming tonight. It is with great pleasure that I am able to announce that I have decided to marry. Especially in a room full of such suitable people. I will marry Latika Bakshmi in two weeks' time. You have my permission to spread the news far and wide, and to publish photographs everywhere. After all, you do know I like the show."

And with that, he grabbed Latika, and pulled her close, kissing her fiercely on the mouth. He might be aiming for a kind of propriety, but he would never be tame.

And that was something Latika would learn. He would help her, but he would never belong to her.

For he belonged to no one.

Not to Bjornland.

Not to his father.

What he did, he did because he *chose* to do it.

He had not gotten where he was by being weak.

He was unable to be brainwashed. Either by verbal suggestion or physical torture.

He'd proved that.

And he'd hidden it.

Because the only other alternative was for Astrid to

know just how desperate their father had been to have her ousted.

And he would never do that to her either.

The only line his father had was that of assassinating his own daughter.

But it had been a thin line.

He had certainly been willing to allow Gunnar to do it if he wanted to.

But Gunnar was strong.

And Gunnar protected what was his.

Now, it seemed that Latika Bakshmi was his, and he would protect her to the end.

On that he was resolved.

CHAPTER FIVE

LATIKA LOOKED TOWARD the back of the room and saw Ragnar, watching the proceedings. For a moment, she wondered what he might do. If he would pull out a weapon and assassinate her there on the spot. But then, her saving grace was the fact that he would never want his name overly sullied. And, that he would not want any physical harm to come to him. It was the biggest reason he would never make a move here. She knew that.

He cared mostly for his own self-preservation, and thanks to that predictability she was insured some level of physical safety.

He was a madman. And he was, in her opinion, nothing less than evil. But he cared for his own skin. For his own money.

And he would do nothing to compromise those things.

And so he simply stood, rendered impotent by the fact that Latika had allied herself with the most powerful man in the room.

That she was now visible.

And that if anything were to happen to her it would create something larger than an international incident.

It would create a wave of global concern.

Because while Gunnar was something of a scorned figure, particularly in his homeland, the world found the Playboy Prince to be captivating and compelling.

He was handsome, and he was roguish, and that was something that won out over respectable every single time.

If you were a man.

Well, thankfully for he was. Because as such, she had been able to use him as her salvation. But she could not escape the feeling that she had jumped from the frying pan and into the fire in many ways.

Although, at least, Gunnar would never harm her. But marriage was marriage. And it was entirely possible that she had gone from one life sentence to another.

You could not just throw yourself onto the altar of marrying a prince and expect that divorce would come easily.

It was possible, certainly. But it would not help Gunnar's reputation. It would not help Astrid's.

Standing there in front of this crowd of people with their eyes on her, putting herself in the exact opposite position to the one she had been attempting to avoid for the past several years, she felt as defeated as she did triumphant.

She had no idea what she was going to do. Not now that she had made herself so vulnerable. Not now that she had cast herself from one jail cell to another.

At least the jail keeper of this one was good-looking.

That was a shameful thought. She despised herself for it.

And even as she did, the enormity of what she had done crashed down around her. Would Gunnar expect that their marriage be real? Would he expect them to have children?

For she would have to marry him. And legally. To be absolutely certain that Ragnar would not simply be able to kidnap her and force her into marriage some other way.

She had to be legally precluded from marriage.

And still, that felt so defeating.

Because she had done all that she could to avoid being in an arranged marriage, and yet, she had gone and arranged one for herself.

Better the devil of your choosing.

Perhaps.

Her lips still burned from Gunnar's kiss. And from the kiss she'd given him earlier.

She had never kissed a man before.

And now she had. Now she had, and in two weeks, was possibly going to be sharing his bed.

And the idea didn't horrify her.

Perhaps there was another solution. Perhaps there was, and you didn't want to. Perhaps it was because you wanted him.

She ignored that voice and attempted to smile.

"Now," Gunnar said quietly to Astrid. "If you'll excuse me. I have to celebrate my engagement with my future bride. In private."

And with that, he looped his arm around her waist and began to walk her toward the door. Once they were out in the corridor, he turned to her. "Not here," she said.

"Then where, Latika? As this is your three-ring circus."

"Your bedroom," she said. "It is protected, and it is private."

"Or are you simply eager to get on with the wedding night? Because I can tell you, there are certain things I'm quite prepared to discuss naked."

"Let us go," she said.

She was trembling as they made their way down the corridor, Gunnar's hand still resting low on her back. And once they arrived in the chamber and he closed the door behind them, he turned to look at her, something cold and vicious in those icy eyes.

"Tell me honestly," he said. "Did you plan this?"

"I told you I didn't. I can take you back to the ballroom and show you the man that I'm running from. Ragnar Stevenson."

Gunnar's lip curled. "I know who he is. He has a... reputation. He has certain sexual interests that I don't approve of. There is little in this world I find distasteful or that I haven't participated in. My line, is consent, and that line is hard. He doesn't seem overly concerned with it."

"Don't you think I know? I heard all about it. I know how much he enjoys pain. Not the kind that both parties agree to enjoy together. He would much prefer to inflict it on women who do not enjoy it."

"How is it that you ended up on his radar?"

"My parents. My parents are very wealthy. They move in elite circles in America. And they wanted his nobility. His connections to Europe. The minute I found out my parents had promised me to a stranger I did as much digging around as I could. In the end it was a friend of mine's father who told me everything. He said I needed to know, and I needed to run. I tried to talk to my parents first. But they didn't believe me when I told them... They didn't believe me. They thought that

I was simply trying to get out of them choosing my husband, something I had always been trying to get out of. They said that I would not have been happy with any of their choices. My friend's father, he encouraged them to sweep my disappearance under the rug. Otherwise he…he threatened to expose them as mercenary enough to marry me to a monster."

"So they did not believe you," he said. "Even when you made it clear that their choice of husband was a sociopath. And they didn't believe your friend's father, yet they swept your disappearance under the rug when threatened with their forcing to wed being exposed?"

"That's the size of it," she said stiffly.

"Where did they tell people you'd gone?"

She rolled her eyes. "To India. To find myself. They couldn't very well tell everyone I'd gone into hiding to lose them."

"How did you find Astrid?"

"She had put out inquiries in my circle about hiring a personal assistant. Of course, a queen does not advertise in the paper. But it made the rounds on the Upper Eastside, and I found out about it. I decided that it would be a fantastic place for me to seek shelter in. I knew a great deal about putting together functions. I had a great many contacts. And I had experience organizing a variety of different events, and schedules. I knew that I could do the job, and whatever I couldn't do I would learn. Because it's really quite amazing what necessity will do for you."

"So Astrid hired you, and did not inquire about your identity?"

Latika shook her head. "I told your sister. I didn't feel right about coming here for shelter without making it very clear that I was running. It wouldn't have been fair."

Some tension drained from his body. "So you have been honest?"

"Yes. Only Astrid knew the truth. But I felt that as long as Astrid *did* know it was fair."

"I can't fault you for that."

"What is it you expect?" Latika asked. As if this had been his idea. As if he were the one who'd flung himself across the ballroom and into her arms. It wasn't fair and she knew it. But she felt slightly helpless just now, and it pained her to feel this way.

"I expect for this to be a marriage," he said. "Because there is little else that will keep him away from you."

"I know," she said, muted. "I did already think that through. An engagement would keep him at bay, and it would certainly give me more visibility. But, when we broke off the relationship I am certain that I would come out looking like the villain."

He chuckled. "How would you come across looking like a villain after the loss of an engagement to a Playboy Prince?"

"There's a very particular appendage you have that makes you much easier to forgive in the eyes of the public."

"True," he said. "I won't pretend that I don't know what you're talking about. Being Astrid's twin has not allowed for me to ignore gender disparity. She has behaved above reproach almost all the years of her life. And still, her ability to rule the country has been questioned, time and time again. I am the one whose competence should be questioned. And regularly. I have never once given the impression that I was overly competent or stable. I am. But I have never demonstrated. Astrid on the other hand has spent a lifetime devoted to Bjornland, and to cultivating a good reputation and yet…it never seems to be enough. It certainly wasn't ever enough for my father, who thought that I would be the superior choice to be on the throne by simple virtue of the fact that I have a penis."

"It is unfair," she said. "But it is true. Additionally, there would be no point in trying to cast you as the villain. The entire point of this ball, the entire point of you getting married in the first place was to improve your reputation. Should we throw up a barrier by deciding to start a rumor that you were unfaithful to me… And infidelity is the only way I could possibly see me coming out the victor… No. I won't do it. I won't do it to Astrid."

"And as you said already, it opens you up to vulnerability. No, legal marriage is likely the only thing that will keep him at bay. And a promise."

"What?"

"We will offer him something. Some sort of diplomatic prize. If he is to set foot in Bjornland again, he will find himself in a jail cell. The fact of the matter is, I have spent a great deal of time running in the circles that he has enjoyed. And I have heard many allegations from women about his behavior. Allegations themselves may not hold up in court, but we have the luxury here in this country of bypassing due process provided the crown sees fit to arrest someone."

"Could you really do that?"

"I could. It would create an incident. Likely a scandal the world over. But, I think that he is conscious enough of his own desire to stay out of prison that it will keep him well away from the borders of this country. Should he set foot over, should he show up in our immigration records, I will have him dealt with. But, that only protects you here. Outside of this place, it would not offer you protection. Only notoriety in marriage would. On that score, he was correct. But he was stupid to tell you. Stupid to think that you, a woman who has been in hiding to escape him for years, would not act in a way that was absolutely necessary to ensure your safety. Clearly, he underestimated you."

"Clearly," Latika agreed. "He underestimates women."

"Likely."

"Can we really have this done in two weeks?" she asked.

"We would be foolish not to. As you said. We must neutralize the threat. Legally tying you to another man, and embroiling you in a media circus so that everyone in the entire world knows your face… It is the easiest way to keep you safe. You must either be invisible or visible to all. And as you have lost your invisibility…"

"How long will the marriage last?" she asked.

"I am sorry, darling, but marriage is forever. At least, from my view it must be."

"But I…"

"If you thought that you could use me as a temporary solution, I'm afraid that you were mistaken. You're very clever, throwing yourself at my mercy and crying sanctuary. But we are a royal family. We cannot subject ourselves to the scandal of divorce."

"Of course not," she said, muted.

"Now, that did not stop my parents from having affairs."

The very thought sent a burst of strange pain through her body. "I have no interest in affairs," she said stiffly.

"Such is your devotion for me?"

"I see no need for it," she said. "It opens us up to pointless censure. The sort of thing we don't need."

"Well then," he said. "Feel free to conduct your business as you see fit."

"And yours?"

"Sadly for you, you are not in a power position."

He was correct. It was the thing that galled her so badly. She had used him. She had used the opportunity presented before her, because how could she not. But Gunnar had only been on his back foot for a few moments, and now it was clear that his was the position of power.

He had been intending to marry anyway, and whether or not it was her or anyone else would hardly matter to him. In fact, all she had done was deliver him an easier bride.

She was the one who would be grafted into a life she had not wanted.

Finding herself potentially shackled to a man she didn't even like.

But you are fascinated by him...

It didn't matter. He was ridiculous. A disreputable playboy.

With a multibillion-dollar company?

That made her wonder if there was more to him.

But she still couldn't... She couldn't fathom sharing a life with him. She could barely share a room with him without wanting to throw something heavy at him.

"I suppose..." She took a breath. This was the only part that would salvage it for her. The one thing that she wanted, above all else. "I suppose there will be children."

"No," he said, firm and decisive.

That shocked her. So much so she couldn't believe he'd said them. "What?"

"I've no desire for children."

The word settled over her skin, a strange, buzzing sensation filling her ears. "You're a prince. Surely you must produce heirs."

"My sister has done so already."

"What if something were to happen to him? God forbid, Gunnar, but it must be considered."

"She will have more children. She and that husband of hers will likely fill the palace. He is Italian."

"That is an incorrigible thing to say."

"I am incorrigible." He shrugged a shoulder. "My father was a tyrant. My time spent in a father-son relationship was unendurable. I have no interest in revisiting it. I have no interest at all in being father to anyone or anything. That word is forever tainted for me. And, as I have no need of producing children..."

"But think of what it would do for your standing in the media."

"Oh, I daresay they will be fine taking photographs of us at various parties. You will be the envy of women the world over."

"Because I'm with you?"

"Obviously." He lifted a shoulder. "I'm rich and handsome. Titled as well. You will be a style icon because you are my wife. Many women would have wanted such an honor. And you have it now."

"But no children."

"Surely your position as one of the top influencers in the world will compensate for that."

Anger vibrated in her core, but she said nothing.

This was worse than she could've possibly imagined. She had not simply trapped herself in a marriage, but she had trapped herself in a childless one. She wanted to be a mother. To fulfill that loneliness inside of her. To repair the distance that she had always felt in her relationship with her own parents, by being a better mother to her children.

And he was not allowing it. He was taking this from her.

It was a thing she could not endure.

But what could she do? She was completely and utterly trapped. Between a madman, and one who had just laid down an edict for her life that she did not know if she can survive. Still, she would have to take Gunnar. Because the alternative may very well actually kill her.

"Well," she said. "If there are to be no children, and you are happy to have affairs. Then I see no point in the two of us having sexual relationships."

Something in his gaze changed. It turned to ice. And then to blue flame. "Is that what you think?"

"As you said. You do not see any reason for a couple in our position to stay faithful, as your parents did not."

"And you think that you can resist me?" he asked.

He was utterly sincere. And she would love to laugh in his face.

Sadly, she wasn't immune to his body, whatever she might want to believe. In fact, his body transfixed her in ways no other man's ever had. Even now, even as he dashed her dreams of the future to dust, she couldn't deny the attraction that flared inside of her.

"It may have escaped your notice, but I have done an admirable job of resisting you for the past three years." That at least was true. She hadn't—as far as she knew—

ever really betrayed her attraction to him. He might suspect, but he didn't know.

"Well, that is because I have never truly tried to seduce you."

She sniffed. "You do have a very high opinion of yourself."

"Well, ask yourself this, Latika. When you needed a port in the storm, where did you look? You looked to me. And I would suggest that that makes me perhaps a bit more than you would like me to be."

"I think perhaps your mind makes you a bit more than you are."

"However you like. Don't think I don't recognize the heat between us. And don't think I don't realize that it is mutual. Whatever I feel for you...you feel it for me."

"How do you know I feel a thing for you?" she asked.

"You were awfully comfortable coming up and kissing me."

Heat stung her face. Shame lashing her like a whip. "When people are in burning buildings, they are awfully comfortable jumping out of five-story windows hoping that they land favorably. I was willing to take my chances with you."

"Call me whatever you like," he said. "A panic button. The fire you jumped to from the frying pan. A last resort. But your mouth doesn't lie when it touches mine. It may when you speak, but you cannot deny chemistry such as ours. Not where it counts."

"I can."

Because he was denying her children. And so, she would deny him her body. There was perhaps no convincing him she didn't want him, but that didn't mean she would weaken in her resolve.

He stared at her, hard. Those blue eyes seeming to look beneath her clothes, beneath her skin. Her heart was thundering, her whole body beginning to tremble. Why did he affect her like this? How?

"You truly expect that we will be married for the rest of our lives and never explore this chemistry between us?" he asked.

She had no defenses left. None but the truth. "It should be no hardship to me. After all, I've reached the age of twenty-four without ever having been with a man. What's twenty-four more years?"

"I did not realize you were so young," he said, his expression strange.

"I don't advertise. Do you think my parents waited until I was very old to try and marry me off? Of course they didn't. They had dynasties to try and make."

"You think we'll only be married twenty-four years? That's not very much time for the rest of your life."

"I was thinking yours," she said, her tone stiff. "After all, your age is much more advanced than mine. And also, I may poison you."

He shrugged. The casual, disaffected gesture such a stereotype she wanted to hit him. "So long as it's in a good whiskey, I may not even mind."

"No commentary on the state of my hymen?"

"I'm not surprised," he said dismissively. "Given how frosty you are, it's little wonder."

Damn. The. Man.

"Well then. It seems that you're not missing anything by being denied my bed and my body. In fact, you should be very happy."

"Consider me overjoyed. I may find a porn star to celebrate our engagement with."

"It's neither here nor there to me, Gunnar. Provided you practice discretion. But then, that's your part. The improving of your reputation. All I need is to be saved."

"I hope you enjoy planning your wedding. We haven't been able to hire you a replacement."

The man was made of ice. She had expected him to protest…to…to something… Act surprised when she threw her virginity down as a gauntlet.

To act disappointed when she said she wouldn't sleep with him, which wounded her feminine pride in ways she would rather not admit. But no. He reacted to nothing.

And he never wanted children.

"Do you care for anyone?" she asked. "Do you even care for your sister really?"

"What does the evidence tell you, darling? For while you may not be able to lie with your body, I can lie with anything I want. I will be much more likely to trust you than me in any situation."

"Well, then I will continue to do so."

She would have to trust herself. She might have used Gunnar, but she couldn't trust him. She would have to remember that. She could trust only herself. And in that regard, while many things felt different in her life at this moment, that one truth remained. She had to rely on herself. And she would. Because she was strong. That truth was the only thing that kept her from slipping completely into despair.

CHAPTER SIX

LATIKA WAS A VIRGIN. Or so she claimed. She was also intent on denying him access to her body. Clearly the last-ditch effort of feelings of control in the situation. Or maybe, an attempt to punish him.

Or maybe… Maybe she truly did not desire him in the way that he did her.

But, that seemed unlikely.

Twenty-four.

She seemed much older than that.

All these revelations had shocked him to his core. And yet, he could not allow her to see it. And she had the nerve to ask him if he even cared for his sister. She had no idea. No idea of why he lived the way he did. He had done everything he could to protect Astrid, not just from his father. But everything he was supposed to learn in his father's name. What Gunnar's father had tried to teach was an abomination.

His father had tried to plant the idea in his mind that women were inferior to men. He'd tried to poison Gunnar's mind. The cost of his resistance had been great.

Latika thought she knew who he was, based on the lies he'd told the world about himself. She was clearly under the impression that he was every inch the debauched playboy.

It could not stand.

He was going to take her to his office in the States. He would show her what he was.

He couldn't tell her. Not everything. Not about his father. But he could show her that he was more.

But he would wait. He would wait until after their wedding. Because the thing that he wanted more than anything in the world was the chance to prove her wrong using nothing more than her own body.

She thought she was kept at night stewing in her irritation over him, but he knew differently.

She was only a woman. And he was only a man. Neither of them were above the basic biology that demanded their bodies mate.

Of course, thinking of it in terms of biology brought him back to the moment Latika had thrown down her virginity revelation.

It had been when he said they would not have children.

He wondered if that was related strictly to practicality, or if for some sort of emotional attachment to the idea of having children herself.

He supposed it wasn't that surprising, given the fact that many women seemed to want children. Most women, he would have thought, would consider a prince enough of a consolation prize. Though, Latika seemed bound and determined to punish him.

She had been avoiding him since the night of the ball. Throwing herself into the melee of planning the wedding.

Meanwhile, Gunnar had been concentrating on the media component.

"There's the groom to be."

He looked up and saw Astrid standing there. She was dressed immaculately, her red hair pulled back into a tight bun.

"Yes. Here I am."

He had been avoiding her since the announcement. Mostly because he didn't want to get into a discussion. He didn't want her questioning him.

She did so, out of habit. A feeling that she was the oldest, and therefore the protector.

"You've been avoiding me," she pointed out.

"Yes," he agreed. "I have definitely been avoiding you."

"Why?"

"Related to the impending lecture."

"How did you know?" She asked, narrowing her eyes at him.

"Oh, just a feeling I had. I was right, wasn't I?"

"I want to be sure that you don't hurt her."

"Interesting," he said. "A different lecture to the one I expected to receive."

"Oh, you expected me to say that you should be on guard in case Latika hurts you? We both know that is impossible."

And he was left to wonder how the whole world seemed to think of him as heartless. Even by a sister he'd worked so hard to save.

"I've no designs on hurting her. She seems a nice woman."

"You're attracted to her. She's attracted to you. But you need to understand that she's inexperienced and..."

"How do you know?"

"Well, I don't really. But, the things that she said seem to imply as much."

He thought of what Latika had said to him. That she had not been with a man in her whole twenty-four years of life.

That, combined with what Astrid said, made him wonder if it was true. "It may surprise you to learn that Latika has already laid out her ground rules. Which, include staying out of my bed."

Astrid frowned. "Really?"

"We are not a love match, Astrid, as you well know. We can barely tolerate being in the same room as each other."

"But she... Yes. But as you so eloquently put it earlier, you... You're attracted to each other."

"It's obvious, I'd think. But, she would happily slit my throat in bed after. Believe me."

"She turned to you when she needed help."

"A person will take their chances with the pavement below when they're trapped in a high-rise building during a fire." He repeated Latika's words back to his sister.

"Oh."

"I'm sorry, you don't need to interfere. The both of us can handle ourselves."

Astrid sighed. "Yes. My concern is that you won't be able to handle each other."

"Dear sister, I make it my business to handle women."

"But Latika is not like your other women. And you will be stuck with her. So whatever you do, you will have to face the aftermath of it. You're not good with consequences, Gunnar."

Just like that, he heard his father's voice echoing in his head. And he was flooded by memories. Days spent in the dungeon of the palace.

Day after day. Spent in isolation, in starvation.

There will be consequences, Gunnar. If you cannot take on board my lessons.

And there had been. Painful consequences.

"No," he said, grinning. "I'm absolutely terrible with consequences. In that I tend not to acknowledge them"

"What about children?"

A poignant question, considering what was on his mind. "There won't be children."

"Why not?"

"Astrid, you know what our childhood was like. I have no desire to father children."

"I love being a mother," she said.

"We lived different childhoods," he said.

"Yes," Astrid said. "I know. Father distrusted me. Mother supported me. She ignored you. But father…"

"You think that I enjoyed getting attention from a man who despised my sister?"

Astrid blinked. "I didn't… I didn't think that might be a problem."

"Of course it is," he said. "You are like a part of me. You are my twin. We are blood in a way few other people on this earth are. Whatever father wanted from me, he was not going to get it."

"That doesn't mean that you shouldn't have children."

"Oh, there are many reasons I shouldn't have children. That's only one of them."

"That breaks my heart," she said.

"It doesn't break mine. I am perfectly happy watching you with your life. Latika and I have come to an agreement. We will live separate lives. I will protect her, she will enrich my reputation. There is nothing to dislike about it."

"If you say so."

"I do. You might rule the country, Astrid, but in my own life, my word is law."

"Of course. I have never thought differently." What he didn't tell his sister was that he wasn't content with the idea of keeping their lives separate. Not completely.

Because he was not a man given to taking commands. Was not a man who bowed to the will of others.

No.

His father had tried. He had tried and tried to break him. But it had forged Gunnar into the strongest steel imaginable.

As his new bride would soon discover.

Yes. Latika would discover it soon enough.

Latika was carried away on the tide of the farce she was currently engaged in. Completely overwhelmed by her role as bride, and retreating as often as possible into the role of planner. It was easy to make decisions when she divorced herself from the narrative. When she thought of it as planning a royal wedding in the generic sense. Rather than her own.

Not that it mattered what her own personal preference was. Not in the context of this arrangement. What mattered was the spectacle. What mattered, was that she took herself out of harm's way. Whether or not she enjoyed the look of the wedding didn't come into it at all.

But there was one piece of it that she found impossible to divorce her emotions from, and indeed her body from. And that was the acquisition of a wedding gown.

She asked Astrid to be there when she made her selection. In part because Astrid was acting as her maid of honor. A farce it might be, but it was a real wedding. And Astrid was her real friend. Much more than Gunnar could ever be considered a real fiancé.

Well, he was real in the sense that she was going to marry him.

She supposed that was the only sense that mattered.

"That one's pretty," Astrid said, but her tone said she did not think it was all that pretty.

Latika looked at herself critically in the mirror. The dress was not to her taste at all, and didn't look particularly flattering on her. For that reason alone, part of her wanted to choose it.

But there would also be pictures, and she was vain enough to not want photographs of her looking anything less than beautiful circulating the world.

But then, maybe she could still find something that didn't feel too personal.

"What I think doesn't matter," Astrid said. "It should be about you."

"It shouldn't be," Latika said. "It is about the spectacle of the royal wedding. It's about putting out into the world what we must."

"And you don't have feelings for my brother." Astrid said, her tone incisive. "Not at all?"

Latika's neck prickled. "It's complicated."

"Is it? It all seems very straightforward to me. Ragnar was at the palace. And I'm very sorry that we failed you in that way."

"Don't apologize to me," Latika said. "The fact of the matter is, I was never going to escape him forever. And I knew it."

"But I said that we would protect you…"

"And you did. You have. And now the crown is protecting me further."

"He told me that you… That you want the marriage to be in name only."

Latika's face flamed. "Why would he tell you that?"

"You may have noticed that my brother doesn't keep secrets."

"Well, it would've been nice of him to keep that to himself," Latika grumbled.

"Why won't you make it a real marriage?"

Latika swallowed. "He doesn't want children. He also said that there was no reason for us to be faithful to one another. If he intends that we sleep with other people, and the two of us don't even have to produce a child, then why bother with each other at all?"

"He *said that* to you?" Astrid asked, incredulous.

"Yes."

"He's an idiot. And I think that he has feelings for you."

Latika laughed. "The only feelings we have for each other are antagonistic. Whatever narrative you've made up in your mind about the two of us… It isn't real. And I appreciate so much that you care about me. About him. You are better than either of us deserve, Astrid. You have been so wonderful to us. But he and I have never had interaction beyond what you've seen. There is nothing secret happening."

"I believe you," Astrid said.

"Your tone says you think I'm telling the truth, but that you don't think I know my own mind."

"I just don't want you to get hurt."

"Believe me. My options are such that I don't fear

any pain from Gunnar." Latika paused for a moment. "You were asking me for advice."

"Well," Astrid said. "I'm married now."

"And I'm still a woman running from overbearing parents and an abusive former fiancé. No offense meant, Astrid, but your relationship with Mauro does not make you an expert on the feelings of every person."

"None taken at all," Astrid said.

But Latika could tell that Astrid still didn't believe her, and she thought it best to say nothing at all. Instead, they continued to rifle through the racks of gowns that had been given to them.

"You should try this," Astrid said, holding up a devastatingly beautiful gown, deceptively simple, and made from the finest white satin. It had long, flowing sleeves and a square neck, a fitted bodice and a skirt that flared out at the bottom.

It was perfect. Sophisticated and sleek, and absolutely something she would've chosen for a wedding to a man she had chosen.

"This one," Astrid said, decisively.

Latika decided she would try it on. But she wasn't certain if she could bring herself to choose it.

The day of the wedding was ominous. Clouds hung thick and low over the mountains, a dramatic effect, the dark green trees piercing through the mist, making it look as if the hills had teeth.

Truly, not an auspicious day for a wedding. But Gunnar did not believe in such things.

He had never been given cause to believe in love at all.

And this was no different. It was not luck that had

brought him here. It was simply a twist of fate, one that he was fine enough to lean into.

He had allowed Latika to continue to evade him up until today. But tonight, tonight he would launch an all-out seduction of her senses.

Why? To prove that you can manipulate her? How does that make you any different than him?

He ignored that inner voice.

He didn't want to manipulate her. He wanted to seduce her. He wanted her. And they were going to be married. The idea that they would only sleep with other people seemed foolish to him, and he had been prepared to offer his wife his fidelity.

He had only said those things to her to get to her, and in many ways, he imagined she had done the same with him. He sincerely doubted that she was actually going to hold to her missish cries anyway. Just as he sincerely doubted she was actually a virgin. The more he thought about it, the more he thought that conversation was designed to give her a power position.

Of course, she would remember that he had said he didn't want a virgin bride. And for whatever reason, she was attempting to prove to him that she was unsuitable in some way.

And again, he felt that had to be about power, rather than any kind of sincere desire to put him off. She needed him to marry her. And given that truth, he didn't actually take any of her nonsense terribly seriously.

He turned and looked in the mirror.

A black suit.

The very thing she told him he didn't require help with for the ball.

He imagined that at that point she had no idea that

the next place she would be seeing him in a suit was their wedding.

He certainly hadn't.

With the decisiveness of a predator, Gunnar turned and walked out of the room, prowling down the halls, making his way to the chapel that was on the grounds of the palace.

Theirs was not a wedding with quite as much fanfare as his sister's. After all, the wedding of the Queen, particularly to someone as famous and outrageous as Mauro, had been an insane spectacle. But, there had been a bit of something as well. The paparazzi was fascinated by her, and of course, a profile had been released about her in the media. Information about her family. They had interviewed her parents, who'd had nothing but good things to say about their daughter.

And he knew that they had contacted the palace and asked for an invitation.

It was a decision that Gunnar had been hard-pressed to make. Because, on the one hand, her parents had clearly tormented her by putting her in the path of Ragnar. But on the other, this marriage solved all of their issues. And keeping her parents away from the wedding might only cause tension, and give Ragnar a foothold.

Indeed, it might also make her parents into problems that he didn't want to deal with. So with regret, he had given them an invite.

He could only hope he didn't regret it. The church was filled already, hundreds of guests in attendance, and millions tuning in on television, and on the computer. And Astrid met him outside the sanctuary.

"Why aren't you already seated?"

"We walk together," she said. She looked up at him,

her green eyes filled with emotion. "I noticed you did not have a best man. Well, I am your twin. And there is no one on this earth who has ever been closer to you than me. So I will walk with you."

His sister's sentimentality hit him hard. At the same time, made great tendrils of acidic emotion churn through his stomach. Because she thought they were close. She thought they shared a bond he wasn't entirely certain they did. She thought she knew him. When he had kept so much back from her. For her own protection.

And yet, she was standing with him. And that mattered. He would let the other things fall from his mind. They walked to the front of the sanctuary together, whispers filling the air, heads turning as they moved. And then he took his position at the head of the altar.

Astrid nodded her head regally, and then went and took her seat by her husband.

Gunnar was very accomplished at not paying attention in church, and he handily tuned out the exhortation given by the priest, and the hymn that went up after. And then, it was time for the bride to walk down the aisle.

The music shifted, swelled, and after a few moments, Latika appeared. Her long black hair was swept up in a bun, her gown made of lace and glimmering beads, the skirt heavy and full, rising and falling elegantly with each step she took. She was an uncommon beauty. And as she walked toward him, his plan became blurry.

Because it was difficult to think straight with Latika there.

Difficult to have a clear-eyed view of his plan. In fact he forgot his plan. Forgot there was anything other than this stark, physical need igniting a fire inside of him. He was in a church, but his thoughts were decidedly less than pure.

In fact, he would not have been surprised to burst into flame at any moment. And when she joined him at the head of the altar, looking all stiff and uncomfortable, he wanted to kiss away those grim lines around her mouth. Wanted to crush her up against his body and kiss her until neither of them could breathe. He already knew how intoxicating a kiss between them could be. How could she deny them? Both of them? They wanted each other, and she was intent on…playing games. Well, it would not stand. She was using him, and he could fully respect that. But that didn't mean she got to be the only one with a say in how their marriage would be conducted.

She turned to face him, wordless. And they both stayed silent until the part came for them to repeat their vows.

It was easy for him, because he had never taken much of anything to heart, or treated anything with reverence, so he didn't know why this should be any different.

Latika, for her part, seemed stilted.

Then she looked over, and he could see the exact moment her eyes came to rest on her parents.

Her face went scarlet, her eyes widening with shock. She finished out her vows tightlipped.

And when time came for the kiss, he determined that he would do his part in loosening that terse expression.

She might not want to desire him, but the fact of the matter was, she did. And he was going to use that.

He lowered his head, capturing her in his arms and holding her firmly against his body. Then he lowered his head and kissed her.

It was nothing like the other two kisses they had shared. For now, they had an audience, it was true. But he was fully in command of the situation.

And it was Latika who melted beneath the heat between them. He crushed her lips beneath his, and forced them apart, sliding his tongue against hers. She was sweet. She was so very sweet.

A prickly, intoxicating beauty.

One that had resisted him far longer than anyone else ever had. One that made his heart beat faster. Made it feel like his body was on fire, and how long had it been since a woman had interested him in such a way?

He couldn't remember.

His image was a blur of glitter, golden brown and red lips. Latika was the only woman in his memory. The only woman that he wanted. He knew that his kiss was pushing the bonds of propriety for a royal wedding— many royal couples did not engage in physical affection such as this, even during the wedding ceremony.

But he didn't care.

As far as he was concerned, being a married man was more legitimate than he had ever intended to be, and he wouldn't be denied this pleasure. Not now. Not now that he finally had her—Latika—beneath his lips.

And it was only a taste. Only a taste of what was to come later. He wanted her. My God how he wanted this woman. It defied everything. Every basic idea he'd ever had about himself.

The world that he lived in where women were interchangeable and one soft body was as good as the next.

Except, no one would do but her. Not now.

When they parted, he was breathing hard. Latika, for her part, was a blank space.

The priest pronounced them man and wife, and he and Latika held onto each other's arms, and walked down the aisle. Once they were free of the audience, free of the church, she jerked away from him.

"How dare you not tell me my parents would be here?"

"I'm sorry," he said. "I miscalculated your response to that. I did not think it would matter."

"How could you think it wouldn't matter? I haven't seen them in more than three years."

"I thought it wouldn't matter because I thought you were a woman of some intellect. One who understood that sometimes the benefits to something outweigh the potential costs. If your parents feel that this marriage will give them more than what your marriage to Ragnar would give, then they will engage in the protection of it as well. You no longer have anything to fear from them. However, should we have excluded them from the happy event, I fear that they might have retaliated. It is all about ensuring that this gives them more than he could have. You must understand that."

She looked away from him, her throat working. "I understand. But you should have told me."

"Perhaps you should have warned me that we were going to get engaged two weeks ago."

"I didn't know…"

"And I simply made a decision when it came across my desk, Latika. One that I thought was best."

"I can't stand this. *I can't stand this.*" She exploded, all her reserve gone now. And not in the way he'd wanted. "None of my life is in my control. And I fear that it never will be."

"Are any of our lives ever in our control?"

"You're a prince," she sputtered, straightening her hands down at her sides, smacking against her full skirt. "You're a man. You have full control over your life. Control to disobey. Control to do whatever you like."

He grabbed hold of her arm and drew her close, something inside of him snapping. "You have no idea what my life has been like. You have no idea what I have been allowed to do, and not allowed to do. Or why I have made the decisions I've made. Do not speak to me about all the freedom you think I have."

He released his hold on her then, as the doors to the sanctuary opened, and Astrid appeared. Along with Mauro. And their child.

"Is everything all right?"

"Gunnar surprised me with a visit from my parents," Latika said, her tone wooden.

"I thought you knew," Astrid said.

"No."

Astrid treated him to an icy glare.

"I refuse to stand in between the two of you when you do that," Gunnar said. "I'm not a naughty child to be scolded. I made a decision that I thought would best protect my wife, Astrid. I will thank you to not undermine me."

His sister looked shocked, but said nothing.

"We are also not attending the reception," he continued.

Astrid looked doubly shocked at that. "What?"

"We are going away on our honeymoon. My wife clearly doesn't wish to be bothered by her parents. They have been given what they wanted. Access to the palace. I assume, Astrid, that you can make them feel welcome, while Latika gets a reprieve."

"Yes," Astrid said. "I can definitely do that."

"Good. Astrid will see to everything," he said to Latika. "Unless you wish to speak to your parents."

"No. I've made a life for myself, a space for myself where I'm not a pawn. And because of them...well, because of them, here we are. I have nothing to say to them."

"Well, this should handle them once and for all, shouldn't it? In the meantime, I have already taken the liberty of packing your things."

"Why are you doing this?" she asked. "You left the entire planning of the wedding to me, and now you're pulling rank?"

"Because, my dear. You're about to discover exactly how this protection is going to work. If you seek shelter with me, then you must deal with my commands. I'm terribly sorry if that interferes in some way with your preferences. But I am not a boy to be manipulated. You leapt out of the burning building into my arms, Latika. And now you must contend with the consequences."

And that was how Latika found herself thirty thousand feet in the air in Gunnar's lavish private jet. She had been in it before, once, when she had needed to meet Astrid somewhere in Europe, when they had been separated. She had thought it gaudy and extravagant then. She did not think it any better now.

Astrid's was all clean lines and taupe leather. Gunnar's was gold and black, a large bed at the center.

"Well, I see you haven't updated," she said waspishly, sitting down on one of the plush leather chairs, designed for a person to sink into the material. Rather than for lovely, modern form.

"It's comfortable," he said. "I believe in substance over style. When it comes to my furniture. In terms of myself, I obviously go with style. But something has to have substance."

"When did you plan for us to leave directly after the wedding?"

"The moment we were standing there and I saw how upset you were."

She couldn't tell if he was sincere. With Gunnar it was nearly impossible to tell. And yet it did something to her stomach to hear him say that. "Really."

"Yes," he said. "I did not mean to distress you by inviting your parents to the wedding. What I told you is true. I genuinely believed that it was the best thing. But there is no reason you should have to socialize with them. Anyway, I was already planning on taking you to the States for a honeymoon. And so that you could see my company."

"New York?"

"No," he said. "San Diego."

That surprised her. But, she also felt just slightly relieved that she didn't have to return to New York. She hadn't been since she had fled her family. And the idea of leaving her parents behind in his land, only to return to a place that she associated with her stifling upbringing didn't suit her.

"I've never been to California," she said.

"How is that possible?"

"We didn't travel that direction. We went to Europe often. Up and down the eastern seaboard. To India. We never had occasion to go to California."

"You'll like it," he said.

"How can you possibly say that with such certainty?" Like he knew her.

"Because it's different than Bjornland. It will be a nice change of pace. For one thing, the ocean is there."

She did miss the ocean. She had always adored visiting the atmospheric beaches of the Atlantic back home. And she adored Goa on holiday. Being introduced to another beach would be nice.

But she was still feeling angry at him, and determined not to allow him to see that she thought it might be nice at all.

It was sour of her, perhaps. But she still felt so very…

Fragile. And a bit like upon being moved around on a chessboard.

Is that fair? You are the one who went to him for help. For this kind of help. You backed him into a corner, and now you're angry with him.

Well. Yes. She was. She couldn't deny that.

"I still don't understand how you managed to keep that a secret."

"And like I told you, people don't go looking for something reputable when someone is wandering around throwing the disreputable in their face. They assume, of course that what I'd like to hide is my scandalous behavior. No one can quite comprehend the fact that I don't care much about that at all. Who would think to look for success?"

"But you go into the office and…"

"Sometimes. Everyone who works there has signed a gag order."

"You're kidding."

"I'm not. Of course, we will be doing away with all of that now. We will be making our debut at the company as husband and wife, and we will be having a proper show for the media. Where all will be revealed."

"Including why you hid it?"

He shook his head. "No. That's not a story I'll ever tell."

"Will you tell me?" Her question seemed to land in a dead space of air. Changing the feel of the room.

Ice blue eyes rested on hers. "No."

She suddenly felt frustrated. She couldn't get a read on him. It was as if this thing she had thought was a puddle all along had turned out to be a fathomless sea. She couldn't see the bottom. And she could not figure out how she had thought it was a puddle in the first place either.

And all of it left her feeling confused, and for a woman who was already feeling at the end of her tether with not knowing what to do in a situation, it was all a bit much.

"I made the right decision, then," she said.

"And that is what?"

"The decision to not share my body with you."

His gaze sharpened. "You think?"

"Yes. Because if you can't even share with me the story of why you started this company, then I don't know how we could ever share anything else."

"Are you so naïve that you imagine a meeting of bodies must also be a meeting of souls?"

She tilted her chin upward, her heart pounding heavily. "I already told you. I'm a virgin. So I wouldn't really know."

"I don't believe you," he said.

Of all the possible responses to that, this was not what she had imagined. "You don't believe me?"

"No. I think you're telling me that because I told you I didn't want to marry a virgin."

"Not everything is about you," she said. "My virginity certainly isn't."

"I don't believe that. Surely most things are about me."

"No, I hate to disappoint you."

"You don't kiss like a virgin."

Her stomach twisted. "How do I kiss?"

"Well, mostly like an indignant cat who would like to scratch my eyes out, and scratch my back, but isn't sure which she wants more."

"Well, that's close enough to the mark," she said.

"So you do want to leave claw marks down my back. Little virgin, that seems like something you couldn't possibly handle."

"If you're trying to goad me into sex, then you've badly miscalculated."

"I'm not trying to goad you into anything. Goading you is simply the natural way we communicate. I assumed it was our love language."

"I'm tired," she said.

She was. But that wasn't the primary reason she needed to be done with this. Because she felt too wounded, too raw, too fragile to deal with him.

"There's a bed just there."

"I won't share it with you."

"Fine by me. I've no interest in sleeping next to you."

"Why do you want me?" Her frustration boiled over. It made no sense. He made no sense. Why did he want her in particular? Particularly after all this time? Why did it seem to be her specifically? They didn't like each other. They didn't get along. And yet something drew her to him, and she could blame her lack of experience. But he... He could have his pick of women who didn't fight with him. Who didn't irritate him. So why he should want her... She just didn't know.

Suddenly, it was as if a wall dropped between them. "I don't know," he said, his voice rough. "And if I had an answer, perhaps I would not feel so driven to get you underneath me. But I don't know. I don't understand it. I have wanted you with a ferocity that defied logic ever since the first time I saw you. And then you opened your mouth, and I wanted, in equal parts to argue with you. I've never understood either compulsion."

Those eyes were such an intense blue. "People don't compel me, Latika. They don't make me do anything. You... You bring out responses in myself that even I don't understand. I don't like it."

She swallowed hard, her heart hammering. "I don't understand how a person can want to slap someone and kiss them."

"I think you and I have far too much chemistry," he said. "The good and the bad. And there doesn't seem to be very clear reason as to why it's so strong."

The talk of chemistry with that big bed right over there, with no escape, terrified her. Because there really was nothing holding her back from being with him.

Yes, there was her sense of self-preservation. Her desire to control the situation in which she had none. But... But she wanted him. And the question now was if she was truly intent on cutting off his nose and hers, which would spite his face, but hers as well.

The look in those blue eyes nearly undid her. And she nearly went to him. Nearly shamed herself by crawling onto his lap, pressing her mouth to his so that she might get another chance to taste him.

But then it hit her. That he was just another jailer. And the last thing she wanted was to end up with feelings for him. She had loved her parents, but it had not changed the fact that she'd been used by them.

This line of thinking made her head throb, because yes, she had been using Gunnar as well. But she was very afraid that her feelings were vulnerable to changing. That she might find herself caring for him, while he simply saw her as a means to an end. A man who had said his vows in a church, without blinking, while he had already made it very plain to her that he had no intention of keeping them.

"I'm tired," she reiterated. "I'm going to sleep."

CHAPTER SEVEN

WHEN LATIKA WOKE, the plane had touched down in San Diego and when she exited the plane, she was stunned by the brilliant blue. The sea, the sky. The Pacific in all its glory.

The sun on her skin was perfection.

She loved her adopted country, but it was a very cold climate. And even though she was used to the intensity of East Coast winters, she had always preferred blue skies.

She could definitely see why Gunnar had chosen to position his business here.

But, she didn't want to tell him that.

"We can go to my house. And then, we will continue on to take the tour of the business."

"You have a house here?" she asked.

"Of course I do. It would be a very silly thing to have offices here, and no house, don't you think?"

She realized that she had imagined that everything Gunnar did was silly. So, it had truly never occurred to her that there could be such hidden depths to him.

"You don't have to tell me the story," she said as they got into the limo that had met them. "But will you at least tell me why you have gone to such great lengths to play the part of court jester, when you're a prince."

"Court jester? I always thought I was quite like Prince Harry."

"Prince Harry is less shameless."

"You must understand," he said, his voice grave. "My father did not want my sister to rule the country. We were twins, with her born five minutes before me. And he did not feel that was sufficient reason to be denied the male heir that he felt the country deserved. My sister had to work so hard to prove to him that she was capable. And I did everything in my power to make them think that I might not be capable."

"All of this… It was a ruse for your father?"

"Not all. But yes, that certainly played into it."

"And you started the business because…"

"Because I was bored. Because a man of my age cannot be happy bouncing from club to club, and bed to bed of anonymous women endlessly."

"Can't they? It seems to me that a great many men would like you to think that they can."

"Without exception, I find the people with the widest smiles on their faces in establishments like that have the biggest holes inside of them."

"Including you?"

He lifted a shoulder. "I'm not entirely convinced that if you knocked on my chest it wouldn't sound hollow."

And yet, it was increasingly difficult for Latika to believe that. She thought that he wanted the world to believe it, but that he wasn't strictly true. She had called into question his caring about his sister, and she regretted that. She regretted it quite bitterly, because she had watched him play the role of protector to Astrid, in spite of the fact that his sister technically inhabited a loftier position than he did. She had the distinct feeling that Gunnar would risk his life for her.

"I don't think it's hollow," she said.

"Don't you?"

"You're helping me."

"I'm helping myself," he responded.

"Yes," she said. "I suppose so."

But there was something in the way he said all that that made her question things. And one of the biggest was if his heart was truly a hollow place, or if the real issue was that it was too full of something darker, that he refused to talk about.

The location of Gunnar's company surprised her. It wasn't situated in the Gaslamp Quarter, or in the business district of downtown. Rather, it was somewhere near old town, back up in the hills and overlooking the ocean. The entire place was built into the side of the mountain, made from shipping containers, glass cut into it, running from floor to ceiling. Parts of it were fashioned with wings from an old Boeing 747, creating a light, steel roof with strange and interesting curves. It blended in with the mountain, just the slightest link of shine, that seemed reflected again in the crystal-clear waves of the Pacific.

"This isn't what I expected," she said.

"Why would anything I do be expected?" he asked.

"I haven't the faintest idea."

The car wound up beside of the mountain, the wide, paved road offering a smooth, easy ride.

What surprised her, more than the appearance of the containers themselves, was that inside it was the epitome of modernity. Neutrals, and incredible natural light filtering in through all the glass and reflecting off the chrome beams that ran the length of the ceiling. The curves, and light metal of the wing that served as the roof offering strange interest to the place, which was more artiste than office.

He smiled when they entered. "Good morning," he said.

There were a great many staff, right there in the room. The building was open, with desks situated all around.

"Good morning," of course came back.

"Is there any news to report?" he asked.

"None," one of the women sitting nearest the door said. She was looking sideways at Gunnar, a questioning expression on her face.

"This is my wife," he said.

"We know that," one of the men toward the back said. "Your wedding was international news. Not that any of us could talk about the fact that we know you."

"I've been avoiding all mentions of it," one of the women said. "I didn't want to let anything slip."

"Well," Gunnar said. "Now you don't have to worry about it. Because the press is going to be here in the next ten minutes. We're going to go on a tour of the facility. This place isn't a secret anymore. The good news is for your trouble, you will all be getting raises."

A cheer erupted from the desks. And Latika couldn't get over just how comfortable everyone seemed to be with him. There was an ease to his interactions with all of these people that she would never have expected to find.

They all spoke to him not even just like he was a normal boss, but like he was a normal person.

Gunnar was neither of those things. Latika couldn't even squint and turn upside down to look at him and pretend it was so.

Latika did a brief circuit of the room, being introduced to everyone here in this portion of the office, and that was when the first reporter arrived.

All told, there were four of them, with cameras and recorders. And they followed Latika and Gunnar around the office, while he made broad, sweeping gestures and talked about the work this company had been doing for years, the strides they had made in both green energy and building.

Innovations that Latika knew about, but that she'd had no idea had been financed by research Gunnar had done.

"Why the secrecy?" One of the reporters asked when they reached the very top shipping crate, that was up two flights of stairs, nestled into a higher part of the mountain. The whole thing served as Gunnar's office, his desk overlooking the pristine ocean.

He was a man that always seemed at ease in his own skin. But here there was something more to it. This was his. The palace in Bjornland was decorated in tradition. And there were updates done now, but they were Astrid's.

This was Gunnar.

Large and at ease. Civilized. But with only a thin veneer between that civility and the wild, raging ocean.

"For a long while I felt it would distract from my efforts. My reputation has never been sterling. And I needed investors. Backers. People who would throw me their best researchers, so that we could make these things happen."

She had a feeling that the words slipping off his tongue were a lie. Very nice lies that everyone around them seemed to be swallowing.

But she didn't.

"And why is this a particular area of interest for you?" one of the reporters asked.

"Bjornland is one of the best examples of the majesty of nature. I grew up surrounded by mountains. Clear sky. I have always loved the outdoors. And I have always felt passionate about preserving it. You may know that I was part of creating a preserve in my home country that left many of the mountains off-limits to development."

He continued. "I was part of that effort in my late teens, and it is something that I found a great deal of satisfaction in. Going out and drinking the night away is fun, but there is little left of that good time in the morning. To be able to invest in something that will last, and to make that investment in the world that we all live in, that is the best thing I can think to do with my money. And it has been a profitable endeavor. Do not imagine that I am entirely altruistic. I assure you that I'm not." He laughed. "But, being with Latika has inspired me to live differently."

"And so the timing of this reveal does coincide with the wedding?" one of the reporters asked.

"How could it not?" Gunnar asked. "It has changed me. This marriage. Being with her. I can make of no better way to mark that, than by laying bare every aspect of who I am. I had to do it with her before we wed. The good and the ugly. I feel that the whole world is fairly apprised of my ugly. For Latika's sake, if nothing else, perhaps more of my good should be out there as well."

He took a few more questions, and then he dismissed them, leaving Gunnar and herself alone in the office.

"Is that all true?" she asked, her voice small in the large space. "About your investment in these projects?"

"Yes," he said. "I blackmailed my father for that preserve. I hope you know."

"You what?"

"I was eighteen, and he was considering an offer from a businessman to build resorts in some of the mountains that surrounded Bjornland. I'm not entirely opposed to development, Latika, you should understand. I'm a businessman in my heart, possibly more than I've ever been a prince. But the proposed plans were grotesque, and the footprint would have been disastrous on the natural wilderness. I went to my father with the proposed plans. That the resorts be put on a side of the country that had mountains already developed, and that we preserve a wilderness area for future generations. He... He did not agree. I reminded him that there were a few skeletons in his closet he would not like to be revealed. He wasn't happy with that. Wasn't happy with the realization that I had ammunition to lobby at him. But there was nothing he could do. So, that's how the preserve came to be. And so it remains. Astrid has expanded those protections. And, it is something that I have made an area of expertise. How we might continue to develop in the world in a smarter, more responsible way. We must live here on this planet. Why should we not live on it more gently?"

"Says a man with a private jet?"

A rueful smile curved his lips. "That was such a predictable statement, Latika, it was nearly boring."

"Then don't be a stereotype," she said.

"I didn't say I was a paragon of any sort of virtue. Simply that I care. And I attempt to affect change in the ways I do care. As humans what else can we do? We can talk about the things that concern us, but if we have the resources to change them and we never do... Better to never even pretend that we care."

She had nothing flippant to say to that. "It's been so long since I've been able to care about anything but myself. It's exhausting."

He frowned. "I have never been given to the impression that you are selfish."

"I am," she said. "The past three years of my life has been entirely devoted to avoiding detection. It doesn't mean that I don't care about Astrid. I always have. But beneath all of it, has been concern for myself. I've had to be wrapped up in the concerns of my own survival all this time. I look forward to being able to care about something else."

She had been so mired in the idea that marrying Gunnar was to submit herself to another version of captivity that she hadn't seen it from that angle. But hearing Gunnar talking about caring for bigger things brought the reality of her own existence sharply to life. It had become closed. It had become small and mean, of necessity and that wasn't the life she wanted.

"Are you hungry?"

She blinked. "My body has no idea what time it is. I think I might be hungry. I might be exhausted. Or ready to run a marathon."

"I find the best thing to do with jet lag is to just start

eating, and keep eating so that you don't fall asleep before you are supposed to. Difficult to go to sleep while chewing steak."

She laughed. "I suppose it would be."

"Come," he said. "And let us return to my house."

CHAPTER EIGHT

GUNNAR KNEW THAT his home was impressive.

A feat of architecture. Made entirely of recycled woods and metals, and constructed into the natural shape of the mountain it was built into. He took for granted the effortless beauty of the place.

But Latika's expression of awe when they pulled up to the house forced him to look at it with new eyes. It created in him a strange sense of pride that was almost entirely unfamiliar.

He had instructed his staff to be absent upon their arrival, and to have dinner laid out and waiting. He was not disappointed, he never was. For he had learned early on that if he surrounded himself with people who thrived on the same level of excellence that he did, then everyone could exist happily.

Every member of his staff had to be almost as type A as he was. Those with less intense personality types would be miserable working for him anyway. And he found, oddly, that surrounding himself with people who had similar levels of intensity created a more serene work environment. Everyone bumped along nicely, no one impeding the progress of anyone else. Gunnar had gone and dressed for dinner, a white shirt and a pair of black pants, and he had asked Latika to do the same. Much like dinner, clothing had been laid out in advance already as well.

Some of her own things had been packed when they had left Bjornland, but he had also taken the liberty of having Astrid's stylist procure some new items.

He had expected the spread set out for them on the expansive terrace that overlooked the ocean to be perfect. And he had expected Latika to look beautiful. She always did. But he had not expected the site of her walking out of the house, wearing a dress that exposed her shapely, brown legs, and showed off her body in a way that would make any man fall to his knees and worship, to leave him utterly breathless.

He had been with some of the most beautiful women in the world. He considered his palate somewhat jaded.

But he had never been with Latika.

And suddenly, that truth felt like too heavy a thing to endure. He wanted her. With ferocity, he wanted her. There was something to her that went beyond beauty. It shimmered across her skin, captured him by the throat, with each shift and slide of that glossy black hair that hung down past her shoulder.

The dress was red. But that didn't matter. Because it *covered* her. Obscured her from his view, and that made it an irritation, rather than anything of note. She seemed oblivious to the fact that she had stunned him completely. That she had reached down inside of him and rearranged things within him so that he could not find his balance.

Like walking into a familiar room and finding the furniture somewhere unexpected.

"This really is quite lovely," she said, crossing the place.

He moved, pulling her chair out for her.

She lifted a brow. "Aren't you the perfect gentleman?"

He chuckled. "I should think a rather imperfect one."

"Perhaps." She pondered that for a moment. "Yes, you do like that story."

"It is isn't a story. It's true. The fact that I put work into a nature preserve, and give a damn about the future of the planet doesn't change these other things about me."

"I suppose not," she said.

"Does it make you feel better to imagine you might be married to someone a bit more decent then you initially thought? After all, ours is not a romantic entanglement. Is it just that you feel the need to have good feelings about partnerships?"

"No," she said. "It's because I find this version of you slightly more interesting."

"Well, I do live to be of interest to you." The words felt true. And he couldn't figure out why, when he'd meant them to be dry.

"I want to know the story," she said. "Because I can't quite piece together all these things I know about you and make one picture. I don't quite understand. I would like to."

"Why?"

"Because from the first moment I met you I… I felt drawn to you. I could not figure out why. I think the answer is in this, and I want the answer."

"Because it damages you so much to think that you want a man you don't like?"

"Maybe," she said. "But I'd like to think it's more complex than that."

"It probably isn't. We people are not overly complex. We want peace. And that's hard to come by, so when we can't find that, we chase oblivion. Through drink. Through drugs. Sex. Our bodies are inclined toward that which is a natural stimulant to us. Oftentimes emotion is separate entirely from that. People will sacrifice whole lives they've built on the offer of being entertained for a few hours. Why should you imagine you're above that?"

"Mostly because I'd like to think I don't even see a carnival ride or a glass of whiskey."

"If you have concerns about that, make it for your own sensibilities, not mine. I for one am completely comfortable being a ride for you."

"Even a ride came into being somehow. Everything was built, Gunnar, even you. And as much as you like to pretend that isn't so, as much as you like to pretend there is no authenticity in you, we both know it isn't true."

"My story is altogether uninteresting. I'm nothing more than a pampered prince, after all."

"If that's what you need me to believe."

It was the boredom in her voice that bothered him. And as they ate their meal, looking out at the ocean beyond, he did his best not to brood on it. It didn't matter whether Latika thought him interesting. He was beyond caring what other people thought, and that included her. They ate in relative silence, and he endeavored to not think overmuch about it.

"It's a strange thing," she said softly. "Growing up in a gilded cage. I understand that better than most. I was nothing but a pawn to my parents. The means by which they could gain some kind of power. I always suspected they weren't able to have more children. Because if they had a son, I think they would have been happy. Except... Maybe not. Because a daughter is an interesting pawn to use to gain greater leverage. Nobility, that was their aim. A daughter is much more useful in that sense."

"I have never thought of it that way, but I imagine so. My own father would have likely been much happier if he could have used me as a ruler, and my sister to consolidate power."

"Of course," Latika said. "My parents' greatest goal was to marry me off to someone like you. They poured every resource into me. Into making me beautiful. Into making me sophisticated. They gave me lessons. I play the piano, you know. And am minorly accomplished in ballet. I learned everything there was to know. Not so much that I would be too smart for whatever man they put me in front of, but just enough that I might be able to carry on a conversation seamlessly. That was very important to them. But none of it was about enriching me. It all about making me into the prettiest of pets."

Gunnar's lip curled. "Like being sent to obedience training."

The idea of Latika being used in that way appalled him.

She continued. "And I understand that so many people on this earth have it worse. That they must worry about their daily survival. In terms of when they might eat again. How they can find shelter. But for so long I was a creation of my parents, and then I spent all those years in hiding. I understand. I understand that you can be surrounded by the greatest beauty in the world, by all the things that money can buy. But if the people around you only want to use you…it's empty."

"Yes, well," he said, "That is very unusual. A couple of poor little rich kids who feel assaulted by their privileged pasts. Actually, that's most dinner parties that I go to on a given day."

He regretted the words as soon as he spoke them, because Latika had been sincere. Sincerity was not something he had a great deal of experience with and it showed here. It made him deeply uncomfortable, her sharing with him. He had given her nothing and yet, she shared things that had wounded her.

But as far as he could see, it wouldn't benefit anyone for him to get into an in-depth discussion of his past.

On the other hand, there was also no reason not to.

He knew why he didn't tell Astrid. She didn't want his sister bearing any measure of burden over the things their father had done to him. But even more so, he didn't want her wounded by the knowledge of just how drastic the measures her father had been willing to take were. She knew that he had opposed her. But, all that their father had ever let Astrid see was vague disapproval. He had set up a council to obstruct her, and that had been an inconvenience. She had certainly felt the sting, the lack of their father's trust. But she didn't know the more sinister elements of his opposition.

And he never wanted her to.

There was no reason to spare Latika from the truth. And indeed, Gunnar was a resilient man. One who might bear some scars on his body, but was otherwise fine in his soul. Such as it was.

"How much has my sister told you about our father?"

"I know that he was opposed to her being the heir. But also that there was nothing he could do."

"Much of that was due to our mother," Gunnar said. "Our mother was a strong-willed woman. I always wondered why she married him. So, I suppose the title speaks for itself. Our mother made it impossible for him to simply install me onto the throne, as much as he would have liked that. Our mother made it known the world over within ten minutes of our birth that it was my sister who was the rightful heir."

"Would you have wanted to be the heir?"

"I would have done it," Gunnar said. "Anyone who wants such a mantle should not have it in the first place."

"That is probably very true."

"The weight of the crown is heavy. And Astrid's crown twice that of what many people in her position would experience. She had to be absolutely perfect. Perfect in a way that I would not have been expected to be. No, I have never envied her. Neither have I resented her. My father wished that I would. My sister's view of things was that our father favored me, but it could not be further from the truth. I am my father's biggest disappointment. What he wished for, more than anything else was for a son who craved power with the kind of avarice that he did. He wanted a son who could be trained to desire power above all else."

He watched as her face shifted, a softness to her dark eyes that he'd never seen directed at him. "But what my father never understood was the bond that twins share. My sister is a part of me. I would die for her. I would no more betray her than myself. For me, it would be impossible. When he found that he could not simply suggest that to me, he tried to force a change of heart.

He tried with everything in him. There is a dungeon in the palace, if you didn't know. And my father was not above making use of it."

Latika's face contorted. "Gunnar..."

"If I tell you this, you must promise me you will not speak of it to my sister."

"Astrid is my best friend..."

"It doesn't matter," he said. "I'm your husband. And if what you desire is intimate knowledge of my secrets, then you must understand why I have kept them."

"I want to know," she said.

"And if you want to protect Astrid, you will swear to me that she will never know."

"I swear it," Latika said, her voice a hushed whisper.

He knew there was dessert in the kitchen, but he decided to leave that bit of information. No matter how good the Princess cake, it would not be good with this story. It would likely curdle soon.

"My father didn't just doubt my sister's ability to rule. He actively despised that she would. For my father, the monarchy and the patriarchy went hand in hand. He wanted me to be his successor. But he knew that he couldn't simply demand it. First of all, we have a government in Bjornland. A council. And while that council was very loyal to my father, while they would certainly have enforced his rule in normal circumstances, the outright replacement of an heir would have been unprecedented, and indeed, would have likely been impossible without inciting some sort of civil war. When the heir to the throne is born, the military swears their allegiance. Their allegiance to the heir is equal to that of the King. It is the same with the council."

"So..."

"Short of killing my sister there was nothing he could do," Gunnar said.

"He would never have done that," Latika said, the horror laced through her tone so pure it made him feel all manner of soft things for her. He wanted to protect her from this too.

"I don't know," Gunnar responded. "But, he didn't. So, I don't know how much of that was out of the grace and goodness of his heart, and how much of that was a desire to never tarnish his legacy. You see, that was what it was all about. The desire to install me as heir was all about the perfect articulation of his legacy. To be caught murdering his own child…"

"I can't believe it," Latika said.

"Because you didn't know my father. But of course, he knew that I would have just as difficult a time taking the throne by force. But he thought that I might be able to…persuade my sister to step down. He began to educate me, as a boy, about the facts of life. He tried to instill in me an idea that women were weak. That a female ruler could never be as strong as a male counterpart. But I knew my sister. I knew my mother. While my mother wasn't perfect, her strength was unsurpassed. That is not up for debate. I can see all around me evidence that what my father said wasn't true. Astrid surpassed me in patience, and kindness. And to me, those things are a particular form of strength. One that has no sense of being threatened. Astrid is, and always will be, to my mind the rightful ruler of our nation. And nothing my father said could make me turn against her. And that was when he decided to try other methods."

"How could he possibly think he would get away with this? He wouldn't come after your sister… You…"

"Yes, he came for me. He would lock me in the dungeon for days at a time. And he would try to get me to say that I was superior. That the country would be better off with me. And I refused. What he did… It had the opposite effect. The decision that I made down in that dungeon was that I would never be manipulated. I swore my allegiance to my sister over and over again in my head, and out loud when my father came. I refused to allow him space in my head."

Gunnar could no longer look at Latika as he continued. "He didn't deserve it. And if I was truly so strong as he kept insisting I was… Well then. I felt that I should show it. Because if I had any piece of a true leader inside of me, then there should be no man on earth who can tell me what. Ironically, it was in opposing him that I found my sense of strength. And then, eventually I was no longer a boy, but closer to being a man, and my father knew that his ability to harm me, his ability to overpower me had come to an end."

"All of this happened when you were a boy?"

"Yes. That is how…bullies like to behave. Is that not what they say?"

"Gunnar," she said. "How did you survive?"

"I had purpose. My purpose was to protect Astrid."

"And then in order to flaunt your freedom from your father you… That's how you became you."

"I took great joy in forcing him to question all that he thought about who his heir should be, and how the country should be run. I took great joy in proving to him that the fact I was born a boy did not make me more suitable than my sister. Rather than her being the real thorn in his side for the rest of his days, I like to think that it was me. Solidifying to the people of the country that Astrid was the clear and rightful heir. By the time Astrid ascended the throne, I daresay there was not a single person in the entire country that wished I were their King. Do not mistake me. I don't think my sister needed my bad example to shine. But…"

"The world is a harsh and old-fashioned place," Latika said. "You don't have to tell me what it's like, you don't have to."

"So there you have it. My origin story. I'm basically a superhero movie."

Latika took a breath, and then she rose up from her seat at the table. And before Gunnar knew what was happening, she dropped to her knees before him, taking his hands in hers. "I don't know what to say."

"Don't get on your knees before me unless you intend to do something of interest with your mouth," he said, his knee-jerk reaction to seeing her sympathy.

As if taking it up as a calling, Latika stood, bending at the waist and grabbing hold of his chin. Then she closed the distance between them, and kissed him.

CHAPTER NINE

LATIKA THOUGHT THAT she might be crazy. Because this emotion and fire running through her blood was something she had never dealt with before. Because it was something that was foreign to her. Utterly and completely foreign. And yet familiar all at the same time.

Gunnar.

She wanted to touch him. She wanted to reach him. Wanted to pour all of her feelings out into his body.

For that boy that he was. That boy who must've been so terrified. Who resisted every attempt at being indoctrinated.

For the man he'd become. Arrogant and exasperating and so utterly brilliant.

She had known that he was strong, but she had only ever seen it in his irreverence. She saw now that it was his shield. That he had used it to protect himself from a Machiavellian father who had perhaps taken more joy in the attempted manipulation of his children than he cared for the outcome.

And Gunnar had kept it to himself. He had hidden it from Astrid so that she would never know the pain he endured on her behalf.

So she would be spared the full brunt of knowing her father's hatred.

The Playboy Prince was not the disgrace of the royal family of Bjornland. He was the crown jewel.

Latika had disdained him from the moment she had met him, but she had wanted him.

And she had been wrong. So utterly and completely wrong.

The man had been tortured by his father.

She kissed him deeper, allowing her thoughts to fall away. Allowing nothing more than the physical home of desire to exist between them. Gunnar growled, pulling her onto his lap.

His hold was strong, his kiss turning desperate. It was deep and intense, his tongue sliding against hers, his whiskers resting against her cheek.

Her Viking marauder who seemed intent on claiming her. No matter that she was the one who had started the kiss.

But that was all right.

If he needed to be the one to stake the claim, she could allow that. She could be that for him.

What she'd said to him had been true. She had gone without sex for twenty-four years. And in this moment, it became clear that what she had been waiting for was this. Not him specifically, but this feeling. For desire to be tattooed on every beat of her heart. For it to be an undeniable, brilliant force that she could not and did not want to deny.

"I want to see you here," he growled.

"I want to…"

"No," he said. "I have a fantasy of you," he said, standing up from the chair, holding on to her. She wrapped her legs around his waist to keep herself from sliding onto the ground. And then he walked her over to the wall and braced her back against it.

She could see him, his eyes a brilliant blue, the same as the sea behind him. Then he lifted her. Lifted her up and maneuvered her so that her thighs were over his shoulders, the wall bracing her up right.

She gasped.

He chuckled.

Then put his face directly between her thighs, with only a thin scrap of underwear keeping him from seeing everything. He held her fast with his arm, and tilted his head, kissing her inner thigh, and then he pushed her dress upward, the fabric bunching around her hips, first on one side and then the other.

"These," he said, "are very pretty." He dragged the back of his knuckle over her crease, and she squirmed. "Pity." Then he gripped the center of her panties and tugged hard, tearing the fabric. It fell free, exposing her to him, and to the open air.

"The beauty of living up on a hill like this," he said, "is that while we have a great view of all this, no one has a view of us. Latika," he whispered, pressing a kiss even higher to her inner thigh. "Latika." Then he turned his head, his tongue painting a hot stripe of pleasure over her flesh as he tasted her, deep and intense.

She gasped, letting her head fall back. She did not know how they had gotten here. With her comforting him only a moment ago, and now with him licking her in her most intimate place up against a wall. He was so big, his shoulders so broad, one large hand bracing her, holding her ass, and the other teasing her as he continued to lavish attention on her with his mouth. He made her feel small, feminine and delicate.

And most important of all, he made her feel wild.

She hadn't known. Oh, she had realized there was something hot and magical that simmered between them. Something dark and rich and unknowable. But she hadn't known that it would feel like this.

No, she'd had no idea.

She hadn't known that anything could be like this. She arched against him as he continued to lick his way to her center, as he moved his hand, sliding one finger inside of her. She gasped, rolling her hips forward, pleasure crashing over her like a wave. A precursor of something that felt like it would be bigger. Deeper.

She was desperate for something to hold onto. She put one hand on the back of his head, pushing her fingers through his blond hair, and gripped his broad, muscular shoulder with the other.

And he continued to eat her like she was dessert.

Continued to tease and torment her with that finger buried deep inside of her. One that became two, the rhythm becoming so slick and beautiful and perfect that she could barely breathe.

And then it hit. Her pleasure breaking her in half. She squeezed her legs together, rolling her hips forward and pushing his head toward her as she rode out the intense peak pleasure. And then she relaxed, letting her head fall back, releasing her hold on him. Then she realized the only thing keeping her from falling down to the earth was the fact that he was holding onto her. He lifted her easily from his shoulders and pulled her into his arms. "You are beyond anything I could have guessed you might be," he said, his voice rough.

"So are you," she said, feeling dizzy.

"I want you," he said. "More than I can remember wanting anything. When I was down in that dungeon I used to think of things that I like. Cars. Cake. My desires were simple then. Moving into adolescence, I thought an awful lot about women. I would picture things I wanted and couldn't have over and over again."

His words were rough. Compelling. Like he was touching her. Over her body. In her body. She was on fire.

"A study in perfect, torturous deprivation," he continued. "And once I got my freedom I never wanted for anything again. I wouldn't allow it. I indulged in everything. Until you. You... I wanted you from the moment I first saw you. And you made me wait. Oh, Latika you don't even know what a sin that is. To a man like me..."

"Have me," she said, her whole body electric with want.

He could. He could have her. Out here if he wanted to. Against the wall. On the floor. Whatever he wanted, he could have. Whatever he needed, she would become. For him, she would do anything.

He growled, picking her up and sweeping her into his arms, blazing a path into the house. He left the door open behind them, but it was clear that he felt secure and isolated up here in his house on the top of the mountain. He carried her up the stairs, and she barely had the chance to take in the beauty before her.

All the clean lines, warm, honey-colored wood panels and open, sun-drenched vistas provided by the windows that overtook each and every wall.

They went up three flights of stairs, to a bedroom that was positioned higher than the rest of the house, built into the side of the hill, made entirely of windows that looked out over the sea that faded from jade to deepest navy. White-capped waves swelled reaching up toward the sky that was open and like the desire the swelling inside of Latika.

So soon.

So *impossibly* soon after the peak he had just brought her to. The bed itself was large, white and spare, upon a raised platform that put it in line with the view below.

And it loomed larger still, as he carried Latika to it, setting her down on the plush surface.

He laid her down on her back, and she blushed when she realized that her legs had fallen open, and that she was still naked beneath her dress.

"Too late for modesty," he said, pushing his hand against her knee and holding her legs open before she could close them.

Then he moved up her body, reaching around behind her and undoing the zipper on the little red dress that had barely gotten an hour's worth of wear. He pulled down, exposing the bra she was wearing beneath. Lacy and insubstantial, with gaps between the intricate flower design, giving him a clear view of the shape of her nipples.

She knew. Because she had put it on and looked in the mirror and wondered what he might think.

Those eyes became a blue flame, the desire in them so clear, so potent, that she didn't have to wonder.

He wanted her. She had been so focused on wanting to make him feel good that she hadn't fully realized what a wonderful thing it was for her to be wanted by him.

No one had ever wanted her. Not her, as she was.

They wanted her to be the perfect daughter and representation of all that they were. Wanted her to be a perfect prisoner and a slave.

She had been the daughter. A fugitive. An assistant.

Never just a woman. And now, with Gunnar's hungry gaze roaming over her curves, woman was exactly what she became. What she felt, straight down to her soul. He pulled the dress the rest of the way from her body and cast it onto the floor.

Then he moved back to her, unhooking her bra and sending it the same direction as the dress. She still had her shoes on, and it should feel ridiculous, her knees bent, her elbows propping her up, her black hair cascading over her body like a wave.

Like she was a pinup, and not a virgin about to surrender to a man with more experience than she could possibly imagine.

But whether she was Madonna or siren, Gunnar didn't seem to mind. He growled, lowering his head and pressing a kiss to her neck, nibbling his way to her jaw, and to her lips, where he treated her to kiss after drugging kiss, ecstasy making her limbs feel heavy.

Then he tore himself away from her mouth again, making his way down, kissing the delicate skin around her breasts, knee, before moving up to suck her nipple.

She gasped, shocked at the arrow of pleasure that pierced her, so deep and so true she wouldn't have thought that she could feel such pleasure again. Not so close to what he had given her release before.

But still she felt it. And it left her utterly transfixed, in desperate need of more.

"You," she murmured even as he moved over to her

other breast, licking and sucking, bringing her nipple into its heightened point. "I need you."

He stood, and began to unbutton his shirt, letting it fall open, revealing that beautiful body she had admired so many times. Those perfect muscles, dusted with just the right amount of hair.

And then he moved his hands to his belt, and her throat went dry. This was the part of him that remained a mystery to her, and the very idea of seeing him now sent little rivulets of pleasure straight through her.

She wanted him.

Wanted *this*.

He pushed his hands down, along with his underwear, and her breath left her body. He was beautiful. Every inch of him.

And there were a great many inches.

No wonder women lost their minds over this man.

He was everything a man should be. Large and broad and thick all over. The most stunning sight she ever beheld. He was art.

A man seemingly carved from marble and made into hot, delicious flesh.

"See anything you like?" His lips tipped upward, that indolent smile she knew so well curving that wicked mouth.

"Just you," she said, breathless. "That's all."

He growled, coming down onto the bed with her, every inch of his naked body touching every inch of hers. She rolled against him, desperately needy.

He kissed her.

Kissed her until she was slick with her need for him. Kissed her until she felt hollow. Until she thought she might die of the need to have him inside of her. He wrapped his hand around his heavy length, pressing the head to the entrance of her body, then drawing the moisture from inside of her and up the sensitive bundle of nerves at the apex of her thighs.

He teased her like that, teased them both, slowly, sensually, the pleasure like a lightning strike as he did. When he finally placed that thick head back in her entrance, she was trembling. Ready to make him come inside of her.

She might not know if it would hurt, and exactly what it would feel like, but she knew it was what she needed. Knew that only this would bring the fulfillment that she craved.

He rocked his hips forward, and she gasped when he reached the much discussed hymen, but he didn't seem to notice, as he rolled his hips forward, filling her completely.

It hurt, but only for a moment. And then it was nothing but a sense of completion. Of desire deep and real, as her internal muscles gripped him and seemed to pull him deeper inside.

She rocked her hips against his body, and it was like gasoline thrown onto a lit match. They combusted. His thrusts were wild, and seeing him like this, feral and without that urbane wit that he used as a shield between himself and the world, seeing him pure and unguarded, his teeth bared like an animal, his ice blue eyes hot and fierce, his entire body reverberating with a growl every time he claimed her body with his own, was the most intoxicating aphrodisiac that Latika could have ever fathomed. She'd never known how wonderful it could be to be desired by a man.

No. Not by a man.

By *this* man.

This man was everything.

He thrust home, grinding his hips against hers, release bursting overhead like fireworks. And then on a growl, he seemed to give up his control, his big body shook as his length pulsed inside of her, as he spilled himself into her.

And then they lay together, breathing hard, slick with sweat, and all tangled up in each other. Then he moved away from her, with shocking speed and the fluid grace of a panther.

"You were a virgin," he said.

She rolled to the side, revealing a spot of blood, shame filling her. "Yes," she said.

"Then tell me, Latika. You don't happen to be taking the pill, do you?"

And that was when she realized, that she and Gunnar did not use protection.

And given the timing of the month, the risk of her getting pregnant was very real.

Gunnar's pulse was hammering wildly out of control. "Are you on anything?" he repeated.

"No," she answered. The answer that he knew she would give. Rage spiraled through his veins.

"I told you that I never want to have children."

"I wasn't thinking," she said, her face getting pale. "I…"

"I don't believe you," he said, rage an unforgiving, unreasonable monster in his gut.

And when he got down past that bright, burning rage, there was something far worse under it. A sense that he had to escape his skin. That his body, his very essence, had betrayed him and there was no fixing it.

Things had been set into motion that could now not be stopped and the absolute terror he felt over that...

Over the possibility of fatherhood.

He couldn't breathe.

"I don't care what you believe," Latika said. "I didn't think of it. You clearly didn't either, so I don't know why I should be the focus of your rage."

"Is there a pill you can take?" There had to be something. A way to turn back the clock. To stop the mistake.

Her expression contorted. Shock. To pain. To rage. "I refuse," she said. "What will be will be, the mistake was ours, and I'm not going to reverse course and make a decision that I will personally regret."

"Because you want a baby," he said. "And that was your goal along."

She frowned. "No. I do want to have a baby. I always have. But to act as if I was somehow using my feminine wiles to manipulate you..." She stood up, hunting for her dress. "There are easier ways to get sperm, Gunnar. Every single one of them involves not having to put up with you."

"Yet, producing a child with me comes as a very hefty reward, I should think."

"I married you already," she snapped. "Where's the benefit of manipulating you? How would that get me money I don't already have access to?"

He knew that what she was saying was true, and that his response was unreasonable. And yet, he could not stop himself. Panic was overtaking him now, and it was an emotion he was not familiar with.

He had spent days locked in a dungeon in the castle

in Bjornland, and not felt panic. He did not know who he was, and if he despised her for anything, it was this most of all.

He felt like his skin was not his own, and that was something that could not be endured.

"I will have nothing to do with the child," he said.

He expected the words to bring with them a rush of relief. Because it was a decision, if nothing else, and it was the unknown that he could not bear above all else.

But he felt no relief. Instead, all he felt was a sick kind of grim determination that settled low in his stomach and refused to be moved.

"You won't have anything to do with your own child?"

"I already told you how things would be. You are the one who refuses to be reasonable here."

"Fine. Then you may have nothing to do with the child. But if there is a child, and that is your stance, you will have nothing to do with me either. You wanted me. You had me. Understand that it is the last time."

"That's it then? Your first time will be your last?"

She whirled around, her eyes a glittering brown blaze. "It will not be my last. I will go about my life as if I do not have a husband who would deny his own child. I will be discreet, but trust that I will find someone who will share my life with me. And if you seek to cast me out, then the world will know of your cruelty. If Ragnar comes and scoops me up because you deny me your protection, when I have your child, then what will the world think of you? And isn't that why you're doing this? So the world will think better of you. I thought… I thought beneath it all was a good man. But no. You're a bad man, Gunnar. And just because you did something good for your sister doesn't erase that."

Fury rose up inside of him and he reached out, grabbing hold of her arm. "Don't you think I know that? Don't you think I already know that I'm dark beyond the telling of it? It doesn't matter how much light I throw onto myself, doesn't matter how much I pretend to be a man filled with nothing but cares for where his next drink might come from, that I don't know that my soul is a pit."

He released his hold on her.

"Even if there is no child, you will not touch me," she said. "I could never be with a man who would say the things that you have. Who thinks the way that you do. I'm appalled by you. Disgusted. As much as I ever wanted you. I'm going to shower now. I need to wash you off of me."

She turned and went into the shower, and he let her go.

He prowled down the hall, pacing back and forth, and then he went into his office. He looked out over the ocean. He would have liked to stay here longer, but their time here was at an end. He had accomplished what he had come for. They had made a show of his company. Had revealed what a fantastically generous soul he was. But he was more than he had always shown the public.

And he had revealed to Latika just how broken he was.

All the sharp edges that lived inside of him that would only cut those who dared come closest to him.

It was time to leave.

He made a phone call to his pilot. "Ready the plane. We depart first thing in the morning."

CHAPTER TEN

THE TRIP BACK to Bjornland was worse than the trip to the States. Latika was reeling from the speed at which they had boomeranged between one continent and another. And if the bed had been uncomfortable and awkward, looming large on the plane on the way over, it was worse now.

Worse now that she had been with him. Worse now she knew all the things he could make her feel in a bed like that.

She felt sick with regret. With sadness.

Because she had felt… For one fleeting moment she had thought maybe she'd found love.

Oh, she wasn't so foolish to think that Gunnar would have immediately fallen in love with her, just because he had bared his soul. But she had felt something for him. Something that had surpassed anything. As if he was what her heart had been waiting for all along. And then it had been for nothing.

Because he had revealed the truth of himself.

He would ignore their child, would hold himself separate. Would sleep with her, and disavow a life they had created.

And she could not endure that. She could not set a child up for that kind of pain.

Nor herself.

She felt sick with worry. Sick with regret.

When they finally arrived in Bjornland, they did not go to the palace, but to Gunnar's apartments.

She didn't know why that surprised her.

"We will be living here," he said. "Your things have already been moved."

"Of course," she said, feeling like she was floating outside of her body.

On numb feet she walked into the bedroom that he had gestured toward. All her things were there. And it was separate from his.

That was a good thing. Because the only thing she could see happening now was the two of them living separate lives.

In this space that was so much smaller than the palace.

She flung herself down onto the bed, and she couldn't cry. Instead she just lay there with eyes that felt like they had been rubbed with sand.

The next week was a blur, the days leading together like strokes of watercolor on a page.

Except they weren't blurry, no. Latika was all too tied in with what was happening in her life.

And worst of all the things she hadn't fully thought through, she was not Astrid's assistant anymore.

She was robbed of the thing that used to keep her occupied. And robbed of an excuse to spend time with her best friend.

On the fourth day since they returned home, Astrid called her.

"You know, it's quite ridiculous that you're acting as if we can't spend time together simply because you don't work for me anymore."

The truth of the matter was, Latika was partly avoiding Astrid, because she didn't want her friend to notice how sad she was.

She couldn't talk to her about Gunnar's revelations, because she had promised, and because she understood why Gunnar felt that way. She agreed with him. To reveal everything would be to harm Astrid, and Latika didn't want to do that. But she was bored, and she and Gunnar hadn't spoken in days. Her husband came and went like a thief in the night, and otherwise was never home.

She wondered—with a brilliant, burning stab in her chest—if he was already in the beds of other women.

And why shouldn't he be?

Just because he'd been with her a few days earlier wouldn't keep him from seeking another lover. It never had before, not with any other woman, so why would it be different with her? He had made it plain she didn't really matter to him.

So when she had been back a week, she entered the palace for the first time since her marriage and walked slowly into Astrid's personal parlor.

"Hi," Astrid said.

"Hello," Latika responded.

"You don't look good," Astrid said.

"It's fine," Latika said.

"Is being married to my brother such a trial?"

She tried to force a smile. "I knew you would ask me about him."

"Is that why you were avoiding me?"

"No," she said slowly. "Things are strange. Things have changed. And I didn't want to assume…"

"Our friendship is more than you working for me. It's even more than you being married to my brother. I care about you because I care about you. It isn't connected to what you can do for me."

Latika was suddenly so very glad she came, because she had never needed to hear something more in her entire life. It was the thing that she had longed to hear from her parents. The thing she had been hungry for in a relationship all her life.

"Thank you," she said, with deep sincerity. "Thank you. I'm not sure anyone else has ever felt that way."

"Then the other people in your life are fools. And if my brother is one of them, so is he."

They let go of talk of Gunnar, and instead enjoyed lunch, until Astrid's phone rang. She picked it up, her brows shooting upward. "Really? You are sure. You are absolutely certain. Because if this is a hoax of some kind… No. I understand. I'll tell her."

Astrid hung up the phone and leveled her gaze at Latika. "Ragnar is dead."

And just like that, her world, that had seemed right for a moment, turned itself on its head again.

Latika waited. She waited until darkness fell. And Gunnar was still not home. Then she procured the use of his private plane, which was available to her even when she had been Astrid's assistant, and was now unquestionably available to her as his wife.

She flew to Italy. Then requested the jet be sent back home.

From there she got a ticket through a commercial airline and flew to England.

She had money in accounts there. And she knew that if he really wanted to, he could likely find her. But, it would take a little bit of time. Because she had secured her money using an alias, as she had done with her credit cards. Saving them for an emergency. For years, she had no need to spend her earnings as Astrid's assistant that she had socked away, hidden from both her parents and Ragnar.

Ragnar was dead. Something so benign as a heart attack seemed so bizarre given how things had been. But that was what had killed him.

And because Ragnar was dead she did not have to stay with Gunnar.

She booked herself into a hotel room near Piccadilly, cursing the proximity to such insanity, but also grateful for the last-minute availability.

Then she collapsed onto the bed.

And this time tears came.

And when they began to fall, she feared they wouldn't stop.

She was free now. Free from everything. But it didn't feel like freedom. It felt like nothing she would've ever wanted for herself, and for the life of her, she couldn't figure out why.

Gunnar.

She didn't want to believe it.

Didn't want to believe that a man who would say those things to her, who would reject his own child like that, could possibly be the reason she suddenly felt like she didn't want the thing she had been craving all her life.

"I have no obligation to anyone," she said into the empty room. "I am free to go where I want. To do what I want."

She waited for that truth to sink in. Waited for it to make her feel good.

It never did.

When Gunnar arrived back home in the wee hours of the morning, something felt strange in the apartment.

But he had spent the evening working at an office that he owned downtown in the capital city of Bjornland—completely unnecessarily, as he could easily work in the palace, or at home—and he was exhausted. He collapsed into bed without investigating the source of the feeling.

He woke the next morning, it persisted.

Typically, he was out until after Latika went to bed, and she was gone by the time he woke up. So the emptiness in the apartment was normal enough. He went to look at her room, and found everything as it should be. Her clothes were hanging in the closet, her shoes lined up.

But then, late that night when he came home again, he checked, and she still hadn't returned.

He called Astrid. "Do you have any idea where my wife is?"

"No," said, her voice filled with concern.

"If that bastard Ragnar…"

"Ragnar is dead," Astrid said.

"What?"

"Latika didn't tell you?"

"No. I haven't seen her. When did you discover this?"

"Early the day before yesterday. You haven't spoken to her since then?"

"I… I haven't seen her."

"Gunnar!" Astrid sounded incredulous. "You haven't seen your wife in two days, your wife has been under threat, and you didn't think to say anything about it?"

"We don't go out of our way to spend much time together," he said, his voice flat.

"I don't know what's going on between the two…"

"Nothing," Gunter said. "Nothing is going on between the two of us."

"That isn't right *when you're married.*"

"You know we didn't marry for conventional reasons."

"Have you tried calling her?" Astrid asked.

"No," he said. "But I will."

He hung up the phone, and dialed Latika's number.

She picked up on the second ring.

"Where are you?" he asked, not waiting for her to speak.

"We don't need to be together," she said, sidestepping the question.

"What the hell are you talking about?"

"Ragnar is dead. And the two of us have no reason to continue on with this farce of a marriage. I've taken myself away from you, for a reason."

"What about my reputation?"

"I'll see that it's handled," she said. "I'll see that there is no doubt that the problem was mine. That it's my fault the marriage dissolved. I will be held responsible, and your reputation will be intact. The response that has been given to you owning your corporation has been overwhelmingly positive. I think that you'll find everything will be just fine without me."

"Latika…"

The line went dead, and she didn't speak after.

Each attempt at calling her after that was met with dead air. She refused to answer. And because of that, he couldn't figure out a way to track her phone. He looked for credit cards, and could find nothing.

Any easy paper trail had been erased.

And then, two weeks after his wife had left home, her name popped up in a database. Her real name had been used at a private physician's office.

One specializing in obstetrics.

Gunnar picked up his phone. "We are going to London."

CHAPTER ELEVEN

LATIKA WAS EXHAUSTED by the time she got home. She didn't know whether to laugh or cry. Honestly, she felt like doing both.

She was pregnant.

Pregnant with Gunnar's baby.

The exact thing that would have driven their marriage to the brink anyway.

She owed Ragnar a thank you note for dying of a heart attack with such excellent timing.

She was surprised by the way he had died. Considering it never seemed as though he had a heart.

The thought made her laugh. And then she realized she was a crazy person, standing in her empty apartment, shaking and laughing. The news she had been given today was life altering. She hadn't wanted to be seen out and about purchasing a pregnancy test, nor had she seen the way she could possibly go to a public hospital.

Thankfully, she had so much money squirreled away, that it hadn't been beyond her to get herself into a private clinic.

She had worn a scarf over her head, and large sunglasses, and it felt ridiculous.

But she seemed to have pulled it off. There were no headlines proclaiming that she was in London, after all.

Incognito still was hindering her new sense of freedom. Perhaps that was why she still felt so heavy.

She was resolute in her purpose. She knew exactly what she needed to do. She only needed a few hours to get everything straight.

And a few hours was all it took. With her press release crafted, she was ready to push it out to new sources.

That her marriage to Gunnar was a sham. That she was the villain. That she had married him under false pretenses, and had later found out she was pregnant with a lover's baby.

And that she had decided to dissolve the marriage as a result.

Not him.

Gunnar, she would say, had offered to raise the child as its own.

Because when her child looked back on the news stories surrounding his or her birth, she wanted to have that child feel as if they were wanted by everyone.

Especially their father.

Even if they never knew that Gunnar was their actual father. It was sad to think that would be how it was, but it would have to be. It would be better for everyone.

And everyone would be protected. She wished desperately she could have a glass of wine with this upsetting turn of events, but she couldn't.

Because of the baby.

She smiled, pressing her hand to her stomach.

If nothing else she had purpose now. Maybe it wasn't

wild, giddy freedom. But purpose would be better. Purpose actually made her much, much happier.

She steeled herself, her finger poised to push Send on the press release. And that was when the door to the hotel room opened.

Latika turned, her mouth falling open when she saw him standing there. His expression was grim, an aura of leashed violence around him that she had never before witnessed.

Gunnar excelled in exuding laconic grace.

She had always sensed that there was the potential for danger lurking beneath that exterior. That the way he lounged about the palace in Bjornland was much like a big cat. Watching. Waiting. Incapable of striking with decisive and fatal force in the time that it would take a person to bat an eyelash.

And here it was now. Raw, unvarnished and unconcealed. How had she never seen this before? Gunnar was not a safe space.

Gunnar was lethal.

And she suspected she had crossed him in a way she had not foreseen.

"Feeling relaxed?" he asked.

"I was," she responded, standing up from the computer and stepping in front of the screen. He walked into the room, closing the door behind him.

"How did you get a key?"

He looked at her, one brow raised. He did not answer her question.

"Ragnar is dead," she said. "I had no reason to hide in Bjornland anymore. I saw the opportunity to claim my freedom, and I did it. Don't worry, I will make sure that there is no…"

"You're pregnant," he said.

Everything inside of her went still. Her heart thundered. She felt very much like a field mouse under the watchful eye of the lion. She had no hope of pulling a thorn out of his paw and making it better. For he was looking at her as if she was the one who had put it there.

"You don't want a baby," she said.

"You should've told me."

"Why? Everything is in hand."

"How dare you? How dare you flee in the night and take my heir from me."

His rage was stark. Palpable. And it took all her strength to find a way to speak with that anger, another entity in the room, pressing in on her.

"First of all," she said, "I took myself from you. I claimed my freedom. I didn't know I was pregnant when I left you. It had to do with me, not a baby. Second of all, you said unequivocally that you did not want a child. That you would have nothing to do with a child that we created."

"That is different than allowing my child to be raised away from the palace, and from its birthright."

"What birthright? You're the spare, Gunnar. Every child that Astrid has will be in line before you, and our child would never be in line at all."

"It doesn't matter. All that matters is that my child receive the rights they are entitled to by birth."

"But you don't want them. And I don't want to subject them to such a thing."

"And I will not allow this. You think that you can walk away from me? What about our bargain? You cannot step into this space and use me as a safety net and then leave when it suits you."

"If you're worried for your precious reputation, don't be." She stepped to the side, revealing her computer screen. "I am prepared to absolve you of any wrong-doing. I have prepared a press release, which I'm ready to push the button on. Wherein I declare that this child belongs to a lover that I took before our marriage, and that you offered to give my child your name, and I refused. My reputation will be in tatters, while yours will remain intact. But I don't care. I care nothing for my reputation, I never wanted notoriety. All I have ever wanted is the chance to live my life on my terms. I'm ready to go off in the country and raise this baby alone. I will be happy doing it."

It wasn't sacrifice on her end. It was the pursuit of freedom. The need to cut ties with him utterly and completely. To uphold her end of their bargain so she might walk owing him nothing.

They had married for his reputation, and for her protection.

She no longer needed protection. And if she just lowered herself, her leaving him would allow him to be blameless.

And the slate would be clean between them.

She would finally be free.

"So," he said, his tone soft. Deadly. "You seek to use me as a sperm donor?"

"Why not?" She lifted her chin up, determined to pour every ounce of defiance she possessed onto him. "Astrid sought to do the same."

"It didn't work out for her, did it?"

"Because Mauro has a heart. Because he was willing to cross borders to claim his child. You don't want yours."

"Have I not crossed borders?" he asked, throwing his arms wide. "Is this the demonstration you were hoping to see? I passed your purity test that I might be able to be father to my own flesh and blood?"

"You were the one who disavowed him," she said, advancing on him. "And in so doing, you disavowed *me*. I will not allow my child a relationship with a father that doesn't want them. If I do, how am I any different than your mother? How am I any different at all? And how are you different from your father? He didn't want Astrid. And his desire to be rid of her made him do appalling things to you. Is that what you want? Is that the place you want your child to grow up?"

He went very still. And Latika knew that she had overplayed her hand.

She had been attempting to manipulate, with a knife straight to the heart. But she could see the moment he grabbed the handle of that metaphorical knife, intent on turning it back around.

He closed the space between them, those ice blue eyes cutting her with the chill in them. He stopped when he was a breath away from her, his chest nearly touching her breasts. He leaned in, his mouth set to a grim line. And then he reached past her, grabbing her laptop and wrenching it free of the charger cord.

He threw it down onto the ground and stomped it beneath his shoe.

The screen went fuzzy, then black. Her heart thundered in abject terror, her entire body trembling.

"The child is mine. So are you. If you want to see what I'm capable of, if you want to see the ruthlessness that my father planted into my soul, then you have given yourself a perfect opportunity to do so. My people are descended of Vikings. Do you know what we do when there is something we desire, and it does not belong to us? We take it, and we make it ours. And you, make no mistake, are mine."

He grabbed hold of her, that large, commanding fist buried in her hair as he pulled her forward, his mouth crashing down on hers. She couldn't breathe. Couldn't think. She was melting, the inferno of his rage demolishing each and every one of her defenses.

She could feel it. Like a rally cry inside of her soul. *Surrender.*

She shouldn't want to surrender. It was a foolish thing to do. And it was one she could not afford. And yet, her Viking marauder would accept nothing less, and somehow her body was intent upon allowing it.

Then he picked her up, swept her straight off of her feet, and carried her into the bedroom.

CHAPTER TWELVE

GUNNAR'S RAGE WAS a living thing. Boiling over, spilling out of control.

Latika had said that he was like his father. And he couldn't find it in himself to fight the ways in which that might be true. He was failing. And yet... She was in his arms. She was clinging to him, kissing him back like liquid fire. And he could do nothing to deny himself. With blinding heat, blinding needs, pulsing behind his eyes, and hard, heady desire pulsing through him he could do nothing but stake his claim.

If it was in his blood, if it was inevitable, then he would surrender.

The bedroom in the hotel suite she was occupying had large windows, overlooking the neon and chaos of the city. It was all noise, next to the sophisticated serenity that Latika possessed. She was dressed simply today, and a black dress that hugged her luscious body, cut off just above the knee.

It was demure, really. And yet, it ignited a fire in his veins that would rival the forge of any dwarf king found in the stories his nannies had told him as a boy.

And indeed, his need was honed to a sharpened edge, like an axe. And when it fell, it would be decisive and deadly. He took her to the window, turned her so that she was facing out.

"You know how I got in here," he said. "I was handed a key. Because you are mine, and the world knows it. Everyone down there... They would not lift a finger to take you out of my custody. You are mine. The whole world knows." He gripped the zipper on her dress and pulled it down, letting it fall off of her body, and pool at her feet.

She was wearing black underwear, lace and revealing, highlighting the curves of her delicious ass. He pushed his hand beneath the waistband, grabbing a handful of soft, plump flesh. Before pushing his hand further between her thighs, feeling how wet she was.

"You desire me even now. You ran from me, and you still desire me."

"We all want things that we despise," she said.

"Do we? Or do bodies sometimes know better than our minds?"

"My heart wants nothing to do with you."

"And yet." He leaned in, toying with her between her legs. "Tell me no. If you don't want this. If you don't want me. Tell me no."

"Bastard," she spat.

"Does my touch disgust you?" He drew his fingers across that place where he knew she was most sensitive. She gasped, rolling her hips forward. "Oh, yes," he said. "I can see the way I disgust you. So much that you're on the verge of coming...out of your skin."

"Let me go," she said. "You don't want me. You don't want the baby."

"Don't tell me what I want," he said, stroking her in time with his words. "Don't speak to me like you know. Tell me what you want. Tell me if you want me to stop."

Again, she did. She simply stood, vibrating with fury and need as he stroked her. And he was filled with just enough rage over her abandonment to continue to push. "Are you afraid that if you push me too hard I'll disappear, never to return? Because you can profess to hate me all you want, because you love what I do to your body. I'm sure being a Duchess doesn't hurt."

"I don't give a damn about being your Duchess."

"But you do give a damn about pleasure, don't you? Is it wounding, to discover you're just as base as the rest of us? So many years of abstinence for you, darling Latika, only to be undone so resolutely by my touch. That must be extremely confronting for you."

"Are you going to do something? Are you going to stand there all night with your hands between my legs halfheartedly pleasuring me."

"Oh," he said. "My mistake. Did you want me to put some effort into it?"

He turned around so that she was facing him, and unhooked her bra, throwing it down to the ground, then he dragged her panties down, pressing a kiss to her ankle, her calf, her thigh before standing. Her eyes glittered with rage, her frame shaking.

"One last chance, darling. Tell me no."

Her dark eyes glittered with rage and desire. "Go to hell."

"I'll take that as an enthusiastic *yes*."

He crushed her up against his body, reveling in the feel of all that soft skin beneath his hands, while he remained fully clothed. He kissed her then, pouring all of the fury and outrage that he felt into her body. Into her soul.

If she thought he was a monster, she would get a monster.

He stripped his clothes off quickly, then lifted her up, set her down on the bed. He maneuvered her so that she was on her knees, her thighs thick and luscious, her waist slim. Her breasts heavy. He stroked himself twice, looking at the picture that she made.

"That's more like it," he said. "On your knees, showing a bit of deference to your King. But I should like a bit of praise from your mouth."

She looked up at him, the reluctant hunger on her face an aphrodisiac. He pressed the head of his masculinity to her lips and he saw the moment she surrendered to her need. Her tongue darted out, touching the tip of him and then she opened wide, taking him and as far as she could.

He grabbed hold of her hair, guiding her movements as she pleasured him. And somehow, the game they were playing got lost. Got all tangled up in the dark, deep pleasure threatening to overwhelm him.

Because he could not remember why he was angry anymore. And he could not remember why he had thought allowing her to put her lips on him would give him the power. For she held in her hand the most vulnerable part of him. And he was a slave to the need that she created, with clever fingers and lips and tongue.

He was the one surrendering.

He growled, pulling her away from him and turning her so that she was facing away. Still on her knees. He pressed himself to the entrance of her body, before thrusting deep, holding tightly to her hips as he led the deep, intense pleasure of being inside of her wash over him. She looked over her shoulder, her black hair covering part of her face, her expression one of dazed wonder.

Then, he began to move.

He lost himself in it. In that rhythm, deep and steady. And whatever he had been thinking to put her in this position, to make her so much less Latika that she was, it didn't work. For there was no other woman who felt like her. Who made him feel like this. There was nothing in all the world had ever felt like this.

Pleasure was like an arrow, piercing him, making it difficult to breathe. It was as though it had punched his lung. His heart. He put his hand between her legs and squeezed her, before moving one finger to either side of the center of her need and stroking, until a hoarse cry left her lips and her internal muscles pulsed around him. Only then did he allow the pleasure in him to rage out of control. He pulsed inside of her, pouring himself into her body, spending everything in her.

And when it was done, he collapsed at her side, laying on his back, feeling like a warrior left for dead on the battlefield.

Latika was laying on her stomach, her head turned to one side, the one visible eye appraising him closely.

"Pack your things," he said. "You're coming back to Bjornland with me."

He had embraced all that he was. He had become the conqueror. The marauder.

And yet somehow, as he headed out the door to the hotel, with Latika mutely walking beside him, he felt more the captive than the captor.

Latika could not untangle the events of the past few hours. And even when she was back in the palace in Bjornland, she felt dazed.

Gunnar had made some noise about the fact the two of them needed to be in residence at the palace for a time, but she hadn't fully understood why. For what all the implications might be. He had their things moved into the same bedroom, and Latika knew that everything between them would be different now. And not necessarily for the better. The way that he had broken that laptop so decisively, and then claimed her body with such force replayed in her mind over and over.

He had left impressions on her and in her that were so deep she could still feel them reverberating within her hours later.

She could not pretend that she hadn't been a willing participant. Could not pretend that part of her hadn't been thrilled that he had come for her.

That he had done exactly what Mauro had done for Astrid, for their child. Crossed borders and made demands.

But she still didn't get the sense that Gunnar wanted their child out of a sense other than…she couldn't even fathom what he was doing.

There was a sense of obligation, that she knew, but it didn't come from a place of love. Not remotely. Either way, it didn't matter. She was here. He had given her a great many opportunities to turn him away, and she had not. However she might regret it now, however she might feel weaker for it now, the choice had been hers. A strange realization. She had choice. She had given it to him.

"You're back," Astrid said, walking with great purpose into Gunnar's living quarters.

"Yes," Latika said.

"Why did you leave?"

"Because Ragnar was dead. And I didn't need to stay."

"But you're back," Astrid pointed out.

Latika knew that she couldn't keep any of this from her friend. There was no real point to it. She would find out eventually.

She only wished that there was some way she could sidestep the fact that of course she and Gunnar had ended up in a sexual relationship. Mostly because she didn't want to sit there and have to bear Astrid being right.

She was raw enough without having to admit that she had been wrong about her own desires.

"Gunnar, for his part, did not think that it was a good time to dissolve our marriage," Latika said.

"Did he not?" Astrid's tone sounded light, casual and wholly unsurprised.

"No," she said, knowing that she was being less than forthcoming.

"And why is that?"

"Perhaps because I'm pregnant," she said crisply.

That succeeded in shocking Astrid into silence. But, Latika could scarcely enjoy that.

"Did you know that when you left?" she asked.

"No," she said defensively. Though, it wouldn't have made a difference in her actions. Not after all that he'd said.

"You said my brother didn't want children."

"He doesn't. And he's quite angry with me. But I seem to recall he was involved in forgetting to use protection."

Astrid grimaced. But then, her expression softened. "I seem to recall having to cope with a very angry man who seems to think that a lack of protection was entirely my fault."

"Amazing creatures, men," Latika said. "Are they not?"

"They are something," Astrid agreed.

"So you're staying married?"

"For the time being," Latika said. Then she sighed. "He does not love me."

"Do you love him?"

She thought about it. For good while. All that he told her about his relationship with his father... It made her feel things for him. But then... There was the way he was acting about this child. All the things he had said. But then, the way he behaved as well. It was difficult to sort out what was true. And it was very hard for her to figure out her response.

"He doesn't want our baby. But he also doesn't want to let it go. I find... I don't know how I can love a man who will not love his child."

Astrid nodded gravely. "Give him time. And a chance to change."

"Some men never do," she said, thinking of their father.

"No," she said. "Some men never do."

"And if he doesn't?" Latika asked.

"Then I will be first in line to help set you free. But barring anything egregious... I think the two of you need to work this out for yourselves."

And as much as Latika would like to disagree, she couldn't. Because she might have been forced into the marriage mess, but no one had forced her into his bed. Twice. She was responsible for her own part in this. And she would not pawn that responsibility off. No matter how difficult it was. And right now, it was all pretty damn stiff.

* * *

Women had never made Gunnar nervous. He was a man who had a certain effect on the fairer sex, and he was well aware of that fact. He had always enjoyed the sort of attention he'd received in that regard. But he was walking on uneven ground with Latika. He felt off balance and out of his depth. He disliked that greatly. "Did you have a good day?" he asked.

"Yes," she responded.

"What did you do?"

"I spent some time with Astrid."

"And?"

"And we had a nice time," she said. "But I always do with your sister."

"Good."

She said nothing. Instead, she began to move about the room, ignoring him pointedly as she sifted through drawers in the large, ornate armoire at the back wall.

"What are you looking for?"

"Something to sleep in," she said.

"I certainly don't require that you wear anything to bed."

She looked at him, her expression verging on incredulous. "Do you expect that I'm going to have sex with you?"

He had. He had very much expected that. After all, she had seemed fully and completely into his body when he had encountered her that morning.

It had only been that morning.

It seemed an eternity now.

"It's no secret that you're attracted to me," he said.

"It's no secret that you have rejected our child. That's why I left. No, I didn't know I was pregnant, but I could not abide the idea of being married to a man who would see a child the way that you do."

"Things are different now that it's a reality," he said, believing that the moment the words left his lips.

"In what way?"

"In the sense that I understand deeply that I have an obligation to this child. And I intend to fulfill that obligation."

"A child should be more than an obligation. Just as a child should be more than a means to an end for an avaricious father intent on having his will be done through his descendants. You should love a child."

"I understand loyalty," he said. "I'm not certain that I understand love."

The look on Latika's face was what made him realize that there was something heavy in those words. Something shocking and wrong. He'd always known that to be true about himself. That he didn't understand that kind of depth.

He had been forced to exist in dark, enclosed spaces and he'd grown armor to protect himself. But it had cost. Because all those layers he'd built up had smothered a flame inside of him.

Or maybe…maybe that flame that existed inside other people had never been in him.

"What about Astrid?"

"You are the one who accused me of not caring for my sister, and now you seek to hold her up as an example of how I do?"

"No I… I'm sorry. I never should have implied that you didn't love Astrid. Of course you do."

"I don't know that I do," he said. "I am bonded to her. She is my twin. We are in many ways pieces of one. She is the head of the nation. And I have been her shield. That's different than love."

"What do you think love is?"

For a man convinced of his own rightness in the universe, his own deep sense of knowing who he was, a question like that was confronting.

Because when he dug down to the bottom of himself and searched for the answer, he found it wasn't there. "I don't know."

"Do you think that maybe it could be the way that you protected your sister. At the expense of yourself."

"No," he said.

"You don't think that love sacrifices itself?"

"If that is love, then love is a cruelty visited on the world. As cruel as hatred."

Her throat worked up and down. "Will you be involved with our child?"

"No," he said, something in his gut twisting, repulsion making his skin crawl.

"I don't understand, Gunnar. I don't understand why you would come for me like you did if you are not willing to offer me anything." She frowned. "Why did you come? How did you know I was pregnant?"

"I tracked your name in a database which attached you to that clinic. I knew why you must've gone there."

"You came to me knowing that I was having a child. And even now you can't bring yourself to admit that you might want to be in that child's life?"

"I don't know," he said. "I cannot explain what drives me. I don't like that. Not at all. I am a man who has always known how to stand firm in his convictions. I had to fight for those convictions. I had to fight my own father. I had to withstand torture. And I am not a man given to change, particularly not quickly. What I have always known is that I did not want to bring a child into the world, but now I am. Now we are. And what I know, with equal ferocity is that I cannot abandon the child." The words were like acid on his tongue, like sharp knives in his chest. "I don't know what love is. And I don't know how to be any sort of decent person. But I do know protection. I know I can offer that. And I offer it to you. To our child. I can pledge allegiance to you. To the baby. I don't know what I can give beyond that. But what I always want my child to know is that I will be a protector. Because Astrid and I never had that. Not from our father. I would have our child know he is loved. *I* don't know how to do that," he said, his voice raw. "I will need to count on you for that. For you to show the child that which I cannot."

She looked at him, and the well of pity in her eyes was almost too much for him to bear.

"Gunnar…"

"Forgive me," he said. "For what I said. I was angry, because I was afraid. And it gets me to say that. All of the things my father did to me and I was never afraid. But it's as if it was all stored inside of me for later. For when I was the one with power. Because I do not wish to use mine in the way that he did. And I thought it best… For the longest time, to avoid what I thought made him the monster he was."

"You thought somehow you made him a monster?"

"If I had not been born, then what choice would he have had? He would have had to accept Astrid. Power corrupts. And in me, my father saw the promise of power."

"I think you've proven that you're incorruptible in those stakes," she said, her voice soft.

"I have never trusted it. Why should I be innately better than my father?"

"Because you want to be?"

She sounded so confident and yet he didn't see how she could be. "Do you ever worry?" he asked. "After what your parents did to you, don't you worry that something inside of you might be broken?"

She looked so serene, and he could not understand it. He could not understand how this woman seemed so utterly and completely without fear for the future. For the child that she carried in her body.

"No," she said. "I worry about some things, but not being like my parents. That life didn't make me happy. And their goal was to have more of that life. They cared so deeply about what other people thought. They cared about power and prestige. I lived there, in that life, and it made me miserable. Their pursuit of more made me miserable. I understand that there is no value in treating people like a commodity. Because I understand not only that more things will never make me happy, but that it does unrelenting damage to the person that you put that on. I know everything I don't want to do. I'm sure along the way I will stumble upon more things I shouldn't do, or things I should do more of. I want to be the best mother that I can be. And I know that that begins with not being like my own. I was raised by nannies and teachers. I was raised by everyone but my parents. Their presence only served to make my life miserable. As they brought their expectations down upon me, as they told me all the ways in which I wasn't meeting them. No, I don't worry that I'll be like my parents. And I don't think you should worry you'll be like your father."

"But we have no guide," he said.

"Even if we did, that child will not be you, and it will not be me. It will be different than either of us, its whole own person. We would not be able to plan perfectly even if our parents had been wonderful."

"You won't use nannies?"

"Oh, I imagine we will to a degree. But we will be involved too. Not because we have to be, but because I want to be."

"What if I'm bad at it? What if it would be better if I weren't involved?"

"We can speak of that as the time comes," she said.

And somehow that was more reassuring than if she had simply told him that everything would be fine. Because the fact of the matter was she didn't know. Gunnar was desperately boggled by this uncertainty inside of him. It was nothing like he usually was, and nothing like he wanted to be at all.

That was the root of all that fear he'd felt when they had first made love without a condom.

Like the world had spun out of his control. And control had been his linchpin ever since he had been a boy, attempting to withstand his father's torture.

That deep base he had built inside of himself had been the only secure and certain thing. It was the thing he relied on. That internal compass. He had no idea how he'd come by it, because it certainly hadn't been taught to him by his father. He had no idea how he'd been so fortunate as to have something like that inside of himself. He had often felt like maybe it was part of that connection with Astrid.

At the very least, Astrid had had something more of a connection with their mother.

Their mother hadn't been interested in Gunnar at all, but she had cared deeply for Astrid.

He had always been grateful that his sister had that.

"We can figure it out together," Latika said. "And if something is going wrong, we can change it. We are not made of stone. Our ways aren't set. We can choose who we want to be. I believe that. All I wanted, all my life was my chance to choose my own path. I'll do so now. And so will you. We can do it. We are not bound by this. We don't have to be."

He didn't want to speak anymore. Not now. Instead, he reached out and picked Latika up off of the seat she was on and carried her over to the bed.

He was desperate for oblivion. He craved it. The future was a bright, blaring light of some uncertainty. Of so many things he had not planned. So many things he had always told himself he didn't want. The only thing he was certain of was that he wanted her. With a desperation that bordered on insanity. Yes, that he was certain of.

He stripped her bare, and he spent the rest of the night proving to her that while he might be uncertain about some things, there were others he was infinitely confident in.

For now, that was enough.

The future would have to handle itself.

CHAPTER THIRTEEN

THE NEXT FEW weeks went by smoothly. Latika felt at ease with Gunnar in a way that she hadn't ever before.

They spent their days companionably enough, Gunnar busying himself with work, but often including her in discussions about new projects. She enjoyed that.

It gave her a purpose.

One beyond dwelling on her current morning sickness.

It was really such a terrible thing, and she found that she could barely rise before ten a.m. Which was completely unusual for her. But she was living on unsweetened herbal tea and dry toast and crystallized ginger candies.

After all that settled, she could bring herself to rise.

She was thankful that Gunnar had suggested they come and live at the palace when they returned. Because that put her in proximity with Astrid very often, and, it meant that they had a whole range of staff available at all times, and given that Latika was currently feeling quite down, it was exceedingly helpful.

Physically, she might be diminished, but emotionally things were going better than she could've possibly asked.

She was having a fortunate moment when she went out onto the terrace to sit in a lounger, in the pale sun making a weak appearance in the pale sky.

That was when Gunnar came out to find her there.

"How are you feeling?"

She smiled, a strange, warm sensation flooding her.

Gunnar had told her a few weeks ago that he didn't know what love was.

Latika was beginning to think that she did. She felt that every time she looked at him. Every time she thought about him.

"I just wanted to come and tell you that I will be heading to San Diego tonight."

That startled her. "Why?"

"There's a big project opportunity, but there's been a snag with some of the planning. I need to see to it in person."

"Let me go with you," she said.

"There's no need," he said.

"Why not?"

"You don't feel well," he said. "In any way, you will be well taken care of here in the palace. And you will have Astrid around you. Wouldn't you prefer that?"

"Would I prefer your sister's company to yours?"

"She's your friend, after all," Gunter said.

"And you're my husband," Latika responded. "I'm not sure why you don't think that takes precedence."

"Ours is not a conventional marriage," he said. The way he said it, so casually, hurt her. And she knew that perhaps that wasn't fair. He wasn't wrong.

Theirs was not a conventional marriage. It never had been. She had thrown herself at him in a crowded ball-room and demanded his protection, when he was in a position of such public visibility he had no choice but to go along with what she done.

But over the past weeks their marriage had felt conventional enough. In fact, it had felt more than conventional. They had slept together, shared with each other. Grown together.

He had begun to feel like the most important, defining piece of her life.

With Gunnar, she had found something that she hadn't found with anyone else.

He seemed to accept her for who she was. More than that, he seemed to enjoy all that she was.

He shared his business information with her, and complimented her on the way her mind worked. He valued her mind, he valued her body. Every piece of her seemed important to Gunnar.

How could she feel anything but adoration for him?

He also got angry with her sometimes, and she liked that even better. Because it showed her that he could want her even when their interaction wasn't companionable. That he didn't require her to be perfect in order to want her company. In order to want to kiss her and pleasure her and be inside of her.

Everyone else had only ever wanted her on their terms, with the exception of Astrid, who had been her truest friend.

And in Gunnar, she had found a man who cared for her that way, and she could not understand why he might think that wasn't earth shattering.

"Our marriage might not be conventional," she said softly. "But it's important. I find that I'm not happy when you aren't around, Gunnar. And I should like to go with you to San Diego."

He regarded her, his expression unreadable.

"It would be best if you stayed home," he said.

"I don't understand. Why would you care either way?"

She suddenly felt very silly. Arguing over whether or not he should bring her. Truthfully, it was kind of sad. Because if he didn't want her there then she should just accept it. It was difficult to do, when she wanted him like she did. It was difficult, because she wished more than anything that he would crave her company in the same way she craved his. But if he didn't… Then, even if he agreed to bring her along it was something of an empty victory. No, it was more than an empty victory.

It was a loss, and she a bad loser. But she wasn't sure right then if she cared, mostly because she wanted to know why. Wanted to know why he was avoiding spending time with her.

Maybe he just needs space. And the fact that for you it's a revelation that someone wants your company some of the time is a bit more of a novelty for you than it is for him.

Perhaps.

Except, she knew all he had been through with his father. And she had a feeling that this wasn't an entirely familiar situation for him either.

"If you want to go by yourself, you can. But I'm not sure why you think I might be an impediment," she said slowly. "Unless there's something happening you don't want me to know about."

She truly didn't think that Gunnar would be unfaithful to her. She didn't know why she thought that. He had never once sworn his fidelity to her, beyond when they had taken their wedding vows, and at that time both of them had been lying, since neither of them had had plans to sleep with each other then.

"I'm not going to be manipulated, Latika," he said, his voice suddenly turning to shards of ice. "That was what my father did to me. Manipulation. All the damn time. And you trying to make me feel guilty, trying to make me feel concerned by the questioning of my character is not going to make me change my mind."

"I wasn't manipulating you," she said. She felt horrified that he might think that, but then she looked closely at his face, and she saw he lacked sincerity.

He didn't think that she was manipulating him. Not really. Not deep in his heart. And that meant he was the one doing the manipulating.

"What's going on? That is not a leading question, neither is it manipulative. But you're being strange. We've been close to each other these past weeks."

"We have been sleeping together."

"More than that. You swore to protect me."

"Leaving you in a palace surrounded by guards, and with your best friend is hardly walking back on my promise to protect you."

That was true enough.

"Well, then maybe it's more than that. Maybe I want more. Gunnar... I have always been surrounded by people who wanted to use me in some fashion. And you... It isn't like that with us."

"Latika, it is the very definition of that with us. You needed protection. I needed a way to improve my reputation. And so here we both are."

She couldn't do this. Not with him. She'd been on a quest for freedom, for the life that she would have been destined for if not for...well, if not for her life.

And that was the problem, she realized.

She couldn't be Latika without her past. Without the years she'd spent with her parents, then the years that followed in Bjornland. It had all been her life, and it had made her into the woman she was.

A woman who loved the man she had married.

She was not waiting on this. She wouldn't let him leave without him knowing.

"No. That was true when it first began. What we have now isn't that. It isn't for me. Gunnar… I've fallen in love with you."

He drew back as though she had slapped him. "No," he said, his voice like iron. "You don't love me."

"I do," she said. "I've been thinking a lot about that. What love is. Because you asked the other day. Because you said you didn't know. But I think… Gunnar, I think that you exemplify love more than anyone I've ever known. With no regard to your own safety or comfort you protected your sister. For no glory and no advancement. You shielded me from Ragnar, even though you could have easily acted like I was a crazy person throwing myself at you the way that I did."

"And put your life at risk? How reasonable is that?"

"Let me finish," she said. "And then you came for me. You came for the baby. Even though you didn't know if you could be a good father. Even though it terrified you."

"How can you possibly act as if I exemplified love in any way through those actions. You remember what I said to you. The night that we first made love."

"I do. I remember it well, because it hurt me. It hurt me deeply. But it wasn't the final thing you did. Those were words, Gunnar. You took the appropriate steps, the appropriate action to fix those words, and that matters more."

"But some things cannot be erased."

"No, but they can be forgiven."

"Just like that?"

"It isn't just like anything," she said. "But we've had weeks where you have demonstrated to me that the things you said that night were spoken in anger. Anger that came from a very understandable place of fear. You had a plan for your life, Gunnar, and this was in it. I understand that. And also, when push came to shove, you came for your child. You came for me. And since then, you have demonstrated all of those things I just said. And through it all, you've shown me what I want for my life."

"It's just another cage, Latika. Don't thank me for putting you in another cage."

"What?"

"You are…conditioned to make the best out of a bunch of very bad situations. You chose to be here, you chose to be Astrid's assistant because the alternatives to you were vile. And our marriage is no different. Now you find yourself with child, and you see the benefits to the two of us being married, over the benefits of us being separated. That doesn't mean it's what you would have chosen. With an entire world at your disposal. I was one of two options placed in front of you, and you took the one that would not result in your abuse and torture. And then, I presented you with very few options when I came to London to collect you."

"You didn't threaten me. And you gave me a great many opportunities to tell you no, if you don't remember."

"But I would have threatened you," he said. "If you

had not come with me, I would have threatened to take your baby from you. And I think on some level you knew that. I wasn't going to let you waft off into the distance with my child, disavow all connection of my blood with me. You knew I wouldn't allow it."

"I didn't know any such thing. I did not make the decision to go with you under duress. I left you under duress. I separated myself from you in San Diego under duress. I wanted to be with you. I was upset when you said those things to me because I wanted you to be a different man. Because the man that I saw hints and glimpses of was one that I knew I could fall in love with. And I wanted more of that man. Well, in the past weeks you have given it to me. And I... I would choose you. With the whole world before me. I would choose you."

"You don't know that."

"I do."

"You've never had enough freedom to be confident in that fact."

"By your standards, does anyone? Maybe only you. Except, even then you had your reputation to consider. Who chooses a partner with nothing in their life coming into play? Who chooses a partner with no consideration for anything? Very few people, Gunnar, so if circumstances make it so that my feelings don't count, then I would say that most relationships are invalidated. People find love. They find it in the strangest places. They find it in adversity. They have always done so. Whether it's because our hearts crave companionship, or because fate finds ways to wind our paths together no matter what, I don't know. But I know that love finds us. And it has found me. It has found me here with you."

"I don't believe in love," he said, his face hard like

stone. "And I certainly don't believe in it with the way things have happened between us. How can it be real? These are trying times, the have found us entwined. It's not fate, but a series of choices. Choices made out of desperation. Choices made by evil men. And none of them yours to be made freely."

"I just told you…"

"And I feel it is something you need to tell yourself. Because otherwise, here you are pregnant with my child and in a sense, it's just sadly inevitable. Because you weren't exposed to other men. Because you were never given the chance to marry another. Because a jailer without sadistic tendencies looks alarmingly attractive next to one who enjoys causing pain."

She would not let him win. She would not let him reduce her. She returned volley. "All of my life I've had people telling me what they thought was good for me. I won't let you do it too. You have trusted me. You gave me selection power over your bride in the first place. You showed me your business, and you've been consulting me on certain things. How can you now decide that I'm ignorant and know nothing?"

"All right, Latika, have it your way. You understand your heart. You understand your mind. You love me. But your love is misguided and misdirected. Because I do not love you. I cannot. Love means nothing to me, so if you're seeking to offer it as some kind of gift or prize, then I think you truly misunderstand who I am."

"How can love mean nothing to you? Look at Astrid. Look at how much she cares for you. And surely your mother…"

He cut her off with cold, decisive words.

"My mother knew that I was being tortured," he said,

his voice hard. "She did nothing. My *loving* mother. She didn't care one bit what my father did to me. Because I wasn't the child that mattered to her. I existed to be a pawn in my father's eyes. And I was nothing in my mother's. Do not ask me to cling to some source of love that believe me never existed."

Latika's heart curled in on itself. Pain lancing through her. "Your mother knew?"

"Why do you think…" He stopped himself, paused for a moment, before continuing. "Why do you think I am so certain that there is no part of me who would do well with a child? It doesn't come from nothing. My own family was so very broken, Latika. I have offered what I can offer. And beyond that…there is nothing."

"I don't believe that. I just don't. I believe there's more. I believe that you have more to give. I do. Down in my soul I believe it."

"Because you want to see this as something you can hope for. Because you want to see it as something you weren't trapped in. But you are. You are trapped, as am I. We are trapped with the child between us, and what can be done? You would have lies. You would lie to yourself. You would lie to me. You would try and make all of this something that you could latch onto. But it is just more of life's cruelty. You are a good woman, to be able to possess the power to feel the way that you do after what you have been through. But you have been shackled to a man who cannot. And there is no fixing it."

"Gunnar…"

"No. I'm going to San Diego. And while I am there I will go about my business as if we are not married. Do you understand me? I will be what I am. Pure. Through and through. And when the world sees that, they will not judge you for leaving me. And that is what you will do. You will leave me."

"What about your reputation?"

"I don't care."

"I thought it was for Astrid."

"Have I not pledged to you to protect you? To protect the child? This is how it will be done. I do not recall making it a discussion. Astrid will find her own way. She is resilient. And what I'm doing… It is simply a holdover from when I was a boy, taking on my father's torture in the name of keeping her safe." A sad smile tipped his lips upward. "Perhaps I was never truly protecting her. I sometimes wonder that. Perhaps she never needed me. For she had all the strength that she possesses now, and she had the protection of my mother. I thought that perhaps my mother saw me as a source of protection for her precious daughter. But I think more she accepted that I was a distraction from my father's rage. He decided to try and use me to do his will, and he found me immovable. And I suspect that my mother imagined it was just as well. I was a worthy sacrifice either way."

"So that's what you're doing again? Martyring yourself?"

"It would only be martyring if it was something I didn't want. And I never wanted this life. Not really. So which one is martyrdom?"

She didn't have an answer for that. Not really. All she knew was that in her heart she felt like she and Gunnar had something special. Something important. But he was standing there with his eyes cold telling her that they didn't. So perhaps it was true. Maybe he did not care for her. Not even a little. Not even at all. Maybe there were no feelings between them, and she had been desperate to conjure them up. Because they were together. Because she had shared her body with him. Because he had given her a child.

"I love you," she said, the words broken. "And I don't care about pride."

Suddenly, she was desperate, emotion clawing at her chest. "I don't care about my safety. Please don't give your body to another woman, Gunnar, it's mine. I love it so much. I love you so much. You're mine, and I would choose you every time. Every single time. And I hated you on site because I knew that I could never have you. Because I knew that a man like you was beyond my reach. And maybe I did manipulate the situation asking you to marry me. Asking for your protection. But your protection was the only one I wanted."

She took a deep, sharking breath and continued, "I could have thrown myself at Astrid's feet. I could have simply used my connection to her to keep myself safe. But I didn't. I didn't mean to manipulate you, but I did. And for that I must apologize, because I know how much you hate it. But don't ever underestimate the power of choice. Because I did choose you. I did. We could go on all day about what my options were, and why you were the best one. But I know in my heart why you were the one I chose. Because you're beautiful. And brilliant. Because I was so enraged by your exploits with other women because I was jealous. Because I found your beauty so magnetic and undeniable I couldn't turn off my response to you when we were in the same room, and it terrified me. I want to be with you," she said. "From now and until always.

When we took our vows I didn't know what I wanted. I was confused."

"You told me that you wouldn't sleep with me," he said.

"Because I wanted children. I was afraid. I was afraid that if I slept with you this would happen. And it did. I was trying to protect myself from the inevitable. Because I knew... Gunnar, I knew that part of you not wanting children was you holding back your emotions. Please don't give what we've shared to someone else. Please don't ask me to go."

"Where do you wish to live?" he asked, not responding to her at all. "I will establish your living quarters there."

"With you, you idiot. In your home, in your bed."

"Anywhere else in the world, Latika. It's yours. But not with me. Not here."

He tilted his chin upward. "I swore my protection to you, to the child, and I will give that. But I will give no more. I hope you will have found a new place to reside when I return. You will want for nothing. My word is binding. Because I never use them to manipulate."

"No. You do. You use them to manipulate yourself, Gunnar. And if you can't see that that I don't know how to help you."

But he said nothing to that. Instead, he turned and strode off the terrace, leaving Latika stunned. Because there was no more discussion. And he had simply walked away. From her. From this. From them.

And it all felt too unreal for her to even believe that it had happened.

But the stunning, intense feeling of being cracked from the inside that overtook her when she drew in her next breath told her that it had. She slid off the chair, on her knees on the terrace, gasping for breath. She had never felt like this before. Ever. And she thought she might be dying. She had run away from her parents, parents who had been intent on marrying her off to a madman. Had seen how little value she had to them.

She had hidden away for years, had been through so many things that should have done this to her. Should have immobilized her. Should have left her completely and utterly breathless with pain. And yet none of it had.

But this... This was beyond what she thought she could endure.

Always in her life when she had been backed into a corner, she had known that she had to move. Had known that she needed to take a step away from the threat so that she would be safe. But here she was immobilized. Because the man who had just hurt her far beyond anything she could have ever fathomed, was also the one person she wanted to be with more than any other. And she found she had for self-protection.

Because all of her walls were gone. She had fallen in love, and it had stolen all of her protection.

It had stolen everything.

And she had no idea how she was going to survive this.

But suddenly, she remembered.

She put her hand on her stomach, covering her body. The place where the baby grew.

The baby was why she would survive. Why she would carry on.

And more than that, why she would find ways to be happy.

Because she would never subject her child to an unhappy, bitter upbringing.

Her chance at love was this baby.

And yes, Gunnar had come and found her, and he had given her hope. But the loss of him didn't mean the death of her hope.

If she had learned one lesson through all of this it was that the amount of hope that existed in her was an incredible thing. She had grown up in a cloistered life, but she had hoped for more than what her parents had chosen for her.

She had hoped for more than a marriage without love.

That hope was strong. And it would carry her through, even when she couldn't carry herself.

That she had to rest on the strength of that hope, because more often than not it was the only strength available.

When Gunnar arrived in San Diego, he was something more than jetlagged. Something worse than hung over. He didn't understand the thing that was happening inside of him. He didn't understand why the hell he couldn't seem to think straight.

He'd needed to get away from Latika for a while. Because the days and nights of time spent with her had begun to erode the walls he'd built in his soul to protect himself and he'd begun to feel battle worn.

Not from torture or isolation.

From her soft touch on his skin. From her kisses on his lips.

And so he'd devised a trip to get away from her for a while and then...then it had all gone to hell.

Everything felt like it was wrong.

Muddled and messed up, and like it would never be right again. He had endured a great many things in his life. Things that would have broken many people. Most people. But he had never felt like he lost his purpose. He did now. He felt like he couldn't remember the reason he was supposed to breathe. Or a reason anyone might keep breathing.

The world seemed dark. Beyond dark. The world seemed like a completely and unutterably foreign and dark place. He could find nothing bright or hopeful in it. And in the past, when he had felt that way, he had been reminded that at least there was alcohol. At least there was sex. But the despair that he felt now could not be dealt with alcohol. And he didn't want women. Not any woman other than Latika. Ever. She was everything. And she was gone. He didn't know what in the hell he was supposed to do with that. Or why in the hell he had behaved the way he had.

Except.

Except. The thing she had been offering to him seemed far too good, far too good to be real. That was something he learned in life. That anything that seemed too good to be true was. The one time his mother had ever shown any interest in him was when he had been a boy. He had spent hours being tormented at his father's hands.

He had spent days confined to the dungeon. Kept in an area that was not large enough for him to lay down. He had been cramped and isolated, and when his mother had seen him again she had acted like she was glad to see him. And then it had become abundantly clear that she didn't wish to hold him or comfort him. But that she was only concerned that his father might have made some headway in convincing him to try and overthrow Astrid. To contest her position for the throne.

It had never been about him.

He had only realized later that of course, if it would have benefited her to liberate him from his father's clutches, she would have done so. But it didn't. Because if she had tried to get him over to her side, then it would perhaps inspire his father to use other means to get his way. And if she had exposed him to the public, well then... The entire reputation of the royal family of Bjornland would be at risk. And that was something that of course neither of his parents could ever chance. It was a terrible realization.

To know that his own mother had weighed and calculated that. That his own father had done the same. And given the way that his parents felt about him, he could not fathom that Latika could feel any different.

His chest felt crushed.

Was he really so simple?

Was he really so simple that he could not face her declaration of love because he feared he might be harmed? Because he feared all the weak and vulnerable places in him that it exposed. The kind of husband and father he could not be.

Because he could not expose himself to such pain.

He was a coward. And yet, he did not know if he possessed the strength to fight against his own cowardice. He was going to go out. He had every intention of going out. Of finding a woman and getting caught in a compromising position with her. Of destroying the reputation that he had built up for himself. Of breaking their marriage apart. Latika had begged him not to touch another woman, so logic dictated that the first thing he should do is go out and touch another woman.

Except the very idea turned his stomach.

He prowled through his house, empty.

This house that had always brought him such satisfaction. A place that he had built far away from himself and the legacy of his father. Yes, this house had been important to him. As had the fact he had built a business across the world. But now, it all seemed trivial.

Because for a while Latika had been in this house. And when Latika had been in this house, it had been something magic.

When he had taken her out against the wall in the terrace, and fulfilled the fantasy he'd had of tasting her as he'd done.

When he had taken her up to bed and taken her virginity. When her innocence had acted like a dagger and stabbed him through the heart. Had made him wonder whose blood it was that was on the sheets.

She made him feel things he hadn't thought possible, and he resented her for it.

He had never depended on another person. Not once in his life.

He knew that Latika loved him. Really, love wasn't the issue.

He didn't know how to need.

Because days spent in solitary confinement at the hands of his father had taught him not to. Because living with a mother who had cared so little for him, who had certainly never held him, not once when he had fallen, had informed him that he could not depend on anyone but himself.

But part of him thought he might need Latika.

And he didn't know what to do with that.

And then she would have a child, one that would need him in return.

He could not fathom it. He didn't want to.

It was painful. Utterly and completely to imagine the scenario, and almost worse to imagine the alternative. He needed her.

He didn't want to need her.

They were having a child. He was desperate for that child. He also didn't want to be desperate. And God help him if he knew what the hell he was supposed to do with either feeling.

He had done what he had become proficient in. Running away. Yes, he was very accomplished at that. It was what he had done, after all. The method by which he had handled his father. He had not exposed the old man—and perhaps the excuse that it might damage Astrid's credibility and harm her was valid enough—but there were other factors. Because it had been more satisfying, because it had been easier, to simply walk. To simply cut ties and care for nothing. To wave a red flag at the bowl in that regard. And to give himself reprieve.

He was a man who had made his own destiny, and who was very proud of it.

But a huge portion of that journey had been about twisting the problem to suit him, rather than killing it once and for all. Perhaps that was what he had done here. Perhaps that was what he had done with Astrid.

But he didn't know who he was, at the end of everything. Didn't know what he was actually capable of.

Because all he ever asked of himself was that he protect Astrid. That he survived.

And suddenly, it hit him like a wall of bricks.

He was accusing Latika of reacting because she had no choice. But he was the one who lived in that world. He was the one who had made every decision he had made because the alternative was so undesirable.

Who would he have been without the abuse of his father? If he'd not had to dedicate his whole life to protecting Astrid? Would he have wanted children. Would he have reacted to the news of Astrid's pregnancy with joy rather than with anger? When Latika had come to the palace to be his sister's assistant, would he have immediately allowed himself to fall for her? How different would everything have been? It was impossible to say. It was impossible to say, because they had not been given that opportunity. Because he had not been given that opportunity.

He put his hand in his pocket, felt the sensor that would start his car. He could go out. He could go out and he could make a scandal. He could destroy his marriage to Latika. It was one of his choices.

Choices. Yes, he had them. He could go back to Bjornland, he could confess his undying love, and what then? What then. What would happen when she tired of him. What would happen when he couldn't be what she needed him to be? In his experience, that meant that he was not worth the effort. And as a man who was not worth the effort, he simply could not believe that he was now.

He gritted his teeth, and turned, walking out of the apartment.

Yes, they all had choices.

And sometimes the choices before you were grim.

But he would do what he had to. To set them both free.

CHAPTER FOURTEEN

WHEN LATIKA CAME down to breakfast the next morning, Astrid's face was guarded.

"What?" Latika asked.

"It has to do with my brother."

Latika felt like a knife had stabbed her through the heart. "I assume you mean he's gone out and found himself a lover."

Astrid blinked. "Did you know he was going to?"

"He told me he would."

"Why?"

"Because I told him I was in love with him, and he did not find that to be satisfactory. But I also begged him not to do this. I told him that we...we could be happy together. We could be. I don't know why he is intent upon hurting himself. I feel..." She sank down into the chair, a tear sliding down her cheek. "Give me the paper."

Astrid pulled it toward her chest. "You don't want to see it."

"I should see it. I need to see it. I really do."

"I know. I would feel better if you didn't."

"Well, this isn't about either of us feeling comfortable."

Astrid slid the paper across the table. And there were

photographs. Of Gunnar with a blonde woman. He was only talking to her over drinks, but his hand was rested low on her back, and the headline implied that the two of them had left together. Trouble for the Royal marriage as the Playboy Prince was caught canoodling a California girl.

Latika surprised herself by grabbing the paper and balling it up, throwing it across the dining room.

"I told you," Astrid said.

"I've never been jealous before. It's awful."

"Yes," Astrid agreed. "Of course it's awful."

"I don't want to hurt like this," Latika said.

"Unfortunately," Astrid replied. "It does hurt when they break your heart."

"Like when Mauro broke yours."

"Yes."

"He didn't sleep with another woman."

"Gunnar might not have either."

Latika knew that was true. And in fact, it did make some sense. Because Gunnar wanted to drive a wedge between them, and he wanted to do something that he thought she might find irreversible. In this… Well, this would be that thing. So of course, it made sense that he might go to such great lengths.

"Maybe." She sighed. "He told me to be gone when he got back."

Astrid looked like she was made of steel. "No. That isn't fair. You don't have to leave. He's the one who should leave."

"Well, good luck kicking him out of his own palace."

"It's my palace. I was born first," Astrid said imperiously.

Latika's breath caught. "Yes."

"Why did you say it like that?"

Latika shook her head. "There are things that… There are things that Gunnar will have to tell you someday. But I can't break his confidence."

"Even now?"

"Even now."

Astrid sighed heavily. And then she stood up, both palms on the table. "Well. If you're bound and determined to be that loyal to him, then I suggest you stay. Stay in your bedroom. Keep your things there too. Refuse to leave. Whatever he needs to see… Prove to him that he cannot get rid of you."

"And if he did cheat on me?"

"Only you can answer that question."

Latika knew the answer in her heart. That no matter what, she was committed to him. Committed to loving him. That whatever actions he committed out of a desire to run…she would forgive.

She truly, truly hoped that she didn't have to. But she was willing. Because she loved him.

And she was tired of living a life where she made subpar choices to run from a bad option.

Gunnar was a good option. Even if he wasn't perfect. She didn't need perfect. She needed love.

And in the end, she would see to it that love conquered all. In the end, she would show him just how strong love was. She only wished that she didn't have to demonstrate it with quite so much intensity. But she would.

By the time Gunnar returned to the palace in Bjornland, he was prepared to find an empty bedroom where Latika should be. Because of course he had done what he needed to do.

He had gone out and found himself a woman. That he had betrayed their marriage vows. And why would she think he had done any differently.

Exactly the way he'd promised he would.

Or at least, made it seem as if he had.

In reality, nothing could have enticed him to touch the blonde woman he had spent approximately ten minutes chatting with. He had asked her to step outside with him, and she had complied. Then he had paid her a significant amount of money to walk away and not go back into the bar.

As he had anticipated, opinion pieces on his behavior began pouring in immediately. It was nothing more than he had expected. And nothing more than he deserved. And it would allow Latika to be free. Truly. She would be a paragon of virtue in the eyes of his people, and indeed, the people of the world. His child would know his father, and even if he had to spend a lifetime atoning for the supposed sins he had committed against Latika, the child would not be denied its parentage, and that, was something of absolute importance to Gunnar.

He had solved everything.

And yet, he felt empty.

He stood at the threshold of the palace in victory.

And yet, he felt defeated.

There was nothing to feel overly proud of. Not in this.

He moved through the corridors of the palace, managing to neatly dodge any of the serving staff, but when he went to the staircase that he knew would take him to his room, he was met by his brother-in-law. Mauro was standing on the stairs, his gaze dark, his arms crossed over his chest.

"I didn't expect a welcoming committee," he said.

"You should have. Of course you should know that I would be aware that you had arrived back at the palace. And that we have all seen the headlines."

"Yes. I suppose I should have realized you were monitoring the border."

"Even you can't go undetected when we would like to see you."

"Well, that's good to know. I'll add espionage and surveillance to the long list of my sister's skills."

"How dare you come back here?" Mauro asked.

"I'm sorry, are *you* of royal blood?"

"Not last time I checked. But I am married to your sister. And I am a faithful husband."

"As far as I know, infidelity is as storied a tradition as the grand Christmas ball that our family throws every year. My people have never much concerned ourselves with anything quite so pedestrian as keeping our vows. I'm not sure why I should be the start of that."

"Astrid and I are the start of that. And she thought well enough of you that you might continue it."

"Well, my sister is optimistic. Especially where I'm concerned. I am nothing immensely exceptional. She should not expect it of me."

He began to move past Mauro, and his brother-in-law planted a firm hand on his shoulder. "Explain yourself."

"I do not have to explain myself to a man such as you."

"Explain yourself," Mauro repeated.

"Sometimes the kindest thing a man can do is set a woman free. I would think you of all people would know that."

Morrow's face darkened. "Are you suggesting it would've been kinder for me to set your sister free?"

"No. But I know you thought that one time. And here you are. You are a good father. A good husband. A man that I am happy my sister has found a life with. But for a while you thought that would not be the case. And you did what you had to. I know myself. I know my heart. And what I have done for Latika was the kindest thing that could be done. Trust me on that."

"You were not here to see her distress. I was. You broke her. If you weren't such a coward that you ran to execute your plan, then you could have seen it yourself, and you could've told her that it was for her own good."

Mauro shook his head. "For my part, I cannot see how harming another person in that way could ever be for their own good."

"Why is it that you're speaking to me instead of Astrid?"

"Astrid didn't trust herself around you. She thought she might execute you."

Gunnar laughed, and then pushed past Mauro. In many ways, he would believe that was true of his sister. She was fearsome, and it was one of the things he respected about her. One of the reasons he had always felt it was important that she be the one who took over the throne. That she be protected at all costs.

But what about yourself?

It didn't matter. The choices were made. And they were done.

He had taken up his mother's charge, and even she had not sworn any kind of loyalty to him.

After of a betrayal such as the one he'd committed, there was no reason to believe that Astrid ever would.

As he continued down the corridor, a door opened, and his sister appeared. "We must talk."

"I just shook off your attack dog."

"Yes I know. Because I told him to speak to you so that I wouldn't have to."

"And yet, here you are."

"Because it's important. It's important that we speak. Latika told me that there was something I didn't know about you. And she refused to elaborate. She said she would not break your confidence. She said this to me even after she had seen the news of your betrayal. Because that is the woman that you have behaved so poorly toward. A woman who would protect you when you absolutely did not deserve it."

He shook his head, a grim weight settling in his chest. "Believe me, Astrid, the question was never whether Latika was good enough for me."

"What don't I know?"

"There is no point rehashing this. There is no point at all. Our lives are what they are. You have found happiness with Mauro, and I am glad for you. I don't need to bring my pain at your feet. My life is also established. It is set. I am what I was made to be."

He looked at his sister, who was like gold plated iron, and he realized he was selling her short. Her strength. Her wisdom.

He had always sought to protect her, but in many ways he had underestimated her.

As his father had always done.

And that…that could not stand.

"Then if everything is set in stone, you might as well tell me. If nothing can be changed…"

"You know how badly our father wanted me to be King."

Astrid stared at him, her eyes wide. "Yes."

"He sought to use me as a weapon against you. He wished to turn me against you. And his method of doing that was to attempt isolation. Torture."

The horror in his sister's eyes was everything he had been trying to avoid for the past twenty years. "And you can see now why I didn't want to tell you this. You can see now why I never wanted any of this."

"Why did you not tell me?" she asked, her voice a broken whisper.

"What purpose would it have served? I had to protect you. It was the most important thing I could do. I had to serve you. You are my Queen. You are my sister. And protecting you all this time has meant shielding you from just how corrupt our father was. Because what does it benefit you to know?"

"So that I could know you," she said. "Not everything is about me, Gunnar. And that is a sentence I never thought I would say to you. Because you have lied all this time about who you are. You let everyone believe that you were selfish. And instead, everything you did was for me. How could you let me go my whole life not knowing that?"

"Because I am still broken. And there is no fixing it."

"How are you broken? It was never you. It was them. All this time it was them. Both of them, Gunnar. Mom and Dad. Don't think I don't realize that. But I was the fulfillment of mother's ambition. And that you are clearly the attempted fulfillment of our father's. When we were lost in the middle. But look at how you have loved me. Look at how loyal you were. How loyal you are. Gunnar, you gave me things I did not deserve with your devotion. No one could possibly hope to deserve. Because how can a person deserve to have someone else sacrifice their safety and comfort for them? You can't. Something like that is never about deserving. It's about love. And love is never something any of us could earn. Not love on the level that you gave me. It is a greater love than most could ever hope to receive."

"I have never felt like I possessed any great love inside of me."

"Because you didn't just let it sit inside of you. You poured it out for me. Love is useless as a feeling. It takes on a new shape when it becomes action. And sometimes that action is a sacrifice, and there is nothing comfortable and sacrifice. But it's real."

"I never wanted to hurt you with knowledge of our father's treachery."

Astrid put her hand on her heart, as if it was in pain and she was trying to minimize that pain. "I'm not hurt for me. I hurt for you. For myself... I have never felt so loved, Gunnar. To have a husband who loves me as he does. To know that my brother loves me in such a way. I cannot fathom how I was born so fortunate."

Gunnar had never thought of it that way, and it was as if everything was turned upside down. That what he'd done for Astrid would make her feel not the betrayal of their parents, but the deep love that he felt for her.

And it was love.

He could see it now. The way that she'd spoken of it. Love that fills you up so very much that you had to pour it out. Love that existed somewhat uncomfortably because it demanded things of you that did not feel good or satisfying.

And now he felt he understood something about love. Something that perhaps might have saved his marriage.

Except... Except what he had done to Latika... She would not forgive him.

Though, he had not betrayed her, he had certainly made the world believe he had. And even if he were to try and fix it now, she might not believe him. And the world certainly wouldn't. So she would always have to be the woman who had gone back to a man that had been unfaithful.

He had created for himself an impossible situation and now, it was too late to fix it. She would be gone now. As he had told her to be. Because he had broken her. Mauro had told him that.

"Excuse me," he said.

Because whether or not it was too late, he was going to try.

Choices. These were the choices. He could live forever without Latika, or he could try. Living without her was unacceptable. And so he had to try, no matter how unlikely it was that he would ever earn her love again.

But love was such a very precious thing, and Latika had put her love for him into action. Had laid herself bare. And that kind of love had to be rewarded. Because that kind of love mattered. When he saw it through the same lens that Astrid did, that bravery and that sacrifice... Latika had done all that for him. She had begged, she had put herself before him raw and naked. And he had given her so little in return. He would make it right. He had to make it right.

He pushed his hands through his hair, making his way down the hall and pushing the door open, expecting to find that same sense of emptiness that had been in his San Diego home.

But instead, he saw her.

Latika was sitting on a bench at the foot of their bed, her long dark hair cascading over her shoulders, her expression set into one of seriousness. He could see that she had been crying. That he had made her cry. He had never despised himself more than he did in that moment.

"I thought I told you to leave," he said.

"You did," she responded. "And you did everything you said you would. You are a man of your word, Gunnar, I will give you that. But I didn't agree to leave you. And I won't leave you. I love you, and I want more than anything for this to work. And I know what they'll say about me. How sad I am. That I'm so desperately delusional for thinking that my husband who was unfaithful to me could ever change."

She shook her head. "I don't care. I don't care what anyone thinks of me. I'm not making decisions for other people anymore. I'm making decisions for myself. From my heart. And what's right for me."

"You would... You would stay with me even now?"

She stood. "Yes. I would. Because I fell in love with you, and I fell in love with each and every broken part of you. The broken part that made you feel you had to run. That made you feel you had no other choice but to try and undo this once and for all by sleeping with another woman. If I believe that love can heal, then I must give it time. I won't stay with a man who cannot love me ever. But if you think there is hope, that we can make a marriage work. That we can love each other, then I will stay. I am...devastated that you would give to someone else what we have shared. But I promise that I will do everything in my power to forgive. To never hold it over your head. I believe that you can be better. And if I believe that, then I need to give you the chance to be."

Her words nearly took Gunnar down to his knees. For what had he ever done to deserve such an offer? Such complete and utter loyalty. He had become his father in many ways now. He had tortured her. And yet, she held fast.

And then, he did find himself on his knees in front of her, taking her hands in his. "I don't deserve such an offer," he said, his voice rough.

"Love isn't about what you deserve," she said softly, her words so closely mirroring Astrid's that the truth of them rang through him like a gong.

"My darling, Latika. I don't know why you would choose to believe me. But I did not sleep with her. I didn't even kiss her. I made all the world think that I did, though, and that means that it will follow us. That means that…you will not be free of the insinuations that will come, and the outright, blatant commentary. And that will be my fault. For I have done that to us."

"You weren't unfaithful to me?"

"No. And I'm sorry that I let you keep talking, and keep thinking it. But I wanted you to understand that I wasn't telling you this to manipulate you into staying. If you would stay either way… And you know I have no reason to lie. I swear to you I wouldn't lie. Not about this."

"I believe you," she said softly. "I swear that I do."

"I was afraid. And I was running. And every single thing that I accused you of… I was the one who felt like I was stuck with a series of choices, handed down to me from others. And I realized that I was continuing to let my father manipulate and control my life. That I was allowing my mother to continue to have dominion over what I was."

He pushed his hands through his hair, and saw they were shaking. "I have always fancied myself a man who lived free. A kind of rogue prince who did whatever he wanted, but that isn't true. And it never has been. I let myself wonder…what kind of man would I have been if not for that?"

"A dangerous thing to wonder," she whispered. "We are what we were made."

"It's true, but I think, Latika, I would have chosen you much sooner. I love you. I don't need time to fall in love with you. I simply needed to find a way to rout the fear out of my heart so that I could give that love space to be felt. And more importantly, so that I could allow myself to act on it. I told you I didn't know what love felt like, but I have come to understand that it isn't important to know what it feels like. It is much more important to know what it looks like."

His throat tightened, making his words rough. "Because love that *feels* like much but looks like nothing is useless. You demonstrated deep and real love for me. The way you chose to stand with me, to be steady. When I was not. You offered me faithfulness when I appeared to have given you none, when for all intents and purposes, I had given you none. You demonstrated bravery in the face of rejection when I couldn't. And that, will always be what love is to me. And it is the love that I will endeavor to give back to you. To be brave when I feel afraid. To give when I feel like being selfish. To love when it would be easier to hate. I will make these choices for the two of us. I swear it. I swear it to you."

She threw her arms around him, a sob racking her shoulders. "I was willing to forgive you, but I'm so glad that I don't have to."

"You will still have to forgive me," he said. "Because whether or not the world will believe that I was faithful to you is another story. And our marriage may forever be tainted by the public perception of what I have done."

"I don't care about public perception. That is the only thing my parents ever cared about, and believe me, it never made any of us happy."

"I don't think I will ever elevate the nation. My reputation may be too far gone."

"Whether or not the world ever knows, you did elevate the nation. You protected their Queen. You protected me. I hope someday the world understands the manner of man that you are. But if they don't… I do. And I will ensure that our child knows it too."

Gunnar took her chin in his hand, stared down into her beautiful brown eyes. "I don't need the world to know a damn thing about me. As long as you trust in me, then I will be happy."

"I trust in you."

"Here I give you vows that I mean with all my heart," he said, holding one of her hands clasped in his. "That I will be faithful. That I would lay down my life for you, and our child. But I will reserve the realest parts of me for you. And only you."

"And I will do the same," she said, one small hand covering his. Then Latika stretched up on her toes and kissed him. Pure and sweet and more than he could have ever hoped to deserve.

But the beautiful thing about love, the real love that had surrounded him for longer than he had allowed himself to see it, was that it transcended what a man deserved.

The best things, Gunnar thought as he carried Latika to bed, were free. They were beyond price. They could not be bought, they could not be worked for, they could only be given.

And Latika had given him her love.

The thing that a man who could afford anything, who had been entrenched in a life that involves no denial, and no deprivation, had never known he was missing.

And as they came together, man and wife in every sense of the word, that hole that had always been there in his soul felt filled.

Completed by this woman. Completed by her love.

EPILOGUE

THE KINGDOM HAD rejoiced when Astrid had given birth to her son, the heir to the throne of Bjornland, but there was no less celebration for the birth of Gunnar and Latika's daughter.

The beautiful Princess with jet-black hair and eyes the same color as her mother's.

And when Gunnar and Latika renewed their vows in an intimate ceremony, attended only by Mauro, Astrid and their children, the photos—of the new baby, and of Latika in a wedding dress made of simple, rich satin, that she'd been so afraid to let herself wear to that first wedding—had helped cement the acceptance of the royal couple as one that would last.

A couple worthy of rooting for. Especially in light of the new revelations that had come to light over the past months.

Gunnar and Latika had been willing to figure out a way to address the issues he had created with his headline within their family. To make sure their daughter understood what Latika believed if ever the time came when she stumbled across those stories.

But Astrid had a different plan. Astrid took it upon herself to demolish the secrets and lies that their parents had lived with. The web of deceit and corruption that had surrounded the castle while they had been alive.

Of course, it had dashed her father's reputation. And it created many questions about the long history of their family.

But it had given the world the truth about Gunnar. About his loyalty to the crown. To his sister.

And to why he had contrived to make it look as if he was unfaithful to his wife.

And of course, there would always be people who believed that Gunnar was not a hero, but a villain involved in a desperate PR campaign.

Though Latika knew the truth. And that was all that mattered.

She knew, beyond a shadow of a doubt that she would love this man forever.

Prince Gunnar von Bjornland, her husband, wonderful father and the pride of his nation. A man she loved with every fiber of her being.

It would be her great joy to be his wife, for all the rest of her days.

* * * * *

MILLS & BOON

Coming next month

CINDERELLA'S ROYAL SEDUCTION
Dani Collins

"You're genuinely asking me to marry you. And if I do, you'll give me this hotel and spa, all the property and rights to the aquifer. Everything," she clarified.

"If you'll live in Verina with me and do what must be done to have my children, yes," he said with a dark smile.

She was still shaking her head at the outrageous proposition but found herself pressing her free hand to her middle, trying to still the flutters of wicked anticipation that teased her with imaginings of how those babies would get made.

She veered her mind from such thoughts.

"Why? I mean, why me?" She lifted her gaze to his, catching a flash of sensual memories reflected in the hot blue of his irises.

"I've already told you. I want you in my bed."

"And that's it? Your fly has spoken? That's the sum total of your motivation?"

His eyes narrowed, becoming flinty and enigmatic. "There are other reasons. I'll share them with you, but they can't leave this room."

That took her aback. "What if I don't want to carry your secrets?"

"You're going to carry my name and my children. Of course you'll keep my secrets. Would you like to tell me yours?" He regarded her over the rim of his glass as he sipped, as though waiting for her to tip her hand in some way.

She shrugged her confusion. "I'm not exactly mysterious," she dismissed. "The most interesting thing that's ever happened to me is happening right now. You realize how eccentric this sounds?"

"Eccentric or not, it's a good offer. You should accept it before I change my mind."

She snorted. "You're quite ruthless, aren't you?" She spoke conversationally but knew it as truth in her bones.

"I do what has to be done to get the results I want. You understand that sort of pragmatism, even if you've pointed your own efforts in dead-end directions. I look forward to seeing what you accomplish when you go after genuinely important goals."

"This is my home. It's important to me."

"Then claim it."

A choke of laughter came out of her. "Just like that? Accept your proposal and—" She glanced at the paperwork. "I'm not going to agree to anything before I've actually reviewed that offer."

"Due diligence is always a sensible action," he said with an ironic curl of his lip. He waved his glass toward the table, inviting her to sit and read.

Gingerly she lowered onto the sofa and set aside her whiskey.

Rhys kept his back to her, gaze fixed across the valley as he continued to sip his drink, saying nothing as she flipped pages.

His behavior was the sort of thing a dominant wolf would do to indicate how little the antics of the lesser pack affected him, but she was glad not to have his unsettling attention aimed directly at her as she compared the two contracts. Aside from the exchange of money on Maude's—and the fact that hers finalized on her wedding day—they were essentially the same.

"I want possession on our engagement. If I decide to accept your proposal," she bluffed, fully expecting him to tell her to go to hell.

"Done. On the condition we begin the making of our children on the day our engagement is announced." He turned, and his eyes were lit with the knowledge his agreement had taken her aback. "We'll keep the conception part as a handshake agreement. No need to write that down in black-and-white."

He brought her a pen. His hand was steady as he offered it. Hers trembled as she hesitantly took it.

"Are you completely serious?" she asked.

"Make the change. Sign it. I'll explain why I want you to marry me. You'll accept my proposal, and Cassiopeia's will be yours."

Continue reading
CINDERELLA'S ROYAL SEDUCTION
Dani Collins

Available next month
www.millsandboon.co.uk

COMING SOON!

We really hope you enjoyed reading this book. If you're looking for more romance, be sure to head to the shops when new books are available on

Thursday 9th January

To see which titles are coming soon, please visit
millsandboon.co.uk/nextmonth

MILLS & BOON
DARE

Sexy. Passionate. Bold.

Sensual love stories featuring smart, sassy heroines you'd want as a best friend, and compelling intense heroes who are worthy of them.